THE JEALOUS KIND

By the same author

Dave Robicheaux Novels

Light of the World
Creole Belle
The Glass Rainbow
Swan Peak
The Tin Roof Blowdown
Pegasus Descending
Crusader's Cross
Last Car to Elysian Fields
Jolie Blon's Bounce
Purple Cane Road
Sunset Limited
Cadillac Jukebox
Burning Angel
Dixie City Jam
In the Electric Mist with Confederate Dead
A Stained White Radiance
A Morning for Flamingos
Black Cherry Blues
Heaven's Prisoners
The Neon Rain

Hackberry Holland Novels

House of the Rising Sun
Wayfaring Stranger
Feast Day of Fools
Rain Gods
Lay Down My Sword and Shield

Billy Bob Holland Novels

In the Moon of Red Ponies
Bitterroot
Heartwood
Cimarron Rose

Other Fiction

Jesus Out to Sea
White Doves at Morning
The Lost Get-Back Boogie
The Convict and Other Stories
Two for Texas
To the Bright and Shining Sun
Half of Paradise

THE JEALOUS KIND

JAMES LEE BURKE

First published in Great Britain in 2016 by Orion Books,
an imprint of The Orion Publishing Group Ltd
Carmelite House, 50 Victoria Embankment
London EC4Y 0DZ
This edition published in 2017.

An Hachette UK company

1 3 5 7 9 10 8 6 4 2

All the characters in this book are fictitious,
and any resemblance to actual persons, living
or dead, is purely coincidental.

A CIP catalogue record for this book
is available from the British Library.

ISBN (Hardback) 978 1 4091 6349 7
ISBN (Export trade paperback) 978 1 4091 6350 3

Printed and bound by
CPI Group (UK) Ltd, Croydon, CR0 4YY

www.orionbooks.co.uk

To Deen Kogan, with thanks for all the support she has given to the arts over the years

THE JEALOUS KIND

Chapter 1

THERE WAS A time in my life when I woke every morning with fear and anxiety and did not know why. For me, fear was a given I factored into the events of the day, like a pebble that never leaves your shoe. In retrospect, an adult might call that a form of courage. If so, it wasn't much fun.

My tale begins on a Saturday at the close of spring term of my junior year in 1952, when my father let me use his car to join my high school buds on Galveston Beach, fifty miles south of Houston. Actually, the car was not his; it was lent to him by his company for business use, with the understanding that only he would drive it. That he would lend it to me was an act of enormous trust. My friends and I had a fine day playing touch football on the sand, and as they built a bonfire toward evening, I decided to swim out to the third sandbar south of the island, the last place your feet could still touch bottom. It was not only deep and cold, it was also hammerhead country. I had never done this by myself, and even when I once swam to the third sandbar with a group, most of us had been drunk.

I waded through the breakers, then inhaled deeply and dove into the first swell and kept stroking through the waves, crossing the first sandbar and then the second, never resting, turning my face sideways to breathe, until I saw the last sandbar, waves undulating across its crest, gulls dipping into the froth.

I stood erect, my back tingling with sunburn. The only sounds were the gulls and the water slapping against my loins. I could see a freighter towing a scow, then they both disappeared beyond the horizon. I dove headlong into a wave and saw the sandy bottom drop away into darkness. The water was suddenly frigid, the waves sliding over me as heavy as concrete. The hotels and palm trees and the amusement pier on the beach had become miniaturized. A triangular-shaped fin sliced through the swell and disappeared beneath a wave, a solitary string of bubbles curling behind it.

Then I felt my heart seize, and not because of a shark. I was surrounded by jellyfish, big ones with bluish-pink air sacs and gossamer tentacles that could wrap around your neck or thighs like swarms of wet yellow jackets.

My experience with the jellyfish seemed to characterize my life. No matter how sun-spangled the day might seem, I always felt a sense of danger. It wasn't imaginary, either. The guttural roar of Hollywood mufflers on a souped-up Ford coupe, a careless glance at the guys in ducktail haircuts and suede stomps and pegged pants called drapes, and in seconds you could be pounded into pulp. Ever watch a television portrayal of the fifties? What a laugh.

A psychiatrist would probably say my fears were an externalization of my problems at home. Maybe he would be right, although I have always wondered how many psychiatrists have gone up against five or six guys who carried chains and switchblades and barber razors, and didn't care if they lived or died, and ate their pain like ice cream. Or maybe I saw the world through a glass darkly and the real problem was me. The point is, I was always scared. Just like swimming through the jellyfish. Contact with just one of them was like touching an electric cable. My fear was so great I was urinating inside my swim trunks, the warmth draining along my thighs. Even after I had escaped the jellyfish and rejoined my high school chums by a bonfire, sparks twisting into a turquoise sky, a bottle of cold Jax in my hand, I could not rid myself of the abiding sense of terror that rested like hot coals in the pit of my stomach.

I never discussed my home life with my friends. My mother consulted fortune-tellers, listened in on the party line, and was always giving me enemas when I was a child. She locked doors and pulled down window shades and inveighed against alcohol and the effect it had on my father. Theatricality and depression and genuine sorrow seemed her constant companions. Sometimes I would see the cautionary look in the eyes of our neighbors when my parents were mentioned in a conversation, as though they needed to protect me from learning about my own home. In moments like these I'd feel shame and guilt and anger and not know why. I'd sit in my bedroom, wanting to hold something that was heavy and hard in my palm, I didn't know what. My uncle Cody was a business partner of Frankie Carbo of Murder, Inc. My uncle introduced me to Bugsy Siegel when he was staying at the Shamrock Hotel with Virginia Hill. Sometimes I would think about these gangsters and the confidence in their expression and the deadness in their eyes when they gazed at someone they didn't like, and I'd wonder what it would be like if I could step inside their skin and possess their power.

The day I swam through the jellyfish without being stung was the day that changed my life forever. I was about to enter a country that had no flag or boundaries, a place where you gave up your cares and your cautionary instincts and deposited your heart on a stone altar. I'm talking about the first time you fall joyously, sick-down-in-your-soul in love, and the prospect of heartbreak never crosses your mind.

Her name was Valerie Epstein. She was sitting in a long-bodied pink Cadillac convertible, what we used to call a boat, in a drive-in restaurant wrapped in neon, near the beach, her bare shoulders powdered with sunburn. Her hair wasn't just auburn; it was thick and freshly washed and had gold streaks in it, and she had tied it up on her head with a bandana, like one of the women who worked in defense plants during the war. She was eating french fries one at a time with her fingers and listening to a guy sitting behind the steering wheel like a tall drink of water. His hair was lightly oiled and sun-bleached, his skin pale and free of tattoos. He wore shades, even though the sun was molten and low in the sky, the day starting to cool. With his left hand he kept working a quarter across the tops of his fingers, like a Las Vegas gambler or a guy with secret skills. His name was Grady Harrelson. He was two years older than I and had already graduated, which meant I knew who *he* was but he didn't know who *I* was. Grady had wide, thin shoulders, like a basketball player, and wore a faded purple T-shirt that on him somehow looked stylish. He had been voted the most handsome boy in the school not once but twice. A guy like me had no trouble hating a guy like Grady.

I don't know why I got out of my car. I was tired, and my back felt stiff and dry and peppered with salt and sand under my shirt, and I had to drive fifty miles back to Houston and return the car to my father before dark. The evening star was already winking inside a blue band of light on the horizon. I had seen Valerie Epstein twice from a distance but never up close. Maybe the fact that I'd swum safely through a school of jellyfish was an omen. Valerie Epstein was a junior at Reagan High School, on the north side of Houston, and known for her smile and singing voice and straight A's. Even the greaseballs who carried chains under their car seats and stilettos in their drapes treated her as royalty.

Get back in the car and finish your crab burger and go home, a voice said.

For me, low self-esteem was not a step down but a step up. I was alone, yet I didn't want to go home. It was Saturday, and I knew that before dark my father would walk unsteadily back from the icehouse, the neighbors looking the other way while they watered their yards. I had friends, but most of them didn't know the real me, nor in reality did I know them. I lived in an envelope of time and space that I wanted to mail to another planet.

I headed for the restroom, on a path between the passenger side of the convertible and a silver-painted metal stanchion with a speaker on it that was playing "Red Sails in the Sunset." Then I realized Valerie Epstein was having an argument with Grady and on the brink of crying.

"Anything wrong?" I said.

Grady turned around, his neck stretching, his eyelids fluttering. "Say again?"

"I thought maybe something was wrong and y'all needed help."

"Get lost, snarf."

"What's a snarf?"

"Are you deaf?"

"I just want to know what a snarf is."

"A guy who gets off on sniffing girls' bicycle seats. Now beat it."

The music speaker went silent. My ears were popping. I could see people's lips moving in the other cars, but I couldn't hear any sound. Then I said, "I don't feel like it."

"I don't think I heard you right."

"It's a free country."

"Not for nosy frumps, it isn't."

"Leave him alone, Grady," Valerie said.

"What's a frump?" I said.

"A guy who farts in the bathtub and bites the bubbles. Somebody put you up to this?"

"I was going to the restroom."

"Then *go*."

This time I didn't reply. Somebody, probably one of Grady's friends, flicked a hot cigarette at my back. Grady opened his car door so he could turn around and speak without getting a crick in his neck. "What's your name, pencil dick?"

"Aaron Holland Broussard."

"I'm about to walk you into the restroom and unscrew your head and stuff it in the commode, Aaron Holland Broussard. Then I'm going to piss on it before I flush. What do you think of that?"

The popping sound in my ears started again. The parking lot and the canvas canopy above the cars seemed to tilt sideways; the red and yellow neon on the restaurant became a blur, like licorice melting, running down the windows.

"Nothing to say?" Grady asked.

"A girl told me the only reason you won 'most handsome' is that all the girls thought you were queer-bait and felt sorry for you. Some of the jocks told me the same thing. They said you used to chug pole under the seats at the football stadium."

I didn't know where the words came from. I felt like the wiring between my thoughts and my words had been severed. Cracking wise to an older guy just didn't happen at my high school, particularly if the older guy lived in River Oaks and his father owned six rice mills and an independent drilling company. But something even more horrible was occurring as I stood next to Grady's convertible. I was looking into the eyes of Valerie Epstein as though hypnotized. They were the most beautiful and mysterious eyes I had ever seen; they were deep-set, luminous, the color of violets. They were also doing something to me I didn't think possible: In the middle of the drive-in, my twanger had gone on autopilot. I put my hand in my pocket and tried to knock down the tent forming in my fly.

"You got a boner?" Grady said, incredulous.

"It's my car keys. They punched a hole in my pocket."

"Right," he said, his face contorting with laughter. "Hey, everybody, dig this guy! He's flying the flag. Anyone got a camera? When's the last time you got your ashes hauled, Snarfus?"

My face was burning. I felt I was in one of those dreams in which you wet your pants at the front of the classroom. Then Valerie Epstein did something I would never be able to repay her for, short of opening my veins. She flung her carton of french fries, ketchup and all, into Grady's face. At first he was too stunned to believe what she had done; he began picking fries from his skin and shirt like bloody leeches and flicking them on the asphalt. "I'm letting this pass. You're not yourself. Settle down. You want me to apologize to this kid? Hey, buddy, I'm sorry. Yeah, you, fuckface. Here, you want some fries? I'll stick a couple up your nose."

She got out of the car and slammed the door. "You're pathetic," she said, jerking a graduation ring and its chain from her neck, hurling it on the convertible seat. "Don't call. Don't come by the house. Don't write. Don't send your friends to make excuses for you, either."

"Come on, Val. We're a team," he said, wiping his face with a paper napkin. "You want another Coke?"

"It's over, Grady. You can't help what you are. You're selfish and dishonest and disrespectful and cruel. In my stupidity, I thought I could change you."

"We'll work this out. I promise."

She wiped her eyes and didn't answer. Her face was calm now, even though her breath was still catching, as though she had hiccups.

"Don't do this to me, Val," he said. "I love you. Get real. Are you going to let a dork like this break us up?"

"Goodbye, Grady."

"How you going to get home?" he said.

"*You* don't have to worry about it."

"I'm not going to leave you on the street. Now get in. You're starting to make me mad."

"What a tragedy for the planet that would be," she said. "You know what my father said of you? 'Grady's not a bad kid. He's simply incapable of being a good one.'"

"Come back. Please."

"I hope you have a great life," she said. "Even though the memory of kissing you makes me want to rinse my mouth with peroxide."

Then she walked away, like Helen of Troy turning her back on Attica. A gust of warm wind blew newspapers along the boulevard into the sky. The light was orange and bleeding out of the clouds in the west, the horizon darkening, the waves crashing on the beach just the other side of Seawall Boulevard, the palm trees rattling dryly in the wind. I could smell the salt and the seaweed and the tiny shellfish that had dried on the beach, like the smell of birth. I watched Valerie walk through the cars to the boulevard, her beach bag swinging from her shoulder and bouncing on her butt. Grady was standing next to me, breathing hard, his gaze locked on Valerie, just as mine was, except there was an irrevocable sense of loss in his eyes that made me think of a groundswell, the kind you see rising from the depths when a storm is about to surge inland.

"Sorry this happened to y'all," I said.

"We're in public, so I can't do what I'm thinking. But you'd better find a rat hole and crawl in it," he said.

"Blaming others won't help your situation," I said.

He wiped a streak of ketchup off his cheek. "I was hoping you'd say something like that."

Chapter 2

MY FATHER AND I went to noon Mass the next day. Even though my mother had been reared Baptist, she did not go to a church of any kind. She had grown up desperately poor, abandoned by her father, and had married a much older man, a traveling salesman, when she was seventeen. She hid her divorce from others as though it had cheapened and made her unworthy of the social approval she always sought. Each Sunday she made a late breakfast for us, and my father and I drove to church in his company car. We seldom spoke on the way.

I never understood why my mother and father married. They didn't kiss or even touch hands, at least not while I was around. There was a loneliness in their eyes that convinced me prisons came in all sizes and shapes.

During Mass, I could smell the faint scent of last night's beer and cigarettes on my father's clothes. Before the priest gave the final blessing, my father whispered that his stomach was upset and he would meet me across the street at Costen's drugstore. When I got there, he was drinking coffee at the counter and talking about LSU football with the owner. "Ready for a lime Coke?" he said.

"No, thank you, sir. Can I use the car this afternoon?" I said.

"*May* I."

"May I use the car?"

“I was planning to go to the bowling alley,” he said. “There’s a league today.”

I nodded. My father didn’t bowl and had no interest in it. The bowling alley was air-conditioned and had a bar.

“Come with me,” he said. “Maybe you can bowl a line or two.”

“I have some things to take care of.”

My father was a handsome man, and genteel in his Victorian way. He never sat at the dining or the breakfast table without putting on his coat, even if he was by himself. He’d lost his best friend in the trenches on November 11, 1918, and despised war and the national adoration of the military and the bellicose rhetoric of politicians who sent others to suffer and die in their stead. But he drank, and somehow those words subsumed and effaced all his virtues. “You dating a new girl?”

“I don’t have an old one.”

“So you’re changing that?” he said.

“I’d like to.”

“Who is she?”

“I don’t know her real good.”

“Real *well.*”

“Yes, sir.”

I took the city bus up to North Houston. The previous winter a friend of mine had pointed out a one-story oak-shaded Victorian house with a wide porch on a residential boulevard, and said it was the home of Valerie Epstein. I couldn’t remember the name of the boulevard, but I knew approximately where it was. When I pulled the cord for the bus driver to stop, I felt my stomach constrict, a tiny flame curling up through my entrails.

I stood in the bus’s fumes as it pulled away, and stared at the palms on the esplanade and the row of houses once owned by the city’s wealthiest people, before the big money moved out to River Oaks. I was deep in the heart of enemy territory, my crew cut and dress shoes and trousers and starched white shirt and tie the equivalent of blood floating in a shark tank.

I started walking. I thought I heard Hollywood mufflers rumbling down another street. On the corner, a woman of color was waiting for the bus behind the bench, her purse crimped in her hands. She looked one way and then the other, leaning forward as though on a ship. There were no other people of color on the boulevard. These were the years when nigger-knocking was in fashion. I tried to smile at her, but she glanced away.

One block later I recognized Valerie's house. There were two live oaks hung with Spanish moss in the front yard and a glider on the porch; the side yard had a vegetable garden, and in the back I could see a desiccated toolshed and a huge pecan tree with a welding truck parked on the grass under it. Behind me I heard the rumble of Hollywood mufflers again. I turned and saw a 1941 Ford that had dual exhausts and Frenched headlights and an engine that sounded much more powerful than a conventional V8. The body was dechromed and leaded in and spray-painted with gray primer. One look at the occupants and I knew I was about to meet some genuine northside badasses, what we called greasers or sometimes greaseballs or hoods or duck-asses or hard guys or swinging dicks.

What was their logo? An indolent stare, slightly rounded shoulders, the shirt unbuttoned to expose the top of the chest, the collar turned up on the neck, the drapes threaded through the loops by a thin suede belt buckled below the navel, shirt cuffs buttoned even in summer, a tablespoon of grease in the sweeps of hair combed into a trench at the back of the head, iron taps on the needle-nose stomps that could be used to shatter someone's teeth on the sidewalk, the *pachuco* cross tattooed on the web between the left forefinger and thumb, and more important, the total absence of pity or mercy in the eyes. I know that anyone reading this today might believe these were misdirected boys and their attire and behavior were masks for their fear. That was seldom my experience. I believed then, as I do now, that most of them would go down with the decks awash and the cannons blazing, as George Orwell once said about people who are truly brave.

The Ford pulled to the curb, the twin custom mufflers throbbing. "Looks like you're lost," said a greaser in the passenger seat.

"I sure am," I replied.

"Or you're selling Bibles."

"I was actually looking for the Assembly of God Church. Y'all know where that's at?"

I saw his eyes take note of the bad grammar and realized he was more intelligent than I thought, and no doubt a more serious challenge.

"You're cute." He put a Lucky Strike in his mouth but didn't light it. His hair was jet-black, his cheeks sunken, his skin pale. He scratched his throat. "Got a match?"

"I don't smoke."

"If you're not selling Bibles and you don't have a light, what good are you? Are you good for something, boy?"

"Probably not. How about not calling me 'boy'? Hey, I dig y'all's heap. Where'd you get the mufflers?"

He removed the cigarette from his mouth and pinched it between his thumb and index finger, shaking it, nodding as though coming to a profound conclusion. "I remember where I've seen you. That bone-smoker joint downtown, what's it called, the Pink Elephant?"

"What's a bone-smoker?"

"Guys who look like you. Where'd you get that belt buckle?"

"Won it at the junior RCA rodeo. Bareback bronc and bull riding both."

"You give blow jobs in the chutes?"

My eyes went off of his. The street was hot and bright, the lawns a deep green, the air swimming with humidity, the houses an eye-watering white. "I can't blame you for saying that. I've shown the same kind of prejudice about people who are made different in the womb."

"Where'd you get that?"

"The Bible."

"You're telling us you're queer?"

"You never know."

"I believe you. You got a nice mouth. You ought to get you some lipstick."

"Go fuck yourself," I said.

He opened the door slowly and stepped out on the asphalt. He was taller than he had looked inside the car. His shirt was unbuttoned, the sleeves filling with wind. His stomach was corrugated, his drapes low on his hips. His eyes roved over my face as though he were studying a lab specimen. "Can you repeat that?"

I heard a screen door squeak on a spring and slam behind me. Then I realized he was no longer looking at me. Valerie Epstein had walked down her porch steps into the yard and was standing under the live oaks, on the edge of the sunlight, shading her eyes with one hand. "Is that you?" she said.

I didn't know if she was talking to me or the greaser on the curb. I pointed at my chest. "You talking to me?"

"Aaron Holland? That's your name, isn't it?" she said.

"Yes," I said, my throat catching.

"Were you looking for me?" she said.

"I wondered if you got home okay."

The greaser got back in the Ford and shut the door. He looked up at me, holding my eyes. "You ought to play the slots. You got a lot of luck," he said. "See you down the track, Jack."

"Looking forward to it. Good to see you."

He and his friends drove away. I looked at Valerie again. She was wearing a white sundress printed with flowers.

"I thought I was marmalade," I said.

"Why?"

"Those hoods."

"They're not hoods."

"How about greaseballs?"

"Sometimes they're overly protective about the neighborhood, that's all."

The wind was flattening her dress against her hips and stomach and thighs. I was so nervous I had to fold my arms on my chest to keep my hands from shaking. I tried to clear my throat. "How'd you get home from Galveston?"

"The Greyhound. You thought you had to check on me?"

"Do you like miniature golf?"

"Miniature golf?"

"It's a lot of fun," I said. "I thought maybe you'd like to play a game or two. If you're not doing anything."

"Come inside. You look a little dehydrated."

"You're asking me in?"

"What did I just say?"

"You told me to come inside."

"So?"

"Yes, I could use some ice water. I didn't mean to call those guys greaseballs. Sometimes I say things I don't mean."

"They'll survive. You coming?"

I would have dragged the Grand Canyon all the way to Texas to sit down with Valerie Epstein. "I hope I'm not disturbing y'all. My conscience bothered me. I didn't go looking for you last night because I had to get my father's car home."

"I think you have a good heart."

"Pardon?"

"You heard me."

I could hear wind chimes tinkling and birds singing and perhaps strings of Chinese firecrackers popping, and I knew I would probably love Valerie Epstein for the rest of my life.

SHE WALKED AHEAD of me into the kitchen and took a pitcher of lemonade from the icebox. The kitchen was glossy and clean, the walls painted yellow and white. She put ice in two glasses and filled them up and slipped a sprig of mint in each and set them on paper napkins. "That's my father in the backyard," she said. "He's a pipeline contractor."

A muscular man wearing strap overalls without a shirt was working on the truck parked under the pecan tree. His skin was dark with tan, the gold curlicues of hair on his shoulders shiny with sweat, his profile cut out of tin.

"He looks like Alexander the Great. I mean the image on the coin," I said.

"That's a funny thing to say."

"History is my favorite subject. I read all of it I can. My father does, too. He's a natural-gas engineer."

I waited for her to say something. She didn't. Then I realized I had just told her my father was educated and her father probably was not. "What I mean is he works in the oil business, too."

"Are you always this nervous?"

We were sitting at the table now, an electric fan oscillating on the counter. "I have a way of making words come out the wrong way. I was going to tell you how my father ended up in the oil patch, but I get to running on."

"Go ahead and tell me."

"He was a sugar chemist in Cuba. He quit after an incident on a ferryboat that sailed from New Orleans to Havana. Then he went to work on the pipeline and got caught by the Depression and never got to do the thing he wanted, which was to be a writer."

"Why would he quit his job as a chemist because of something that happened on a passenger boat?"

"He was in World War One. The German artillery was knocking their trench to pieces. The German commander came out under a white flag and asked my father's captain to surrender. He said the wounded would be taken care of and the others would be treated well. The captain refused the offer. A German biplane wagged its wings over the lines to show it was on a peaceful mission, and threw leaflets all over the wire and the trench, but the captain still wouldn't surrender. The Germans had moved some cannons up on train cars. When they cut loose, they killed half my father's unit in thirty minutes.

"Ten years later, he was on the ferry headed to Havana when he saw his ex–commanding officer on the deck. My father insisted they have a drink together, mostly because he wanted a chance to forgive and forget. That night his ex–commanding officer jumped off the rail. My father always blamed himself."

"That's a sad story."

"Most true stories are."

"You should be a writer yourself."

"Why?"

"Because I think you're a nice boy."

"Somehow those statements don't fit together," I said.

"Maybe they're not supposed to." She smiled, then took a breath, the light in her eyes changing. "You need to be more careful."

"Because I came up to the Heights?"

"I'm talking about Grady and his friends."

"I think Grady Harrelson is a fraud."

"Grady has a dark side. There's nothing fraudulent about it. The same with his friends. Don't underestimate them."

"I'm not afraid of them."

She jiggled her sprig of mint up and down in the ice. "Caution and fear aren't the same thing."

"Maybe I've got things wrong with me that nobody knows about. Those guys might get a surprise."

"Number one, I don't believe you. Number two, it's not normal to brag about your character defects."

"Sometimes I believe I have two or three people living inside me. One of them has a horn like Harpo Marx."

"How interesting."

"My mother says I'm fanciful."

I could see her attention fading.

"I have a term paper on John Steinbeck due tomorrow," she said. "I'd better get started on it."

"I see."

"I'm glad you came by."

I tried not to look as stupid as I felt. I could see her father working on his truck, the muscles in his forearm swelling as he pulled on a wrench. I wanted her to introduce me to him. I wanted to talk about trucks and pipelines and drill bits. I didn't want to leave. "Sunday night is a good time to play miniature golf. The stars are out and the breeze is blowing from the south, and there's a watermelon stand with picnic tables close by."

"See? You talk like a writer. Let's get together another time."

"Sure," I replied. I hadn't finished my lemonade. "I can show myself out. You'd better get started on your paper."

"Don't be mad."

"I'm not, Miss Valerie. Thank you for inviting me in."

"You don't have to call me 'miss.'"

I got up from the table. "My father is from Louisiana. He gets on me about manners and proper grammar and such."

"I think that's nice."

I waited, hoping she'd ask me to stay.

"I'll walk out with you," she said.

We went through a dark hallway that smelled of wood polish. A man's work cap and raincoat, a 4-H Club sweater, and a denim jacket with lace sewn on the cuffs hung from wood pegs on the wall. A man's galoshes and a pair of white rubber boots, the kind a teenage girl would wear, rested on the floor. There was no housecoat or woman's hat or house shoes or parasol or shawl or scarf in the hallway.

Also, there was a solemnity about the living room that I hadn't noticed before. Maybe the effect was created by the nineteenth-century furniture and the radio/record player with a potted plant on top of it and the empty fireplace and the couch and chairs that looked as though no one sat in them. I had thought Valerie Epstein lived in the perfect home. Now I wondered.

"Is your mother here?" I asked.

"She died during the war."

"I'm sorry."

"She's not. She did what she thought was right."

"Pardon?"

"Her brother got left behind when her family fled Paris. My mother had herself smuggled back into the country. The Gestapo caught her. We think she was shipped to Dachau."

"Gee, Miss Valerie."

"Come on, I'll walk outside with you," she said. She put her arm through mine.

The porch glider was swaying in the wind, the trees swelling, yellow dust rising into the sky. I could smell the odor of rain striking a hot sidewalk. "Can I have your phone number?"

"It's in the book. You'd better hurry." She glanced at the sky. "Don't get into trouble. You understand? Stay away from Grady, no matter how much he tries to provoke you."

"My father will let me have the car tonight. We can go to the watermelon stand. I'll pick you up at eight and have you back home in less than an hour."

"Nobody is this stubborn."

"I call it conviction."

"Back home by nine?"

"Promise," I said.

Her eyes crinkled.

IT RAINED MOST of the night. When I woke in the morning, the sun was pink, the sky blue, the sidewalks streaked with shadow and moisture. I loved the dead-end street where we lived in our small brick bungalow. All the houses on the street were built of brick and had fruit trees and flower gardens in the yards, and there was a wall of bamboo on the cul-de-sac and, on the other side, a pasture dotted with live oaks that were two hundred years old. I sat down on the front steps with my sack lunch and waited for my ride to school. Saber Bledsoe, my best friend, picked me up every school day in his 1936 wreck of a Chevy, one he had chopped and channeled and modified and customized and bought junk replacement parts for, although it remained a smoking wreck you could smell and hear coming from a block away.

There was nothing Saber wouldn't do, particularly on a dare. At school he flushed M-80s down the plumbing and blew water out of commodes all over the building, usually between classes, when people were seated on them. The most hated teacher in the school, or maybe the whole city, was Mr. Krauser. Saber sneaked into the teachers' lounge and stuffed a formaldehyde-soaked frog in Mr. Krauser's container of coleslaw and caused him to puke in the faculty sink. Saber also unzipped his pants and got down on his stomach and stuck his flopper through a hole in the floor above Krauser's classroom, letting it hang there like an obscene lightbulb until Krauser figured out why all his students' faces looked like grinning balloons about to pop.

I was determined this would be a good day. Probably nobody noticed my erection in the middle of the drive-in. So what if I had gotten into it with Grady Harrelson? What could he do? He'd had his chance. The hoods in the Heights? Valerie had said they were just neighborhood guys. I had taken Valerie Epstein to the watermelon stand and driven her back home and sat with her on the glider and even patted the top of her hand when a streak of lightning crashed in the park. Nobody paid any attention to us.

Maybe in the Heights I had found a part of town free of my problems. Maybe I had found a place where fear wasn't a way of life.

Wrong.

As soon as I got into the car, I could tell Saber was agitated. He backed into the street and headed toward Westheimer, the floor stick vibrating in his palm, his T-shirt rolled up to his armpits. He looked at me, then his head started bobbing on a spring, and he gave me what was known as the Saber Bledsoe stare, a cross-eyed, openmouthed reconfiguration of his face indicating disbelief at your stupidity.

"Why mess around? Just join some suicide unit and go to Korea," he said.

"You have to run that by me again, Sabe."

"The word is you got into it with Grady Harrelson at a Galveston drive-in. Then you went up to the Heights and were driving around with Valerie Epstein."

"Where'd you hear that?"

"Where did I *not* hear it? You told some greaseballs to go fuck themselves, one greaseball in particular?"

"There's no way you can know this."

"The guy you almost got it on with was Loren Nichols. He shot a man in the chest with a dart gun at Prince's drive-in."

Saber had light red hair he wore in a flattop combed back on the sides, and green slits for eyes and the innocuous stare of a lizard and a peckerwood accent and a level of nervous energy that made you think of a door slamming. He pulled a cigarette from a pack of Camels with his mouth.

"They came by my house last night, Aaron," he said, the cigarette bouncing on his lip. "Somebody must have given them my name."

"Who came by?"

"Loren and three other greasers."

I felt a hole yawning open in my stomach. "What did they want?"

"You."

"What did you tell them?"

"I told them my old man was drunk and had a baseball bat, and they'd better drag their sorry asses out of my driveway. Guess what? Before I could get the words out of my mouth, the old man came stumbling out of the garage with a Stillson in his hand."

"We need to forget this, Saber."

"It'll be all over school by second period. You helped bust up Grady Harrelson and Valerie Epstein?"

"No."

"Doesn't matter. The story will be a legend by this afternoon. You actually went out with her?"

"More or less."

"That's like getting laid by Doris Day. You're a hero, man. Does she have a sister? I'm ready."

Chapter 3

FOURTH PERIOD, SABER and I had metal shop. The teacher was Mr. Krauser, living proof we'd descended from apes. He had been a tank commander in France and Germany during the war and used to tell stories about how he and his fellow tankers smashed their Shermans through French farmhouses for fun. One of the vandal tanks crashed into a cellar, which Krauser thought was hilarious. He also told us how, as an object lesson for his men, he dragged an elderly German civilian by the collar into the street and occupied his home. Once while drunk at the bowling alley, he borrowed a knife from a student and sawed off a bowler's necktie.

Saber was the only kid in school who knew how to stick porcupine quills in Krauser and keep the wounds green on a daily basis. Krauser believed it was Saber who'd hung his plunger through the hole in the ceiling, but he couldn't prove it and was always trying to find another reason to nail Saber to the wall. But Saber never misbehaved in metal shop, whereas other guys did and in serious fashion.

Our school was located close to River Oaks, a tree-shaded paradise filled with palatial homes. But the school district was huge and extended into hard-core blue-collar areas of North Houston and even over to Wayside and Jensen Drive, where some of the roughest kids on earth lived. Metal shop was a natural for the latter. Three guys commandeered the foundry and cast molds in the sandbox and poured aluminum reproductions of brass knuckles they sold for a dollar apiece, the outer edges ground smooth or left ragged and sharp. These were things Krauser had a way of not seeing, just as he didn't see bullies shoving other kids around. It wasn't out of fear, either. I think at heart Krauser was one of them. He liked coming up on a spindly kid and squeezing his thumb into the kid's upper arm, pressing it into the bone, then saying, "Not much meat there."

That was when Saber would find ways to get even for the victim, like going up to Krauser and saying, "What should I do with this paintbrush, Mr. Krauser? While you were taking a whiz, Kyle Firestone told Jimmy McDougal to put his hands in his pockets and shoved the brush into his mouth. Look, it's got spit all over it. You want it, or should I wash it in the lavatory?"

This morning was different. Mr. Krauser wasn't watching Saber; he was looking out the door at a 1941 Ford sprayed with primer that had just pulled up on the shale bib by the baseball diamond. Four guys got out, combing their hair, all of them wearing drapes and needle-nose stomps. They leaned against the fenders and headlights of their car and lit up, even though they were on school property. Krauser rotated his head, then looked over his shoulder. "Come here, Broussard."

I put down my term project, a gear puller I was polishing on the electric brush, and walked toward him. "Yes, sir?"

Krauser had a broad upper lip and wide-set eyes and a bold stare and long sideburns and black hair growing out of his shirt cuffs. His facial features seemed squeezed together as though he carried an invisible weight on top of his head. As soon as you saw him, you wanted to glance away, at the same time fearing he would know how you felt about him.

"Heard you had an adventure in the Heights."

"Not me."

"You know that bunch out there?"

I shook my head, my expression vague.

"You don't want to mess with them," he said.

"I don't want trouble, Mr. Krauser."

"I bet you don't."

"Sir?"

His eyes went up and down my body. "Been working out lately?"

"I have jobs at the neighborhood grocery and the filling station."

"Not exactly what I had in mind. Tuck your shirt in and come with me."

"What's going on?"

"I'm going to show you how it's done. They think you were hunting in their snatch patch. Dumb move, Broussard."

"How did you know I was in the Heights?"

"Heard about it during homeroom. I've seen that bunch before. There's only one way to deal with them, son. If you've got a bad tooth, you pull the bad tooth."

"I really don't want to do this, sir."

"Who said you had a choice?"

I didn't know what Krauser was up to. He was no friend. Nor did he care about justice. I could hear him breathing and could smell the testosterone that seemed ironed into his clothes. By the time we reached the ball diamond, I was seeing spots before my eyes.

"What are you guys doing here?" Krauser said to them.

The tall guy who had braced me in front of Valerie's house was combing his hair with both hands as if Krauser weren't there. He was wearing gray drapes and a black suede belt and a long-sleeved purple rayon shirt. He reminded me of the photographs I had seen of the jazz cornetist Chet Baker: the same hollow cheeks and dark eyes, an expression that was less like aggression than acceptance of death. It was a strange look for a guy who was probably not over nineteen.

"Did you hear me?" Krauser said.

"You got a rule against people having a smoke?" the tall greaser said.

"There's a 'no loitering' sign right behind you," Krauser said.

"That's a police station across the street, right? Tell them Loren Nichols is here. Tell them to kiss my ass. You can do the same."

"You shot a man in a drive-in."

"With an air-pump pistol. A grown man who put his hand up my sister's dress at a junior high school picnic. I don't know if that was in the paper or not."

I heard the bell ring and classes start emptying out in the hallways and concourses. Neither Loren Nichols nor his friends had looked at me, and I thought the incident might pass, that I might go to the cafeteria with Saber and forget about everything bad that had happened since Saturday evening. Maybe I could even make peace with Loren Nichols. I had to give it to him. He was an impressive guy. The moment was like an interlude in time when the potential for good or bad could go either way.

Mr. Krauser rested his hand on my shoulder. I felt an icicle run down my side. "My young friend Aaron has told me how you boys treated him," he said. "Now you're here to pick on him some more. What do y'all think we should do about that?"

Loren's gaze shifted from Krauser to me, his head tilting. "Buy him a dress? He's a cute kid, all right."

"The kids in our school respect authority," Krauser said. "They report guys like you. They don't put themselves on your level."

"I didn't say anything to anybody. That's a goddamn lie," I said, my eyes stinging with moisture, the sunlight dissolving into needles. "Tell them, Mr. Krauser."

"I want y'all to leave Aaron alone," he said. "If you bother him again, I'd better not hear about it. Don't you be bothering Saber Bledsoe, either."

"You got a sissy farm here?"

"Look at me, boy. I'll rip out your package and wrap it around your throat," Krauser said.

Loren propped one foot on the bumper and scratched the inside of his thigh, gazing at the school. "Glad to have made your acquaintance. You got yourself quite a crew here. That's River Oaks across the street? We'd better get back to our part of town."

"Smart boy. Keep being a smart boy and leave Aaron and Saber alone," Krauser said.

They got into their car and drove away, the dual exhausts purring on the asphalt. My knees were shaking with shame and sickness and fear. Krauser squeezed my shoulder with one hand, massaging it, tightening his fingers until they bit into the nerves like a dentist's drill. "You're safe now, Aaron, bless your heart. I always like to help out one of Saber's friends. Let me know if I can do anything else for y'all."

He dropped his hand from my shoulder and left me standing on the grass like a wood post. I couldn't hear any sound at all, not even the chain rattling on the flagpole by the ball diamond.

"I'M GOING TO get that cocksucker," Saber said that afternoon as he drove, a quart of Jax between his thighs.

"Which cocksucker?" I asked.

"Krauser, who else? I'm going to call in a few markers. I know a guy who's a master of photographic surveillance. I bet Krauser is a sexual nightmare. I'm going to catch him muffing the meter maid or pronging sheep, then air-drop photos all over the school."

I looked straight ahead and didn't speak. I could still feel Krauser's fingers digging into my shoulder, probing for a weak spot.

"Don't let him get to you," Saber said. "God, I hate that bastard. You're a stand-up guy, you hear me? You called Krauser a liar? Nobody in the school has that kind of guts. I bet he won't sleep tonight. You showed him up in front of the greaseballs. You're a musician, Aaron. What's Krauser? A nothing."

"They think I'm a snitch."

"Fuck *them*. You're a model for guys like me. I think there's a stink to this. Loren Nichols was in Gatesville. Guys with Loren's record don't start a beef in this part of town unless they want to pick state cotton."

"I went into his territory."

"So does the garbage collector. Trust me, there's something bigger involved here. Krauser has awakened a sleeping giant—the Army of Bledsoe."

"He wants to suck you in, Sabe."

"He succeeded."

At the red light, Saber began gargling with beer, swallowing it with his neck stretched back on the seat, revving his engine, indifferent to the stares from other cars.

My father kept a small office at the back of the house. He had inherited the secretary bookcase from his father, a lawyer appointed head of the Public Works Administration in Louisiana by Franklin Roosevelt and one of the few men in the state with the courage to testify against Huey Long at the impeachment hearing. My father worked for years on a history of his family, his grandfather in particular, a young Confederate lieutenant who was with Jackson through the entirety of the Shenandoah campaign.

He never typed, writing page after page in longhand, sometimes late into the night, smoking cigarettes he left floating in the toilet bowl. On his shelves were boxes of letters written at First and Second Manassas, First and Second Fredericksburg, Cross Keys, Malvern Hill, Chantilly, Chancellorsville, Gettysburg, and a prison camp at Johnson's Island, Ohio. My father's tragedy was one shared by almost all his family. Their patriarch had been a generous and honest man and, as a result, died a pauper at the onset of World War II. His family believed their genteel, privileged world had died with him, and they began to drink and substitute the past for the present and let their own lives slip away.

I walked into my father's office and sat down. He wrote with a fat, obsolete fountain pen that leaked ink. A cigarette burned on the cusp of his ashtray; a thermos of coffee rested on his desk; the window was cracked to let the attic fan draw the evening air from outside. The sky was filled with crimson and purple and black clouds that resembled plumes from an industrial furnace. I could probably say a lot about my father's writing, but for me the most memorable words he ever wrote were contained in a single sentence on the first page of his manuscript: "Never in human history have so many fine men fought so nobly in defense of such an ignominious cause."

"How you doing there, pal?" he said.

It was a rare moment. He was happy and did not smell of alcohol. I sat next to him.

"I've got a problem," I said.

"It can't be that bad, can it?"

"I got into it with some guys from the Heights."

"Try not to say 'guys,' Aaron."

"These aren't kids, Daddy."

"They insulted you?"

"They came to school today. Mr. Krauser made me walk with him to their car. He said he was going to show me how to deal with them."

"Maybe he was acting like a good fellow. I had a teacher like that at St. Peter's when I was a boy. All the boys looked up to him. I've always had fond memories of him."

"Mr. Krauser shamed me."

"I don't understand."

"He said I snitched on them. One guy said I should wear a dress."

"Your teacher was probably making them accountable."

"Mr. Krauser is out to get Saber. He went through me to do it."

"It's good to stick up for your chum. But Saber can take care of himself. I bet you'll never see those fellows again."

"The trouble started over a girl from the Heights. Saturday night I got involved in an argument between her and her boyfriend. He lives in River Oaks. I think he's a bad guy."

"Don't say—"

"I know. But he's a bad guy, Daddy. I don't know what to do."

"Maybe we should all have a talk. I mean if they come back. If there's going to be a fight, there's going to be a fight."

"This isn't about a fight. This guy Loren Nichols shot a man with an air pistol."

"A BB gun?"

"The kind that shoots steel darts. It hits like a twenty-two."

"This sounds like one of Saber's stories. Do you want me to talk with Mr. Krauser?"

"Mr. Krauser is a liar. Why would he tell you the truth if he lied about me to a bunch of greaseballs?"

"Don't use language like that. You want to go for a Grapette?"

My efforts were useless. I folded my hands between my legs and hung my head. "No, sir."

"Let's sleep on this. Tomorrow everything will look different. You'll see."

He adjusted his rimless glasses and looked down at the page he had been working on, his attention already far away, perhaps on a hillside in Virginia where grapeshot and canister hummed louder than bees through the warm air, while a drummer boy about to die stood mute and powerless amid the horror taking place around him.

I went into the kitchen, where my mother was pulling a pie from the oven. She was an attractive woman and often caught the eye of other men, in whom she had no interest, even as flatterers. She always seemed to be waking from a reverie whenever someone walked up to her unexpectedly. On occasion she cried without cause and walked in circles, knotting her hands, her lips moving as though she were conversing with someone. Her peculiarities were so much a part of her life that they seemed normal. "Why, hey there, sleepyhead. Did you have a nice nap?"

"I wasn't sleeping."

"Where have you been?"

"Talking with Daddy."

"Tell him dinner is ready. Have you done your homework?"

"I'm not feeling well. I'd better not eat."

"What's wrong?"

"Nothing. I'm going outside."

"Outside? What are you going to do outside? Why are you behaving so strangely?"

"Everything is fine, Mother."

"Why do you have that wrinkle between your eyes? I don't like it when you have that. Come back here, Aaron."

I went out the screen door and down the driveway through the porte cochere and began walking down the block. I walked until my feet hurt. Then I hitchhiked with no destination in mind and by dark was in a part of town where sundowners and people in the life frolicked and Judaic-Christian law held no sway.

THE JUKE AND barbecue joints were loud, the doors wide open, the elevated sidewalks inset with tethering rings and littered with paper cups and beer cans, rust-stained where the rain spouts bled across the concrete. Outside speakers at the beauty parlors and barbershops played Ruth Brown, Big Joe Turner, Guitar Slim, LaVern Baker, and Gatemouth Brown. Mexicans and blue-collar whites and people of color melded together in dress and dialect and the addictions and poverty and lucre they shared. The only authority figures were black Houston cops who drove battered patrol cars and parked inconspicuously at an abandoned filling station under an oak tree on a corner and were prohibited from arresting a white person. The prostitutes often carried either a gun or a barber's razor; the pimps and dope dealers stood on the sidewalks, dressed in the zoot style of the forties; for a free beer, a kind soul was always willing to go inside a liquor store and buy what a white teenager needed. For me that was one can of malt liquor.

I sat down on the curb and drank it. It was hot and tasted like wheat germ with lighter fluid poured in it. I kept hearing a sound like an electrical wire shorting in a rain puddle, and I thought the buzzing sound might be coming from the neon sign over the pawnshop behind me. Except there was nothing wrong with the sign. I got up from the curb and dropped my empty malt liquor can in a garbage barrel and looked at the glittering display of saxophones and trumpets and trombones and drums inside the pawnshop's windows. There was even a J50 acoustic Gibson in one window, just like mine, along with rows of private-investigator badges, handcuffs, brass knuckles, blackjacks and slapjacks, and pistols of every kind.

I had seven dollars in my wallet. I went inside and bought a stiletto with a thin black handle and a tight spring and a six-inch rippling blade. One touch of the thumb and the blade sprang to life, and I felt a sense of power in my palm that was almost sexual.

I walked back down the street toward the police car parked at the filling station, the switchblade riding in the back pocket of my jeans. I was sure the cops in the patrol car were watching. But they were black and I was white, and I knew they would not bother me. That I was taking advantage of the unjust way colored police officers were treated made me ashamed, but not enough to cause me to turn back from my destination.

What was my plan? Where was I bound? I had no idea. I knew only that I was going somewhere to do something that seemed disconnected from the person I was. It was like stepping onto a carousel and disappearing inside the music of the calliope and the mirrors on its hub while the horses and children spun round and round, unaware that I had become their guardian.

Or at least that was what I told myself.

Chapter 4

In the early a.m. I found myself by a phone booth under a streetlight ringed with humidity somewhere in North Houston. I had fifteen cents in my pocket and no bills in my wallet. The air smelled of sewer gas and dead beetles in the gutters and a coulee where the owners of a filling station had poured fifty-gallon barrels of oil. I dropped a nickel into the pay phone and woke up Saber. "I need a ride."

"Where are you?" he said.

I looked through the window of the booth at the street signs and gave him their names. "I think I'm not far from North Shepherd. I've got some blank spaces in my head."

"You had one of your spells?" he said.

"About three hours' worth."

"My folks are going to brown their pants."

"I can walk."

"Stay where you're at. The Army of Bledsoe does not leave its wounded on the field. Did you do anything we need to worry about?"

I reached into my back pocket. The knife was still there. I removed it and pressed the release button. The blade leaped into the air, clean and glazed with a clear lubricant, the way I bought it. "Everything is copacetic."

"Keep a cool stool. I'm on my way."

* * *

MY PARENTS WERE furious. I told them I fell asleep in the hammock in Saber's backyard and that he and his parents thought I'd gone home until I knocked on the screen door, confused and mosquito-bitten.

"Why didn't you tell anyone you were going to Saber's?" my father asked. He was wearing his pajamas; the lights were on all over the house.

"I'm sorry I made y'all worry," I said.

"We'll talk about this later," he said, his mouth bitter.

My mother's eyes were full of tears, her nails hooked into the heels of her hands. "You're going to give me a nervous breakdown. I've had a lifetime of your father's drinking, and now this. I can smell it on you. Where did you go?"

"You saw Saber drive me home," I replied.

"Don't lie," she said.

My father went into his office and turned on the desk lamp and stared at the manuscript pages on the desk blotter. He picked up a page and read it, then sat down at the desk and looked out the window into the darkness, like a man for whom a black box was a way of life.

THE NEXT MORNING I missed the first three periods at school and barely made metal shop before the bell rang. I dropped my book bag on my worktable. With luck, Mr. Krauser would give me a hall pass to the restroom so I could wash my face and sit on the toilet and deliberately turn my head into an ice cube. But hall pass or not, I was safe from my parents and the consequences of my actions, whatever they were, until three P.M. I sat at my worktable and lowered my eyes and tried to doze. The windows in the shop were ajar, and I could smell mowed grass on the wind, like a pastoral hint of summer vacation and release from all my problems at school. When I opened my eyes, I saw Mr. Krauser framed against the open door of his office, his finger pointed at me. "Inside, Broussard," he said.

He closed the door behind me and turned the key in the lock. There were streaks of color in his face and perspiration on his upper lip, as though he had been standing over the foundry.

"I do something wrong, sir?" I asked.

"I want to get something straight before I walk you across the street to the River Oaks substation."

"The police station?"

"You guys aren't dragging me into your shit, you got that?"

"I don't know what we're talking about, sir."

"A plainclothes cop was just here. He called your house, and your mother said you overslept and were on your way to school. I told him I'd deliver you to the station. I also told him you had never been in trouble and were a good kid. You owe me a big favor."

"What's a cop want with me?"

"That is not the issue. The issue is the conversation we had with the four hoods in the souped-up Ford. I told them they were on school property without authorization. I told them to get off campus. That was the entire substance of the conversation. *Right?*"

He was nodding while he spoke, waiting for me to agree with him, his eyes as hard as marbles, locked on mine. There was no window in his office; his body odor seemed to eat up the oxygen in the room.

"You made out I was a snitch. You set me up, Mr. Krauser. Has something happened?"

"Don't you dare lay this on me, you little son of a bitch."

"You told Loren Nichols you'd rip out his package and wrap it around his throat. Has somebody hurt him? Is that why you're so afraid?"

"I hope that cop sticks a baton so far up your ass, you'll be coughing splinters."

AT THE SUBSTATION, a patrolman ushered me into a small room and left me alone with a huge thick-necked man gazing through the window at the high school campus across the street. He wore cowboy boots and a brown suit and white shirt and a tie with a swampy sunset painted on it. Behind him, a fedora rested crown-down on an army-surplus metal desk that was otherwise bare. He turned around and stared into my face, his eyes the color of lead. A snub-nose chrome-plated revolver and a badge were clipped on his belt. "I'm Detective Merton Jenks. Sit down," he said.

"Are my folks here?"

He pawed at his cheek, his gaze never leaving my face. The skin around his eyes was grainy, like scales fanning back into his hairline. I thought of a reptile breaking out of its shell, perhaps millions of years ago. I sat down and looked up at him. He had not answered my question. I tried to hold his stare.

"You carry a shank?" he asked.

"A knife? No, sir."

"Turn your pockets out. Put everything on the desk."

"Yes, sir."

"Did I tell you to stand up?"

"No, sir."

My hands were shaking as I removed my belongings from my pockets. He sat on the corner of the desk and watched me. "What do you call this?" he said.

"It's a penknife. I use it to cut string at the grocery."

"You sack groceries?"

"I tote them outside, too. Sometimes I work at a service station."

"That's a good job for a boy. Pumping gasoline, fixing tires, and all that," he said, half smiling. "That's what you do, right?"

"Yes, sir, oil changes, too."

"What were you doing last night?"

"Not much. I took a walk."

"Where'bouts did you walk?"

"I can't rightly say. I have spells."

"What kind of spells?"

"Like down in the dumps. They pass. They run in my family."

"Know who Loren Nichols is?"

"A guy I had trouble with up in the Heights. He came to the

school with his friends yesterday." I straightened my back and took a fresh breath. Maybe this was about Loren Nichols and his buddies, not me.

"Were they in a 1941 Ford that belongs to Loren and his brother?"

"It was a '41 Ford. I don't know who owns it."

"You wouldn't have vandalized his car, would you?"

"No, I don't do things like that. Are my folks on their way?"

"You mean 'no, sir'?"

"Yes, sir, that's what I meant."

"Loren says he saw you in the Heights last night, not far from his house. Were you in the Heights?"

"I never bothered those guys. They came after me. I don't know what's going on, Mr. Jenks."

"Detective Jenks. You didn't answer my question. Were you in the Heights or not?"

"I don't know where I was. Did somebody cut their tires? Is that why you asked if I had a knife?"

"You have no memory of where you were or what you did? I'd better get this down." He felt his pockets as though he didn't know where his pencil and pad were, then removed them from his shirt pocket and began writing, pressing the pencil hard into the paper, dotting an "i" as if throwing a dart.

"I know I didn't cut anybody's tires," I said.

"If you were in a blackout, how do you know *what* you did?"

He had me.

"Would you set fire to a car?"

"No, that's crazy."

"Because that's what somebody did. Cutting the valve stems wasn't enough."

"Loren Nichols says I burned his car?"

He looked at what he had written on the pad. "One step at a time. You did or did not cut his tires?"

"There's a girl in the Heights I wanted to see. Maybe that's why I was in the neighborhood. Her name is Valerie Epstein."

"You were chasing some new puss? That's why you were in the Heights? It's coincidence you were seen in proximity to the Ford, owned by guys you admit to having trouble with?"

"You don't have the right to talk about Miss Valerie like that."

"Get up."

"Sir?"

He ripped the chair from under me and threw it against the wall, spilling me on the floor. "You think I came from downtown over a burned car owned by two punks who were in Gatesville? Are you that dumb?"

I pushed myself up, swaying, my knees not locking properly. "You didn't have the right to say what you said."

This time I held his stare and my eyes didn't water. He picked up the chair with one hand and slammed it down in front of the desk. "Sit down." When I didn't move, he opened a desk drawer and removed a telephone book. "I'll take your head off, boy."

I sat down but never took my eyes off his face, even though I couldn't stop blinking. He removed a five-by-seven black-and-white photo from his coat pocket and set it on the desk. "You know this girl?"

"No."

"Look at the girl, not me."

"I don't know her."

There were two images on the same sheet of paper, a side view and a frontal of the same young woman. She was wearing an oversize cotton jumper with gray and white stripes on it. At the bottom of the frontal photo was her prison number. She was hardly out of her teens, if that. Her hair was awry, like thread caught in a comb. Her eyes seemed to well with sadness and despair.

"You never saw her anywhere? You're sure about that?" he said.

"Yes, I'm sure."

"You didn't decide to try some Mexican poon?"

"Why are you asking me questions like this?"

"Her name was Wanda Estevan. She was a prostitute in Galveston."

"*Was* a prostitute?"

"Somebody broke her neck. Maybe she was thrown from a car. Or maybe somebody broke her neck in the car, then bounced her in the street. About two blocks from where the Ford was torched."

"What does her death have to do with the car?"

"There was gasoline and detergent on her jeans. The same combination that was used to burn the car. Quite a puzzle, don't you think? You have gasoline cans at your filling station?"

"Sure. For people who run out."

"How about in your garage?"

"No, sir."

"Were you out with Saber Bledsoe early this morning?"

"Yes, sir, he picked me up in the Heights and drove me home."

"You said you didn't know if you were in the Heights or not. Rats must have eaten holes in your memory bank."

He had me again. He put a Pall Mall in his mouth and scratched a match on the desk, the flame flaring on his cigarette. He took a couple of puffs and removed a piece of tobacco from his lip. "We found a gas can in his garage. The can has soap detergent in it. I'd say your friend has shit on his nose."

WHEN I GOT HOME, I threw up in the toilet. Then I recovered the stiletto from under my mattress and flicked it open. I saw on one side of the blade, barely visible, a trace of rubber, the kind that might be left from slicing off a valve stem. My father came into the room without knocking. "Want to explain that?"

"This frog sticker?"

"I'd call it a weapon a criminal would have. Where did you get it?"

"In a pawn store."

His eyes rested on the shelf above my desk where I kept my arrowhead collection and antique fishing lures and minié balls and a rusted revolver that had no cylinder and a cigar box full of Indianhead pennies. He didn't speak for a long time. "Put it on the shelf. It doesn't leave the room."

"Yes, sir."

"As a rule, when members of our church's clergy talk about sin, what are they referring to?"

"Sex."

"That's correct. They don't mention much about war, nor about violence in general. But that's the real enemy, that and greed. Don't let anybody tell you different. A man who carries a knife like that one is a man who's afraid."

When my father spoke this way, he was a different man, more regal and just and clearheaded than any man I ever met. He allowed no guns in our home and hunted ducks only one day a year, with the president of his company, in a blind over by Anahuac. After a prowler broke into our garage a couple of times, my father placed a brick in a hatbox and wrapped the hatbox in satin paper and tied a ribbon on it, then he set the box on the front seat of the automobile. He also put a note in it that read:

Dear Burglar,

While you were stealing this brick, a twelve-gauge shotgun was aimed at your back. If you return, you will not be received in a gracious manner. I do not wish to offend you, but you seem very inept. I suggest you join a church or practice your profession somewhere else. Give serious thought to this.

Best regards,

Your victim,

James Eustace Broussard

Our burglar friend never returned.

I closed the stiletto and placed it on the shelf and sat down on my bed. My Gibson was lying facedown on the spread. I picked it up and propped the curve in the sound box across my knee and formed an E chord on the neck. "I feel a mite sick, Daddy," I said.

"Your stomach acting up again?"

"It's not acting up. It's always like that. Like I have a boil on the lining."

A shadow slid across his face. "Did that police detective touch you?"

"He tore the chair out from under me and threw me on the floor. That's not the problem, though."

"If that's not the problem, *what* is?"

"He said a Mexican woman, a prostitute, was killed two blocks from the burned car. He thinks she was mixed up in the burning of the car. He says the cops found the gasoline can that did the job. It was in Saber's garage."

There was a long silence. I couldn't look at him. "Daddy?" I said. But he didn't answer. "Daddy, say something."

"What have you got us into, son?"

SABER WASN'T AT school the next day. I didn't know if his father had beat him up or if he had just cut school. Mr. Bledsoe was from rural Alabama. He wasn't a bad man, but he was uneducated and insecure and frightened and each day had to scrub off the grime from his job at a rendering plant with Ajax and a bar of Lava soap and a stiff brush. Whenever I saw a bruise on Saber, I didn't ask about it. I didn't think Mr. Bledsoe meant to hurt his son. When he was drunk, he made me think of a sightless pig trapped inside a circle of javelins.

At three o'clock I hitched a ride to Saber's small frame house on the edge of the West University district. He was under his Chevy on a creeper board, his legs on the grass. I grabbed him by the ankle and pulled him out. He had a wrench in one hand; he rubbed at a piece of rust in his eye. "What the hell," he said.

"Why weren't you at school?"

"Didn't feel like answering questions all over campus. Besides, I wanted to put my split manifold on the engine and hang my new mufflers. I filled them with oil first and set the oil on fire. The carbon gives it that throaty sound."

"You're thinking about putting dual exhausts on your heap when the cops are trying to send us to Gatesville?"

He pulled his knees up in front of him, his skin dark in the shade of the car. He used his shirt to wipe the grease off his cheek. "I don't know where that gasoline can came from. I told that to the detective.

So did my old man. I was proud of him. He told the detective to pack his shit up both nostrils."

"I hate to tell you this, Sabe, but that's not smart."

"I thought it was. They're after us, Aaron. I told you."

"Who is 'they'?"

"Ask yourself where all this started."

I shook my head.

"Don't play dumb," he said. "This is about Valerie Epstein."

"No, it's not."

"You went to see her, and the next thing you know, Loren Nichols and his greaseballs show up in front of her house. The next day the same guys show up at school and in my driveway. In the meantime, Mr. Krauser is twirling his joint in the punch bowl."

"I can't tell you what that image does to my brain."

"Who's the guy getting a free pass on all this?" he asked.

"You tell me."

"Stop acting like a simp. You're talking to the Bledsoe, the Delphic oracle of Houston, Texas." He cocked back his head and spat in the air, catching his saliva on the return trip in his mouth.

"You're unbelievable."

"I know. I also know Grady Harrelson is a prick from his hairline to the soles of his feet. I think we should make some home calls."

He pulled himself back under the car and finished hanging one of his dual mufflers on a bracket, oblivious to the rest of the world.

RIVER OAKS WAS foreign territory. It wasn't simply a section of the city that contained some of the most beautiful homes in America or perhaps the world; it was a state of mind. Unlike the Garden District in New Orleans, the mansions of River Oaks were not connected to the antebellum South and not stained by association with the lash and branding iron and auction block. Inside an urban forest were homes as white and pure as a wedding cake, the St. Augustine lawns a deep blue-green in the shade, the gardens and trellises and gazebos blooming with flowers as big as grapefruit, almost all of it bought and paid for by oil that sprang like chocolate syrup from the ground, oceans of it put there by a loving Creator.

Police cruisers rarely patrolled the streets. They didn't need to; no professional criminal would invade a sanctuary like River Oaks. The afternoon was cooling, the streets dropping into shadow as we motored toward Grady Harrelson's house, Saber's new mufflers rumbling off the asphalt. I asked him how he knew where Grady lived.

"A year ago he shoved my cousin into the Shamrock swimming pool with all her clothes on. On prom night I followed him and his girlfriend to his house. His folks were away, and he thought he'd use the opportunity to get his knob polished at home. I bagged up a dead skunk and shoved it through his mail slot with a broom handle."

"I don't believe you."

"So ask him about it. His girlfriend was screaming, and every light in the house was on when I left."

I looked at the side of his face. His expression was serene. The Bledsoe never lied, at least not about his one-man crusade against hypocrisy and phoniness. Sometimes I longed to know his secrets, but even at my young age, I knew he had paid a high price for them. "I don't know if this is a good idea."

"You got to do recon," he said. "Write down license numbers. See who's going in and out of the house. I've got connections at the motor vehicle department."

"Grady Harrelson's father will have us ground into salt."

"That's my point. We'll get the coordinates on these guys and call in the artillery."

"Have you lost your mind?"

"Grady is out to hurt you, Aaron. I'm not going to let that happen." He put his hand on my forearm and squeezed it, maybe for longer than he should. "You're the only real family I got."

WE WERE NOW on the outer edge of River Oaks, in an area where the yards were banked and measured in acres, the houses three stories high with white-columned porches, the driveways circular and shaded by trees that creaked in the wind. The sky was a soft blue, the lawns deep in shadow, the air scented with flowers and chlorine and meat fires. The interior of every house tinkled with golden light.

Saber began reciting the encyclopedic levels of information he had on the Harrelson family; I would have dismissed most everything he said if it had come from anyone else. But he had a brain like flypaper and never forgot anything.

"See, the old man isn't just a rice farmer and oil driller. He's mixed up with these Galveston mobsters who're moving out to Vegas," he said. "You know their names."

"What do you mean, I know?"

"Your uncle is buddies with some of these guys. It's no big deal, Aaron."

"Don't be talking about my family like that. You get this stuff out of men's magazines with Japs on the cover, strafing naked women tied to stakes in the Amazon."

"The best source of information in the nation," he said. "Look at what we read in school, *Silas Marner* and *The House of the Seven Gables.* I bet that's what people in hell have to read for all eternity. Hitler and Tojo and guys like that."

He coasted to the curb, under the limbs of a spreading oak, the engine coughing like a sick animal. Up ahead we could see the floodlamps shining on the front of Grady's house and a party taking place by the swimming pool in the side yard. Saber took a pair of binoculars from the glove box. I could feel my heart thudding against my ribs. He read my mind. "They cain't see us," he said. "I'm going to read off these license plate numbers. You write them down."

"This is nuts."

"Take off the blinders, Aaron. How do you think these people got their money? Hard work? I bet this place is full of gangsters. How did Grady get discharged from the Marine Corps?"

"Grady Harrelson was in the marines?"

"He enlisted after he graduated. Except, when he was about to be shipped to Korea, he discovered he had asthma. His old man pulled strings. The guy's not just a tumblebug, he's yellow."

"He might be a bad guy, but I don't think he's yellow."

Saber began reading off license numbers, then stopped and took the binoculars from his eyes and wiped the lenses and looked through them again. "I don't need this."

"Need what?"

He squeezed his scrotum. "My big boy just woke up with a vengeance. Check it out. You ever see a pair of cantaloupes like that? Those bongos were made in heaven."

I took the binoculars from him and focused them on the pool. Nine or ten guys Grady's age were swimming or barbecuing or springing off the board. The obvious center of attention was a black-haired, dark-skinned woman who must have been in her late twenties. She was lying on a recliner, her white swimsuit like wet Kleenex.

"Who is she?" I said.

"Mexico's answer to Esther Williams." He pulled the binoculars from my hands and looked through again. "Didn't I tell you the Harrelsons had ties to Galveston?"

"She's a pro?"

"No, she's the kindergarten teacher at St. Anne's Elementary. Say a prayer of thanks you have me to escort you through these situations. Oh, man, I'm about to shoot my wad. Look at that broad. It's criminal that a woman can be that beautiful."

"You know those guys?" I asked.

"It's his regular crowd. Guys who went to military school because their parents don't want them. Know what makes them different from us?"

"They're rich?"

"They don't have feelings. After we do our recon, I'll drive you over to Valerie's. That's what's really on your mind, isn't it?"

"I want to tell her we didn't have anything to do with burning Loren Nichols's car."

"Right, otherwise she'd be heartbroken."

"Lay off it, Saber."

But his attention had shifted to a kid who'd climbed up to the high board and was looking straight at us.

"Start the car," I said.

Saber shook a cigarette out of his pack. "Bad form. There's a tire iron under your seat. I'd love to bash one of these guys. Maybe sling brains all over the bushes."

"Are you serious? What's the matter with you? Start the car."

"Too late. Don't rattle. You got to brass it out. Look upon this as an opportunity."

A sea-green Cadillac with fins bounced out of the entrance to the driveway, and a Buick with a grille like a chromium mouth came up behind us, sealing off the street. We were shark meat. Grady's friends piled out of the cars. Grady, with the woman behind him, walked through the camellia bushes in his yard and opened the door to a piked fence and stepped out on the swale in his swim trunks and a pair of sandals. He tied a towel around his hair, like a turban, exposing his armpits. He was probably the most handsome young guy I'd ever seen. I could not understand how a kid who had so much could be the bastard he was. He leaned down to see who was in the car. "Bledsoe?"

"The chosen one himself," Saber said. "How's it hangin', Harrelson? Love your pad. I hear you bonked the maid in your atom bomb shelter."

"I dig your pipes."

"I always knew you had taste."

"But why is your shit machine parked in front of my house?"

"We got a situation we thought you could help us with," Saber replied. "Aaron didn't mean to cause you any trouble at the drive-in restaurant, but you blamed your breakup with your girlfriend on him because he happened to say hello at the wrong time. That's definitely uncool. In the meantime, somebody has been trying to kick a telephone pole up our asses."

"A telephone pole? Man, that's a sad story."

"Framing us for a car arson, stoking up some hoods in the Heights, that sort of thing."

Grady propped his hands on the Chevy's roof and seemed to reflect on Saber's words. The woman had hung a blue silk robe on her shoulders and was watching from the other side of the piked fence. Her sloe eyes and her black hair curling damply around her neck made me think of a villainous movie actress.

"Do you see anyone else on this street, Bledsoe?" Grady asked.

"Not a soul."

"Does that indicate the nature of your situation?"

"You mean y'all could rip us apart and stuff us down the storm drain and nobody would care?"

"I can tell nobody is putting anything over on you. But we don't want to see you hurt. You're a nice little guy. So I'll ask you again: What are you doing with your shit machine in front of my house, nice little guy?"

Saber sniffed at the air. "Y'all got skunks around here?"

"What?"

"Smell it? One of them must have come out of the coulee or the sewer. Maybe you could call in the marines and clean the place up. You know, semper fi, motherfucker, let's take names and kick ass and exterminate the smelly little varmints before they perfume the whole neighborhood and people stop believing our shit don't stink."

Don't do this, Saber. Please, please, please don't.

"You been getting high on lighter fluid again, turd blossom?" Grady said.

"Heard you were in the Corps for a while. So was my old man. He was at Iwo Jima. Did you make it over to Korea before you got sent home?"

"Go back to that business about the skunks."

"Before you know it, they'll be coming through your mailbox, maybe while you're muffing the town pump. What do they call that? Climax interruptus?"

"Get out of the car."

"Up your nose," Saber said.

I opened the door and stepped out on the asphalt and looked across the roof at Grady. "This is between you and me. Saber isn't involved. We shouldn't have come here. We'll leave."

"You'll leave when I tell you to. You haven't answered the question. Why are you parked in front of my fucking house?"

"I want to know if you sicced Loren Nichols on me," I said.

I saw a tic under Grady's left eye, as though someone had touched the skin with a needle. "Who the fuck is Loren Nichols?"

"The guy whose car got burned," Saber said.

"Step out of your heap, you slit-eyed freak," Grady said.

The change in his tone was like an elixir to his friends. They tightened the circle around us, their bodies hard and tan, beaded with water. Saber had said Grady's kind was different, incapable of empathy. He wasn't wrong. They threw trash out of their cars, were profane around people they believed to be of no value, and were unfazed by the suffering of the poor and infirm. But for me, the open sore on every one of them was unnecessary cruelty. As I looked at them gathered around Saber's pitiful excuse for a hot rod, I remembered a scene from years before. There was a coulee and a piney-woods pond on the backside of River Oaks Country Club. It contained bream and sun perch, and kids from other neighborhoods came there and fished with bobbers and bamboo poles. One week after Christmas, on a warm, sunny day, a little boy had parked his new Schwinn bicycle at the top of the incline and was fishing among the lily pads when a carful of kids who were country-club members stopped their car. A tall kid got out, picked up the Schwinn, and hurled it end over end down the slope into the water, scratching the paint, denting the fenders. The little boy cried. The kids in the car sped away, laughing.

I thought about Saber's mention of the tire iron under the seat, and I thought about it not because of the danger we were in but because of the memory of the Schwinn bicycle.

"All is fair in love and war," I said.

Grady's gaze shifted sideways into neutral space. "You're speaking in code?"

"That means do your worst."

"I think you and Saber need a dip in the pool."

The passenger door was still ajar. I leaned inside and felt under the seat and pulled out the tire iron. I let it hang from my right hand, the end with the socket touching my knee.

Grady looked at his friends. "Do you believe this asshole?"

"You dealt it, Grady," I said. "Want to boogie?"

"With one phone call, I can make your life miserable," he said.

"My life is already miserable."

"Maybe you need an around-the-world. I'll call Valerie. She gives the best I ever had."

I kept my eyes on his and didn't blink or show any expression. I felt my fingers tightening on the shaft of the lug wrench. He looked again at his friends, as though sharing his amusement with them. None of them met his eyes. He looked back at me. "What's with you? You got some kind of mental defect?"

"Nothing is with me. I won't be a senior till next week. You already graduated. You're a wheel. I'm nobody."

"You're trying to provoke an incident and then file a suit. It's not going to work, Broussard." He flexed his shoulders and rotated his head like a boxer loosening up. His confidence was starting to slip, and the others knew it.

"Call the shot, Grady. Or apologize for that remark about Valerie."

"You start a beef at my house and I'm supposed to apologize? That's great, man. You almost make me laugh."

The woman in the blue robe stepped out on the swale. She was wearing huaraches. There was a smear of lipstick on one of her canine teeth. She cupped her hand on the back of Grady's neck, one pointy fingernail teasing his hairline. She was whispering in his ear, but her eyes were on me. He seemed to be listening to her as a child would to its mother.

"Get back in the car, Aaron," I heard Saber say.

"We're fine," I said.

"No, get in the car," he said.

"Listen to your friend," the woman said to me.

"Who are you?" I asked.

She winked, her lips compressing into a glossy red flower, her eyes darker and more lustrous than they were a second earlier.

I stuck the tire iron under the seat, and in seconds Saber and I were headed down a long tunnel of live oaks, his dual exhausts echoing off the tree trunks. My right hand was trembling, the shaft of the tire iron printed as red as a burn across my palm.

Chapter 5

SABER TURNED NORTH, toward the Heights and Valerie Epstein's house. "What happened back there?" he said. "Who's that broad?"

"You got me."

"It's like she has some kind of control over them. Why is she wasting herself on guys like that when I'm available? Have you seen me do the dirty bop?"

"I missed that."

"It's not funny. I'm a good dancer." He tugged on his dork, trying to straighten it in his pants. "This is killing me. I've got to have some relief."

"Will you act your age?"

"I am."

"I didn't know your father was in the marines."

"He wasn't. He was in the Seabees. He spent most of the war in San Diego."

"Why did you tell Harrelson he was in the marines?"

"To make him feel like he's worse butt crust than he already is. Any time I can screw up the head of a guy like Harrelson, I'm on it."

He shifted down, flooring the Chevy, blowing birds out of the trees into a maroon sky as we plowed deep into the Heights.

* * *

KNOW WHAT IT was like back then? It's not the way everybody thinks. Not one person I knew listened to Frank Sinatra or Bing Crosby or Perry Como. We thought their music was shit and Lawrence Welk was water torture. In jazz, there was the cool school and the honk school. Pres Young was from the cool school. Flip Phillips was honk, in the best way. He and Pres and Buck Clayton and Norman Granz toured the country with Jazz at the Philharmonic. Hank and Lefty were on every blue-collar jukebox in America. The seminal recording in R&B was Jackie Brenston's "Rocket 88," featuring Ike Turner on piano. Politics? What was that? My father said Senator McCarthy had the warmth and depth of a bowling ball. Saber asked him who Senator McCarthy was.

The real story was the class war. We just didn't know we were in it.

"What's that?" Saber said, slowing the Chevy.

On the street a short distance from Valerie's house, I saw a scorched area the size of a car and fractured glass and scraps of rubber on the asphalt. I realized that once again Saber had driven us into the belly of the beast.

"That's where Loren Nichols's car got burned. Get us out of here," I said.

"He lives in that dump?"

A sagging nineteenth-century two-story white house, with a dirt yard and rain gutters that had rusted into lace, stood on cinder blocks among live oaks whose lichen-crusted limbs seemed about to crush the roof. Loren Nichols was drinking a beer, bare-chested and wearing suspenders, behind a hair-tangled old woman sitting in a wooden chair. Her skin was shriveled like dry paste, her neck tilted as though she had been dropped from a hangman's noose. Loren was down the steps in a blink, the beer can in his hand, coming hard across the yard. "Come back here, boy. Your ass is grass," he hollered.

Saber shot him the bone and kept driving. The beer can smacked against the trunk and rolled across the asphalt.

"Stop the car," I said.

"Over a beer can?" Saber said.

"Let me out."

"No, that guy's a mean motor scooter, Aaron. Anybody is who survives Gatesville."

I pushed open the door and stepped out with the car still moving. Loren came toward me, his torso as pale and hard-looking as whalebone. I stepped back, raising one hand. "It wasn't me who torched your heap. Maybe I cut your tires, but I didn't set the fire."

"Who did?"

"Probably the guys who threw the Mexican girl out of their car a couple of blocks from here."

"What do you know about the Mexican girl?"

"Nothing."

"Then shut your mouth, asshole. She was my cousin."

"Don't be calling me names."

"Who the fuck do you think you are?"

"A guy who wasn't looking for a beef until you and your brother and your friends 'fronted me on the street."

There were nests of green veins in his forearms and chest. He was breathing through his mouth, his eyes out of focus. He hit me in the sternum with the heel of his hand.

"Don't do that," I said.

"I'll do it all day. You got a shank?"

"No."

"How'd you cut our tires if you don't carry a shank?"

"I said *maybe* I cut your tires."

He thumped me in the forehead. "I can take your skin off, boy."

"I know that."

"Admit you burned my car."

"I didn't."

He slapped me. "Lie to me again."

The side of my face was on fire. I felt tears running down my cheeks. "I didn't do anything to you guys."

"You think you can come up to the Heights and wipe your feet on us? You come up here to dip your wick?"

"I didn't wipe my feet on anyone."

He raised his hand as though to slap me again. "I'll knock your head into the storm sewer. I mean it, I'll tear it clean off your shoulders. Who he'ped you do it?"

"No one," I said, wiping my face.

Saber had gotten out of the Chevy. The passenger door was still open. I saw him reach under the seat for the tire iron.

"You chickenshit?" Loren said.

"People who fight are weak."

He tried to catch my nose between two knuckles. "Don't jerk away from me, boy. You're about to get on your knees. That's the only way this is going to end."

I tried to push his hand aside. Saber was walking toward us now, the tire iron behind his leg.

"Why were you spying on my house?" Loren said.

"Why would I want to spy on your house? I couldn't care less about your house."

"Because that's what dingleberries do. I hear you're a momma's boy and your old man is a lush."

"You don't know anything about me."

"Go wash your face. You can use my garden hose."

"Get back, Saber," I said.

Loren realized he had forgotten about Saber. He turned in Saber's direction as though in a dream.

"Put it away, Saber," I said.

"Well, you little shit," Loren said, sliding his right hand into his pocket.

"Look at me, Loren," I said.

"What is it now?" he said.

I thought about saying something clever, but I didn't. I felt like a helpless child watching his best friend about to cross a line and perhaps ruin his life. The wind was as warm as blood; I could feel the tears drying on my cheeks.

I caught Loren Nichols on the mouth, bursting his lips against his teeth. I never saw anyone look so surprised. He cupped his hand to keep the flow from his mouth off his chest and drapes. I had never been in a fight and did not know what I was supposed to do next.

Then I saw the pain and shock go out of his eyes. From that point on, I didn't think.

I used both fists and hit him so hard, I knew the blood on my knuckles was from me and not from him. He tripped backward over the curb and tried to lift his forearm across his face, but I clubbed his head and the back of his neck and drove one punch into his eye when he looked up at me for mercy.

My mother had been the first to call the blank spaces in my days "spells," maybe because spells and blackouts ran in her family. The Hollands were a violent people, capable of turning their weapons on themselves as well as others. My grandfather was a Texas Ranger who put John Wesley Hardin in jail, something Wild Bill Hickok tried and couldn't do. My mother often went to places in her head that no normal person dared visit. I believe Loren Nichols realized his mistake and wanted to undo it even as I drove him across the dirt yard onto the rotting steps of his house, even as I continued to beat and stomp him in front of the old woman, who had madness in her eyes but seemed to see nothing.

For the first time in my life, I understood that I was capable of killing a man with my bare hands. The world turned to a red and purple melt while Loren Nichols's face was coming apart. Then I felt Saber's arms grab me from behind, his hands locking on my chest, pulling me backward as I kicked at Loren and missed.

I tried to get loose, but I was finished, the adrenaline gone, my strength draining like water through the soles of my feet. The old woman was making a keening sound, her body shaking. Loren rolled into a ball on the ground. His face didn't look human.

"We're in the skillet," Saber said. "Did you hear me? We're deep in Indian country, Aaron. Snap out of it. His friends will pull our teeth with pliers."

He carried me upright to the street as he would an upended hogshead, and body-slammed me on the swale. I stared up at him, the sky and the trees and the houses along the block spinning out of control.

"Is that you, Saber?" I asked. "Did you just throw me on the ground? What in the world is the matter with you?"

* * *

I MADE HIM DRIVE me to the alley that led behind Valerie Epstein's house.

"You're going up to her door like that?" he said, looking at my clothes and hands.

"I'm going to use her hose."

Valerie's yard was deep in shadow, the fronds of the banana plants next to her garage rattling in the wind. The air smelled of fertilizer and the damp soil in the flower beds, an odor like a fresh wound in the earth. An odor like a grave. I heard a siren several blocks away.

"They're coming," Saber said.

"Nichols started it."

"I'm scared," he said.

"They're just cops. It's our word against his."

"No. It was the look on your face. It wasn't you."

"Don't talk that way."

But I couldn't get his words out of my mind.

I squatted down by the garage and removed my shirt and turned on the garden hose. I washed off my hands and arms and soaked my shirt and squeezed it out and put it back on and dried my hands on my pants. I saw Valerie through the back screen. I got to my feet. I didn't know what to say to Saber.

"I hurt Nichols pretty bad?" I asked him.

"He won't want to look in the mirror for a while."

"Was that his grandmother?"

"I think that's his mother. I heard she was in the asylum in Wichita Falls."

"If they catch you with me, they'll put you in the can."

"You're telling me to beat it?"

"No, I'm saying I might not go home."

"Because of Nichols?"

"I'm not supposed to bring problems into my house. It's an unwritten commandment. My father once said if I ever run away, not to come back."

"Your old man said that?"

"That's the way he is sometimes."

Valerie opened the screen and stepped outside.

"Want me to leave?" Saber asked. "Just tell me."

"Do what you want."

"I'm not stupid."

"Don't be that way," I said.

He threw his car keys in the air and caught them. "You sure know how to kick a guy in the teeth."

He fired up his Chevy and drove down the alley, gunning the engine with the clutch depressed, as though the roar of his mufflers could shut out the injury I had inflicted on him.

Valerie was holding the door open with her rump. She wore a white dress with black trim and tiny red hearts all over it. "What happened to you?"

"I got into it with Loren Nichols."

"Are you hurt?"

"Not really."

"Did Loren attack you?"

"He thinks I burned his car."

"That's ridiculous. You look awful."

"It's part of my mystique. Is your father home?"

"Why do you ask?"

"Because I'm a little embarrassed."

"Over what?"

"Everything. I busted up Loren Nichols. Where's your father?"

"Working in Beaumont. You did what?"

"If Saber hadn't stopped me, maybe I would have finished the job. I don't feel too good about it."

I saw the light go out of her eyes. She studied my face and blinked and looked at the alleyway and the dust rising into the sky. "Come in."

"What for? I just wanted to tell you I didn't burn his car."

She pulled me inside and latched the screen. She bolted the inside door and looked through the window at the alley again. I could hear her breathing. "Say all that again."

"I hit him and then I couldn't stop. I've never felt that way before."

"I'll talk to him. I know his brother, too. We have to do something and do it now."

"You said he wasn't a hood, just a neighborhood guy."

"You can't come into the Heights and beat up somebody and walk away."

"That's what I just did. He asked for it, too."

"What you did was insane."

"You think you know these guys, Valerie, but you don't. They're mean to the bone."

"I grew up here, a Jew in a neighborhood where people like me are called Christ killers. Don't tell me what they're like. Sit down."

"What for?"

"You have a cut in your scalp. I don't believe you beat up Loren. Or you're exaggerating about it."

"Tell him that. I feel sick. I hurt Saber's feelings. Saber says I'm the only family he has."

"We'll call him up. We can go out together. We can play miniature golf."

I think in that moment I fell in love with Valerie Epstein all over again, and this time I knew I loved her more than life itself.

"Why are you smiling?" she asked.

"Because I can't stop thinking about you."

A wood-bladed fan spun above us, its shadows breaking across her face. Her gaze fixed on mine; she didn't speak.

"You're the only person in the world I want to be with," I said. "I care about you more than my parents, more than Saber, more than anyone I've ever known. I'd do anything for you."

She was looking at me in a different way now. She placed her hand on my forehead as though I had a fever. "You're such a strange boy. You want to believe bad things about yourself. That's wrong, did you know that?"

"Would you run off with me?"

"Don't talk foolish," she said, taking her hand away. "I'll fix coffee for you. We can make sandwiches."

"I don't want any." I stood up. We were almost the same height, her face inches from mine. I could feel her eyes go inside me. "I want to be with you forever, Valerie. We could go to Louisiana. I could work in the oil field. I know everything about horses and cattle, too."

I took her wrist and placed her hand on my heart.

"Aaron," she said.

"You're stuck with me. For me, there'll never be another girl. I don't care if Loren Nichols and his friends kill me."

"Aaron, please."

I put my arms around her and spread my fingers over her back and smelled her hair and the heat in her skin. Her head was framed against the window, the late sun lighting the skein of auburn and gold strands in her hair, the shadows from the fan spinning like a vortex around us.

Then I felt her step on top of my feet and mold herself against me. My entire body felt as though it were being lowered into warm water, my phallus rising, my fingers biting into her back. I walked with her on top of my feet into the living room, as though we were dancing. Then she stepped away from me, and I felt my head reel as if I were floating away on the wind, alone, like a balloon with a broken string.

"Did I do something wrong?"

"No, of course not," she said. She took my hand and led me up the stairs to her bedroom. The window curtains were open, and I could see the top of the pecan tree in her backyard and clouds that were like streaks of blood in the western sky. We were both trembling as we undressed. My words clotted in my throat, and I can't remember what I said to her when I saw her naked. I had never seen a woman undress, and I had never been to a burlesque club, and I had never done more with a girl than kiss her, and that was at the drive-in movie.

She pulled back the covers and lay down and waited, her arms at her sides, her fingers curling and uncurling with anxiety. I kissed her on the mouth and eyes and breasts and stomach, my head hammering, the cuts on my knuckles from the fight streaking the pillows and sheets like wisps of pink thread. When she took me inside her, I put my face in her hair and swore I could smell the ocean and hear wind blowing and feel myself slipping into an underwater cave filled with gossamer fans and electric eels, each tidal surge taking me deeper and deeper into a place I never wanted to leave.

Then I closed my eyes and surrendered myself to the fates, and saw a single bottle rocket rise into the sky and burst in a shower of stars that floated down through the ceiling onto our bed.

Chapter 6

I RODE THE CITY bus home. My father had come home from work late and gone to the icehouse. He did not know of my absence from the supper table. My mother met me at the door, her face like a piece of crumpled paper, a mole peeking from the deteriorating makeup on her chin. "I've called all over town."

"I went to see a girl in the Heights and lost my ride. I called twice. The line was busy. I'm sorry."

"Which girl? Your father doesn't want you in the Heights." Her eyes were jittering, her hands clenching.

I started for my room, exhausted, wanting to lie down on my teester bed; I wanted to sleep as if I'd been swallowed by a hole in the earth, safe from all the violence and cruelty surrounding me. My mother circled my wrist with her thumb and forefinger and lifted my arm and studied my knuckles. "Did you hit someone?"

I was surprised. My mother dealt with reality only in teaspoons. She'd had a hysterectomy and a nervous breakdown and electroshock therapy, an experience that had left her shaking and filled with dread. I'd realized long ago that there are people who are not liars but are incapable of telling the truth or dealing with it. There is a great difference between the two.

"A run-in with a fellow," I said. "It's nothing to worry about."

"Dr. Bienville increased my medication. It makes me confused. Why did you have a run-in with someone? Has a bully bothered you? Is that what all this strange behavior is about? Go get your father, would you? There's a television set at the icehouse now. Something to sell more beer."

"I'll get him, Mother."

"Tell him about this trouble you had."

"I will," I said.

"And leave that girl in the Heights alone. Your father won't like it."

"I understand."

I went to the icehouse and walked back home with my father. Heat lightning rippled through the clouds; hurricane warnings were up along the Louisiana-Texas coast; and earlier I had lost my virginity and tried to beat a greaseball to death. But there was not one subject of either substance or insignificance that my father and I could discuss. I wondered what it would be like to stroll with one's father along a sidewalk, like two friends out on a warm evening that smelled of flowers and water sprinklers slapping on the lawns. Maybe one fine evening that would happen, I told myself, if I just had faith.

I LAY IN BED and stared at the ceiling until one A.M. and woke to what I expected to be the worst day of my life—cops at the door, handcuffs, a felony assault charge, or maybe Mr. Epstein charging into the house, enraged at what I had done with his daughter. All day at school I waited for a police cruiser to turn in to the faculty parking lot, then a call to the principal's office. It didn't happen. The only unusual element in the morning was Mr. Krauser's behavior. During metal shop he kept staring at Saber and me as though he wanted to say something to us but couldn't.

At seven-fifteen that evening, I looked out the window and saw Mr. Krauser park at the curb and get out and stand uncertainly on the edge of the lawn, flattening his tie, straightening his shoulders. There was a young guy I recognized in the passenger seat. His name was Jimmy McDougal; he was an effeminate kid whose body was almost hairless, his eyebrows blond wisps. I'd see him shooting baskets at the YMCA after he dropped out of school, his gym shorts barely clinging to his hips when he leaped to make a shot.

"Who's that man?" my mother said.

"Satan," I replied.

"Who?" she asked.

"It's Mr. Krauser," I said, more to my father than my mother.

My father was reading under a lamp. The book was *Men Without Women* by Ernest Hemingway. "The teacher who tried to help you with these bad kids from the Heights?" he said.

"They're more than bad kids, Daddy. And Mr. Krauser doesn't help anybody with anything."

He looked at his pocket watch. The ball game would soon be starting on the small-screen television at the icehouse, although my father usually sat at one of the plank tables under the canvas awning and drank by himself and took little interest in the game. "So let's see what he wants," he said.

It was obvious that Mr. Krauser had not bathed or changed clothes before coming to the house. As I held the door for him, I could smell the dried sweat in his shirt, an odor that was as thick and gray and palpable as a towel left in a gym locker. His smile made me think of a grin painted on a muskmelon. "I hope I'm not disturbing anyone," he announced in the middle of the living room. "I like your house. What do you call that overhang on the side?"

My father put away his book and rose from his chair to shake hands. "I'm James Broussard, Mr. Krauser. In Louisiana it's called a porte cochere. What can I do for you?"

"I understand we have much in common."

"Oh?" my father said.

"My tank was the first armored vehicle across Remagen Bridge. In the Great War, you were at—"

"No place of any import. What's the nature of your visit, sir?"

In moments like these I believed my old man was the best guy on earth, although he hated the word "guy."

"I work as a counselor at one of the summer camps on the Guadalupe River, up in the hill country," Mr. Krauser said. "There're a couple of slots available for assistant counselors. I had Aaron and his friend Saber in mind."

Many high school and junior high school coaches worked at summer vacation camps and received twenty-five dollars for each kid they signed up. I pitied the kid who looked forward to camp all year and arrived only to find out that Mr. Krauser was his cabin supervisor.

"That's good of you," my father said. "Why did you choose my son for such an honor? Not to mention Saber."

"Both have leadership potential. Lots of potential. We start the day with reveille at oh-seven-hundred hours. Boys learn discipline up there, Mr. Broussard. Not that Aaron needs it."

My father had lean hands that were sun-browned and freckled and webbed on the backs with purplish veins that looked like knotted twine. Whenever he was bothered by an inconsistency in other people's words, he rubbed the fingers of one hand on the back of the other, his thoughts known only to himself. "If I wanted to start a second American revolution, I'd turn loose ten like Saber Bledsoe in the middle of Boston."

"Saber isn't a bad boy. A little imaginative, maybe, but that's why I'd like to work with him now. Catch things in the bud."

"What did you say to all this, Aaron?" my father asked.

"I'm working at the filling station this summer," I replied.

"So there you have it," my father said to Mr. Krauser.

"One hundred dollars a month and room and board," Krauser said.

He waited. My mother stood in the background, her eyes fixed strangely on the back of his head.

"I say something wrong?" Krauser asked.

"Not a thing. Have a fine evening, sir," my father replied.

"What's that McDougal boy doing in your car?" my mother said.

"He helps me with household chores and cutting the lawn," Krauser said.

"He's ill," my mother said.

"Ma'am?"

"The boy is an outpatient at a clinic. He had a harsh childhood. He needs care."

Krauser nodded. "That's true. That's why I do what I can for him."

She stepped closer to him. "I know your kind."

"Beg pardon?"

"Your kind of man. I've seen you on many occasions. The clothes and the rhetoric are different, but the persona isn't."

"I don't know what you're saying, Miz Broussard."

"Oh, you certainly do."

Krauser's gaze went from my father to me. He looked through the screen door at our yard and the shadows that fell on our two white cats, Snuggs and Bugs, who each slept in a flower box on the front porch. "I think I shouldn't have come here," he said.

"It's been a pleasure," my father said. "Have a grand time at summer camp, and tell us about it sometime."

Then Krauser was out the door. His stink hung in the air like a soiled flag.

"YOUR FOLKS EIGHTY-SIXED Krauser?" Saber said early Saturday morning at the filling station in West University where I worked part-time.

"I don't think he's figured it out yet."

Saber had come to the station with a thermos of coffee at seven A.M., full of forgiveness for my going in the house with Valerie and leaving him alone. I promised myself I would never hurt him again.

"What's Krauser up to?" he asked.

"You got me. He's scared about something."

"You're right," he said, watching a long-legged girl in shorts pedal past the station. "He probably knows I got the goods on him."

"What goods?"

"My sources saw him hanging around the Pink Elephant. He may be a closet stool-packer."

"Come on, Saber."

"I'm not knocking those guys. They don't bother anybody. I'm knocking this ass-wipe who's declared war on us. What did I ever do to Krauser besides drop my johnson through a hole in the ceiling of his classroom? Did you ever notice how he always looks constipated? I bet he has some kind of blockage that's backed up into his brain. I got to ask you something."

"About what?"

"Valerie Epstein." His eyes went away from mine, then came back. "Did you?"

"Did I what?"

"You know."

"End of conversation."

"Am I your best friend or not? Who keeps you out of trouble? Huh? Answer that."

"I appreciate your efforts."

"You don't need that kind of grief. When you get the urge, just flog your rod."

"Shut up, Saber."

Sometimes Saber had inclinations and said things I didn't like to dwell on. Saber never had girlfriends or asked a girl to a dance. He didn't even go on Coke dates. He talked about movie actresses but always eased away from the group when we visited a slumber party or hung out with a mixed crowd in the back row at the drive-in theater, drinking beer and necking and sometimes having to lift a car bumper to get rid of a discomfiting condition.

"Loren Nichols didn't give us up," he said.

"Maybe he has character," I said.

"Save it for Mass. This isn't nearly over."

A Cadillac pulled up to one of the pumps; the driver honked. I ignored him and said to Saber, "Will you take the collard greens out of your mouth?"

"This is about Grady Harrelson. It's always about a guy like Harrelson, not a greaseball from North Houston."

"You don't like rich people, Saber."

"Why should I?" he said.

I thought about it. I couldn't come up with an answer.

* * *

DETECTIVE JENKS PULLED into the station in an unmarked car at six that evening, just as we were closing up. The only other employees, two black men, were rolling dice in back on a flattened cardboard box for fun. In those days white kids were hired in filling stations because black men were not allowed to handle money or deal with the customers. Other than making change, our skills were virtually nil. The owner of the station had already gone home. I looked at the two black men and wondered at the composure that seemed to characterize their lives in spite of the hard times they'd had. The younger man had been with the Big Red One in Korea and come home with a Bronze Star and a Purple Heart. The older man had a scar like a braided rope on the back of his neck, where he had been stabbed by a cuckolded husband in Mississippi. Both men, like most men of color in that era, knew a cop when they saw one. They put away their dice and began washing up under a faucet, their backs turned to me and Jenks. I was on my own.

"Get in," Jenks said.

I tossed my sponge into a bucket and slung a chamois over my shoulder. I even tried to smile. "What for?"

"Don't make me say it twice."

I got into the front seat. The inside of his car was hot and smelled of dust and old fabric. With his fedora and necktie and suit coat on, he looked like he wouldn't fit inside the car and was about to break the seat or headliner or steering wheel with his size and weight. "Close the door."

"Yes, sir."

"You beat the crap out of the Nichols kid?"

"I defended myself."

"You use a two-by-four?"

"I got lucky. Is he all right?"

"No thanks to you. You ought to be in the ring. Know who Lefty Felix Baker is?"

"The best boxer in Houston. Middleweight Golden Gloves champion of Texas five years running."

"I was one of his coaches. Lefty is a good kid. He could have gone the wrong road, like some kids he grew up with. But he didn't."

"Am I in trouble, Detective Jenks?"

"As a detective, I cover the entire metro area. You know the kids I have the most trouble with? You pissants in Southwest Houston. You think you're better than other people. I'll take the nigras or the Mexicans over y'all any day. They might steal, but some of them don't have much choice. Y'all vandalize property because you think it's your right. Sometimes I fantasize about stuffing the bunch of you into a tree shredder."

"What do you want from me?"

"For starters, you'd better choose your words more carefully."

As bad luck would have it, Saber's 1936 Chevy roared out of a side street and bounced up the dip into the station lot. Saber had a bottle of Jax in one hand, the radio and the stolen speakers from the drive-in theater blaring. His face lost its color when he saw me in the car with the detective.

"Turn off your engine, lose the beer, and get in the backseat," Jenks said to Saber.

Saber got out and set the beer down by his front tire.

"I said, lose it."

"Yes, sir," Saber said. He threw the bottle up on the patch of lawn by the boulevard and opened the back door of Jenks's car and sat down as though taking up residence in a tiger's cage.

Jenks turned around. "You going to give me a bad time, Bledsoe?"

"No, sir," Saber said.

"When we're done, pick up that bottle and put it in a trash can."

"Yes, sir."

"Would you boys like to continue drag racing, feeling up the girls at the drive-in, running your money through your peckers on beer and whores, and maybe even graduating from that brat factory you call a high school?"

"Yes, sir, we're on board for all of that," Saber said.

Shut up, Saber.

Jenks went to the trunk of the car and returned with a canvas haversack full of file folders. He sat behind the wheel, the door hanging open, and began sorting through sheaves of typewritten pages and black-and-white photographs. "Here's a mug shot you've already seen. I want you to look at it again. This is one time in your life you don't want to lie. Did you ever see this girl?"

"That's the girl named Wanda, Loren Nichols's cousin, the one whose neck was broken," I said.

"Where did you see her?"

"I saw her in that mug shot you showed me," I said.

"Nowhere else? You haven't changed your mind?"

"No, sir."

"Because I think she pulled a train for a bunch of high school guys more than once. You know what I mean by pulling a train?"

"No," I said.

"How about you?" he said to Saber.

"Same as Aaron."

Jenks scratched the tip of his nose. "Strange she ends up with a broken neck two blocks from where you boys might have torched Loren's vehicle."

"We didn't do that, sir," I said.

"I admit that might take more smarts than either of you seems to have," he said. "I got some other photos in here."

He pulled out about fifteen of them, all of different sizes and origins, like photographs someone had thrown in a box and put away in a closet: elegantly dressed men and women eating in a supper club, evening gowns glittering like melted sherbet; a man in a summer tux with his hair parted down the middle, shaking hands with Tommy Dorsey; a racehorse dripping with roses in the winner's circle, its owner wearing round glasses as dark as welders' goggles; a casino under construction in a desert; a jailhouse photo of a man in a wide-brimmed fedora; and a nude woman with glorious breasts leaning back on a polar-bear rug in front of a fireplace, one eye closed in a lascivious wink.

Jenks made each of us look through the photos one at a time. Neither of us spoke.

"Big blank?" he said.

"I recognize the man in the mug shot," I said.

Jenks looked out at the boulevard, amused or bored, I couldn't tell which. "Care to tell me his name?"

"Benjamin Siegel."

"Which magazine did you see his photo in?"

"My uncle introduced me to him at the Shamrock Hotel. My father has never forgiven him for that."

"What's your uncle's name?"

"Cody Holland. Mr. Siegel was at the Shamrock with Frankie Carbo."

Jenks rolled his eyes. "Cody Holland the boxing promoter?"

"He's an oilman, too."

"Do you know who Frankie Carbo is?"

"He's my uncle's business partner."

"Business partner? Where'd you pick up that language, boy? Frankie Carbo was a member of Murder, Incorporated."

"That's why my father was upset."

"You know anyone else in these photos?"

I could see Saber out of the corner of my eye. His upper lip was moist with perspiration. "Not exactly," I said.

"What the hell does that mean?"

"I might have seen the lady who's sitting on the rug in front of the fire."

"She's on your paper route and she pays you in trade?"

"I don't think she's that type of lady," I said.

"Son, did your mother's doctor drag you out of the womb with forceps? Where did you see this woman?"

"I don't remember. I just remember seeing a woman who seemed kind and looked like her, that's all."

"This woman was kind? The woman wearing no clothes?"

"I'm probably mixed up," I said.

"That photo was taken from the suitcase of a dead man. He was frozen in a snowbank two thousand feet above Reno, Nevada. He was so scared he tried to get over the Sierra Nevada Mountains barefoot with no coat on. You saw this woman in Houston?"

"At Grady Harrelson's house in River Oaks," Saber said.

I wanted to yell in Saber's face, stuff a cork in his mouth, use his head for a kettledrum.

"You're talking about the home of Clint Harrelson?" Jenks said.

Saber nodded. "Two days ago. They were having a swim party. Grady has a hard-on for Aaron because he thinks Aaron took his girlfriend. We thought we'd straighten things out."

"You're sure it was her?"

"How many women look like that?" Saber said.

"You're in the know when it comes to women?" Jenks said.

"I've been around," Saber said.

Jenks propped the photo on the dashboard and studied it. "This is Cisco Napolitano, boys. She's screwed every major wop in the Mob. How tight are y'all with the Harrelson kid?"

"Not at all," I replied.

"You just happened to go to his house in River Oaks while he was having a swim party?"

"I think Grady sicced Loren Nichols on me," I said.

"Why would Harrelson be mixed up with a northside punk like Nichols?" Jenks said.

"That's what we cain't figure out," Saber said.

"Why didn't you want to tell me you'd seen the naked woman?" Jenks said.

"She seemed nice. She kept Harrelson's guys off us," I said.

"He's got hard guys around?" Jenks said.

"I've seen them spread-eagle a guy on a car hood and put out his lights."

Jenks crumpled an empty package of Pall Malls and threw it out the window, then fumbled another pack out of the glove box. He peeled off the red cellophane strip while he stared at nothing, my words lost in the wind.

"Sir, did you hear me?" I said. "I've seen Grady and his friends gang up on a guy and hurt him real bad."

"Okay, I got it."

"What do you want us to do, sir?"

His skin had the texture of ham rind. "Get out. Pick up that beer bottle while you're at it."

"Did we say something?" I asked.

"Don't go near Cisco Napolitano. She'll have your body parts hung on hooks. How did you dipshits get involved in this?"

"I don't think we're the problem," I said.

He gave me a look, then drove away as though we weren't there. Saber was writing in the notebook he carried in his shirt pocket. "He said Cisco Napolitano? How do you spell that? I'll be haunted by those lovely eggplants the rest of my life."

"She's mixed up with Vegas and the syndicate," I said.

"So what? She seems to go for younger guys. Maybe she's a nympho. Did you see the way she was eyeing my heap? I think she dug us."

Chapter 7

SIX DAYS LATER, school was out for the summer, and all I could think about was Valerie Epstein. I had three hundred and eighty-five dollars in a checking account and thirteen silver dollars in an army-surplus ammunition box, and because I was now a senior, my father had given me permission to buy a 1939 Ford from a neighbor who'd just been drafted and probably headed for Korea. So I had my own heap and could drive up to the Heights whenever I wanted. The Ford wasn't just a heap, either. It had twin pipes and Zephyr gears and a Merc engine with milled heads and a hot cam and a high-speed rear end. It could hit sixty in five seconds.

I couldn't believe my good fortune. Each evening I bathed and changed clothes after work and motored into the Heights to pick up Valerie Epstein, arguably the most beautiful and intelligent teenage girl in Houston. Her name had the melodic cadence of a sonnet or a prayer. I went to bed with Valerie on my mind and woke with images of her printed on the backs of my eyelids.

It was the hurricane season, but we had no hurricanes. Instead there were purple and crimson and orange clouds in the sky at sunset, and Gulf breezes that smelled of flowers and rain. We ate fried chicken off paper plates at Bill Williams's drive-in restaurant by Rice University and skated at the roller rink on South Main to organ music under a tent billowing with the cool air blown by huge electric fans. We went swimming once at the Shamrock Hotel, across the street from a cow pasture spiked with oil derricks pumping fortunes into the pockets of men who had eighth-grade educations. Somehow being in love with Valerie made me fall in love with the whole world.

We danced at one of the many nightclubs that served underage kids, and rode the roller coaster on Galveston Beach in spite of the Condemned sign nailed above the ticket window. I felt anointed by Valerie's presence, and my fear of hoods and greaseballs disappeared, as though the two of us had a passport to go wherever we wanted. A jalopy packed with rough kids drinking quart beer seemed no more than what it was, a car packed with kids who were born less fortunate than I and wanted to pretend for just one night they were happy.

TEN DAYS AFTER I had seen Jenks, I was in the grease pit draining a crank case when I heard a voice I did not ever want to hear again. My ears popped, and I opened and closed my mouth, hoping the wind inside the breezeway had distorted the voice and words I heard.

Walter, the black man who had been wounded and decorated for bravery in Korea, leaned down so he could see me under the car. "A guy here wants to see you, Aaron."

"What did he say to you?"

"Ask him."

I climbed out of the pit, wiping my hands on a machinist cloth. A tall kid was framed against the sunlight; he was wearing drapes and suede stomps and a shirt with the collar turned up on the neck, his hair greased and combed in ducktails. He stepped out of the glare into the shade, a toothpick rolling across his teeth. The swelling and discoloration were almost gone from his face, but one eyebrow looked like a broken zipper.

"What do you want?" I said.

"Did you know my cousin Wanda?"

"The girl whose neck was broken? No, why would I know her?"

"You cracking wise?"

"I've got a better question for you. You said 'Go get him, boy' to Walter?"

"The nigger?"

I threw the machinist rag aside. "He has the Bronze Star and the Purple Heart. How would you like to have your face broken again?"

"Just take it easy and hear me out."

"I'm through with this stuff, Loren."

"Somebody gave you permission to call me by my first name?"

"Excuse me, Mr. Nichols. I didn't know you were so important."

"You better climb down off it, man."

A skinned-up dirty-vanilla pickup was parked in the shadow of a live oak by the boulevard. The driver was wearing a denim shirt and a baseball cap and looked like a farmworker. He had been among Nichols's group when they badgered me earlier. For the first time, I noticed the resemblance.

"Is that your brother out there?"

"I'm here about my cousin. The cops aren't going to lose sleep over a dead Mexican girl. But my brother and me do. I think you know something."

"You're asking *me* about your cousin? I was walking down the street in the Heights on a Sunday morning when you guys decided to mess up my life. I don't know anything about you or your family, and I don't want to."

"You set fire to my car or you didn't. Which is it?"

"I didn't do it, and neither did Saber."

He took the toothpick from his mouth and slipped it into his shirt pocket. "Your family is connected?"

"Connected?"

"I hear your uncle knows people."

"He's an oilman and he manages prizefighters. That doesn't mean he's a criminal."

"Yeah, but he knows people. Maybe you know people, too."

I couldn't believe his naïveté. In his mind I belonged to a world where the solutions to his troubles were easily available to people who lived in high-income neighborhoods, which I didn't.

I said, "I don't think anything I say to you is going to work. I'm sorry I hurt you. You could have snitched me off, but you didn't. I think that's stand-up, man."

"Don't flatter yourself."

"Grady Harrelson told you to bird-dog me, didn't he?"

He combed his ducks. "*No,* motherfucker, he didn't tell me anything."

"Then why did you and your brother and hard-guy friends try to get it on with me in front of Valerie's house?"

"General principles."

"Look me in the face and say that," I said.

"See you around, kid."

He walked toward the pickup. I couldn't let it go. "Listen, Nichols, no matter how this plays out, you've got a lot of Kool-Aid. You cut it in Gatesville. That's not lost on people. But don't go calling me a kid and acting like you're hot shit."

He turned around. "It doesn't take brains to stack time. It takes brains not to stack time."

"Square with me. Maybe we're on the same side. Harrelson has something on you?"

"A punk like that?"

"So how do you know who he is?"

"He's like all you guys. He slums. He hunts on the game reserve. For him, that's our neighborhood."

"I don't think your neighborhood is a slum. And I'm not Grady Harrelson."

He gazed at my 1939 Ford. The hood was up, exposing the twin carbs on the V8 Mercury engine. "Those your wheels?"

"Yeah, it is."

"Not bad," he said. "Do yourself a favor, Holland. Drive your heap, date your girl, stay out of the kitchen. You're not up to the heat."

"I didn't do a bad job with you."

He stuck his comb into his mouth and combed his hair again, this time with both hands. "You got lucky. Next time bring a blade."

* * *

AFTER I WENT home and bathed and changed clothes, I drove to Valerie's house and told her about Loren Nichols's visit to the filling station. "I can't figure that guy out. He's got guts. Why does he act like such a shit?"

We were sitting on the porch swing. She was wearing a white blouse with flower-print shorts like a little girl would wear. Her father was inside. She said, "He's like most of the boys around here. They aren't afraid of the world they live in. They're afraid of the world that's waiting for them."

"How'd you get so smart?"

She kicked me in the ankle.

"You want to go for some ice cream?" I said.

"Sure."

I looked over my shoulder. "Would your father like to come with us?"

"He's going to a movie with a lady friend." She put a piece of Juicy Fruit into her mouth and looked at me and chewed it with her mouth open. The lawn sprinkler flopped across the flower bed.

"We could go for ice cream another time. I mean when your father is here and can go with us," I said.

"He wants to talk to you."

"Pardon?" I felt as though I had just stepped backward into an elevator shaft.

"About what?"

"Guess."

"Jesus Christ, Valerie."

"Come on," she said.

She picked up my hand and led me inside. Her father was talking on the telephone in the kitchen, looking through the hallway at me. Inside a glassed-in case in the hallway was a photo of him on one knee by a campfire, with several bushy-haired and mutton-chopped men who wore filthy clothes and rags wrapped on their heads, all of them armed with U.S. paratrooper grease guns, the kind that had folding wire stocks. Only three men in the photo were clean-shaven. One of them was Mr. Epstein; the second was Marshal Tito; the third resembled the actor who starred in *The Asphalt Jungle*.

Mr. Epstein hung up the phone and motioned for me to enter the kitchen. He was olive-skinned, his hair flaxen and curly on the tips, his short sleeves tight-fitting on his biceps. "Sit down."

"Is anything wrong?" I asked.

"We'll see. What do you have to say?"

"About what?"

"You and Valerie."

"About us going out?" I replied, my vocal cords beginning to atrophy.

"Call it that if you want. You seem like a nice kid. At least that's what my daughter thinks, and that's all that counts. Here are the rules in my house. I don't impose my way on Valerie. She's like her mother. Not afraid and not receptive to control by others. That said, she's still my little girl, and that means no boy or man will ever abuse or disrespect her. If that happens, I get involved. Are you reading me?"

"Yes, sir."

"You have any questions?"

"No, sir."

"That's it." He picked up a teacup and drank from it.

"That's it?"

"Yep."

How about that for clarity of line?

"Is that Sterling Hayden in the photograph?" I asked.

He nodded and waited for me to go on. But I thought the less said, the better.

"What do you know about him?" he asked.

"He gave names to the House Un-American Activities Committee."

"What are your thoughts on that?" he asked.

"I don't have any."

"How about your parents? What do they think?"

"My father said the ones who gave names should have taken their medicine. My father hates war. He was in the trenches in 1918. He says Russia's objective is to bleed us white through its proxies."

Mr. Epstein nodded, his eyes hazing in the way of adults when they're no longer listening. "You ever meet Clint Harrelson?"

"Grady Harrelson's father? I know who he is."

"He's the founder of a right-wing organization that would enjoy seeing people like me put in a soap dispenser. I've had a couple of personal run-ins with him. His organization called me a Communist in its newspaper."

"You're not a Communist, are you, Mr. Epstein?"

"Not now."

"Sir?"

"I think his son was after Valerie to prove something to his father. I told the father in front of the Rice Hotel that if either he or his son brought harm to my family, I'd shoot him."

He drank from his teacup. It looked small in his hand.

"You said you'd shoot Clint Harrelson?"

"That was a mistake. I won't do it again."

"I'm not sure I'm following you, sir."

"You don't threaten a man. If he comes at you, you put him out of business. An evil man is not scared by threats. He's scared when you don't speak."

He winked at me.

THAT NIGHT I WENT home and sat for a long time in my bedroom without turning on the light. The attic fan was droning above the hallway, drawing the air through the screened windows. I tuned the strings on my Gibson and played one song after another without thinking about the chords my fingers were shaping. I could not believe what had occurred earlier. In his house, within earshot of his daughter, Mr. Epstein had talked about the possibility of killing another man, the father of a student with whom I had gone to school. That the object of his hatred was Clint Harrelson didn't matter. Mr. Epstein had been talking about murder. To compound my discomfort, I was sleeping with his daughter.

You have to understand that we felt differently about certain things years ago. I was a Catholic, and the idea of killing someone except in self-defense was not tenable. My other problem was Valerie. In the eyes of others, we were breaking a commandment. Except emotionally, that wasn't how I felt. I loved Valerie, and it was through her that my entire life had changed. There was nothing impure about our love; it was bright and clean and innocent and natural, like the flame on a votive candle. I did not believe that God saw it differently. When I tried to work my way through my thoughts, I felt a pressure band along the side of my head, as though I were wearing a hat.

I had never needed to talk with my father as badly as I needed to talk with him that night. He was reading in the living room, but I didn't seek him out. I let Snuggs and Bugs and my tabby cat named Skippy and my toy bird dog named Major climb up on the bed with me, each pointing its muzzle into the cool air flowing through the screen.

I tried to imagine a conversation with my father about Mr. Epstein's threat and about my sleeping with Mr. Epstein's daughter. How would my father react? Sometimes he went into rages over the use of a vulgar word.

I could try to talk with my mother, except that prospect gave me an even deeper sense of angst and foreboding. It wasn't her fault. Her father had farmed her out to the kindness of strangers and resentful relatives. The bad memories of her childhood seemed to crawl under her skin. She reminded me of a crystal glass teetering on the edge of the drainboard, about to shatter in the sink. When I deceived her about where I had been or what I had done on a particular day, I did not feel I was committing a sin.

So I added one more day to my conspiracy of silence and put away my guitar and tried to shut Mr. Epstein's words out of my ears. I turned on my radio with the volume low and, among all my animals, laid my head on my pillow in the breeze and the smells of the night and listened to Jo Stafford sing as she had to millions of GIs.

* * *

SABER WAS AT the house early the next morning, after both my parents had gone to work. Saber had two jobs: racking pins in the pits at the bowling alley, a job that only men of color and the roughest white kids in town did; and throwing the *Houston Chronicle.* For anyone else, a paper route was just a paper route. For Saber, it was similar to Charlemagne fighting his way up the canyons of Roncevaux Pass. After he rolled 115 newspapers with string, he packed them like artillery rounds into the passenger and backseat of his heap, and set out on the route, heaving a paper over the roof through a sprinkler onto a porch, when he easily could have dropped it onto a dry spot on the walk; smacking a leashed bulldog that attacked him while he was collecting; nailing a flowerpot of someone who was in arrears; parking just long enough to run through an entire apartment building with his canvas bag on his shoulder, stomping up and down the stairways, dropping papers in front of doorways, crashing out the back door like a deep-sea diver emerging into light.

He drank a cup of coffee on the back steps and watched me fill the bowls of all my animals. "Things all right with you and Valerie?" he asked.

"Why wouldn't they be?"

"Because you always busy yourself with your cats and Major when you got something on your mind."

"Pets can't fill their own bowls, so give it a break."

"Krauser is dogging me," he said.

"Stop it," I said.

"I saw him in my rearview mirror last night. I saw him this morning, too."

"It's coincidence. He lives a few blocks from your house."

"More like a half mile. I saw his car at the Pink Elephant."

"Saber, I don't want to hear this. What were you doing there, anyway?"

"Surveilling Asshole. Jimmy McDougal was sitting in his car. Then Asshole came out of the club and drove away. Remember Jimmy?

Two quarts down the day he was born? Why's Krauser taking him to a dump like the Pink Elephant?"

"It's not our business."

"It is when he's following us around," Saber said.

"Are you sure about all this?"

"You think I want to believe somebody is copping that poor kid's joint?"

"You really know how to say it, Saber."

He looked at the animals eating from their bowls. "I'm thinking about joining the marines."

"You're just seventeen."

"I can forge the old man's signature. I'll be at Parris Island before he can do anything about it."

"Stop talking crazy."

"Every day we seem to get deeper in a hole. It's busting us up."

"What?"

"You heard me," he said.

"Don't talk like that. We've always been buds. I won't ever let you down."

"You told me to beat it because you wanted to get in the sack with a girl. I don't hold it against you, but it doesn't make me feel too good, either."

"I wasn't thinking."

"Yeah, you were. You thought me right out of the picture," he said.

"Valerie and I are both sorry."

"*She's* sorry? What the hell does she have to be sorry about?"

"She's got feelings. She's got a conscience. You don't know her."

"She was Grady Harrelson's girlfriend. She didn't know he was a dickhead? Why'd they break up? She just discovered out of nowhere what kind of guy he is? 'Oh, hey, Grady, a flashbulb just went off in my head. You're a prick. Here's your class ring.'"

"I never asked her."

"I bet there's a lot you didn't ask her."

"Say that again?"

"Did she get it on with Harrelson before she got it on with you? Were there other guys before him?"

"You can't talk about her like that."

"Why are you letting these people hurt us, Aaron?"

There were tears in his eyes. I tried to catch him in the porte cochere, but he fired up his Chevy and peeled rubber down the street, an acrid black cloud blooming from his pipes.

Chapter 8

No matter which way I turned, I saw only darkness. A Mexican girl was dead, and her death may have been related to me. My girlfriend's father was threatening to kill a man and telling me about it in advance. Saber believed Mr. Krauser was part of a conspiracy involving homosexuality or pedophilia, and that he was following us around. Worse, Saber had made me doubt the nature of Valerie's relationship with Grady Harrelson. She was too intelligent not to have realized the kind of guy he was. Why did she let him take her virginity? Or had someone else already done that?

I could not rid myself of the image of Grady and Valerie entwined naked in each other's arms. I called her house, but no one answered. Didn't she remember it was my day off? We had talked about cane-pole fishing off the jetties in Galveston. I called her house three times within ten minutes.

Think, I told myself. I hadn't done anything wrong. Or at least I hadn't intended to do anything wrong. I had a right to confront the people who were working out their problems on my back and Saber's. Suddenly the man who had always seemed a scourge in my life seemed a minor player, someone whose job security demanded he conform to masculine and brutish parameters, a man who was more dolt than villain and not a threat. I'm talking about Mr. Krauser.

He lived by himself in a squat gravel-roofed house that resembled a machine-gun bunker, built of glazed brick that looked like plastic. There were no shrubs or flower beds in the yard; the St. Augustine grass was chemical green and as stiff and unnatural in appearance as the spikes in a rubber mat. The backyard contained an archery target stuffed with straw, a swimming pool made of plastic tarps, and a doghouse where a Doberman stayed unless it was killing the neighbors' cats or the wild rabbits that lived in the neighborhood. The grass was pocked with yellow depressions from the mounds of dog shit that Krauser shoveled into a garbage can humming with flies.

He answered the door in a sweat-soaked Texas A&M jersey cut off at the armpits and a pair of gym trunks rolled to the crotch. He seemed surprised to see me, even pleased. "Broussard, what's up, big man?"

"Need to talk to you, Mr. Krauser."

"About what?"

"A delicate subject."

"Come in. Get yourself in girl trouble?"

"No, sir."

He closed the door behind me and turned the dead bolt, then cracked the curtain and looked through the window. The air conditioners were turned up full blast, the air frigid. "Where's Saber?"

"He's part of the reason I'm here."

"If this is about the counselor job, it's too late. Come in back. I'm lifting. Get yourself a soda out of the icebox."

I followed him into a windowless room. The floor was concrete. There was a sweat-printed, leather-padded black bench in it, and a rack of barbells along the wall, and at least two hundred pounds of steel plates on the weight bar racked above the bench. On the wall were certificates of merit from booster organizations, a framed collection of military medals and ribbons and chevrons and a unit patch, a pair of women's black panties pressed on pink felt under glass with a card that said "Liberating France one piece at a time," a plaque with crossed cavalry swords on it, photos of Krauser bowling and performing on a trapeze and hitting softballs to young boys and playing with the Doberman, a letter of commendation from a group in Dallas called Patriots Unlimited, and a Confederate battle flag. In the corner was an old wooden desk with a lamp on it made from a German helmet and an artillery shell. There was an SS insignia on the helmet and a silver-smooth bullet hole an inch from that. A chrome-bladed dagger, the white handle inlaid with gold lightning bolts, lay on the desk blotter.

Krauser began curling a ninety-pound bar, his biceps swelling into white cantaloupes corded with veins. "Spit it out."

"Saber and I have bad people on our backs, Mr. Krauser. The problem is, we don't know why."

"This is about those punks from the Heights?"

"I think it has to do with people in the underworld."

"Oh, bullshit."

"I don't think it is."

He continued to pump the bar, eight and nine and ten times, the steel plates rattling, sweat popping on his face, his odor blooming.

"Sir, I'm asking for your help," I said.

"You think too much."

"This isn't just a beef with some rough guys from the Heights. I think we're dealing with evil people, people with no mercy. There's some things about you that don't make sense, Mr. Krauser."

He dropped the bar on a rubber pad, breathing deeply, his nostrils dilating. "What was that again?"

"Saber says you were following him."

"What, I follow Mongolian idiots around town in my off hours?"

"Why would you come to my house and offer Saber and me jobs? You don't like either one of us."

"I tried to do a good deed, that's why. I didn't exactly get a warm welcome from your parents." He picked up a thirty-pound dumbbell in each hand and began pumping, his eyes sinking in his face.

"Saber saw you at the Pink Elephant with Jimmy McDougal."

Krauser inverted the dumbbells, lifting them straight out from his chest, counting to ten under his breath, a drop of moisture hanging off his nose. He dropped them heavily on the rack. "Get this straight. There're kids who frequent that neighborhood because nobody else cares about them. Others go down there because they like beating up queers. Most of them are queers themselves but don't know it. Jimmy McDougal is a kid with nobody to take care of him. I told the faggot who picked him up what I'd do if he ever tried it again. I even gave him a preview. By the way, the reason Bledsoe saw me at the Pink Elephant is that's where he hangs out, even though he pretends he's got some other reason to be there. Tell me if I'm right or wrong on that."

"You're wrong."

"Good try, son."

He gave me a threatening stare. I looked him straight in the face and didn't blink. His stare broke. He blotted the sweat out of his eyes with the back of his wrist. "I got to shower. A lady friend is coming over. I don't want you here when she arrives."

"Why'd you bolt the door?"

"We have break-ins. Now get out of here."

"I think you're scared, Mr. Krauser."

"Scared?" His forehead was strung with tiny knots. He pulled up his jersey and pointed. "That's where an SS lieutenant cut me open. I took his knife away from him and sliced off his nose. Then I put a bullet through his brain. That's his helmet on my desk, his knife on the blotter. I wouldn't wipe my ass with you, Broussard."

It was classic Krauser: the self-laudatory rhetoric, followed by the attack on the sensibilities. This time I was ready for him. I stepped closer to him, holding my breath so I wouldn't have to breathe his fog of testosterone and BO and halitosis. Involuntarily he stepped backward, as though unsure of his footing.

"You're cruel because you wake up scared every day of your life, Mr. Krauser. I know this because I used to be like you. Now I'm not. So I owe you a debt. You're the model for what none of us ever want to become."

I unbolted the door and went outside into the heat. I thought he might follow me into the yard and take a swing at me. But he didn't. I even waited by my car to see if he would come out. The sun went behind a cloud, and I got into my heap and drove away, no plan in mind.

Headed toward home, I saw a black-and-red Oldsmobile Rocket 88 convertible with a starched-white top. The driver was slowing as though looking for a house number. The Rocket 88 was state-of-the-art, hoodoo cool, too cool in my opinion for losers like Mr. Krauser and his friends. I slowed my car until I was abreast of the driver. She came to a complete stop and took off her sunglasses and shook out her hair, then removed a strand from her mouth. "What's the haps?" she said.

"You're the lady who was at Grady Harrelson's house," I said. "You're Miss Cisco."

"Who told you my name?"

"A Houston police detective."

She raised her eyebrows. "Must have been a slow day at the precinct."

"Are you looking for Mr. Krauser?"

"Maybe. Want to take a ride? I'll let you drive. How about a cherry milkshake? I can drink them all day long."

"I'm pretty tied up right now."

"Bussing tables?"

"I work at a filling station."

"You have a girlfriend? I bet you do, a handsome kid like you. Clean-cut and wholesome. A little reckless, maybe. Girls like that. I always did."

"Why are you talking to me like this?"

"Because you remind me of someone I used to know. Hop in. Don't be scared." She was wearing a white blouse that exposed her shoulders, the kind Jane Russell wore in her films. There was a mole by her mouth, a purple shine to her hair.

"If you like nice guys, why do you hang around with douchebags like Grady Harrelson?"

"Boy, you have a potty mouth, don't you? Get in. Live dangerously. I dare you."

I felt foolish and stupid in front of her but didn't know why. "I knew Benny Siegel."

"You shot craps with him at the Flamingo?"

"My uncle is Cody Holland. He was a runaway and a vagabond when he was twelve years old. He became a bouncer at the Cotton Club and a bodyguard for Owney Madden and put himself through NYCC on a boxing scholarship. He's business partners with a guy who was in Murder, Incorporated."

She laughed. "You're cute. I just wish you weren't a fly in the ointment."

"I'm a what?"

"You're getting yourself into stormy weather, kiddo. You should stay in your part of town."

"What kind of crap is that?"

"I knew a boy who looked and talked just like you. I'm not making fun of you. You could be his twin. Tell your sweetheart she's a lucky girl. I wasn't fooling about that cherry shake."

"You pick up high school guys?"

"What's a girl to do? Will you not look so serious? By the way, you're right about Grady Harrelson and his friends. They're shitheads. That's my point. Why let them fuck up your life?"

"So why are you with them?"

"It beats getting your ass pinched in a cocktail lounge. Your parents did a good job. You're a good kid. Keep me in mind if you want that cherry shake."

She blew a kiss at me, then drove off to park in front of Krauser's house. My head was a basket of snakes by the time I reached the Stop sign.

A HALF HOUR LATER I pulled into the deep shade of Valerie's driveway rather than park on the street, where my heap might be recognized and vandalized by Loren's friends. I twisted the bell on the door. No answer. I walked up the driveway, beneath the tall windows, and tried to see inside by jumping above the ledges. I saw Valerie's face behind a dining room screen, a towel wrapped around her hair.

"Are you out of your mind?" she said. "Why are you looking through the windows?"

"I've been calling all morning. Where have you been?"

"I went to the grocery."

"I have to talk with you. It's urgent. Call it of global significance."

"I thought we were going to Galveston," she said.

"Once we get some things out of the way."

"Stop shouting."

She went to the back door and pushed it open. I brushed against her as I stepped into the house. I could smell a scent like strawberries on her skin. She was dressed in faded jeans and a short-sleeve blue denim shirt with cacti and yellow and red flowers sewn on it. She had unwrapped the towel from her head. Her hair was damp and hung in ringlets on her cheeks and neck.

"Let's go for a cherry milkshake," I said.

"Cherry milkshake? We're not going to Galveston?"

"I can't think straight. I just talked with a woman who's probably in the Mob. She was talking about cherry milkshakes, so I have milkshakes on my mind. She was talking about you. Or seemed to be. So was Saber. How long did you go out with Grady Harrelson?"

"What does that have to do with anything now?" When I didn't answer, she said, "I went out with him for two months. Why?"

"It took you that long to discover what kind of guy he is?"

"*Yes,* it did. What is wrong with you?"

"I don't believe it would take that long."

"I don't care what you believe. It's the truth. Grady can be thoughtful and kind when it suits his purpose. But I saw another side to him the night you walked up on us at the drive-in."

"Saw what side to him?"

Her mouth was a tight seam, as though she were deciding how long she would tolerate my behavior. "A Mexican girl got out of one of the cars and came over to say hello. She had a *pachuco* cross on the web of her left hand, like a street kid might wear. She got confused and didn't know what to say and kept looking around. I felt sorry for her. She walked off, humiliated in front of Grady's worthless friends. He swore to me he didn't know who she was. So I went to the restroom. When I came back, he was talking to one of his friends, the guy who flipped a cigarette against your back. Grady didn't see me. He said, 'Get that bitch out of here. Tell her she's going to be a grease spot if she bothers me again.' "

"You never had a clue about him before that?"

"I don't know what's gotten into you, but if you're trying to hurt me, you're doing a good job of it."

"I just wondered why you were with a guy like Grady. It doesn't make sense. How could it? You're everything that's—"

"A woman in the Mob said something about me?"

"I saw her at Harrelson's house. She was asking me if I had a girlfriend."

"Why are you telling me all this crap? Why now? We were going fishing on the jetties."

"I was trying to tell you you're everything that's good. That's why I couldn't understand how you could go out with Harrelson. I'm not the same since that night at the drive-in."

"Don't talk stupid. People don't change," she said. "They grow into what they've always been. They just stop pretending, that's all."

My head felt small and tight. My cheeks were burning. I couldn't speak.

"Some people are the jealous kind," she said. "They don't love themselves, so they can't love or trust anyone else. There's no way to fix them. That's why you're really upsetting me."

"I think that's the worst thing anyone ever said to me."

"I'm going upstairs now and lie down," she said. "I don't feel well. Or maybe I'm going to take a long walk by myself. You can let yourself out."

I don't know how long I stood in the middle of the living room while the house swelled with wind and her footsteps creaked across the ceiling. "Come down, Valerie!" I shouted.

I heard a door slam and thought perhaps she was having a tantrum, which meant her mood would pass and at some point we would make up. But doors began slamming all over the house, and I realized the wind was perpetrating an innocent deceit upon me, unlike the pernicious deception I had just perpetrated on myself. I had let suspicion winnow away my faith in the girl I loved, and as a consequence the gift presented to me had been taken away and probably would be given to someone else. Worse, I knew the fault was my own.

That's about as close to a definition of hell as it gets, if there is such a place.

MY MOTHER WORKED in a bank and each afternoon came home earlier than my father. I was sitting at our redwood picnic table in the backyard with the cats and Major and my Gibson when I saw her through the back screen, a glass of sun tea in each hand. She came down the steps and sat across from me, her expression thoughtful rather than irritated or anxious. "Are you worried about something, Aaron?"

"Nothing in particular."

"Worry robs us of happiness and gives power to the forces of darkness."

"You learned that in a log-house church in San Angelo. I'd leave it there."

"I learned it in 1931, picking cotton from cain't-see to cain't-see. If you have enough to eat for the day, the next day will take care of itself."

I looked at the simplicity and repose in her face. These moments came to my mother rarely, but when they did, the transformation in her manner was as though she had undergone an exorcism. Today it's called bipolar. Back then, people didn't have a name for it.

"I went to Mr. Krauser's house," I said. "He told me he had been protecting Jimmy McDougal from a homosexual who hangs out at the Pink Elephant. He said Saber hangs out at the Pink Elephant, too."

"Mr. Krauser believes Saber is a homosexual?"

"That's what I gathered."

She ticked her nails on the side of her glass. "What's your opinion?"

I was hesitant to confide in her. Her mercurial nature was similar to my father's, but rather than rage, she would find pills in the cabinet or solitude and darkness in her bedroom. My mother's prison was her mind, and she took its dark potential with her wherever she went.

"One time at Saber's house when we were fifteen, he asked if we could get naked and wrestle." I gazed at my hands, my ears ringing in the silence. I saw her pick up her glass and remove the napkin from it and slowly wad the napkin in her palm.

"So what did you all do?" she asked.

"I made a joke about it. Then he said he was just kidding."

"And that's the way to remember it. It's nothing to worry about. What occurred then was not bad, and it's not bad now. That's the way you must think about it."

"Really?" I said, looking her in the face.

"Mr. Krauser said he's protecting Jimmy McDougal?" she said, the subject already behind her.

"Do you know something about Mr. Krauser I don't?"

"You could put it that way. I know a liar and a bully and white trash when I see it. Is Mr. Krauser in the directory?"

OUR TELEPHONE WAS in the hallway. I sat in the living room and could hear her dialing Krauser's number. The cats and Major had followed us inside. They perched on the furniture like an audience anticipating a stage presentation. My mother's voice was clear, without emotion, her accent less like Texas than the boarding school she briefly attended in New Orleans through the generosity of a charitable family.

"This is Mrs. Broussard, Aaron's mother, Mr. Krauser. I understand you think his friend Saber Bledsoe is of questionable character. . . . You saw him at the Pink Elephant? Can you please tell me what you were doing there? I see. Why would you have Jimmy McDougal in your automobile at the nightclub if in fact you did not want Jimmy to be in the company of the men who frequent the nightclub? Mr. Krauser, I'm not going to report you for your activities. Instead, if I hear you have lied about or mistreated either my son or any of his friends, I'm going to take a horse quirt to you in public, in front of witnesses. Then you can explain your shameful behavior to others, in particular the superintendent of schools. Thank you for your time."

There are good days you never forget. There are also days when people can throw a cup full of kerosene into a smoldering, wood-fueled stove, not pausing to think about the evaporation process and its effect when they casually toss a match through the grate.

That evening I called Saber and told him I was sorry I had ever hurt his feelings or done anything bad to him. I also told him he was the best guy I ever knew, and that Valerie felt the same about him, although that was a lie. I also told him it was time to visit one of our favorite nightspots, Cook's Hoedown, the honky-tonk where Elvis said he loved to perform more than any other. I snapped my Gibson into its case and put it into the backseat of my heap and headed for Saber's house. It was a bad choice.

Chapter 9

THE CLUB WAS on Capitol Street, and all the big Western bands and stars played there during the 1930s and '40s, including Hank Williams. A disk jockey named Biff Collie used to let me in through the back door and allow me to sit in with a couple of the bands at the back of the stage. To this day I tell people I played with Floyd Tillman, who wrote "Slipping Around," and Jimmy Heap, who recorded the most famous song in the history of country music, "The Wild Side of Life." I don't tell them I sat in the shadows, my acoustic Gibson lost among the drums and amplified instruments of the band.

It was a beer joint with a small dance floor and an earthy crowd. My parents wouldn't have approved of my being there, and few kids from my section of Houston wanted to go there unless they had an agenda that had to do with the availability of uneducated blue-collar girls. But for me the coarse physicality of the culture, the hand-painted neckties, the slim-cut trousers, the two-toned needle-nose boots, the drooping Stetsons, the sequined snap-button shirts that sparkled like snow, all somehow created a meretricious artwork that was greater than itself, one that told the audience that fame and the glitter of stardom were only a callused handshake away. Even Saber seemed in awe of me when I stepped down from the back of the stage and returned my Gibson to its case. "Jesus Christ, I cain't believe it's you up there with those people," he said.

"It's not a big deal," I said.

"Fuck it's not. That's Leon Payne."

Payne wrote "The Lost Highway" for Hank Williams. I didn't want to let on how proud I was, so I didn't say anything.

"Let's get a beer," Saber said. "My best friend plays acoustic guitar for Leon Payne. How about that, music fans everywhere? Hey, those girls over there are looking at us."

They weren't, but I didn't want to disillusion poor Saber. Cook's Hoedown wouldn't serve minors, as many of the nightclubs and beer joints did. So we went to a place called the Copacabana, over on Main. It had fake palm trees, the cloth trunks wrapped with strings of white lights by the entrance, and shades made of bamboo on the windows. It was a dark, refrigerated club, with only a jukebox on weekday nights. You could order beer or Champale from the waitress or at the bar; if you wanted anything harder, you had to bring your own bottle and order setups, which meant glasses, a small bucket of ice, and carbonated water or Coca-Cola or Collins mix at premium prices. Also, the bottle had to stay behind the bar. On Friday and Saturday nights there was a jazz trio and sometimes a female singer. There was a uniformed cop stationed by the men's room, but he never interfered with the sale of alcohol to minors or bothered the patrons unless someone started a fight or he recognized a parolee.

Saber and I sat in the darkest corner of the room and ordered two bottles of Champale from the waitress. Saber lit a cigarette, bending his face to the cupped match, his eyes tiny with secret knowledge. "Did you see who was in the parking lot at Cook's?"

"Whoever it was, why did you wait until now to tell me?"

"I didn't want to stoke you up."

"Then I don't want to know."

"It was Harrelson. With three other guys. They were in his pink convertible."

"What's Harrelson doing at Cook's?"

"Girls from the welfare project are always hanging at the back door. He gets them to blow him, then drops them on a country road."

"Stop making up lurid tales, Saber. The guy is bad enough as it is."

"Anyway, I shot him twin bones and double eat-shit signs, plus the Italian up-your-ass salute. I don't know if he saw me or not. Man, it's cold in here. Check out those guys in the corner."

A conversation with Saber was like talking to the driver of a concrete mixer while he was backing his vehicle through a clock shop. "Which guys?"

"In the suits. Tell me they're not gangsters."

"Lower your voice," I said.

"The flight from Palermo must have just landed."

I turned around slowly, as though looking for the men's room. The waitress had brought out a tray on wheels and was setting silverware and a battery-powered electric candle on a table. Three men sat around a bottle of champagne wedged into an ice bucket. She served steaks with Irish potatoes wrapped in tinfoil to the two older men, although the club had no kitchen and to my knowledge never served food. The younger man wasn't served a meal; he sipped from a champagne glass, one arm hanging on the back of the chair. None of the men spoke. When the waitress went away, the oldest of the three men tucked a napkin into his collar and bent to his food.

He was Frankie Carbo, my uncle's business partner, the man who fixed fights the way Arnold Rothstein fixed the 1919 World Series. I had shaken hands with both him and Benny Siegel, and it would take years before I could acquire the words to describe the peculiarity in both men's eyes. They saw you but did not see you; or they saw you and dismissed you as not worth seeing; or they saw you and filed you into a category that involved use or self-gratification.

Carbo probably was handsome at one time, but his face had become fleshy, his throat distended, his dark hair curling with gray on the tips. I saw his eyes cut toward me. I looked away.

"Told you," Saber said.

"That's Franke Carbo," I whispered. "Don't say another word."

"The gangster you met at the Shamrock? I knew it. See the young guy?"

"No."

"That's Vick Atlas. The guy who looks like Mickey Mouse without ears is his old man. He's supposed to be a nutcase. The son is a half-bubble off, too. They're hooked up with the cathouses in Galveston."

"Keep your eyes on me, Saber. Do not look at that table again. Do you hear me? And lower your voice."

"Don't get in a panic," he replied, his fingers drumming the table. "You should go on medication. I won't always be here to get you out of trouble."

"Let's go back to Cook's," I said. "Harrelson and his friends have probably left."

Saber's gaze shifted sideways and stayed there.

"What is it?" I said.

"Bogies at two o'clock."

"Who?" I said, not wanting to look, my stomach on fire.

He grinned painfully. "Harrelson left Cook's, all right. My ram-it-up-your-ass semaphore usually gets their attention when all else fails."

GRADY AND HIS friends took a table by the jukebox, close to Carbo's table, and Grady went over to shake hands with Vick Atlas. Then he returned to his table. At first I thought he was going to ignore me. I should have known better. He pointed at me, then said something to his friends.

"Don't react," Saber said. "Watch me and go with the flow. Look upon this as an opportunity. It's time Harrelson got exposed in public."

"Exposed for what?"

"I don't know. A guy like that has all kinds of secrets. All you've got to do is tap on the right nerve. Relax. I've got it under control."

The waitress brought a round of longneck beers to Harrelson's table. He sipped from the bottle, hunching his shoulders forward as he told a story to his friends. Each time they laughed, he glanced at me, smiling. I heard a sound inside my head like someone tightening a treble string on a guitar. Harrelson got up and walked toward me.

He wore black drapes and a thin crimson suede belt and tasseled loafers and a Hawaiian shirt with blue birds on it, the top of his shirt unbuttoned, a gold chain and cross around his neck. He fingered a pimple on his chest.

"What do you want, Grady?" I said.

"She eighty-sixed you?" he said.

"Who eighty-sixed me?"

"Valerie."

"Where'd you get that?" I said, my heart turning to gelatin.

"She called me. She didn't put it in those terms, but that was her drift."

"You talked to Valerie?"

"What did I just say?"

"I don't believe you."

"So how do I know she gave you the gate? Want the rest of the story?"

"Not interested."

"I bet. I motored on over and calmed her down." He took a swig from his bottle. "She hadn't been long-dicked in a while."

I saw the look on Saber's face, and felt his hand grab my forearm and hold it tight against the table. "You're a lying bastard, Harrelson," he said. "Go back with your greaseball friends."

"What did you say?"

"Look at your threads," Saber said. "You couldn't cut it in the Corps, so you wear drapes and Mexican stomps and pretend you're a hood. When did you start hanging with Mickey Mouse, Jr.? It's a drop even to be seen with that guy. By the way, I got some pix of you getting it on with that broad, what's-her-name. That's sick stuff, man."

"You asked for it," Grady said. He crooked his finger at his friends. "You got to hear this, y'all. Tell Vick to come, too. This guy here wants to repeat something he just said about Italians."

Saber knew how to do it.

"Your beef is with me, Grady," I said.

"No, it isn't. You're out of the picture and out of the saddle, Broussard. Got it? Anything you had going with Valerie is over."

"I don't believe you were at her house. I don't believe she would let you in."

"You need a blow-by-blow? She puts her tongue in your mouth when she comes. She likes to get on top. She can have three climaxes in one session. Sound familiar? Or did you get that far?"

I stood up from the chair, knocking it backward, and hit him across the face with the flat of my hand, hard, snapping his chin on his shoulder. He stepped back, a smear like ketchup on his mouth. I had never seen anyone's eyes look at me the way his did at that moment, as though I had awakened a darkness in him that no one else knew about.

Vick Atlas stepped in front of him. He was short and thick-bodied and looked full of contradictions. He had a damaged lip and whiskers like a patina of steel filings etched with a razor, as though he cultivated an unshaved look; he wore elevator shoes and a pressed suit without a tie and a rumpled white shirt with a belt and suspenders. He was probably in his early twenties but could have passed for forty. "That's my friend you hit," he said to me.

"He asked for it," I said.

"Wrong thing to say, kid."

"Who are you to call anybody kid?" I said.

"You know who you're wising off to?" he said. "You just get in town from the South Pole? You got a penguin stuck up your ass?" A drop of his spittle struck my chin.

"I'll take care of this later, Vick," Grady said.

"You made a crack about Italians?"

"His friend called you Mickey Mouse, Jr.," Grady said. "Believe me, Vick, this guy is going to be walking on stumps."

"I think y'all came in here to make your bones," Vick said.

I wanted to believe he was a caricature, that his black satinlike hair was a wig, that the mindless ferocity in his glare was a reflection of the light and not an indicator of bottomless rage because of his father's abuse or a plastic surgeon's failure. Minutes earlier we had been worried about dealing with a collection of spoiled rich kids; now we were a few feet away from men who fixed prizefights and trafficked in narcotics and prostitution and committed murder for no other reason than greed.

"Grady slandered my girlfriend," I said. "What would you do in my situation?"

"I wouldn't ever be in your situation. You and your friend mouthed off about Italians. A lot of my friends are Italian. So there's principle involved. The question is what we should do about it. Hey, you listening to me?"

"Yeah, and we're leaving," I said.

Vick Atlas looked at Saber. "You're the one called me Mickey Mouse, Jr.?"

Saber squinted at him. "Yeah, I guess I did."

"A guy with slits for eyes shouldn't be calling other people names."

"I apologize."

"You looking at my lip? You think I'm a freak? The sight of me offends you?"

"No," Saber said.

"You're saying you feel pity? That's why you got a change of attitude? You think that's going to save you? Don't look away from me. I'll pull your nose off."

"I told you I'm sorry. If you won't accept my apology, blow me," Saber said.

I saw Frankie Carbo turn in his chair and snap his fingers at the uniformed police officer by the men's room. The officer was a huge man, one shirt pocket stuffed with cigars, his shield pinned to the other. He walked toward us, an avuncular smile on his face.

"How you doin', Mike?" Vick Atlas said, shaking hands. "Everything is okay here."

"Little discussion, huh?" the policeman said.

"You know how it is," Atlas said. He took a money clip from his pocket. "I'm going to buy these guys a round so we can get out of here. At least if they'll let me. How about some Champale, you guys?"

"Screw the round," Saber said.

"See what I mean?" Atlas said.

Saber started to get up.

"Whoa," the policeman said. "I need y'all to keep me company. It's a lonely job."

"We just want to go home, Officer," I said.

"You will. All things come to those who wait. Trust me," the officer said.

He winked at me and patted Vick on the shoulder and walked away. Then Vick and Grady and his friends went out the front door in a group. The senior Atlas and Carbo never looked in our direction. I put a dime into the jukebox and went back to the table. The police officer smiled at me from his station by the men's room.

"My stomach's sick," Saber said.

"I think we can go now."

"We can go now? Listen to yourself. I feel like somebody held me down and put his spit in my ear."

"It could be worse."

"How?" Saber said. He waved at the policeman. "Hey, Officer, is the coast clear?"

The policeman gestured at the front door as though telling us the world was ours.

"Thanks! Keep up the good work!" Saber said. "The eyes of Texas are upon you!" He punched the air with his fist. The policeman looked at us sleepily.

Grady had outwitted us. He had managed to make us the personal enemy of Vick Atlas while pretending to be Atlas's friend and protector. Saber had walked right into it, but as always, I couldn't be mad at him.

We went outside into the humidity of the night and the smell of road tar and the heat stored in the asphalt. Somehow the club seemed shabby, the bamboo blinds crooked, the neon lighting shorted out. I could see my car where I had parked it under a light pole, its windows down, its doors unlocked. Back then we believed in our own mythology about the safety of the places we lived, and we didn't worry about car break-ins. Fortunately I had put my Gibson in the trunk.

* * *

THE INTERIOR WAS crosshatched with urine. The driver's seat was puddled with it, the dashboard and steering wheel dripping. We had no way to wipe it off or wash it out in the parking lot. We sat down in a world of beer piss and drove to a filling station and hosed out the interior. Then we stripped off our shirts and trousers behind the station and washed ourselves in the lavatory and got back in the car wearing only our boxers while bystanders gaped and cars on the road blew their horns. I saw Saber pick up a half piece of brick behind the station and drop it onto the car floor.

"What are you doing with that?" I asked.

"I'm tired of being shoved around," he said.

"Get rid of it."

"The best defense is a good offense."

"That's the kind of thing people say when they develop jock rash of the brain," I said.

"There's a lot of wisdom in a locker room."

"Saber!"

"Lighten up and get us out of here, will you? I feel sick. We've got their piss all over us."

I started the engine and pulled out of the station into the street, almost hitting an oncoming car. Saber hunched forward, his ribs stenciled against his sides. He turned on the radio, then turned it off.

"Don't let these guys get to you," I said. "You did great in there. You tried to take the heat off me."

"Those guys need a lesson," he said.

"What kind?"

"One they're not expecting. We need to put our mark on them. If we don't, we're going to be anybody's pump."

I didn't try to argue with him. I had never felt comfortable with the pacifism of my father, as much as I respected it. He had earned his in the trenches. When I tried to forgive those who transgressed against me, I felt weak and insignificant and deserving of the injury done to me. Now the seats and door handles and steering wheel, and even the radio knobs of my car stuck to my skin like adhesive tape, courtesy of Grady Harrelson and his friends.

We drove down South Main.

"Go to Herman Park," Saber said.

"What for?"

"Harrelson rat-races out there. He's probably going to give Atlas a thrill."

"What are we going to do when we get there?"

"I'll think of something."

"No."

"There's a faucet and a garden hose by the zoo. I cain't go in the house smelling this way."

Herman Park was a spacious urban forest full of live oaks and pine trees, located right off South Main Boulevard not far from Rice University; it contained a zoo and a playground and picnic tables and barbecue pits. It sometimes hosted another culture at night, one in which kids fought not for the fun of fighting but to do felonious levels of injury to one another. It also offered crowned asphalt-paved roadways that wound through acres of trees strung with Spanish moss, their leaves flickering in the headlights, their shadows as shaggy as the outlines of mythic behemoths.

I heard two cars coming fast beyond a bend. One sounded like a smaller vehicle, the engine whining, the driver squeezing everything he could from his lower gears, shifting up and then down, squealing into the turn, a bigger car coming hard behind him, the chassis swaying on the springs, a hubcap bouncing loose, clanging on its rim along the asphalt.

"It's him," Saber said.

"How do you know?"

"I got a sense. It's us against them."

"We're not talking about the big picture, Sabe. This is about Grady Harrelson and his punks."

"You saw the look on his face after you hit him. I'd like to do him in. I'd like to pop a cap on every one of them. Pull over. Here those cocksuckers come."

He was right. A red Austin-Healey came around the bend, sliding sideways, three guys in the front seat. They were laughing and had beer cans in their hands. Hard behind them was Grady's pink convertible, one guy standing up, holding on to the windshield. I thought he was yelling and shaking his fist. He wasn't. He was holding a firecracker while a guy in back was lighting it. He threw it just before it exploded, almost in his face.

I pulled onto the grass and cut the lights. Both cars went past us.

"We're going to find that hose and get out of here," I said.

"You know the edge they've got on us?"

"They don't have an edge."

"They never have to pay a price," he said. "We do. That's why we always back off. They've got a lock on the game before it starts, and they know it."

I stared at Saber. He had a gift for seeing the corruption in people's hearts when others saw only the monk's robe.

"That's a breakthrough?" he said. "Why would a rodent like Vick Atlas start a beef in front of a flatfoot?"

"I get the point."

"No, you don't get anything, Aaron. My old man said it. You and your old man are water-walkers."

"Cut it out."

He found a stick of gum in the glove box. He peeled it and stuck it into his mouth. He sighed. "You should be playing in one of those bands at Cook's. I was proud of you up there on the stage."

"Grin and walk through the cannon smoke," I said. "It drives the bad guys up the wall. A great man said that."

"Who?"

"Me."

But he was like a bird that had lost its song. He stared out the window, his eyes dead. In the distance I heard the two cars coming down the road again, engines wide open, headlights whipping around the curve, sweeping across the trees. I rested my hand on the keys, preparing to start the engine.

"Let them get past," Saber said.

I clicked on the radio. Hank Williams was singing "Cold, Cold Heart." I thought of Valerie and wanted to cry. The Austin-Healey and Grady's convertible were barreling toward us, leaves blowing in their wake. I heard another firecracker pop. As they roared past, I started the engine. I saw Saber stick his arm out the window and heave something over the roof. I thought I heard glass break.

"What did you just do?" I said.

"You told me to get rid of the brick."

I looked in the rearview mirror. The convertible was swaying all over the road; then it slowed as though the engine had died, and coasted onto the grass. People flung open the doors and piled out, silhouetting against the headlights like confused stick figures in an animation.

"Haul ass," Saber said.

My hands were shaking. I couldn't think.

"Snap out of it! Get us out of here!" he said.

I started the engine and drove onto the asphalt, slowly accelerating so my twin mufflers didn't come to life. I followed the bend in second gear, the headlights off. The road was winding and gray and humped, speckled in the moonlight like the scales on a snake. We drove in silence all the way to South Main, neither of us willing to look at the other lest we recognize the deed we had done.

Chapter 10

Two days passed. I called Valerie four times. I would have gone to her house, but I didn't want more trouble on the northside, at least not until I was sure about what had happened during the incident in Herman Park. (That was the way I had come to think of a brick flying into an oncoming automobile: "The Incident.") At 9:14 A.M. Wednesday, I glanced through the living room window and saw Detective Merton Jenks pull into our driveway and get out. The fact that he parked in the driveway indicated he knew I was alone and my parents had gone to work. I met him on the front porch. He carried two small ice cream cups and a pair of tiny wood spoons in one hand. "I bought these at that ice cream store by the firehouse on Westheimer. This is a nice neighborhood you have."

"I'm fixing to go to work," I lied.

"You need to talk to me. Don't try to jump me over the hurdles, either. If you cain't tell me the truth, don't say anything. But the one thing you need to do is listen. Sit your ass down."

"Don't talk to me that way."

"I'll talk to you any way I goddamn please."

He wore his fedora but no coat. His sleeves were rolled, and I saw a red parachute and the scrolled caption "101 Airborne" tattooed on his forearm. He put an ice cream cup and spoon in my hand.

"Somebody threw a brick at Grady Harrelson's car in Herman Park. Were you aware of that?"

"No, sir, I haven't heard talk of it. Is Grady okay?"

"The last I saw him, he was. On occasion do you drive through the park at night?"

"Not often."

"A couple of guys say your car was parked by the zoo a couple of nights ago. Maybe you and your girl were making out. You see any vandals cruising around?"

"No, sir, no vandals and no smoochers. I don't hang out at Herman Park at night."

"How about Bledsoe? Maybe he borrowed your heap and was making out?"

"No, sir, he didn't do that."

"Glad to hear that. Eat your ice cream."

"Was Grady's car hurt?"

"The brick went through the windshield and caught a guy named Vick Atlas in the eye. He might lose it."

"Lose his eye?"

"That's what I said. Makes you wonder why anybody would do that. You got something you want to say?"

"No, sir," I replied, my insides turning to water.

"This is my guess. If you did it, you'll tell me. If Bledsoe did it, you won't. You'll turn DDD on me."

"What's that?"

"Deaf, dumb, and don't know."

I didn't reply.

"Two guys say they saw your car. These are Harrelson's friends, not Atlas's. Atlas says he didn't see anything but the brick. He also says he never heard of you or Bledsoe. What does that tell you, Aaron?"

"I don't know."

"I think you do."

The ice cream was melting in my cup. I had eaten none of it. I felt sick all over, as though a toxic cloud had invaded my lungs and fouled my blood.

Jenks set his ice cream cup on the brick step. Snuggs and Bugs walked out of the hydrangeas and looked at him. Jenks picked up Bugs and petted her. "I'm going to tell you some things I normally wouldn't tell a suspect in an investigation. You think your problem is with the Harrelson kid. It's not. It's his father. He's the closest thing to a Nazi we have in Texas. You wonder why Loren Nichols came after you? Nichols's brother works in one of the Harrelson rice mills. You wonder why Grady is hanging with a lowlife like Atlas? The Mob does Clint Harrelson's dirty work. Harrelson is building youth camps around the country. If he has his way, your children will be brownshirts."

"You're going to arrest me, sir?"

He set Bugs down on the walk. He looked at me for a long time. I had a hard time holding his eyes. His gaze dropped to my stomach. "I like your belt buckle. You a rodeo man?"

"Amateur ranking only."

"The Atlases will hurt you. Maybe not kill you. But they'll do something to you that you'll carry with you a long time. Both the father and the son are depraved. If I had my way, I'd cap both of them. But people like me don't get their way."

The sky seemed a darker blue than it should be, too pure and unblemished to be real, more like bottled ink than air, the trees a deeper green, every color of the rainbow spilling out of the flower beds along the street, sunlight dancing crazily on the neighbors' rooftops, all of it deceptive and not to be trusted. "My grandfather was a Texas Ranger. He put John Wesley Hardin in jail."

"Talking about what our ancestors did isn't going to he'p. Talk it over with your parents. Don't try to handle this on your own. They'll cannibalize you, boy."

"My parents don't need this kind of grief."

"Then confide in me. Learn who your friends are."

"Saber Bledsoe is my friend."

I saw Jenks's jawbone flex. He placed the cover on his ice cream cup and put it and the spoon into my hand. "Stick this in the trash for me."

"I know you're trying to help, Detective Jenks. I just don't know any good way out of this."

He wiped his hands with a handkerchief. The tips of his cowboy boots had been spit-shined into mirrors. He cracked his knuckles. "You know why young men go to war?"

"They want to defend their country?"

"No, wars are there to solve a young man's problems. Do you understand what I'm saying to you?"

"I'm not sure."

"That's what I thought."

Then he did something I didn't expect. He patted me on the shoulder. A minute later he was driving away. I looked at the sky. It wasn't blue at all. It was streaked with rain clouds that resembled dirty rags, the wind filled with dust and desiccated animal manure blowing from the pasture at the end of our street. Drops of water were evaporating on the sidewalk, the air blooming with an odor like fish spawn and stagnant mud and carrion and waste buckets poured in a privy, as though the mystical cycle of creation had been preempted and replaced with a universe at war with itself. I thought I was losing my mind.

I NEEDED TO TALK to Valerie. A thunderstorm had just burst over the city when I drove into the Heights. The rain was blinding, the palm trees on the boulevard thrashing, lightning crashing in the park. On the main boulevard, the drains were plugged with floating trash, and rainwater had already backed over the curbs and sidewalks into people's yards. The explosions of thunder were deafening. Out in the park a solitary figure splashed through the puddles, bent forward into the wind, a clutch of books held against her breast.

I recognized her from afar as I would have in a crowd the size of China. No one else had auburn hair with gold streaks in it; no one else wore pink tennis shoes without socks and white shorts printed with flowers and a baseball cap and a shirt like cheesecloth with lace sewn on it; no one else would try to cross a softball diamond in the midst of an electric storm while hugging library books to her chest to keep them dry rather than cover her head with them.

I shifted down and pulled onto the swale and drove across the sidewalk into the park, my tires unable to find purchase, spinning water and mud and divots of grass into the air. I left the engine running and the door open and sprinted through the rain, slipping and almost falling. I could see her squinting at me through the rain, the sky black and unmerciful overhead.

I took the books from her hands and grabbed her arm and started running for the car. She tripped and fell, and I picked her up around the waist and held her against me, my arm tight around her ribs. When we reached the car, I pushed her across the seat and jumped in after her and slammed the door, both of us breathless, books spilling on the floor.

"Where did you come from?" she said.

"Home."

"How did you know where I was?"

"Who else would be out in an electric storm in the middle of a field?"

She moved the strings of wet hair from her eyes and stared into my face. She smiled. Slowly at first. Then she looked through the windshield as we worked our way out of the park.

SHE GAVE ME two bath towels so I could dry off in the living room while she changed clothes upstairs. Then she went into the kitchen and got a bowl of potato salad and cold fried chicken out of the icebox. I couldn't eat, not until I unloaded the nest of fish hooks in my head and the guilt that lived like weevil worms in my heart. "Grady Harrelson said some ugly things about you at the Copacabana."

"What things?"

"Personal things about y'all being together."

"Be specific, Aaron."

"About making love with you."

"He said he slept with me?"

I looked out the window at the raindrops sliding like quicksilver off the banana fronds, my eyes empty. "He went into detail. I hit him."

"Whatever he told you, he made up," she said.

"You didn't sleep—"

"Did you hear what I said?"

"He claimed you told him we'd broken up."

"Grady calls every day, no matter how many times I hang up. The other day he asked where you were. I told him I didn't know because I wasn't seeing either one of you. I'm sorry I said that."

She waited for me to speak, but I didn't.

"You're still worried I wasn't a virgin when we met?" she said.

"No, I don't care about that at all."

"The boy was a senior and I was a sophomore. We were going to be married. At least that was what we told ourselves. His reserve unit was called up just after his graduation. He was killed at Heartbreak Ridge."

"I'm sorry, Valerie. I didn't know any of that."

"I'm all right now. I wasn't for a long time."

"There's something I need to tell you," I said. "Maybe you won't like being around me anymore."

"It can't be that bad, can it?"

But I heard the resolve slip in her voice.

"Saber threw a brick out of my car at Grady's convertible in Herman Park." I could hear the rain beating on the window in the silence. "It hit a guy named Vick Atlas."

"Vick Atlas from Galveston?"

"Yes."

I saw the blood drain from her face.

"He might lose an eye," I said. "A detective was at my house this morning."

"Oh, Aaron."

I looked away from her.

"Do your parents know?" she asked.

"Neither one of them has had a very good life. I try not to add to their problems." I felt like a fool, someone who had gotten himself in trouble and wanted others to save him from himself. "I don't see any way out, not unless I give up Saber."

"He has to go to the cops. On his own. You didn't do it," she said.

"They'll send him to Gatesville."

"He didn't mean to hurt anyone. They'll take that into consideration."

"Loren Nichols went to Gatesville for shooting a guy with an air pistol after the guy molested his sister."

"Your friend is not acting like a friend."

"Saber always stood up for me when nobody else would. He'd always get even with the bullies. He doesn't have anybody except me."

It was obvious she didn't know what to say. How could she? She was seventeen. I wanted to go back into the ferocity of the storm and take her with me so we could disappear inside the rain or be gathered up by a giant funnel and carried out to sea.

"Maybe I could talk with Vick Atlas," I said.

"My father knows the Atlas family. Don't go near them."

"How could your father know them?"

"He was with the OSS. It became the CIA. The Atlas family helped Lucky Luciano get out of prison. They also helped him set up gambling operations close to navy shipyards so the workers would lose their money and stay on the job. You don't 'talk' to people like the Atlases."

"Can I use your phone? I'm supposed to be at work by three. The traffic lights are probably out."

"Stay with me," she said. "You have to stop doing things on your own without talking to somebody first. You understand that?"

"What should I do, Valerie?"

"Nothing. Stay with me. That's all. Just stay with me. I want you here."

"I don't want you hurt."

"They won't hurt me. They know better."

"What do you mean?"

"Nobody messes with my father."

"He's not actually a violent man, is he?"

"He doesn't have to be," she replied. She went to the window and looked at the rain and at the wind tormenting the trees. "We come from different worlds. The difference between Jews and gentiles isn't a religious one. The difference is in our knowledge of what human beings are capable of. Do you know you're the sweetest boy I've ever met?" She turned around. I could almost see her unspoken words in the fogged place she had left on the windowpane. "Do you understand what I just said?"

"I believe the guy who died at Heartbreak Ridge was the best guy on earth."

She came behind my chair and hugged my head against her, kissing my hair, her breath in my ear. "I'll always be with you," she said. "I give you my word. You're my Pegasus, my winged horse taking me out of the storm."

I tried to twist my head. But she wouldn't let go of me. I never wanted to leave her embrace; nor did I want the storm to end. And if it had to end, I prayed the world would be washed clean and a light as bright as creation would burst on the ocean's rim.

But in the morning the sun came up hot and sultry, and the air was leaden with the stench of dead beetles in the drains, and from baitfish that meteorologists claimed had fallen from the clouds. At eight sharp, Saber's father was fired from the rendering plant where he had worked for nine years.

SABER CAME TO the filling station to tell me. The gas pump island was littered with leaves and twigs, a live oak across the boulevard uprooted from a yard like a raw tooth. We were standing under the shed by the pumps while I fueled a car. Saber kept looking over his shoulder while he talked.

"What did your father's boss say?" I asked.

"They have to cut back on overhead, and some of the old guys have to go."

"What did your father say?"

"He's the only one they canned. What's to say besides 'Thanks for the memory, motherfuckers'?"

I looked around to see if anyone had heard. The city bus stopped on the corner. Saber's face twitched when the collapsible doors opened. Several black people exited from the back door, and the bus pulled away. Saber's eyes kept blinking, as though the light were too harsh. "Somebody tied black crepe on our doorknob last night. It had dog shit on it so the person who tore it off would get it on his hands."

"Maybe the cops can lift fingerprints off it," I said.

"Try dusting dog shit for fingerprints."

"Maybe it's kids."

"Quit it, Aaron."

"Has Jenks been to your house?"

"No." He waited, his eyes drawing close together. "Has he been to yours?"

I finished fueling the car and made change for the driver and watched him drive onto the boulevard. "Jenks was at the house yesterday. The brick caught Atlas in the eye."

Saber made a sound like someone had punched him in the stomach.

"You haven't told your dad what happened?" I said.

"No. My old man didn't go past the seventh grade. He doesn't have a job, and it's my fault. I want to go to Korea and get killed."

"We've got to tell somebody," I said.

"You're kidding. Don't even think that."

"We can't hide this, Saber," I said. "The Atlases are criminals. What if they try to hurt my parents and I don't warn them first?"

I thought he was going to cry. I finished fueling another car and clanged the hose spout on the pump. Saber stared emptily at the boulevard as though he had no idea where he was. I would have given anything to undo the bad decisions I had made and the pain they had brought my best friend. Just a few weeks earlier we had been part of a postwar era that had no antecedent. No other country had our power or influence. Music was everywhere. Regular was eighteen cents a gallon. All the services on a car—window washing, oil check, tire inflation—were free. Those small and inglorious things somehow translated into a confidence that seemed to dispel mortality itself, even though Joseph McCarthy was ripping up the Constitution and GIs were dying in large numbers in places no one could locate on a map or would take the time to spit on.

I walked over to Saber and placed my hand on his shoulder. "You've got to trust me, Sabe. If we do the right thing, we don't need to be afraid."

"You're going to tell your dad what happened?"

"What if I do?"

"My old man worries when baloney goes up ten cents a pound. Your old man thinks it's noble to burn your own house down while the band plays 'Dixie.' Gee, who's about to get it without grease?"

Chapter 11

My mother didn't allow my father to keep liquor in the house. In order to drink, he went to the icehouse or the bowling alley or the garage, where he kept a bottle under the spare tire in the trunk of the car. It was a shameful way for him to live, and a shameful way for my mother to behave, but it was the only way they knew.

After supper I sat at the redwood table in the backyard and played my Gibson. By chance I once heard Lightnin' Hopkins playing in front of a bar on Dowling Street, in the heart of Houston's black district. He was singing "Down by the Riverside." It was the saddest and most beautiful blues rendition I had ever heard. I did not know the song's origin, but I understood its content, and when I would feel one of my spells coming on, I would get out my Gibson and sing it:

Gonna lay down my sword and shield,
Down by the riverside,
I ain't gonna study war no more,
Down by the riverside,
Ain't gonna study war no more.

Somehow I knew he was not singing about war but about something even worse, perhaps the destruction of the spirit or the mortgaging of one's soul. I wondered how anyone could prevail over the unhappiness that had been imposed on Lightning and his people. I wondered if the Texas prison he had served time in was worse than the prison I had constructed for myself.

I heard my father open the screen door and head for the garage. "Daddy?"

He looked at me, startled.

"I've got to tell you something," I said.

He looked at the garage door. "I might have a low tire. Can it wait a few minutes?"

"Yes, sir."

I heard him scrape the door back on the concrete, then pause and push the door in place without going inside. He walked across the grass toward me, fishing in his pocket for his Lucky Strikes. He had left them in the house.

"Go get a smoke if you want one," I said.

"It's all right. I'm trying to cut down. What's on your mind?"

Saint Augustine said not to use the truth to injure. I don't think he used those words lightly. My father tried to remain impassive as I described the events at the Copacabana and in Herman Park, but his expression was like that of a man walking barefoot on a rocky road. There was a tremble in his right hand, the fingertips vibrating slightly on the tabletop, a blue vein pulsing in his temple.

When I finished, he cleared his throat and looked at my mother's silhouette in the kitchen window, where she was washing dishes. "You and I are supposed to be doing that."

"I'll go help her."

"No, she'll understand. The boy is going to lose his eye?"

"He's not a boy."

"It doesn't matter."

"Yes, sir, that's what the detective said."

"And Saber wants to keep quiet about it?"

"He's scared. His father just got fired."

"Fired? When?"

"This morning."

"For doing what?"

"Nothing."

"You think these criminals are behind it?"

"Or Grady Harrelson's father."

My father cleared his throat again and stared at the garage.

"Want me to get you a glass of water?" I asked.

"The boy's name is Atlas?"

"Yes, sir."

"What do you know about him?"

"He's no good."

"Did you have words with his father in the nightclub?"

"No, sir."

"You're not to have any contact with them. If they try to talk to you on the street, if they yell insults at you from a car, if they make threatening phone calls in the middle of the night, you do not respond, not under any circumstances. Clear?"

"Yes, sir, but what does it matter?"

"Every word you utter to an evil man either degrades you or empowers him. Evil men fear solitude because they have to hear their own thoughts." He glanced at the evening sky. The moon was yellow, surrounded by a rain ring that looked like a halo on the painting of a Byzantine saint. "Get an umbrella. I'll back the car out and meet you in front."

"Where are we going?"

"Where do you think?"

I was beginning to regret confiding in my father. Maybe Saber had been right. My father belonged to that generation of Southerners drawn to self-destruction and impoverishment as though neurosis and penury represented virtue.

"You want your hat and coat?" I asked.

"Yes, I'd appreciate that. Thank you," he said. "Tell your mother we'll be back soon."

My FATHER PULLED to the curb in front of Saber's house. The only light inside came from the television set. The same was true of most of the houses on the street. Saber's house looked like a railroad shack someone had forgotten to bulldoze before building a modern subdivision around it. The television had a small black-and-white screen encased in plastic and had been manufactured by a man named Madman Muntz, who came to Houston in 1951 and sold thousands of them for fifty dollars apiece. The warranty was thirty days. The lawn mower was dead-stopped in the grass, a long swath behind it. The garbage can, emptied that day or the day before, was still on the swale.

My father removed his hat and tapped on the screen door. I could see Saber and his mother sitting on the cloth-covered couch in front of the television. Neither of them looked away from the program. Mr. Bledsoe got up from his stuffed chair and came to the door in slippers and cutoff shorts and a T-shirt. His hair looked like weeds growing on a rock. He stared straight into our faces and did not unlatch the screen. "I know why you're here."

"We'd like to talk with you and Saber," my father said.

"We're fixing to go to bed."

"Our difficulty is not going away that easily, sir," my father said.

"We don't have difficulty. Nothing happened."

Neither Saber nor his mother looked in our direction.

"That's right, isn't it, Saber?" Mr. Bledsoe said.

Saber didn't answer or turn around.

"Obviously your son told you what happened, or you would not know the purpose of our visit," my father said.

Mr. Bledsoe gazed through the screen, a tired man whose vocabulary was probably no more than a few hundred words, a man with no self-knowledge and neither moat nor castle except for his shack and the broken screen that separated him from the rest of the world.

"Will you invite us in?" my father said.

"They took my job. They'll take my house and they'll take my boy, too. Don't tell me they won't, either."

"We need to go to the police," my father said.

"Like heck I will."

"You're putting the burden on my son, Mr. Bledsoe."

"It's not him that's at risk. If he wants to go to the cops, that's his damn business."

"You just admitted Saber threw the brick."

"I didn't admit anything. No, sir."

"My son isn't an informer."

Mr. Bledsoe's gaze had shifted into space, as though he saw content there that no one else did. "We look after our own."

"Would you step out here and talk to me, please?"

"There's nothing to talk about. I already took a belt to him."

"For telling you the truth?"

Mr. Bledsoe tilted up his chin, defiant. "Maybe if you'd disciplined your own son, he wouldn't have drove Saber to a nightclub, then to a park where they didn't have no business."

"So Aaron must either inform on your boy or bear the consequence of Saber's throwing the brick?"

"I didn't say anything about a brick. You want to talk about that, you take your conversation somewhere else."

"I'd like you to forgive me for what I have to say, Mr. Bledsoe."

"I got no idea what you're talking about."

My father started to speak, then stopped. "We wish you and your family the best. If we can be of assistance to you, please call."

"That won't be happening," Mr. Bledsoe said.

My father put his hat back on. It was a classic fedora, the front brim bent down. He had small eyes and dark hair and clean features that belied his age and the alcohol he consumed. I wondered what he would look like if he didn't drink or smoke. We got into the car and he started the engine. He looked up at the gaseous yellow glow of the moon; it had a peculiar radiance, like a campfire burning inside snow.

"What were you fixing to say to Mr. Bledsoe?" I said.

"That his conduct is dishonorable."

"Why didn't you?"

"He's an uneducated and poor man. We won't make him a better one by criticizing him."

We drove home in silence. After he pulled into the garage, I hoped he would follow me into the house and the two of us would clean up the kitchen, working as a team. Instead, he said he had to check the tire. Ten minutes later, I went back outside. The moon had gone behind clouds, and the yard was filled with shadows as pointed as swords. My father was sitting in the passenger seat, the car door open, drinking from a paper cup one sip at a time, his eyes closed as though he were involved in a secular benediction whose nature no one else would ever understand.

I WENT IN TO work early the next morning so I could get off that afternoon and take Valerie to play miniature golf. I wasn't expecting to see Cisco Napolitano's black-and-red Olds convertible coming down the boulevard. Miss Cisco was behind the wheel. She turned in to the station and stopped at the pumps. She was wearing a scarf and shades and white shorts and a pink halter that barely contained her breasts. "What's the haps, darlin'?" she said to me.

"Are you from New Orleans?"

"Why would you think that?"

"Because that's the way people talk in New Orleans."

She removed her shades and let her eyes adjust on my face. "Take a ride with me. No argument this time."

"What for?"

"You got yourself in a lot of trouble. I can get you out of it."

I told the other kid who worked in the station that I'd be back soon. He took one look at the Olds and the gorgeous woman behind the wheel and stared at me in disbelief. I got into her car and settled back in the comfortable softness of the leather. She stepped on the gas before I had the door closed.

"Where we headed?"

She squeezed me on the thigh, grinning behind her shades.

"What are you doing?" I said, alarmed.

"Don't be so serious. Your virginity is safe. You're a virgin, right? Anyway, I don't molest young boys."

She turned off the boulevard into the Rice University campus and parked in the shadow of the football stadium. She took a small leather-bound photo album from the glove box and marked one page with her thumb, then handed me the album. "Tell me who that is."

"Benny Siegel and Virginia Hill."

"Who's that with them?"

"You?"

"At age twenty."

"Who's the guy with you?"

"Who's he look like?"

I lifted my eyes to her. "Like me?"

"He was an actor. I met him at a lawn party at Jack Warner's, next door to Siegel's house. He was my first real love."

"What happened to him?"

"He died from a heroin overdose. It was probably a hotshot. You know what that is?"

"No."

"The dealer slips the user some high-grade stuff he's not ready for. He was going to another studio. Hollywood is a place where you don't break the rules. Vegas works the same way, Aaron. You come into their world, you play by their rules. You don't sue the Mafia. You listening?"

"I didn't choose to be involved in any of this."

"Jesus, you're thick. There's a hot-dog cart by the street. Go get me one."

"*What?*"

"I'm hungry. Now go do it. What's the matter with you?" She handed me three dollars from her purse. "With relish and ketchup and mustard and onions. Buy yourself one. Bring us a couple of Cokes, too. I have to pee. I'm going into the stadium. Hurry up, now."

I went after the hot dogs. When I got back, she was fixing her hair in the mirror, examining a sun blemish under one eye. She patted the dashboard, indicating where I should place the food and drinks.

"What did you think of Benny Siegel?" I said.

She picked up her hot dog and bit off a huge hunk of sausage and bread and onions, catching the drippings on the back of her hand. "He was a psychopath. Which returns us to the subject at hand."

"I wish you wouldn't put it in that context."

"You fucked yourself, kiddo. Now let's see if we can unfuck you. Our problem is not Vick Shit-for-Brains. It's his father, Jaime Atlas. Do not get the idea that he's a devoted father who wants to get even for his son. Shit-for-Brains is Jaime's possession, and you and your buddy threw a brick through a windshield into his face."

"I didn't throw anything."

"Your friend did?"

"Why did you bring me here, Miss Cisco?"

"Tell your friend to turn himself in. In the meantime, think about the army. Your parents can sign for you. When you finish your enlistment, this will probably be forgotten."

She wiped her fingers with a paper napkin. A campus security car pulled up next to us; behind the wheel was a guy wearing aviator shades and a cap with a lacquered bill. "You cain't park here without a sticker, ma'am."

"I'm moving in just a minute, Officer."

"You have to move now, ma'am."

She shot him the finger without looking at him, then started the engine and drove out to the street and parked under a live oak.

"Is that how you deal with everybody?" I asked.

"Shut up. Do you know what 'in the life' means?"

"No."

"I don't know why I'm doing this. I should let you drown. I feel like throwing an anchor chain around your neck myself."

"I don't know why you're doing this, either."

She looked straight ahead and blew out her breath. "Grady Harrelson's father is a silent partner with some nasty people. Jaime Atlas will get his pound of flesh, or he will no longer be doing business with Clint Harrelson. It's you or your friend. But there're no guarantees on that. It could be both of you."

"I can't change that."

She pushed a strand of hair out of my eyes. I moved my head away from her hand.

"I go out of the way for you, and that's how you feel?" she said. "You're a strange kid. Maybe you're a lost cause, not worth the effort. What's your opinion?"

"I didn't want any of this to happen."

"Tell that to the people who voted for Hitler."

She put on her shades and started the engine, then clicked on the radio. I thought she might play some music. She turned the dial to the stock market report and didn't speak on the way back to the filling station. When I got out, I turned around and thanked her. She drove away without replying.

I WENT HOME AT three P.M. and bathed and changed clothes. I was about to go to Valerie's house when my father pulled into the driveway and parked in the porte cochere. He got out of the car with a paper bag in his hand.

I met him outside. "You're home a little early."

"Where's your mother?" he said.

"At the grocery."

"If you have a minute, come in the backyard."

He opened the gate and sat down on the back steps and waited for me to sit down with him; the bag rested on his knees.

"Yes, sir?"

"The most frightened I've ever been was the first time I had to go over the top in early 1918. I went over it four more times, but nothing could equal the fear I felt the first time. No one who was not there can understand what that moment is like. No one."

He rarely spoke of the Great War, and when he alluded to it, he never mentioned his experiences as a soldier. Most people who thought they knew him well were not even aware he had been to Europe. When others began to speak of war—especially when they spoke in a grandiose fashion—he left the room. The paper bag was folded in an oblong, humped shape, as though it might contain a rump roast or a couple of odd-sized books.

"You think I'm quitting school and joining the army?" I said.

"No, I think you're worried about evil men coming into your life. That's what I want to talk to you about. When we went up the steps on the trench wall, it was likely that the man in front of you had soiled himself. You had to breathe his odor and stiff-arm him in the back so he didn't fall on you, and you hated him for it. Once you were in the open, there was no going back. You had to run through their wire into hundreds of bullets while your chums fell on either side of you. I did it once and thought I could never do it again. I told this to the lieutenant. He was a Brit serving in the AEF and a fine fellow. He said, 'Corporal Broussard, never think about it before it happens, and never think about it after it's over.' I remembered that the rest of the war. It gave me peace when others had none."

I didn't know why he was telling me any of this, and I said so.

"Can't blame you," he said. "These men who wish us harm may come to see us or they may not. If that happens, we'll confront them as necessity demands."

He unfolded the paper bag and removed a heavy blue-steel sidearm with checkered grips stuffed in an army-issue canvas holster. "This is the 1911-model .45-caliber automatic. It's simple to operate. Its effect can be devastating. You drop the magazine from the frame, you load the magazine by pressing these cartridges here against the spring, then you reinsert the magazine and pull back the slide. You do not take it from the holster unless you plan to shoot it."

"Does Mother know about this?"

"She's the one who told me to buy it. Aaron?"

"Yes, sir?"

"When you kill a man, his face stays with you the rest of your life."

"Can I hold it?" I said.

He placed the .45 in my hand. The magazine was not in it. The frame and checkered grips felt cold and heavy. There was a reassuring solidity about its heft, a potential that was dreamlike and almost erotic. I put my finger through the trigger guard and aimed at a caladium in the flower bed my mother had dug along the neighbor's garage wall, just as my dog, Major, emerged from the plants and stared at the gun's muzzle and at me. He backed among the caladiums and elephant ears as though he didn't know who I was.

"It's all right, Major," I said. "Hey, come out here, little guy. Don't be afraid."

My father took the .45 from me and shoved the magazine into the frame with the heel of his hand, returned it to the holster, and snapped down the flap.

"Why is Major scared?" I said. "He's never seen a firearm."

"They have an instinct," my father replied. "It will be in the right-hand bottom drawer of my desk. It will stay there unless we have urgent need of it. Do not play with it. Do not show it to your friends. You with me on that?"

"Yes, sir," I said. "A woman named Cisco Napolitano came by the station today. She's mixed up with the guys who run Las Vegas. She said Jaime Atlas won't rest till he gets his pound of flesh."

My father got up from the steps. "Good. Tell her thanks for the advance notice. If any of these criminals call, would you tell them I'm at the icehouse and I'll have to get back to them?"

I LOVED MINIATURE GOLF, and I loved playing it with Valerie. It was fun putting down the lanes of pale red fabric, watching the ball rumble over tiny bridges and waterways and through the bottoms of Dutch windmills, then see it plunk neatly into the cup.

The evening was cool and breezy and smelled of water sprinklers and meat fires, and after we played nine holes, we ate watermelon at the stand across the street while Tommy Dorsey's "Song of India" moaned from a loudspeaker in the fork of an oak with its trunk painted white. Then I heard a pair of dual exhausts that were like none other—operatic, deep-throated, throbbing like the motorized equivalent of a classic ode, produced by Saber's homemade mufflers and the oil he had set aflame inside them. He pulled his heap to the curb and got out wearing jeans and a white T-shirt and half-top boots with chains on them, combing his hair with both hands, affecting a confidence I suspected would crumble any second.

I was happy to see him. I couldn't bear to think of Saber as a Benedict Arnold. People like Saber died on crosses or were lobotomized but were never compromised or absorbed by the herd.

"Thought y'all would be here," he said, his eyes going from me to Valerie.

"This is Saber, Valerie," I said.

"How you, Miss Valerie?" he said, sitting down at the picnic table.

"You don't have to call me 'miss.' "

"I get it from Aaron." His eyes went everywhere except on her face. Saber was a wreck around girls. One time he climbed out a second-floor window when a girl tried to drag him onto a dance floor.

"What happened to your arms?" Valerie said.

"Fell off the roof." He folded his forearms and tried to cover the stripes on them. There was a fresh stripe on his cheek, the same shade of red as the ones on his arms, all of them the width of a belt. "I could stand some of that melon. Those are Hempstead melons. That's the best kind."

"Did your dad go after you again?" I said.

"He's not thinking straight. He's all right when he sobers up."

"Your father did that to you?" Valerie said.

He looked straight ahead, trapped inside his shame. Valerie cut off a piece of watermelon from her slice and put it on a paper napkin and pushed it toward him. "Aaron says you're the best friend he's ever had. He says everybody respects you."

There were strings of electric lights in the trees, and I could not tell if the shine in Saber's eyes was from their reflection or not.

"How'd you know where we were?" I said.

"Called your mom. Krauser popped up today. He came by the house right after Jenks did."

"What's Krauser want?"

Saber looked at Valerie, not sure how much he should say. "He works part-time for the probation department. He says he knows I'm going to end up in Gatesville. He can get me into a youth camp of some kind that'll protect me."

"You mean summer camp?"

"No, it's some kind of political crap."

"What did your parents say?" I said.

"Neither of them finished grammar school. They think Krauser is big shit, the intellectual of the Houston school system." He glanced at Valerie. "Sorry."

She smiled at him with her eyes.

"Stay away from Krauser. Don't listen to anything he tells you," I said.

"Tell that to my old man. He eats up Krauser's war stories. 'Ole boy from South Carolina blew the treads on a SS Panzer and put a flamethrower on it. We nicknamed him Hotfoot.'"

"You okay, Sabe?" I said.

"Sure."

"You could fool me," I said.

"I think I'm going to turn myself in," he said.

"You're sure that's what you want to do?"

"Jenks says they found the brick and they're going to dust it for fingerprints."

"Then why tell you about it?" I said. "Why not just bring you in?"

"I don't know. I don't know anything."

A car passed. It had straight pipes, and the engine roared like a garbage truck. The guys inside it were big, their arms tattooed and hanging out the window, the sleeves cut off or rolled to the shoulder. One of them yelled something. Saber kept his eyes on the car until it turned the corner at the end of the block. "You know who those guys are?" he said to Valerie.

"I couldn't see their faces."

"How about the car? A '49 Hudson."

"No, I don't remember seeing it," she said.

"Did you recognize them?" he said to me.

"No."

"They look like bad news," he said. He stared at the street, then at me. "I think they're dogging us."

"They're just guys. If they wanted a beef, they would have stopped."

"You don't know that."

"What's going on, Sabe?" I said.

"Nothing. I don't take guys like that for granted. I've had my fill of them."

"You want to play a round of miniature golf?" I said.

"No, I got to get home. I don't feel too hot. I got to get off the dime. You don't let the enemy take the high ground. Rule one of the Army of Bledsoe, right?"

"Why not spend more time with Aaron and me?" Valerie said.

"Me?" he said.

"The rodeo and the livestock show are coming up," she said. "My 4-H club has some exhibits."

"That would be pretty simpatico," he said.

"Can I tell you something?" she said.

"Go ahead."

"Quit fighting with these people," she said. "One way or another, they'll all disappear."

"I don't think it works that way."

"Yes, it does. Don't go seeing things, either," she said. She reached across the table and squeezed his hand. I think she almost had him convinced.

The car loaded with big guys came by again, slower this time, one guy sitting up on the passenger window bare-chested, shooting us the bone across the roof. Saber stood up from the table. A narrow object protruded from his boot, stiffening inside the leg of his jeans.

"Sit down," I said.

"I'm tired of these guys," he said. He gave them the Italian salute.

The car kept going, crossing the intersection, its straight pipes shaking the air. I pulled up the cuff of his jeans. "What are you doing with that?"

"Taking care of myself. Not taking any more shit. Sorry, Miss Valerie."

"Give it to me, Saber," I said.

"I'll give it to you when people like Krauser and guys like that bunch in the Hudson get off our backs."

He had a sheathed British commando knife strapped to his calf. It was doubled-edged and dark blue and made of steel, including the handle, the blade tapering to a razor-sharp tip, an absolutely murderous gut-ripper you could buy for $2.95 and a coupon from any men's magazine.

Saber wiped his place clean and threw the napkin into a trash can.

"Stay with us," Valerie said.

"Thanks. See y'all later," he said. "Let me know if those guys come back. Maybe get their license number. I think it's time to start doing some home calls."

He lit a cigarette as he walked to his car, not even bothering to hook his pants cuff back over the knife's handle, flicking the match angrily at the air.

Valerie stared at me. "He said Jenks?"

"That's the detective who's been giving us a bad time since Loren Nichols's car was torched and the Mexican girl was killed," I said.

"Merton Jenks?"

"Yeah, that's his name. You know him?"

"Jenks was in the OSS with my father," she replied.

Chapter 12

I HAD NEVER WORN handcuffs before. Or been pushed face-first against a car and probed under the arms and in the crotch. It happened at the filling station the next morning in front of my boss and our customers. A plainclothes detective pulled my arms behind me and snipped the steel tongs into the locks and squeezed them into my wrists, bunching the skin, then turned me around and set me on the backseat. "Stick your feet outside."

"Outside?"

He had a narrow face and large ears and nicotine breath and a level of irritability and malevolence in his eyes that seemed disconnected from the situation, as though he carried an invisible cross and wanted to visit as much damage on the world as possible. "You go to school. You don't understand English?"

"You want my legs outside the car?"

I looked at his eyes again and didn't wait for an answer. I hung my legs out the door. He pulled off my shoes, glanced at the soles, and dropped the shoes into a paper bag.

"Sir, what are we doing?" I said.

"Watch your feet," he said, and slammed the door.

It was a short ride to Mr. Krauser's house. A cruiser and a cage truck from the SPCA were parked in front. I could see Saber's head through the back window of the cruiser. Krauser was standing in the front yard, wearing tennis shoes and a yellow strap workout shirt and slacks dotted with paint, his shoulders and upper arms ridged with hair. His face was dilated, as though it had been stung by bees. The man who cuffed me was named Hopkins. He had taken off his hat inside the cruiser; there was a pale line across the top of his forehead. He looked at me through the wire mesh. "I talked about you boys with Detective Jenks. I don't know why he's put up with you. But that's him, not me. That man standing in the yard has the Purple Heart and the Bronze Star. Somebody should beat the shit out of both y'all. Your buddy in the cruiser says it was your idea. Is that true?"

"What idea?"

"Last chance. It's you or him or both y'all. He's already put your tit in the ringer."

"Saber said I committed a crime?"

"His words were 'It was Aaron's idea. I just went along.'"

"It looks to me like he just got here. When did you talk to him?"

His gaze went away from me. "Saw your belt buckle. Don't try to ride this one to the buzzer. You'll end up in Gatesville."

"I didn't do anything."

"You've already got a jacket, boy. You think your shit don't stink? You think you're going to get away with this?"

"With what?"

I could see the hair moving in his nostrils. He got out and pulled open the back door. The pupils in his eyes looked like burnt match heads. He fastened his hand around my bicep. "Don't speak unless you're spoken to," he said. "Don't be eyeballing, either."

Krauser stared at me as we went up the driveway. His face was razor-nicked, a piece of blood-spotted toilet paper plastered to his chin, one of his eyes bulging and the other recessed and watery, as though diseased.

"I don't know what happened here, Mr. Krauser, but I didn't have anything to do with it," I said.

"Broussard?"

"Yes, sir."

He blinked and looked at Hopkins. "What did he tell you?"

"Maybe you should go inside and cool off, have a glass of water," the detective said. "Don't worry. We'll get the truth from these boys."

"Bledsoe is the ringleader," Krauser said. "He belongs in a juvenile facility. This one here is a snake. Don't turn your back on him."

The other cops were taking Saber out of the cruiser. He was handcuffed and barefoot, his T-shirt stretched out of shape on his neck, one knee grass-stained, his elbows raw and bleeding. Hopkins pushed me up the driveway.

"I want to call my parents," I said.

He didn't answer. I stepped on a bottle cap or a rock and had to hop on one foot. Then we rounded the corner of the house. The yard was in full sunlight, the humidity like spun glass, the air thick with the smell of feces. Flies buzzed around the trash can. The Doberman was stretched out on the grass, inches from an empty water bowl. A piece of butcher paper streaked with a copper-colored liquid had blown against the chain-link fence.

"You think we did this?" I said.

"You wear a ten and a half?" he said.

"Shoe?"

"No, your hat size."

"Yes, a ten-and-a-half shoe."

"Go up the steps."

"The Harrelsons or the Atlases are behind this."

"The who?"

"If you talked with Jenks, he told you about them."

"What he told me is you boys may have caused a boy to lose his eye. Now, get your ass inside."

"I want to call my parents."

"You don't make the rules, boy."

"I'm not going to cooperate with this."

"You're going to do as you're told."

The back door was open. So was the screen, slashed diagonally by a sharp knife or a box cutter. The dead bolt had been prized out of the doorjamb. Hopkins pressed his knuckle into my spine. Sweat was running down my nose; the sun was the hot yellow of an egg yolk, the heat from the concrete and St. Augustine grass a wool blanket on my skin. I could feel my wrists peeling and salt running into the cuts, when I tried to twist them inside the cuffs. Hopkins worked his knuckle into my spine again.

"You son of a bitch," I said.

"Didn't quite catch that."

My nose was dripping, my eyes burning, the yard and house slipping out of focus. "I apologize."

"Get inside," he said.

"What for? I was playing miniature golf with a friend last night. I went from my house to work this morning. I couldn't have done whatever it is that happened here."

"Inside, boy. I won't say it again."

"I want a witness."

"Witness to what."

"Whatever you're going to do."

There was no one else in the yard. I could hear Saber and the other cops out on the driveway. Saber had either fallen or sat down and was making them drag him into the backyard. Hopkins lit a Camel and took a puff and let the smoke out slowly. He looked at his cigarette, then raised his eyes to me. "You smoke?"

"No, sir."

"Good for you. I got to quit these things one day."

He stiff-armed me through the door. I stumbled against the wall. "I never did anything to Mr. Krauser. You probably cost me my job. Everybody in school hates Mr. Krauser's guts. He's a cruel, mean-spirited shithead, and everybody knows it. I want my damn phone call."

"You'll get it at the jail."

I knew that nothing I said would make any difference. He belonged to the huge army of people who believed that authority over others was an achievement and that violence was proof of a man's bravery.

Hopkins flipped his cigarette through the ripped screen into the yard and led me into a foyer shiny with fresh paint and tracked with shoeprints. He stood on the edge of the foyer and took one of my shoes from the paper bag and squatted down and fitted it inside a print. Then he did the same with the other shoe. "Both shoes fit, wouldn't you say?"

"What does it matter? I didn't walk through that paint. I wasn't here. At least not yesterday or today."

He didn't answer. The other cops brought Saber through the back door, one of them carrying his shoes. The cop handed the shoes to Hopkins. It took three tries before Hopkins could fit one of Saber's shoes into a print. Then he pressed the other shoe inside another print and stood up, flexing his back. "Neither one of you were here? That's your story?"

"Those tracks could have been put there by anyone," Saber said.

Hopkins turned up the soles of our shoes. "How'd the same paint get on here?"

"You put it there," Saber said. "We saw you do it."

"That paint has been dry for hours." He squatted down again and touched the floor and rubbed his thumb across his fingertips. "See?"

Through the back door, I saw the SPCA man wrap Krauser's Doberman in a piece of canvas and carry it out of the yard. Hopkins walked into the weight room and turned around. "Bring those two in here. I want to see if they're proud of their work."

I went ahead of Saber, the paint in the foyer sticking to the bottoms of my feet. At first glance, everything in the weight room seemed to be in order. The dumbbells were racked, the weight bar loaded with fifty-pound plates notched on the stanchions above the leather-padded bench, the memorabilia hanging on the walls. As my eyes adjusted to the poor lighting, I saw the methodical thoroughness the vandal or vandals had used in destroying everything that daily reassured Krauser who he was.

They had broken the glass out of the frames on the walls, then cut and shredded the citations and photos and military decorations inside them, reducing them to confetti and miniaturizing Krauser's life. They had used pliers or vise grips to mutilate Krauser's medals for valor and his combat infantryman badge. The Confederate battle flag hung in strips from the wall, each strip tied in a bow. The lamp made from a German helmet was upside down on the floor, propped against the wall. Hopkins tipped it with the point of his shoe. A rivulet of yellow liquid ran onto the concrete. The white-handled Nazi dagger with the incised gold SS lightning bolts was gone.

No one spoke. The air-conditioning unit in the window was dripping with moisture, its motor throbbing. As much as I disliked Krauser, I felt sorry for him.

"What would make y'all do something like this?" Hopkins said. "That man served his country. That's how y'all pay him back?"

"We never did anything to that motherfucker," Saber said.

"What do you call this?" Hopkins said.

"You're asking *me*?" Saber said.

"That's his Purple Heart by your foot. Yes, I'm asking you."

"I hung my swizzle stick through a hole in the ceiling above his biology class. I put a dead frog inside his coleslaw. But you want my opinion on this mess here?"

"We're burning to know," Hopkins said.

A sound came out of Saber that was like air wheezing from a slow leak in a basketball. He was trying to hold it in, his face splitting; his knees started to buckle, his suppressed laughter shaking his chest, his tear ducts kicking into overdrive.

"What do I call it?" he said. "What do I call it? What do you think, man? It's a fucking masterpiece."

I NEVER KNEW THAT jails were loud. The Harris County jail boomed with noise of all kinds: people yelling down corridors and out windows, cell doors slamming, radios blaring, cleaning buckets grating on concrete, a dozen court-bound men coming down a steel spiral staircase on a wrist chain, a lunatic banging a tin tray outside the food slot of an isolation unit. The level of cacophony never grew or decreased in volume; the building seemed to subsume it the way a storm does; you could actually feel the noise if you pressed your palm against the wall, as if the building had a vascular system.

There were eight of us inside a rectangular cell that had four iron bunks hinged and suspended from the walls on chains. The toilet seat was gone, the bowl striped with tea-colored stains. Our compatriots were a drunk who'd started a fight at the blood bank, a handbill passer accused of window peeping, a check writer who had been out of jail six days before he wrote another bad check, a four-time loser picked up for parole violation, and two bare-chested Mexican car thieves whose torsos were wrapped with knife scars and jailhouse art. They all seemed to know one another or have friends in common, and to accept the system for what it was and not argue with either their surroundings or their fate.

I was allowed one phone call. I called my father's office. He was out and I had to leave the message with a secretary, knowing the embarrassment it would bring him. At four o'clock a trusty in white cotton pants and a white T-shirt with HARRIS COUNTY PRISON stenciled on the back stopped a food cart at the bars and handed a tray through the food slot with eight baloney sandwiches and eight tin cups of Kool-Aid.

"When's the bondsman come around?" Saber said.

"You got to go to arraignment first."

"When's arraignment?"

"In the morning."

"I'm not planning on being here in the morning."

"We got Cream of Wheat and sausage and coffee for breakfast. It's pretty good."

The trusty pushed the cart down the corridor.

"Come back here!" Saber shouted. "Hey, I'm talking to you!" He pressed his head to the bars, then gripped them with both hands and tried to shake them.

"Relax," one of the Mexicans said. "You got to be cool. Don't be shouting at the trusties. They'll spit in your food."

"I got news for them. I ain't eating it."

"That ain't smart," the Mexican said. "You got to get in step, man. You're in jail."

"Thanks for telling me that."

I put my hand on Saber's shoulder. "Your dad or mine will be here soon."

I was wrong. The hours passed and the electric lights went on in the corridor, then at 11:01 P.M. they went off with a *klatch* all at once, dropping the building into darkness except for the fire exits and a guard box by the main gate.

At seven A.M. the trusty was back with a cauldron of Cream of Wheat and an aluminum bucket of sausages and a huge pot of coffee. One hour later we went to arraignment on a long wrist chain. My father was among a handful of spectators in the courtroom. Saber's was not. We were charged with breaking and entering and destruction and theft of private property. Our bail was set at five hundred dollars, a great amount back then.

My father had brought cash. Saber kept craning his neck, looking at the entrance to the courtroom. Mr. Bledsoe never arrived. It took a half hour for me to be processed back on the street. Saber was issued jailhouse denims and told to change for transfer to a unit upstairs. I could see the fear and hurt in his eyes. "Your dad is probably putting the money together," I said.

"No, he's not. He's drunk. He doesn't care."

"I'm sorry, Saber. Don't mouth off to these guys. No matter what they say or do."

"I can do this standing on my hands." He missed an eyelet as he buttoned his denim shirt, as though his fingers had gone numb.

I lowered my voice. "Be careful about what you say to *everybody,* got it? There are no secrets in a place like this."

"So maybe I'll make some new friends."

"What do you mean?"

"It's the way things worked out. I'm here. You're going home. I told you they were out to get us. I was half right."

Outside, in the freshness of the morning and the sound of traffic amid Houston's tall buildings, I walked with my father toward his car while Saber was put in lockdown with mainline cons.

"Did you do it?" my father said.

"No, sir."

"Your word on that?"

"Yes, sir."

"What about Saber?"

"He wouldn't kill Mr. Krauser's dog. I'm sure of that."

"I talked with this fellow Hopkins, the one who arrested you all. He said the SPCA man thought the dog was fed sleeping pills, not poison."

"How could he tell?"

"Poison would have caused convulsions and vomiting. The dog simply went to sleep. You still think Saber wasn't involved?"

He waited for my reply.

"Can we get him a bondsman?" I asked.

"He might be better off in jail. Anyway, we can't mix in the family business of other people."

"Hopkins rubbed the soles of our shoes in the paint on Mr. Krauser's floor."

"I think it's time we have a talk with Mr. Harrelson."

"Grady?"

"No, his father."

We crossed the street to Kelly's steak house, one of my father's favorite downtown spots. His face was untroubled, perhaps even at peace, his fedora tilted over one eye, his clothes free of cigarette smoke. I wondered if we had entered a new day.

Chapter 13

I WAS SURPRISED HOW easily we gained access to Clint Harrelson, since he was known as a recluse and an introvert. My father called him, and he invited us to his home. As we opened the piked gate and entered the main grounds of the estate, I noticed how my father looked at the details surrounding him; I knew what he was thinking. The Harrelson estate was a replica, at least generically, of the Louisiana home where my father was born in 1899, except the brick walkways and live oaks and camellia bushes and creamy columns and emerald-green lawn and clumps of pink and lavender wisteria and subterranean garage of the Harrelson estate were real. They were not an abstraction or part of a postbellum era that had become little more than a decaying memory on a polluted bayou.

Grady had no siblings nor a mother. Grady told others she had died of breast cancer in a Mexico City clinic. Others said she'd died in a plane crash with her Brazilian lover, a famous polo player and owner of a coffee plantation. Regardless of how she died, all of her genes and physical characteristics must have gone into her son, because Grady looked nothing like his father. Texas was full of loud, porcine oilmen who made fortunes during the war. They combined a predatory form of capitalism with down-home John Wayne folksiness and couldn't wait to spit a mouthful of Red Man on the lawn of a country-club terrace. Mr. Harrelson was not one of these. He was a slight ascetic-looking man with a thin, bloodless nose and a V-shaped chin and a broad forehead and steel-rimmed glasses and white-gold hair cut short. He wore a white robe and slippers on his small feet and had a book in one hand. "Oh, yes, you're Mr. Broussard." He glanced at his watch. "Right on time. Come in."

He didn't bother to acknowledge me. My father waited for him to extend his hand, but he didn't.

"This is Aaron, my son," my father said.

"Yes, how are you?" Mr. Harrelson said. "Follow me, if you would." He paused at the staircase. It was wide enough to drive a truck up, the handrail and steps made of restored cypress, the grain polished to a glossy amber. "Our guests are here, Grady!"

His voice had no inflection, no regional accent. His eyes were a grayish blue. They showed neither interest nor dislike and seemed to look inward rather than out. He made me think of a mathematician or a chemist, not the owner of rice mills and a drilling company. There was an antiseptic cleanliness about him that made me wonder if his glands were capable of secretion. If he had a botanical equivalent, it was a hothouse plant that had never seen sunlight or one that had been leeched of its chlorophyll.

He went into the living room and sat down in a stuffed chair by the fireplace. There was a tea service on the coffee table with a cup for one. He raised his eyebrows and gestured toward a divan on the other side of the fireplace. "Let's see if I have everything straight. It started with the Epstein girl and progressed to a brick being thrown through the windshield of Grady's car, right? So your son wishes to own up and apologize or pay damages, or you want me to speak to the Atlas boy's father? Or some combination thereof? Does that sum it up?"

I stole a glance at my father. I could not count the number of social indiscretions that, in his eyes, Mr. Harrelson had already committed.

"You have a very attractive home," my father said. "I was admiring your camellia bushes. They put me in mind of the place where I grew up."

Mr. Harrelson set his book facedown on the table, splayed open against the spine; he crossed his legs, his robe falling loose. He pawed at a place below one eye. There were white bookcases on either side of the fireplace. The titles of the books had to do with history and economics. The only novelist I recognized was Ayn Rand.

"Can you tell me why you're here?" Mr. Harrelson asked.

"My son has been accused of things he hasn't done. This morning he was charged with a break-in. The possibility that someone is doing this to him deliberately is difficult to abide." He held his gaze on Mr. Harrelson.

"Does your indignation extend to the Atlas boy losing an eye?" Mr. Harrelson said.

"Yes, it does. I'm bothered by another factor as well. The Atlas family are criminals. Your son was in the company of both the father and the son and a gangster named Frankie Carbo. Does that seem normal to you?"

Mr. Harrelson touched at his nose with one knuckle. He looked toward the staircase. "Come down here, Grady."

Barefoot, Grady walked down the stairs and into the living room. He was wearing a T-shirt cut off at the mid-abdomen and beltless Levi's that hung below the navel. His tan had deepened, and his body tone was as supple and smooth as warm tallow. "What's going on, Pop?"

"This gentleman says you were with a gangster named Carbo."

"Not so. I saw Vick Atlas at a nightclub. Vick was at another table and joined us. That's about all there was to it."

"You urinated in Aaron's car," my father said.

"With respect, I don't do things like that, sir."

I tried to make Grady look at me. He wouldn't.

"Well, there you have it," Mr. Harrelson said. "We seem to have different perceptions about past events. I'd like to let it go at that. An investigation into the brick incident is in progress. I'll abide by its outcome." He turned toward his son. "I think the real issue is the Epstein girl. I think she's better left alone. Her father is a Communist. Usually the acorn doesn't fall far from the tree. That's just one man's opinion. Do you want to say anything to Mr. Broussard or Aaron, Grady?"

"I'm willing to shake hands," Grady said.

"How about it?" Harrelson said. "Then let the law handle it. Grady has never been in trouble. He's never hurt anyone, either."

Grady had his arms folded on his chest, his gaze focused on the floor, a study in humility. Outside, the underground sprinkler system sprang to life. I had never seen one before. Jets of water spiraled and twisted throughout the yard, swinging across the patio, clicking against the live-oak trunks and trellises and French doors, misting in the twilight. Simultaneously, the underwater lights in the swimming pool came on, creating a turquoise radiance on the surface that resembled colored smoke. Could a person live in a more perfect setting? And there in the midst of all this stood Grady Harrelson, lying through his teeth while Saber Bledsoe was probably eating grits and beans out of a tin plate, wondering about the visitors who might come to his bunk when the count screw dropped the building into blackness.

I stared at Grady's father, forcing him to look at me. "Grady *does* hurt people, Mr. Harrelson. Last summer some hoods from across town crashed a party on Sunset Boulevard. Grady and his friends beat them so bad they begged. They stretched one guy backward over a car hood and pounded his face in."

"That might have been wrong, but it sounds like these fellows were asking for it," Mr. Harrelson said.

"Maybe you should talk with Detective Jenks," my father said. "A Mexican girl, a prostitute, was killed in the Heights. Someone broke her neck two blocks from where a car was burned. Detective Jenks thinks the two events are related. It appears someone is trying to place the blame on my son and his friend Saber Bledsoe."

Mr. Harrelson wrinkled his nose under his glasses and smiled. "This has nothing to do with us," he said. "At this point I think we should say good evening and next time speak to the authorities if we have questions about my son's behavior or the behavior of his friends. I must say one thing, though, before we conclude: There seems to be little concern about the damage done to the Atlas boy. From what I understand, he's lucky he wasn't decapitated. I'm sorry, I didn't mean to get into that again. Grady, would you make sure the outside lights are on for Mr. Broussard and Aaron."

My father looked into space. His hat lay on the table, crown-down. He picked it up and straightened the brim. Then he rose from the chair. He hadn't slept well the night before and had gotten up early to go to the bank and withdraw the five hundred dollars he needed to pay my bail. He looked ten years older than he was.

"We'll find our way out. Please don't get up," he said.

Mr. Harrelson nodded and opened his book and began reading. I didn't think I had ever met a more arrogant man in my life.

Grady opened the front door and held it while we walked outside. The night was sweet with the smell of flowers and lichen and the haze from the sprinkler system. Grady started to close the door. My father turned around and stiff-armed it back open. "Ask your father to come out here."

"He's done talking," Grady said. "It's just his way. He's a funny guy sometimes."

My father had not put his hat back on. He held it pinched by the crown and pointed it at Grady. "Go get him, young man. I don't wish to embarrass you, but you need to do as I've asked you. *Now.*"

"If that's what you want."

Grady went back into the living room and returned a moment later with Mr. Harrelson, who was still holding his book, his thumb marking his place. For the first time I could see the front of the jacket. The book was a collection of essays by Harry H. Laughlin.

"Yes?" he said.

"Your ungracious manner is probably related to a lack of breeding and background, Mr. Harrelson, so you should not be held accountable for it," my father said. "However, the degree of your rudeness seems to indicate contempt for the civilized world rather than ignorance of it. You seem to lack what William James called 'the critical sense.' This is the faculty in us that works a bit like God's fingerprint on the soul. It's not a faculty that can be acquired. One is either born with it or he is not born with it. Obviously, in your case, it's the latter." My father fitted on his hat. "You have a grand place here. As I said, it reminds me of another setting, one I don't think you would understand. Good evening, sir. Come on, son."

We walked along the gravel drive to our car. I didn't hear the door close behind us. I did not look back. I had the feeling it would take Clint Harrelson a while to absorb what he had just been told. I also had the feeling Grady was about to become a pincushion.

I was right. But I found out about Grady's private torment in a way I never thought possible.

In the meantime, I treated my old man to a cherry milkshake at the Walgreens on Westheimer, where we sat side by side at the counter, the jukebox playing, a big fan on the wall shaking to the beat of the band.

I KEPT MY JOB at the filling station, I think in part because the other white kid who worked there had been drafted, leaving only me to handle money when the owner wasn't around. But I had to come in on Sundays, too, which meant if I wanted to attend Mass, I had to go at seven A.M. The church was located not far from the eastern border of River Oaks.

I hadn't eaten, and after Mass I went across the street to Costen's drugstore and ordered toast and a cup of coffee at the counter, then realized I had left my missal in the pew. The church was empty. Or at least I thought it was. I gathered up my missal and was going back out the side exit when I heard someone leave the confessional, either knocking the kneeler against the cubicle or banging the door. A moment later Grady Harrelson came through the exit. We were standing a few feet from each other in a shady patch of lawn between the church and the convent and a covered walkway with no one else around. The morning was still cool, the stucco walls of the church and convent streaked with moisture.

"Are you following me?" he said.

His eyes were red, his face pinched, perhaps heated, perhaps embarrassed, perhaps remorseful, I couldn't tell. I didn't feel any anger toward him. Or even resentment. If anything, I felt pity. "How you doin', Grady?"

"I asked if you're bird-dogging me."

"This is where I go to church. I didn't know you were Catholic."

"I'm not."

"Just visiting?" I said.

"You being a wisenheimer?"

"No," I said. "I'm glad to see you."

"That's a tough sell."

"Did something happen in there?" I asked.

He looked at me warily. "Can those guys tell other people about what you say to them? I mean, if you're not Catholic, can they tell?"

"Not to my knowledge."

"What does that mean?"

"No, they can't tell anyone."

He looked back at the church door, then at me. Then he stared at his convertible parked in the sunlight. The top was down, the white folds snapped against the body, every inch of the paint a creamy pink you could eat with a spoon.

"It's not over between us," he said.

"What isn't?"

"Nobody slaps me in the face."

"If I could undo it, I would. Anyway, it's over for me."

He had tried to change the subject, but it hadn't worked. He humped his shoulders and scratched at his upper arm, narrowing his eyes, imitating the slouch and look of the street hoods he probably envied. "Sometimes you can do some shit you don't set out to, know what I mean?"

"I'm not sure," I replied.

"That stuff I told you about Valerie, about getting it on with her? It's not true."

I nodded. I didn't want to say anything more. He wrapped his arms across his chest. "You tell anybody about this, you know what's going to happen, right?"

"Tell anybody about what?" I asked.

"Me being here."

"Don't get mad at me, Grady, but I've got news for you. Nobody cares whether either one of us is here. A bird just splattered your windshield. Nobody cares about that, either. These are not big events."

"You've always got the cute comeback," he said.

What do you say? I wondered what had occurred inside the confessional. I didn't want to ask, but I thought I knew. "Can I help you, Grady? I've had a few hard times. We got off to a bad start. It doesn't always have to be that way."

His face was like a portrait painted on air, the eyes flat, the lips still. "No," he said.

"No, what?"

"No, I don't need help with anything."

"I'd better get to work. See you another time," I said.

The sun hadn't climbed above the church, and the air was blue with shadow in the lee of the building. Purple roses bloomed against the stucco wall. He shook his collar as though he had overdressed and his body heat was trapped inside his shirt. He coughed on the back of his wrist. "How's she doing?"

"Who?"

"Val."

"She's fine."

"That's good. Make sure she stays that way," he said.

Why did he say that? What had Valerie told me about the jealous kind? They were unteachable and incapable of change? "What was that last part?"

"What I said."

"You volunteered for the service," I said. "You would have ended up in Korea if you didn't have a medical condition. Why don't you drop the hard-guy bullshit?"

"You don't know anything about my military service, so shut your mouth, Broussard."

"Don't be telling me how I should treat Valerie."

"You think you have to tell me I'm not yellow? You told my old man I helped tear up those guys who crashed a party on Sunset. Let me give *you* a news bulletin. I didn't gang anybody. The guy behind most of it was Vick Atlas, the same guy who wants to chain-drag you and Bledsoe from his bumper. That's not exaggeration."

Maybe I shouldn't have said anything else. I was talking to a kid who would never be anything except a kid. But I had been at the party on Sunset Boulevard and seen what had happened, and I just couldn't abide his lying, or maybe I couldn't abide his proprietary attitude about Valerie. Even now, over sixty years later, I have a hard time with it. He called her "Val"?

"Those were your friends who spread-eagled that guy," I said. "You could have stopped them. You were laughing when y'all walked off. The guy had to go to the hospital, at Jeff Davis, as a charity case. I thought that was pretty chickenshit."

He didn't reply. He bit his bottom lip, his body turned sideways, positioned to throw a hook straight into my face.

"You want to say something?" I asked.

"I can't tell you what I feel like doing to you right now."

"Then do it. I want you to."

There was a blood clot in the corner of his left eye. His eyelids were fluttering.

"You think you're a swinging dick because your old man told off my father?" he said. "My father could have your old man cleaning toilets, except he wouldn't waste his time. Your old man's a drunk. Your mother has been through electroshock. We could have you ground into paste if we wanted to."

"The priest told you to turn yourself in," I said.

His face went white. "What'd you say?"

"You owned up to something bad. Maybe it had to do with the dead Mexican girl. But you won't turn yourself in because you're a bum, Harrelson, and not worth spitting on."

I walked away from him and didn't look back. At the corner I saw him drive slowly out of the parking lot onto the street, too slow for the traffic. A car blew its horn. Grady didn't react or accelerate and instead pulled to the light as though frozen in thought. When the light changed, he steered with the heel of one hand, not heeding a truck trying to turn in front of him. He seemed to have every characteristic of a man without a past worth remembering or a future worth living. But the words he had spoken about my father and mother had robbed me of all sympathy for him. The pity and charity I had felt only minutes ago were gone. I was the less for them.

My missal was still in my hand. I wondered what Saint Paul would have to say regarding my role as a bearer of the good news.

Chapter 14

THE DAYS PASSED, and Saber's father took out a second mortgage on the Bledsoes' run-down home and used the money to put up Saber's bail and consult with an attorney, one he had found in the Yellow Pages. Saber called me as soon as he got home. I thought he wanted to get together. That wasn't the case.

"We're down to rat cheese and crackers at the house," he said. "The old man is collecting newspapers to haul out to the mill. Ever been to the paper mill?"

The mill was located on several hundred square acres of piled trash swarming with seagulls. It was a wretched place peopled by the desperate and the poor who eked out a living by going door-to-door, asking others for their old newspapers and cardboard boxes and later selling them for a penny a pound at best. They had the despair in their faces of medieval ragpickers.

"You want me to ask my father if he can get your dad a job on a pipeline?"

"My old man thinks your dad talks to him like he's a nigger. Those were his words."

"That's ridiculous."

"If you don't see me for a while, it's not because I ran off to the army," he said.

"You going somewhere?" I said.

"I made some connections in the can. Remember the Mexican guys in the holding cell?"

"Those guys are *pachucos.* They'll cut you from your liver to your lights," I said.

"Been to some KKK meetings lately?"

"You know what I'm talking about," I replied, my face flushing.

"See you in the funny papers, Aaron. Keep it in your pants. Oops, too late for that. How's Valerie doing?"

I hung up.

I LOVED THE SUMMERTIME. The afternoon thunderstorms were the kind you stood in and took joy in the rain. When the sky cleared and turned a soft blue again, the clouds in the west were like strips of fire, or sometimes piles of plums and peaches. Every new day was a cause for celebration, no matter its content. And the explanation for the joy I felt was easy: I was not only in love with the season; I loved Valerie Epstein and I knew Valerie loved me.

I loved her smell and the smoothness of her skin and the way her eyes crinkled when she laughed. There was not enough time in the evening to do all the things that seemed created just for the two of us. Whatever we did was an adventure. We went to the ice rink in one of Houston's poorest neighborhoods and to baseball games at Buffalo Stadium and to R&B concerts at the city auditorium, where whites had to sit in the balcony because the best seats and the dance floor were reserved for Mexicans and people of color.

For a dollar and a quarter we saw B.B. and Albert King, Big Mama Thornton, and Johnny Ace. On a Friday night we drove to Galveston and the Balinese Club, run by the Maceo family on a six-hundred-foot pier. The moon was up, the Gulf slate green, the waves tumbling through the pilings. The entranceway was framed with neon and hung with Japanese lanterns, the sky black and sprinkled with stars, the air heavy with the smell of an impending storm. We could hear a dance orchestra playing.

Valerie took my hand as we were about to go inside. "This is really uptown, isn't it?" she said.

"Yeah, Frank Sinatra has sung here."

"You're kidding."

"Bob Hope played here, too."

She started inside, tugging my hand. For no reason that I could explain, I hesitated. It wasn't because the Maceo family owned the club. They owned casinos, bingo parlors, nightclubs, restaurants, and the slot machines in beer joints all over the island. I felt a vibration in my chest, the pressure band along the side of my head reappearing, warning signs I sometimes experienced before I had a spell. I glanced down the boulevard. "Maybe we should go to the Jack Tar and have a big fried-shrimp dinner."

"Don't they serve seafood here? I always heard it was special."

"It's real good, all right," I said, touching the side of my head.

The front door opened, and a blond man in a summer tux and a glamorous woman in an evening dress came down the steps, confetti in their hair. The orchestra had just gone into "Tommy Dorsey's Boogie-Woogie." Valerie had worn a new white dress.

"Let's go," I said. "I'll show you Sinatra's and Hope's pictures on the wall."

Why had I hesitated? It wasn't the club itself; it was the locale. Galveston was the turf of the Mob. The club was a reminder of something Grady Harrelson had said outside the church, that Vick Atlas wanted to chain-drag me and Saber from his car bumper. It was hard to shake the image from my mind, and I had not told either my father or Saber about Grady's statement, trying in my futile fashion to avoid giving evil a second life.

At the far end of the pier was a casino. Only select guests and high rollers were allowed inside. But every kind of person was at the dining tables and on the dance floors that telescoped room after room down to the casino area. Seven French sailors were dancing together, unshaved, wearing their caps. We got a table by an open window and could smell the salt in the wind and hear the waves slapping against the pilings under the building. There was a checkered cloth on our table, and a candle burning inside a glass chimney, and silverware wrapped in bright red napkins. Valerie reached across the table and squeezed my hand. I had never seen her so happy. We ordered crab cocktails and a sample tray of everything on the menu and a pitcher of iced tea with spearmint leaves floating in it.

Then I saw him, the way you notice an aberrant person among a crowd of ordinary people, the way you take note of a smile that doesn't go with someone's eyes, the way the oily imprint of a man's handshake can send a wave of nausea up your arm and into your stomach.

She followed my eyes. "Puke-o," she said.

"You recognize him on sight?"

"He used to go to all the Reagan–San Jacinto games. Nobody wanted him there, especially the cheerleaders. He was always trying to make out with them."

Vick Atlas was looking at us from a table across the dance floor, grinning in spite of the black patch he wore over one eye. He wiggled his fingers. I pretended not to see him. "Let's dance."

"I think we should stay where we are."

"Why?"

"He'll try to cut in."

"We'll tell him to drop dead."

We danced, then came back to the table. A green bottle of champagne waited for us in a silver ice bucket. I called our waiter to the table. "This must be for somebody else."

"No, sir, Mr. Atlas sent it to you with his compliments." The waiter was wearing a starched white jacket and a black bow tie and high-waisted black trousers. "I think Mr. Atlas wants you to have it."

"We're hard-shell Baptists. Tell him we appreciate the thought."

The waiter picked up the bucket with both hands, his expression dead, and walked to the bar, careful not to look in Atlas's direction.

"You shouldn't have done that," Valerie said.

"We don't have room on the table for it," I said. "Here comes our food."

We started eating, neither of us looking up from our plates. I felt rather than saw Atlas walking toward our table. A shadow fell across my arm. "How you doin'?" he said.

"We're doing all right," I replied.

"You don't like champagne?"

"Not tonight."

"Because I saw you drinking beer at the Copacabana. Maybe y'all would like a beer. How about some German beer?"

I didn't answer. Valerie was taking small bites of her food, her eyes lowered.

"No?" he said. "If you look out the window, you can see the bait-fish jumping in the waves. That's because a sand shark or a barracuda is after them. It's a rough world out there. Underwater, I mean."

"Those barracuda are bad guys, all right," I said.

"Not as bad as some I know. Real bums. What do you think of my patch?"

I stopped eating and looked at the flame burning inside the glass chimney of the candleholder. "I didn't notice."

"What's a guy have to do to get your attention? I might end up with an empty socket."

"I'm sorry to hear that."

"I guess that's the breaks. Is that the way you read it? Just a bad break?"

"I didn't do it to you, Vick."

"Did I say you did?"

"Leave us alone," Valerie said.

"You're Valerie Epstein," he said. "You go to Reagan. I know some of your girlfriends."

She looked out the window at the waves swelling as black and slick as oil under the moon, the candlelight flickering on her face. Her cheeks were red, as though windburned.

"How about a little slack, Vick?" I said.

"You want slack? You got it, Jack. I was just asking about my champagne. I thought maybe you didn't like the year. Next time I'll send over iced tea. Will you dance with me, Miss Valerie?"

"We're eating," she replied.

"I mean after you eat. I want to dance with you. Okay with you, Aaron?"

"Let's go," Valerie said to me.

"No," I said.

"No, he says. Way to go, Aaron. You're a stand-up guy. Did you know somebody boosted Grady's pink convertible last night?"

"No, I didn't."

"An expert. Not many people can hot-wire a Caddy. Grady is torn up about it."

"That's a heartbreaking story," I said.

"That's why my father has got some of his friends looking for the guy who did it. Can I sit down before we dance?"

"What do you want, Vick? We haven't done you any harm."

"I know that now because you told me. If a guy like you tells me something, I know it's gold. That's straight up. From the heart. I wouldn't feed you a line." He dragged a chair from another table and sat down. "Where's the Bledsoe kid tonight? Still in the can? Or out doing mischief? What a card."

"We need to go," Valerie said.

"Hang on, little lady," Atlas said. "We've got to dance. Nobody will believe a story like this. I meet Aaron, get my eye put out, then dance with his girl. I mean, provided he doesn't mind. You're simpatico with that, aren't you, Val?"

"Why did you ask about Saber?" I said.

"He's a fascinating guy. I heard a lot of the parts on his heap are stolen. A guy who steals car parts is probably one jump away from boosting the whole car. But you probably wouldn't hang with a guy like that. Give me an answer on this dancing situation, will you? My lady is waiting over there. You know her."

I followed his eyes across the dance floor. At a long table in the corner, Cisco Napolitano was sitting with a group of people who looked like they'd just arrived from Miami. She was wearing a strapless black evening gown and a pink corsage. For just a second I thought she was looking back at me.

"So what's it going to be, Aaron?" Atlas said. "I'm not talking about slow dancing. We'll wait for a fast number. I dig the bop. Jitterbug is out, the bop is in. There's even a dirty bop, did you know that? We can do it, Val, you and me. I mean the regular bop."

"I don't want to dance with you," Valerie said. "Do we have that settled now? Please leave our table."

"The lady is direct. I respect that. Too bad you didn't step up to the plate on that, Aaron." He leaned closer to me. I could feel his breath on my cheek. "Doesn't matter, though. We're buds. Right? Talk to me. The right kind of bud is a bud for life." He grinned at Valerie and put his arm across my shoulder. Unconsciously I put my hand on the steak knife that lay by my plate. He jiggled his arm. I could smell the staleness in his armpit. "Friends?"

"Yeah," I said, my eyes straight ahead.

"That's the way to talk, Jack."

He removed his arm. I thought he was done. I should have known better. He wet his finger and reached around the side of my head and put his saliva inside my ear.

I had never experienced a greater sense of revulsion and violation. I drove my elbow into Atlas's face and, at the same time, pressed my napkin into my ear. In my mind's eye, I saw myself tearing him apart, stomping his face into jelly, breaking his jawbone, snapping ribs like Popsicle sticks. But I didn't do it. I doubt I drew blood. The orchestra was blowing down the walls with "One O'Clock Jump"; few if any people seemed to notice a problem at our table.

Valerie handed me her napkin. I dipped it in my water glass and cleaned my ear with it. Atlas was pressing his fingers against his cheekbone, otherwise unruffled. Then I realized he had paid a price he hadn't anticipated. His patch had popped up from his eye, exposing the true nature of the injury. The eye was a blue orb the size of a dime, oozing liquid, either infection or medication or both, but the surrounding tissue was not cut or bruised or stitched; the tissue was puckered, the eyelid seared. Atlas's eye had been burned, not hit with a brick.

"It was a firecracker," I said.

"Firecracker? What are you talking about?" he said, popping the patch back in place.

"Y'all were throwing firecrackers," I said. "Maybe Baby Giants or M-80s. A firecracker blew up in your face. You and Grady framed us, Vick."

"You just admitted you were in the park, smart guy."

"Get away from our table. If you don't, I'm going to do something that will embarrass you for the rest of your life."

There was a beat. His good eye was watering. His bottom lip had started to puff where my elbow had hit him. "You're going to do what?"

"You don't want to know. Nobody watching will forget it."

The band finished "The One O'Clock Jump." Vick looked over his shoulder at the orchestra as though somehow it contained the solution to his problem. "I'm going to write this off for now. But I'm coming for you."

"No, you'll send somebody else. All you guys are the same. You never go it on your own."

He rose from his chair and looked around casually. "Good night, Miss Val. You got class. I'm a big respecter of that. Anything I can do for you, let me know. It's an honor to have sat at your table."

He waited for her to speak. She looked at her plate.

"So be it," he said. "Good night to both of you. Maybe I'll see Aaron again. Maybe not. Who knows? It's a big universe out there."

"Not big enough," I said.

"We'll see, smart guy."

The band started playing again. He walked through the dancers to his table rather than around the dance floor.

Valerie lifted her face and opened her eyes. "I never saw anything like that in my life. What was the embarrassing thing you were going to do?"

"Nothing."

She looked at me a long time. "You're the best boy I've ever known."

There are compliments you never forget and you never tell anyone about; instead, you hide them in an invisible place, and for the rest of your life, when the world about you is in tatters, you take them out and read them to relearn who you are.

Chapter 15

AFTER I PAID THE check, Valerie and I walked out the front door into the warmth of the evening and the wind blowing the palm trees on Seawall Boulevard. A minute earlier I had seen Cisco Napolitano go out the door by herself, while Atlas was still talking with his friends at the table in the corner. As Valerie and I walked toward my car, Cisco drove a dark blue Buick out of the parking lot and pulled to the curb across the street, waiting for Atlas, I figured.

"Is that the woman you told me about, the one who knew Bugsy Siegel?" Valerie asked.

"That's the one."

"Why is she staring at us?"

"I think she's messed up. Maybe her life would have been different if she hadn't gotten mixed up with some bad guys. You want to meet her?"

"No."

But Cisco didn't give us an option. As we passed the Buick, she opened the door and got out. Her sun-browned skin and black evening dress and pink orchid corsage were marbled with the reflection of the neon; her hair was twisted like snakes around her throat. "Is Shit-for-Brains coming?"

"I didn't pay him any mind. What are you doing with a creep like that, Miss Cisco?" I said.

"Doing penance for being born. Tried to warn you, but you wouldn't listen, kid. Now fuck off."

How's that for getting the message across?

But it wasn't over. Atlas came out of the club just as we were walking away. When he saw us, he opened the trunk of the Buick and took something out, then got into the passenger seat with it and closed the door. Cisco Napolitano made a U-turn so she could drive past us. Atlas hung a chain out the window. Four rope loops were threaded through the links. He shook the chain as he passed us. "Meet your future, asshole."

I CALLED SABER THE next morning. No one answered. I called that night and Mr. Bledsoe hung up on me. I tried again the next morning and Mrs. Bledsoe answered. "He's not with you?" she said.

Two days later Saber came by the house in his heap. The windows were filmed with dirt, the fenders and hubcaps caked. My parents were at work. He didn't cut the engine until he was in the porte cochere. When he got out, he looked back at the street, even though there was no traffic nor anyone in the yards. An envelope protruded from his back pocket, rounded to the shape of his buttocks. He was chewing gum, smacking it; his eyes were behaving like Mexican jumping beans. "My mom said you were looking for me."

"I had a run-in with Vick Atlas at the Balinese Club in Galveston. His eyepatch came loose. Remember the firecrackers those guys were throwing? His eye was burned. That brick might have hit the windshield, but it's not what did the damage to his face."

"The cops never knew that?"

"They probably didn't look at the medical report. Or maybe they don't care."

"Son of a bitch."

"We're off the hook," I said. "All they've got is that bogus charge on the Krauser break-in."

He began chewing more rapidly, his eyes burning holes in the air.

"The charge is bogus, right?" I said.

"Who cares? Krauser and those pinheads who knocked me around are going to hang it on us anyway."

"My father talked to my boss at the filling station," I said. "My boss saw the detective examine my shoes. He said there wasn't any paint on them. The detective rubbed paint on them at Krauser's house."

"It doesn't matter. If they cain't get us one way, they'll get us another. Nothing has changed." He pulled the envelope from his back pocket and handed it to me. The flap was glued down. "Open it in the house."

"What's in it?"

"Eight hundred spendolies."

"How much?"

"For your bail and for your car getting pissed in and for any legal fees your dad had to pay. If you need more, I got it."

"Where'd this come from?"

"Midnight auto supply. Houston is lighter one pink Caddy convertible, formerly owned by Grady Harrelson."

"That's what Vick Atlas said. I thought he was crazy. You boosted Grady's car?"

"The Mexican guys from the jail gave me a little help. A police chief in Nuevo León loves his new car."

"I can't believe you've done this. How much did you get for it?"

"Not a lot. It was a three-way split, and we had to pay off some guys at the border. So we pooled resources and made another business connection. This one was a real score. My cut was twenty-eight hundred."

"Doing what?" I said, my heart tripping.

"Transporting a little laughing grass and a shitload of yellow jackets and redwings across the Rio Grande."

I put the envelope back in his hand. "I don't want to hear this, Saber. Leave the money in a church. Throw it out the window in the Fifth Ward. Don't bring it here."

"That's the way you feel?" he said.

"In spades."

He took the gum out of his mouth and tossed it into my mother's hydrangea bed. "What are we supposed to do? Keep squatting down for our daily nose lube?"

"Stay away from those Mexican guys."

"Manny and Cholo are my friends. They were both in Gatesville. Manny did a one-bit in Huntsville. They don't take shit off anybody."

"Listen to yourself," I said.

"Take the money."

"Not on your life."

He got into his car and shut the door, then fired up the engine, revving it, filling the porte cochere with oil smoke. I walked around to his window. His shoulder was pointed into the door, the way teenage hoods drove. He looked up into my face, his T-shirt rolled into his armpits, an unlit cigarette hanging off his lip, the carefree Saber of old.

"Grady Harrelson told me Vick Atlas made a threat about chain-dragging the pair of us," I said. "When I saw him in Galveston, he hung a chain out of his car window and said, 'Meet your future, asshole.'"

"And I'm the guy whose life is screwed up? That's a howl."

He backed into the street and drove away, his stolen loudspeakers blasting out Lloyd Price's "Lawdy Miss Clawdy."

I WENT TO POLICE headquarters downtown and asked to speak with Detective Merton Jenks.

The officer at the reception desk didn't look up. "He's at lunch."

"It's eleven o'clock."

"He eats five times a day."

"What time will he be back?"

"He didn't say."

"Where does he eat lunch?"

The officer looked up. "Two blocks down the street. It's the place with the gurney and the stomach pump by the door."

I thought he was kidding until I got to a poolroom with a lunch counter and saw Jenks through the window. There was also a wood booth where customers could cash welfare checks and process bail bonds. Jenks sat hunched over a meatball sandwich and a bowl of pinto beans he was eating with a spoon. I had to go to the restroom badly. I walked the length of the poolroom through smoke that was as thick and toxic as cotton poison, and used the toilet and washed my hands and dried them on my pants. Then I waited for somebody to push open the door so I wouldn't have to touch the knob. I went out and sat down next to Jenks without being invited. "Have you seen that washroom?"

"You ought to see the kitchen," he replied.

"Why do you eat here?"

"The philosophic insight." He wiped his mouth with a paper napkin. "What do you want?"

"You heard about the medical information on Vick Atlas, right?"

"Your old man's lawyer did a good job on that. So what do you want?"

"My dad found a witness who can prove Saber and I are innocent of the break-in at Mr. Krauser's house."

"Correct. You still haven't told me what you want."

The last time I had seen him, he had acted in a friendly manner, and I didn't understand his irritability. I told him that.

"I'm a homicide detective, son," he said. "I have more on my mind than this teenage bullshit."

"Vick Atlas is threatening to chain-drag me and Saber behind his car. Tell me what we have to do to get clear of all this."

"What you have to do? You ask me a question like that?"

"Who else can I ask? What's with this Detective Hopkins, the guy who tried to frame us for the break-in at Mr. Krauser's house?"

Two loud, unshaven men in unironed clothes stacked their pool cues and sat down beside us. They picked up menus and started to order.

"These seats are taken," Jenks said.

"By who?" one man said.

"Me," Jenks said.

They got up, one of them spinning the seat on the stool, looking back at us.

"Hopkins worked vice in Galveston," Jenks said.

"Yeah?"

He looked straight ahead, widening his eyes in mock dismay. "I'll have a run at it another way. Hopkins has the same fascist politics as your metal-shop teacher. He also has chewing tobacco for brains. Put that together with his background in Galveston and you have your answer." He bit into his sandwich.

"I'm lost."

"Jesus." He put down his sandwich. "There's a fortune going out of Galveston to the casinos and hotels in Vegas and Reno. The grease-balls are becoming respectable. Clint Harrelson is a big player, but he's not going to keep financing greaseballs till they clean up the mess you started. The issue is the dead Mexican girl. Did you kill her?"

"No, of course not."

"If you didn't, who did?"

"Grady Harrelson and his friends?"

"I knew you'd work it out."

"I saw Grady at my church. He went into the confessional. He's not a Catholic."

Jenks had started in on his sandwich again. He replaced it on the plate. "He told you something?"

"Not directly. He was afraid the priest would inform on him."

"What'd you tell him?"

"The confession is sealed, whether the person is Catholic or not," I said.

"Tell me exactly what Grady Harrelson said to you."

I told Jenks every detail I could remember. He was shaking his head before I finished. "That's not going to do it."

"I think he was admitting he killed the girl," I said.

His sleeves were rolled, his coat folded on the counter. He pinched his temples. I could see the tattoo of the red parachute on his arm, a green vein running through it.

"My girlfriend said you and her father were in the OSS together," I said.

"What's your girlfriend's name?"

"Valerie Epstein."

I saw the recognition in his eyes. "Her father is Goldie Epstein?"

"I don't know his first name. She's right? You were in the OSS?"

He stared into space, his thumb working up and down on the shaft of the spoon.

"Did I say something wrong?" I asked.

"What's Mr. Epstein's attitude on all this?"

"I know he doesn't like Grady Harrelson's father. He told Mr. Harrelson that he'd kill him if Mr. Harrelson tried to hurt Valerie or him."

"Those were his words?"

"Yes, sir."

Jenks picked up his coffee cup but didn't drink from it.

"You think Mr. Epstein was exaggerating?" I said.

The two loud pool shooters had grown louder. "You boys shut up before I come down there," Jenks said. He turned back to me. He was breathing through his nose, obviously thinking about how much he should say. "Here's the short version: Mr. Harrelson should make sure his life insurance policies are up to date."

"You never answered my question, sir."

"What question, for God's sake? I swear, my heart goes out to your parents."

"How do I get clear of all this?"

"I'll ask *you* a question: Where's your buddy Bledsoe? For some reason, you haven't mentioned a word about him."

"I'm worried about him."

"Worry about yourself. That kid is a born brig rat."

"I think I know how to get out of this, sir. I need you to help me."

"You're seventeen years old and you've got the magic solution? Does that strike you as a little vain?"

"The dead Mexican girl was Loren Nichols's cousin."

"So?"

"He knows who did it, but he's scared. I want to talk to him. I'll have to give him some assurances."

"Why do you think a kid like Nichols is going to do anything for a kid like you?"

"I know what it's like to be him."

Jenks signaled the waiter. "Wrap up my sandwich and get my check, will you?"

AFTER WORK, I FOUND Loren Nichols's number in the city directory. When I called, he picked up on the second ring.

"I need to talk. Can I come to your house?" I said.

"Broussard?"

"Yep."

"Tell me over the phone."

"Not a good idea."

"Mommy and Daddy are standing close by?" he said.

"Don't be disrespectful of my parents. I think Grady Harrelson killed your cousin. You want to pull your head out of your ass or not?"

"Come up to the Heights and say that."

"Count on it," I said, and hung up.

But I didn't get to keep my word.

Chapter 16

IT STARTED WITH my mother. Some days she took off early from work and rode the bus to a clinic where she talked to a counselor. There she sometimes saw the effeminate and odd kid named Jimmy McDougal. Poor Jimmy. He was the butt of everyone's jokes, homely and awkward and gullible if someone showed him a teaspoon of kindness. He was in the corner of the waiting room, his hands clenched between his thighs, his face downcast as though he had wet his pants. My mother sat beside him and placed her hand on his back. "What's wrong, Jimmy? It can't be that bad, can it?"

"No, ma'am," he said, the soles of his shoes tapping up and down. "I'm tops."

"You don't have to hide things, Jimmy. You want to tell me what's troubling you all the time?"

He shook his head adamantly. "I'm doing okay. That's a fact, Miz Broussard."

"Has Mr. Krauser hurt you?"

"Mr. Krauser takes me to ball games and shoots baskets with me at the Y. Leastways that's how it's been."

"Tell me the truth, Jimmy."

He crouched over, his fingers tightening, the blood leaving his knuckles. "I don't want to talk about it anymore, Miz Broussard."

"Come home with me. We're going to get to the bottom of this. I've already warned Mr. Krauser."

"Oh, Miz Broussard, I don't want you doing that."

"I told that vile man he'd better leave you alone or I'd take a quirt to him."

"I'm already in trouble, Miz Broussard. I cain't handle any more."

"What are you in trouble about?"

"I say the wrong things sometimes. I rehearse the right thing to say, but it always comes out wrong. It doesn't matter. I end up being a fool in front of others."

"Is that your baseball cap?"

"Yes, ma'am."

"Get it," she said.

They took a crowded bus in traffic and diesel smoke and hundred-degree heat down West Alabama, and got off at the icehouse where my father drank, and walked to our small ivy-covered brick home on Hawthorne Street. I was just about to head for the Heights and Loren Nichols's house when they came through the front door.

"Aaron, fix us some ice water, please, while I talk to Jimmy," my mother said. She pulled the long pin out of her pillbox hat and removed the hat and clicked on the ceiling fan in the living room.

"What's going on?" I said.

"I ran into Jimmy at the clinic, and now he and I are going to have a talk."

I went into the kitchen, but I could hear every word through the open door.

"I know the signs, Jimmy. Where did that man touch you?"

"It was on accident. The first time, I mean."

"The first time he touched you?"

"I took a shower at his house. We'd been working out. He was waiting for me to finish so he could take his shower. He bumped into me when I was coming out."

"Out of the shower?" she said. "You were undressed?"

"Was I—"

"Were you naked?"

"Yes, I was naked. He almost knocked me down. He picked me up. That's when he leaned over me and it touched me. On accident."

"It? You mean—"

"Yes, ma'am."

"Then he did it on another occasion but not on accident?" she said.

"The next week I stayed over at his house. I woke up in the middle of the night on the couch. He was doing something."

"You don't have to say any more, Jimmy."

"I have to, Miz Broussard. He was rubbing my leg. He said I had a charley horse and was yelling in my sleep."

"It's all right, Jimmy. Where's that ice water, Aaron?"

I didn't want to go into the living room. I didn't want to bring Jimmy more shame and embarrassment. In those days we didn't have adequate ways of reporting sexual abuse or pedophilia. The victim was usually blamed or accused of lying; the issue would be buried, and anyone who raised it again was excoriated.

I put two glasses of ice water on a tray and set it down in the living room, then sat on the brick steps in the porte cochere with Bugs and Snuggs and Skippy and Major. The windows were open, and I could still hear my mother talking with Jimmy.

"You're not fixing to call him up, are you?" he said.

"I'm so angry I can't rightly say."

"He's not going to do it anymore. He's done with me because of that woman."

"Which woman?"

"Miss Cisco. She's got a Rocket Eighty-eight and comes from Las Vegas or somewhere. Mr. Krauser said he'd be spending most of his time with her and I shouldn't be hanging out at his place. Then she flushed him. I'm glad."

"She broke up with him?"

"I was there when she did it. I went over there to get my bicycle after he said he was going to fix it and then stuck it in the garage on a nail. She said he'd broke his word to somebody about sending boys to a camp, and he was on Clint Harrelson's S-list."

"His what?"

"It's a bad word."

"I think I can survive it."

"She said Mr. Krauser was on Clint Harrelson's shit list."

"I don't care about any of that. I care about you, Jimmy, and what's been done to you. We're going to have a talk with Mr. Krauser."

My mother's manic personality had just shifted into overdrive. I knew nothing good would come of it. I got up from the steps and went through the side screen into the living room. "Mother, I think we should take Jimmy home and forget this."

"We will not. Drive us to Mr. Krauser's house, Aaron."

"Bad idea, Mother. Mr. Krauser isn't going to change his stripes because people take him to task."

"There is only one way you treat white trash," she replied. "As white trash. This man is not only white trash, he's a deviant. Now drive us there, please."

"Yes, ma'am."

The events that would follow remain among the most embarrassing and tragic in my life. Even today I have a hard time writing about them.

I DROVE THE THREE of us to Krauser's machine-gun bunker of a house, my mother in the passenger seat, Jimmy McDougal in back. With his high forehead and wispy blond hair and milk-white skin and lack of definable eyebrows, he looked like a space alien that had been trapped and stuck in a cage. My mother was holding her riding quirt in her lap.

"You're not going to use that, are you?" I said.

"That's up to him," she replied.

I pulled to the curb in front of Krauser's house.

"No, in the driveway," she said. "So he doesn't try to escape in his car."

After I cut the engine, she reached over and blew the horn and got out and banged on Krauser's door. When he answered, he was wearing a navy blue suit and dress shirt without a tie, his hair wet-combed, as though he were preparing to go somewhere. I never saw a man look so stunned.

"Step out here, Mr. Krauser," my mother said.

"Do you want to come in?" he said.

"No, I do not. You come out here right now and you apologize to this boy. You also will promise in front of me and him and Aaron and God and anyone else listening that you will never go near him again."

I could see the confusion and fear in Krauser's eyes. But something else was at work in his psyche or his metabolism that was far worse. I was too young to understand how mortality can steal its way without apparent cause into the life of a man who should have been in his prime. His skin was gray and beginning to sag; hair grew from his ears and nose; he had buttoned his shirt crookedly. He looked like he had gone through the long night of the soul.

"I was on my way to the doctor," he said.

"You should probably call your minister instead," my mother said.

"Aaron, you and Saber broke into my home, didn't you?" he said. "Tell me the truth. I won't hold it against you. I need to know this."

"No, we didn't, Mr. Krauser," I said.

"You step out here right now, you terrible man, or I'll come in after you," my mother said.

"Mother, please," I said.

The next-door neighbors had come out of their house. The postman and a woman on her porch across the street were watching. A car slowed in the street, the driver and a woman looking at us.

"Damn you," my mother said. I was sure at this moment that she was no longer addressing Krauser but somebody in her past, a featureless man who had violated her in her sleep.

She struck the first cut across his face, then beat him methodically, slashing him every place she could. The quirt was stiff and hard, the leather sewed tightly around a metal rod, with a braided knot on the end. Krauser cupped his hands over his head as though he were being attacked by bees. I had to pin my mother's arms to her sides to make her stop.

We left Mr. Krauser bleeding in the doorway and drove home, all of us silent, numbed by what we had done or seen.

Back home, my mother went into the bathroom and locked the door and stayed there. When my father came home from work, I told him what had happened. He tapped on the bathroom door, his eyes lowered. When there was no response, he put on his hat and walked to the icehouse.

That night Mr. Krauser managed to get inside one of the tallest buildings in downtown Houston. Then he worked his way up a stairwell and found a fire exit that led to the roof. He plunged fifteen floors to the concrete.

I TALKED TO SABER at Costen's drugstore the next morning. "It was almost like he wanted us to be the guys who tore up his awards and medals rather than somebody else."

"Why would he want it to be us?" Saber said, sucking a strawberry milkshake through a pair of straws.

"Because he thought it was somebody Clint Harrelson or his people sent."

"Why would they want to do that?"

"I don't have the answers, Sabe. My mother stayed home from work, then went to church. She never goes to church."

"You think Krauser lost sleep while we were in jail? You think he cared about my father getting fired? He was mixed up with Grady Harrelson's old man. All of them deserve whatever happens to them."

Through the window I could see our two heaps in the parking lot. Coincidentally, we had parked next to each other, our hoods pointed in opposite directions. A Studebaker was parked next to Saber's heap. Two Mexicans in drapes were in the front seat, the doors open to let in the breeze.

"I saw Jenks yesterday," I said. "He asked about you."

Saber raised his eyes. A big electric fan was oscillating near the comic book rack, flipping hundreds of pages with each sweep. "What'd you tell him?" he said.

"Nothing of importance."

"Screw him, anyway."

"Get loose from those guys out there," I said.

"Which guys?"

"The ones in the Studie."

He stabbed at his milkshake with his straws.

"Did they boost it?" I asked.

"Who's going to boost a Studie?"

"Somebody who knows they're already collectibles."

He glanced at the parking lot, then back at me. I thought he might say something indicating the old Saber was still with me. *Come on, Sabe. Two or three words. Or just one.*

But the only sound I heard was the comic book pages rippling. I looked through the window at the two Mexicans. They were relaxing, the seats pushed back, their eyes closed. They had unbuttoned their shirts, exposing the hair and ink on their chests. For just a moment I hated them, or at least I hated what they represented.

"Why do you have that look on your face?" Saber asked.

"They're drug pushers," I said. "They're worse than pimps. They betray their own people."

"Who's worse? Guys born in a bean field who get called pepper-bellies and spics all their lives, or a ball of shit like that detective who tried to frame us?"

"Why did Krauser want to believe you and I broke into his house?"

"When we have some free time, we can dig him up and ask."

I got up from the booth. "I'll see you, Sabe."

"Aaron?" he said.

He took a long, dry drag off the dregs of his milkshake. I was smiling at him. *Say it, Sabe. Be the innocent kid you are. Be my old-time bud.*

"I lost my virginity in Reynosa," he said. "Outlawry has got its upside. The downside is I probably picked up a nail. Krauser was a prick. I hope the devil throws him a beer once in a while."

He grinned as though he had neutralized the enormous gulf that lay between us.

On the way out of the drugstore, I bought a Captain Marvel comic book so I could pretend to read it and not acknowledge the Mexicans who had been our cellmates. I heard one of them sink an opener into a beer can, then smelled the beer spraying in the air and splattering on the asphalt. When I looked back, both of them were laughing and wiping beer out of their hair, indifferent to the family people wheeling grocery baskets through the parking lot.

I started my engine and headed for Loren Nichols's house.

AS SABER WOULD have said, I was back in Indian country, more specifically in Loren's two-track dirt driveway, next to his termite-eaten, two-story nineteenth-century house sitting on cinder blocks. The old woman with the maniacal glare was sitting in her rocking chair, her hair tangled like wire. I got out of the car. "Is Loren home, ma'am?"

She made no reply. Her body was withered, her dugs exposed, her hands little more than bird claws.

"I'm back here, if you want to talk to me," a voice said.

Loren was standing in the doorway of a paintless garage, barechested, a screwdriver in his hand. The woman took no notice of him. I didn't know if her face was twisted in fear or silent rage. But I didn't want to be rude and walk away from her. "Thank you, ma'am," I said. "There's Loren now. It was nice meeting you."

Why did she bother me so? Because I had seen the same look in my mother's eyes, no different in portent than a cave filled with startled bats. I walked to the garage. "Is that your grandmother?" I asked Loren.

"That's my mother."

"Sorry. Is your dad here?"

"What's it to you?"

"I don't know. I just asked. I wasn't thinking."

"He's in Huntsville."

"He's doing time?" I said.

"No, he's a gun bull. You ask too many questions. Is this about your teacher who bailed off a building?"

"It's about your cousin Wanda Estevan."

"You put me in mind of a hemorrhoid, Broussard. No matter where I go, there you are."

"You want Vick Atlas and his old man on your case? He threatened to drag me behind his car. You know who Vick Atlas is, right?"

His attention seemed to wander, linger in space. He flipped the screwdriver in the air and caught it. "Atlas said that to your face?"

"More or less."

"Talk to me while I work. Don't lean against the wall. The whole place will fall down." He went inside the garage to a workbench that had an amplifier and a soldering iron and a cherry-red electric guitar on it. He propped his hands on the bench and stared at the motes floating in a shaft of sunlight. His spine was etched against his skin, both sides of his back crosshatched with scars, some as fine as a cat's whiskers. When we'd fought, he had been bare-chested, but I hadn't seen the injury someone had done to his body.

"I'm going to line it out for you," he said. "You tell anybody we're talking to each other, you and me are going to have another go at it. *Comprendo?* Wanda was hooking out of a couple of clubs in Galveston and sometimes in Big D because a lot of political guys live there. The clubs were a setup to blackmail politicians and big shots in the oil business. That's where she met Harrelson."

"He was a customer?"

"No, he hangs with Atlas and pretends he's a hood and a rich-boy badass. He took Wanda out a couple of times, and he probably got it on with her, since that was her line of work. Except she fell in love with him. Then he dumped her and she went nuts. That's when you came along."

"At the drive-in in Galveston?"

"Harrelson knew you'd be coming to Valerie Epstein's house, and he told us to mess you up."

"And you did it because he told you?"

He began soldering a wire inside the amplifier. Then he set down the iron. The scars across his back looked like lesions that had healed badly. "Harrelson said if we ran you off, he'd get Wanda cut loose from her job and send her to beautician school. He promised to get my brother a Teamster card."

"Cut her loose?" I said.

"Where've you been? You think you resign from the Mafia and file for unemployment?"

"What happened to your back?"

"Poison ivy."

"Anyone ever tell you that you look like Chet Baker?"

"Yeah, I hear that all the time. What's with you, man? You got a black carrot growing on your brain?"

"Can I see your guitar?"

"He'p yourself."

I picked it up and worked the strap over my shoulder. The cherry finish was chipped, but the neck was straight, all the surfaces clean, the tuning pegs lightly oiled, the strings new and hovering just above the frets.

"It's a little out of tune. Mind?"

"Do whatever you want," he said, and went back to working on the amplifier. But he was looking out the side of his eye and was not as disinterested as he pretended.

"Know what a problem of conscience is?" I said, twisting the tuning pegs.

"Lay off that stuff, man."

"I hear you. I can't take unctuous people."

"Take *what* kind?"

"When we fought, I wanted to kill you, Loren. I would have done it if Saber hadn't stopped me."

"I told you to shut that down, didn't I? I don't owe anybody, and that means they don't owe me. You asked about my old man. My mother had me when she was forty. That was when my father traded her in on a pair of twenties. I grew up rolling winos and breaking into vending machines. Anything Gatesville could throw at me, I'd already seen. I said fuck you to all of them then; I say fuck you now. That's my flag, a big fuck-you in capital letters. You got my drift?"

"You bet." I took a plectrum from my watch pocket and formed an E chord on the guitar neck. I drew the plectrum across the strings. "Where'd you get it?"

"Eddy Pearl's pawnshop on Congress."

"It has a nice touch. No rattle in the frets."

Again, he pretended not to care about my interest in his instrument. He bent over the amplifier, smoke from the soldering iron rising into his face, his scars stretching into pale wisps.

"You ever see a photo of the Shroud of Turin?" I asked.

"The *what*?"

"Forget it."

"Pardon me for asking this, but do you drop yellow jackets?" he said. "Because frankly, you're a little strange. No, don't say anything else. Plug the guitar in. Let's see what happens. I'm not kidding you, man. I think you fried your Spam somewhere along the track."

"Thanks," I said. He rolled his eyes.

I plugged the guitar into the jack on the amplifier and stroked the E chord again. All six notes of the configuration bloomed like magic from the speakers. For the first time since I met him, Loren Nichols smiled. "Man," he said.

I started to take off the strap and hand him his instrument.

"No, I learned G and D, but that's it," he said.

"I'll show you something," I said. "You already know D. So this is how you make E, except you turn it into what is called a covered E and run it up and down the neck. Watch, I'm just using E and D."

I began picking out "The Steel Guitar Rag." He folded his arms on his chest and raised his eyebrows. "That's something else, man."

"You know 'Malaguena'? Same key of E." I ran through the first three chords of the famous Andalusian song by Ernesto Lecuona.

"Shit, man," Loren said.

"Try it." I handed him the guitar.

He struggled with the chords at first. I fitted his fingertips on each string, then showed him how to slip the chord up the frets, covering all six strings.

"You're better than you thought," I said.

"I don't know about that." He took a cigarette from behind his ear and put it into his mouth. He slipped a match folder from his jeans, then flipped it onto the workbench without lighting his cigarette and tried sliding the chord up and down the guitar neck again.

"I need to square with you about something, Loren. I'd be lying if I told you I wasn't worried about Vick Atlas's threat."

"You scared?"

"Call it what you want."

"You want it straight up?" he said.

I waited.

"You *should* be worried," he said. "Atlas has brain damage. His old man hit him in the head or something. When you 'front a guy like that, you don't let him deal the play."

"I'm supposed to go after him?" I said.

"No, that's what he wants. You wait for him to come to you. And believe me, he will. A dipshit like that wants an audience. So you let him put on his show. You dummy up. You don't act cute. You don't try to be a nice guy. You're D, D, and D. You know what that is, right?"

I nodded.

"So he's having a ball. About to get his rocks. Maybe his girlfriend is watching. He thinks you're browning your Fruit of the Looms. That's when you tag his ass."

"Tag?"

He put the guitar on the blanket and opened a drawer under the workbench. "This is a thirty-two. All the numbers have been burned with acid. The electrician's tape is inside out so your prints cain't be lifted. You put a pill between his eyes. If you have time, you put extras in his ear and mouth. If you take it with you, pour motor oil on it and throw it in a bayou or saltwater. Take it. It's yours."

"No, thanks."

"You're making a mistake."

"I guess it will just have to be my mistake."

"A minute ago you said something about a Shroud of Whatever. What is it?"

"The burial cloth of Christ."

"Are you out of your fucking mind?" he said.

"Probably," I said.

He dropped the revolver in the drawer and shut it. "You don't want to smoke Atlas, that's your choice, Broussard. There's a possibility we didn't discuss. What if he gets his hands on Valerie? Close your eyes and let your imagination go. Tell me what kind of pictures you see."

A drop of sweat slid like an icicle down my side into my underwear.

Chapter 17

FIVE DAYS AFTER Mr. Krauser jumped to his death, my mother and I attended his funeral in a small Protestant church near his house. The casket was closed. There were perhaps a dozen people in the pews. One was the assistant principal. Two were faculty members. There were no students. Mr. Krauser's father, a stooped man with dandruff on his shoulders who carried an oxygen bottle on a strap, placed a yellow rose on the coffin. The minister read three passages from the Book of Psalms that seemed to have little to do with Mr. Krauser. A man from his bowling team tried to read a tribute, then dropped his notes and couldn't straighten them out and had to ad-lib the rest of the testimonial. He concluded by saying, "Give them hell wherever you're at, Krausey." Outside, a woodpecker hammered its beak into a telephone pole.

Maybe Mr. Krauser had virtues. Maybe he refused to deliver up young people to Clint Harrelson's indoctrination camps and paid a price for it. Maybe he was driven by compulsions he didn't understand. Regardless, I didn't feel sorry for him. He used his power to humiliate and degrade and to inculcate shame and self-hatred in others. To me there was no lower form of life on earth, including drug pushers and pimps.

I believed there was only one victim in the church, and that was my mother. Her eyes didn't see; her speech was lifeless, her attention span nonexistent. The clinical depression that had been passed down in the Holland family like an heirloom had taken up residence in her soul once again. Over the years, pharmaceutical and vitamin injections and hospitalization and electroshock treatments had been like raindrops blowing against the bulletproof glass of her neurosis. I learned early on that people do not have to die to go to hell. As I sat next to her in the pew, I knew she had already departed from us and taken up residence in the privation and abandonment of her youth.

If I felt any emotion toward Mr. Krauser at all, it was resentment. Like most suicides who stage their departure in Technicolor, showering the walls or sidewalk with their blood, Krauser had left a legacy of sackcloth and ashes for someone like my mother to wear. As we walked out of the church, I put my arm around her. Her bones felt as frail and hollow as a bird's. I wanted to kick Krauser's coffin off its gurney.

If there was any drama at the funeral, it took place across the street, where I saw Jimmy McDougal sitting on his bike under a live oak. I put my mother into the car and caught him as he was about to pedal away. I believed that Krauser had molested him in one way or another. Jimmy's parents were uneducated and poor, and often he wore clothes that came from the welfare store. I also believed he was experiencing the same kind of guilt over Krauser's death as my mother was.

"Where you goin', partner?" I said.

"Nowhere."

His legs were forked on either side of the bike frame, his hands clenched on the rubber grips. An army-surplus haversack, one with pockets on it, was in the delivery basket mounted on the front fender.

"You got your lunch in there?" I said. "It smells good."

"I'm working at the drugstore. I just came by, that's all. I got to get going."

"Jimmy, you can't let this worry you. You didn't do anything wrong."

"Yeah, that's right," he said.

"You're a good guy. Everybody knows that. Mr. Krauser was no good."

"How come you're here?"

"My mother feels bad. But she shouldn't feel that way, and neither should you."

"I'm late, Aaron."

"Come by if you feel like it. We can go to a show or out to Buffalo Stadium for a ball game. How about that?"

"Sure, Aaron. Thanks. I'll see you."

He put his right foot on the pedal and was almost gone when I saw a smooth white cylindrical object protruding from a pocket on the haversack. I grabbed the handlebars. "Hold on."

"Let go," he said.

"No, what's that sticking out of your bag?"

"Nothing," he said, pulling the flap down.

But I had already seen the two gold SS lightning bolts inlaid in the handle of the knife that had been on Krauser's desk.

"How did you get this?" I asked.

"Mr. Krauser gave it to me."

"A guy like Krauser doesn't give away his war souvenirs."

"He did. I swear he did."

"You and Saber broke into his house and tore up his things. Tell me the truth. Come on, buddy."

He tried to twist the handlebars from my grasp, then bounced the front tire up and down, rattling the basket. "I've got to go. I'll get fired."

"I'm not going to tell anyone, Jimmy. But you have to level with me. Saber has been taking me over the hurdles. Now he's running with some really bad guys. In the meantime, I got arrested for what you guys did."

"I'll go to Gatesville. You ever hear what it's like in there? Why are you doing this to me? You know what they'll do to me?"

He was right. The law was enforced on the people it could be enforced on. In this case it was a retarded boy who hadn't had a chance from the day he was born. I let go of the handlebars. "You were just getting back at Mr. Krauser for what he did to you, Jimmy. Come with me to the rodeo. I'm riding bulls this year in the adult competition."

I tried to smile. But Jimmy was terrified. He pushed off with one foot, careening out of the shade, fighting to gain control of his bike, his pale skin and wispy hair almost translucent in the raw light of the sun.

THAT EVENING I TOOK Valerie to a movie. I don't remember the name of the movie or what it was about. I discovered that my memory had taken on an odd aspect. When I was with Valerie, I remembered only having been with Valerie. Everything else was an adverb. Wherever we went, I was conscious of her touch, the smell of her hair, the light in her eyes.

She wore pleated skirts and oxfords and pink tennis shoes and white blouses with frills, and was easily recognizable as a member of her generation, but she was somehow always above it. She chewed gum constantly. I never knew anyone who chewed so much gum, boxcar loads of it. She was a member of the National Honor Society, the drama club, 4-H, the chess club, and the debate team. I felt proud any place I went with her. I always wondered if her dead mother or her widowed father had the greater influence on her. Perhaps neither of them did. The Nazis had killed her mother during the war, and Mr. Epstein's work caused him to be out of town more than he was at home. As far as I knew, she had raised herself. That night I asked her what kind of rules her dad had taught her.

"None," she replied, as though surprised by the question. "He took me dancing when I had my first period. He said I was a young woman now, and that meant he would always honor my choices as a woman and he would not impose his way upon me. He said he would never judge me but would always be there in my defense, regardless of the circumstances. He said if a man ever violated or tried to molest me, he would kill him and the people with him."

The gospel according to Mr. Epstein.

She kissed me on the cheek.

"What's that for?"

"For being the good boy you are," she replied.

"I'll be eighteen this fall."

She kissed me again.

You wonder why I always wanted to be with Valerie?

Valerie's greatest time commitment wasn't to her clubs or school assignments; it was to reading in the public library. The great gift of the government to our generation was the WPA program known simply as the bookmobile. Those of us who loved books didn't learn to love them at school; we learned a love of literature by reading the adventures of Nancy Drew and the Hardy Boys and Richard Halliburton. One day Valerie would probably become a librarian. For now she had formed an almost religious faith in the knowledge a person could discover on her own in the musty shelves of a small library in North Houston.

We went for a soda after the show, and I told her that Saber and Jimmy McDougal had vandalized Krauser's home and that Saber had betrayed me.

"You can't be sure of that, can you?" she said. "Jimmy what's-his-name didn't actually tell you that?"

"He didn't have to. I always thought Saber was involved. When I asked him, he slipped the punch. The funny thing is that Krauser wanted to believe we did it."

"Why?"

"Because he was afraid of Clint Harrelson and the kind of people who work for him. He probably thought he and Saber and I were being set up, and Cisco Napolitano dumped him because he wouldn't use his influence to get kids into Harrelson's indoctrination camps. A guy who went all the way to the Elbe River killed himself for no reason."

Maybe my reasoning was self-serving and I was exonerating my mother at the expense of a suicide victim, but I didn't care. She had paid enough dues in this world, and Krauser had not, no matter how many Nazis he had killed.

She pushed aside her black cow and took a pencil and pad from her purse. "What was the title of that book Clint Harrelson was reading when you and your father went to his house?"

"I saw the word 'eugenical' on the cover. It was written by a guy named Laughlin."

She wrote it down. "I'll get right on this."

"Maybe you shouldn't get too involved," I said.

She gave me a look that made me blink. That was the downside of being in love with Valerie Epstein. You didn't tell her what to do.

"I mean, Detective Jenks has evidently been after these guys for years. The only thing he's gotten for it is indigestion."

"Where is Saber now?"

"With a couple of Mexican drug dealers."

"Tell him I want to talk to him."

"What about?"

"He let you get arrested for a crime he committed. I'm going to give him a piece of my mind."

"Let's take a pass on that," I said.

Under the table, she put both of her tennis shoes on top of my cowboy boots.

"If I see him, I'll tell him," I said.

She pounded her feet up and down.

"I'll call him," I said.

"You never know when I'm kidding you, do you," she replied.

I never saw anyone who had so much light in her eyes.

SHE MADE CLINT Harrelson the subject of her private investigation at her neighborhood public library, then expanded her operation to the library at Rice University. The filling station where I worked was a short distance away. The campus was green through the summer and winter and filled with oak trees, the buildings deep in shadow at sunset. As I approached her in the reading room and saw her at one of the tables, writing in her notepad, books spread open around her, I was reminded of Nancy Drew waging war with her fountain pen against the sinister forces that threatened to destroy River Heights. Even though Valerie's mother had been murdered by Nazis, she believed that people were basically good. I did not think she would find anything in either a public or university library that would tell us anything we didn't know about Clint Harrelson or the people who ran the Galveston underworld. But I dared not tell her that.

"What'd you find?" I said, sitting down across from her, still wearing my green-and-white-striped gas station shirt.

"Clint Harrelson went to a military academy in Virginia," she said. "He had a senatorial appointment to West Point, but he was expelled for hazing another cadet. Guess what? He did it again at Northwestern. Mr. Harrelson and his fraternity brothers hung a boy by his feet off a pier and ending up dropping him on the rocks. They not only killed him and hid the body, they did the same thing to another kid later on, although he survived."

"Where'd you get all this?"

"The Chicago newspapers are on microfilm. Guess what Mr. Harrelson has a degree in. Anthropology. Look what I found on the Atlas family and the Mob's operations on the Gulf Coast."

I didn't want to see it. I had no doubt about the kind of people the Harrelson and Atlas families were. They and others just like them did business with baseball bats while the law and decent people looked the other way. There were brothels and gambling joints along the entire rim of the Gulf of Mexico, even in Mississippi, which was supposedly a dry state, and they operated openly and with sanction by the authorities. Slot and racehorse machines were everywhere, and Louisiana cops in uniform with their badges pinned to their shirts worked behind the bar and served mixed drinks to underage kids. But I didn't want Valerie to know how I felt about the information she had worked so hard to find. Who wanted to offend Nancy Drew?

I read her notes and looked at the marked pages in the books and feigned as much interest as I could. "I haven't eaten supper yet. How about we go over to Bill Williams's for some fried chicken?"

"I have to go home and help my father with the income tax," she said.

"You have time for a cold drink?"

"I'd better not. I'll see you tomorrow, Aaron."

I walked her to her car. It was her father's, a four-door Chevrolet. Back then most families had only one car; many had none. The Epstein car was parked in a cul-de-sac in the shadows of slash pines silhouetted against the sun. It had just rained, and the windows and roof were showered with pine needles. The lights were on in the dormitories and the offices of a few professors; I wanted to believe they were a reminder that civilization was a constant and evil was not. But I couldn't shake the trepidation in my chest. It was the way I had felt before I swam out to the third sandbar south of Galveston Island into a school of jellyfish. I didn't want to let go of her.

"I'll follow you home," I said.

"No, you will not."

"Please."

She kissed me lightly on the mouth. "See you in the morning, Kemosabe."

The sun dropped below the campus buildings. I watched her drive away, her taillights winking like rubies in the shadows.

Chapter 18

IT WAS A weeknight, and few vehicles were on the two-lane street she took into the north end of the city. The sky was black, creaking with electricity, like someone crumpling cellophane. Her windows were down. She could smell the clean odor of a storm and the coldness of the dust blowing in the street. Then at a stoplight, at an intersection where there were no other cars, she smelled gasoline. The light changed and she shifted into first gear and drove through the intersection, then looked in the rearview mirror just as heat lightning flared in the clouds. For an instant she thought she saw a drip line on the asphalt that led to her back bumper. She looked at the gas gauge. It was on empty.

There was a weed-grown vacant lot on each side of the road, a deserted house on one corner, a spreading oak on the other, a few lighted houses a block farther on. She was two miles from home, but she remembered a filling station three blocks back that was still open. She made a U-turn and drove slowly toward the stoplight. Then her engine coughed and shook once and died. She shifted into second and popped the clutch, trying to restart it. Her right front tire struck the curb, her headlights dimming as the battery went down. A car going in the same direction passed her. She tried to wave the driver down, but he kept going. The wind began blowing harder, buffeting her car, the first raindrops hitting the windshield as hard as hail.

She rolled up all the windows. A pair of headlights came around the corner and approached the rear of her car. The driver had his high beams on. He pulled to the curb forty feet behind her and cut his engine but left the lights on. The sky was black, the raindrops on the windshield as big as nickels. No one got out of the car.

She pumped the accelerator and pushed the starter, then gave up and pulled the keys from the ignition and bunched them in her right hand, allowing one key to protrude between her index and middle fingers. She stared into the rearview mirror until her eyes watered. The driver turned off his lights. The windows in the car were as dark as slate, impossible to see through; steam was rising off the hood. She opened her door and stepped into the rain.

"Who are you?" she called.

There was no response.

"I have a pistol. I'll use it," she said.

The car was a 1949 or '50 Ford, with an outside spotlight on the driver's side. When lightning split the sky, she saw a man's face behind the wheel. He was wearing a dark cap with a lacquered bill. The door made a screeching sound when the driver opened it. He had on a heavy rubber slicker and unshined black shoes and trousers with a stripe down the leg. Another man stepped out on the passenger side. He was also wearing a slicker and a cap with a bill; he carried a flashlight and a one-gallon gasoline can. The two men walked toward her. The driver was tall, blade-faced, in his thirties, his expression calm, reassuring. He was standing four feet away.

"Saw you sputter. Figured it was a fuel problem," he said. The rain was sliding off his cap and slicker. He felt under the bumper and smelled his hand. "You probably got a hole in your tank."

"You're not cops," she said.

"Why do you think that?"

"Your coats are wrong."

"We're not Harris County cops, but we're cops," he said. "You're lucky we came along. This is a bad neighborhood."

"I live here. There's nothing bad about this neighborhood," she said.

A car was coming up the street. The other man waved it by with his flashlight.

"I can walk to my house," she said.

"We'll take you," the driver said.

"No, you won't."

"That's a strange attitude, missy," he said. "We're police officers trying to help. Is there something in your car you don't want us to see?"

"You're not cops of any kind," she said. "Your shoes have eyelets in them. They reflect light."

The two men looked at each other. "You need to get out of the rain," the driver said. "We also need to take a look inside your car."

"Get away from me," she said.

The driver twisted her wrist and pulled the keys from her hand. Then he threw them on the floor of the car and shoved her inside. When she tried to get out, he slammed her down again and handcuffed her to the steering wheel. He looked over his shoulder. A car was coming, its tires whirring on the asphalt. Its lights flashed across his face. His hair was uncut and his mouth had an overbite; he was older than she had thought. He blocked her from view while his friend waved the car on.

"My father will be looking for me," she said. "He knows the streets I take to get home."

The driver rubbed the back of his hand along her cheek. "I hate to do this to you, missy. But a job is a job. You should have stuck to your studies and such."

The other man opened the passenger door and leaned inside.

"What are you all doing?" she said.

She heard the second man unscrew the cap from the can, and smelled the gasoline splashing on the floor and the plastic seat covers. She jerked against the handcuffs.

"Listen to me, missy," the driver said. "I want to make this as easy as possible. I'm going to give you a shot. I guarantee in ten seconds you won't feel a thing. Close your eyes."

She thought the size of her heart would shut down her lungs. Her eyes welled with tears. "Why are you doing this?"

"People always try to buy time. It won't change the outcome, sweetheart."

"Don't call me that."

"You're in a bad position to be giving orders."

She spat in his face.

"I don't blame you," he said. He wiped her spittle off his cheek and mouth. "But you're on your own now. Back away, Seth."

The other man capped the can and stepped back into the rain, then kicked the passenger door shut, not touching any of the surfaces with his hands. The driver took a book of matches from his shirt pocket and pulled one loose. He shielded the matchbook with his body and dragged the match across the striker.

She held her eyes on his and pressed down on the horn with both her forearms. She never blinked, even when all the match heads flamed into a miniature torch.

"You should have let me inject you," he said. "You're pretty. I hate to do this. But you dealt it, little girl."

Chapter 19

THE FLAME BURNED down to his fingertips and died in his hand. He dropped the remnants of the matchbook and stepped back from Valerie's car. A big Buick with a grille that resembled chromed teeth roared down the street and came to a lurching stop two feet from Valerie's fender. The driver's door flew open, and Vick Atlas was in the street, his suit coat unbuttoned, a pearl-handled pistol pushed down in his belt. He was wearing his eyepatch. "What do you guys think you're doing?"

"Mr. Atlas?" the driver of the Ford said.

"Get away from her car," Atlas said.

"Yes, sir," the driver said. He brushed the soot from the dead matches off his fingers and held up his hands to show they were empty.

"You with the can," Atlas said. "Set it on the ground."

"You got it," the man said.

Atlas walked closer so he could see inside Valerie's car. "Get those handcuffs off her."

The driver reached inside with a tiny key and inserted it in each lock. His overbite and the vacuity in his eyes made her think of a barracuda swimming along the glass wall of an aquarium. He removed the handcuffs and dropped them into his pocket, never looking at her.

"I'll get you for this, buster," she said.

He didn't answer. His attention was concentrated on Vick Atlas. "We were going to scare her."

"Who you working for?" Atlas said.

"I don't know."

"You're telling me you don't know who you work for? You think I'm dumb? That's what you're saying? You insult me to my face?"

"We get a phone call. We do the job," the driver said.

"I know who you are," Atlas said. "I'll be dialing you up, know what I mean?"

"We're gone, Mr. Atlas," the driver said, stepping back toward his car, his hands raised.

"You're gone, all right," Atlas said. "You got till three."

Both men got into their Ford. The man with the overbite started the engine and backed straight to the next intersection, then turned on his lights and headed down a side street. Atlas reached into Valerie's car and offered his hand. "I'll take you home, Miss Valerie. I'll be dealing with those guys tomorrow. You'll never see them again."

She didn't move.

"You don't trust me?" he asked.

"How do you know my car won't start?"

"If you could start it, you would have driven away from those bums. That's what they are. Bums. They're going to pay a price."

"They were dressed like police officers. They could have pulled me over. I might have a tank full of gas. There's no way you could know that someone punched a hole in my tank or damaged my fuel line."

He smiled. "I'm getting confused here. I offered to take you home because I figured you were a little shaken up and didn't want to be driving. I'm getting wet. You want a ride or not?"

"How did you know where I was?"

"Because I was coming to your house," he said. "Because I wanted to tell you I heard somebody was going to do something bad to you. Can I get in the backseat? I'm getting soaked. I felt bad about what happened at the Balinese Club. That's not my style."

"Yes, it is. You're a criminal."

"Jesus Christ, are you nuts? I saved your life. Those are bad guys. I'm getting in the back. You don't like it, that's tough."

She tried to lock the back door, but he pulled it open and got inside before she could push down the door button. He took out a handkerchief and blotted his face and hair. "Those guys are freelancers. You wonder who sent them after you? Probably Grady. You heard the guy—they wanted to scare you so you'd run back to Grady."

"Grady wouldn't do that."

"You study psychology? He was strapped on the pot too long. He'll do anything to get his way. His old man got him discharged from the Marine Corps so he wouldn't have to go to Korea."

"All right, you saved my life. Now please get out."

"Do you have brain damage?" he said, tapping the side of his head. "I'm your friend. Look, you need a ride somewhere, call me. I'll send a car service for you. You got guys bothering you, call me. I'll put them out of business. You ask, you get."

"I'm going to walk home now. Please don't follow me."

He leaned forward and cupped his hands on her shoulders. His breath was moist on her ear. He seemed to be gathering his words, his thoughts, before he spoke, as though about to say something he had never said and did not want anyone to hear him say again. "I got a thing for you. You're like nobody I ever saw or met. I'm just a reg'lar guy. That means I'm not a bad guy, even though I look different and other people say I'm a bad guy. I'm not like my father. He hurts people because he likes it. I defend people. I stand up for myself and my friends. I'll defend you. I'm different from other people. That's all I wanted to say, Miss Valerie."

The smell of the gasoline was overwhelming, dense and wet, clinging to the inside of her head and lungs. She couldn't begin to sort out his words. She thought she was going to faint. She felt his fingers sinking into her shoulders. He shook her as though waking someone from a nap. "Talk to me."

"Thank you, Vick," she said. "But you must let me alone."

He pressed his face into her hair. The rain was slacking, the windshield clearing. Then his breath left the nape of her neck.

"I'll take you home now," he said. "You can call the cops, or you can trust me to take care of what happened here. I hear your father is a war hero. Maybe he's got some ideas of his own, the same kind I got. Hop in my car. Don't dishonor what we got here."

What we got here?

She opened the door and got out, her purse and her book bag gripped to her chest. Her blood had pooled in her legs; her body had turned to lead. He was getting out of the backseat, unable to hide his male arousal, his hair as slick as sealskin, his teeth showing behind his disfigured lip, his visible eye glimmering like a stone at the bottom of a dirty fish tank. "Hey, where you going? I'm not an ogre! Don't treat me like this!"

She began running toward the intersection, gaining the curb, running along the edge of the vacant lot toward the lighted houses on the next block. She heard him open and slam the door of his car, then start the engine, pressing on the gas while in neutral. The moon had broken through the clouds, flooding the sidewalk and the vacant lot and the oaks and the yards with a glow the color of pewter. She ran into the lot so he couldn't follow her with the car; she jumped across weed-spiked piles of building debris, a moldy mattress with a used condom on it, a pile of broken glass, the carcass of a dog whose skin had turned to a lampshade. She passed a horse shed built of slat wood and RC Cola signs and gained another sidewalk and ran across a lighted intersection into a neighborhood thick with live oaks and magnolia trees, the wide front porches hung with flower baskets and gliders and wind chimes, all the iconic images that should have offered reassurance and sanctuary but tonight did nothing of the sort.

She had given herself over to her worst imaginings, but she didn't care. They were preferable to the memories that three men had just visited upon her and from which she would never escape. She didn't look back until she had rounded the corner of the next block and saw her house. There was no traffic anywhere, nor anyone on the sidewalks or front porches or even in representation on a window shade, as though the earth had been vacuumed of humanity and turned into a stage set.

* * *

I TOOK OFF FROM work and stayed with her the next day. A tow truck pulled the Epstein car to the shop. Mr. Epstein talked to some uniformed cops, then to a plainclothes detective. None of them seemed convinced of Valerie's account. Vick Atlas had a penthouse apartment in the Montrose district but had not been seen by anyone in three days. The father's lawyer said he was in Mexico. No one answered the phone at the family compound in Galveston. Two days after the fake cops had terrorized Valerie, Detective Merton Jenks showed up at her house while I was there. I hadn't thought I would ever be happy to see Merton Jenks again. When he knocked on the door, the living room shook. I answered the door. He took one look through the screen and said, "I should have known."

"That doesn't seem quite fair, sir," I said.

"Where's the girl?"

"Her name is Valerie."

"Go get her. Her old man, too."

"He's not here."

"Great," he said in disgust. He opened the door and came in without asking. "Where is she?"

I called upstairs. Jenks's eyes kept boring into my face, the source of his agitation a mystery, at least to me.

"Nothing I say to you kids seems to get across," he said. "There's not a lot of sympathy for you downtown. The consensus is trouble either follows you or you go out and find it. Right now I'm the only friend you've got."

"Sir, they almost set her on fire."

He walked to the stairs and hit on the banister with his fist. "We need you down here, Miss Epstein. Let's go."

"Why don't you show some respect?" I said.

"You'd better shut up."

"When you guys get scared, you take out your anger on people who have no power," I said.

"When's Goldie going to be here?"

"Mr. Epstein?"

"Who do you think?"

"He's at work," I said.

I realized he wasn't looking at me anymore. He was staring up the stairway at Valerie. She was wearing jeans and sandals and a tan cowboy shirt with rearing horses sewn on the pockets.

"I'm Detective Merton Jenks," he said. "I want to get a confirmation of your account and ask you a few questions. It won't take long, miss."

"Did you find Vick Atlas?" she said.

"Not yet," Jenks said.

"Then who is going to believe my story?"

"I'm not sure what your story is. That's why I'm here."

We sat in the living room under the ceiling fan, and she went through it again in detail.

"Atlas couldn't explain how he knew you had run out of gas?" Jenks said.

"That's right. How did he know those phony cops didn't pull me over? They had a spotlight on the driver's side like police cars have."

"You think Atlas set up the situation?"

"That's what I'd like to believe."

"Why?"

"Because otherwise they intended to burn me to death."

"You spat in one guy's face?"

"The one with the overbite."

He removed a manila folder from his coat pocket. "I have two sets of mug shots here. Do these men look familiar?"

She took the photos from his hand and looked at them. She pointed at the profile of a man whose upper teeth extended over his lower lip. "This is the one who handcuffed me. I can't be sure about the other one. His friend called him Seth."

"That's Seth Roberts. He was in Huntsville and Raiford in Florida. The guy you spat on, the one with the matches, spent nine years in the Nevada state prison for suffocating his common-law wife. I'm going to show you two more photos. The purpose is not to disturb you or to satisfy any desire for revenge that you might have. The purpose is to make sure the men in the second set of photos are the ones who handcuffed you and poured gasoline inside your car. Maybe your father will object to me showing you these pictures, but that's the way it is."

"Please show me the photos, Mr. Jenks," she said.

"It's Detective Jenks."

The photos were eight-by-tens. The two bodies in them were naked and curled up inside a ditch. The hands had been cut off. The gunshot wounds were in the ear, the mouth, and the forehead.

"I recognize the man who handcuffed me," she said. "I don't know about the other one."

"That's Seth Roberts."

"Who killed them?" she asked.

"Vick Atlas said he was going to square things for you?" Jenks said.

"He didn't use those words."

"But he was going to get even for you?"

"That's what he said."

Jenks put the photos away. "How you feeling?"

"Guess," she replied.

"You're a brave girl," he said.

"Do you believe Vick Atlas killed those men?"

"He's twenty-one years old. He looks forty. His old man is a sociopath. If I had a son like Vick, I'd have my genitalia surgically removed and buried in concrete." Jenks shook his head and rubbed his palms on his knees. "I don't know who killed them."

"What are you not telling us?" I asked.

"Vick Atlas doesn't decide who dies and who lives. His father gives the orders. If the old man has somebody tagged, it's about money. This isn't about money."

"How do you know that?" she asked.

"I don't. If I had to guess, I'd say Vick Atlas created a setup where he'd be your savior, Miss Epstein. Then somebody else got involved."

"Who?" I said.

"Somebody with no conscience at all," he said. "Have you seen a woman named Cisco Napolitano around recently?"

* * *

THAT AFTERNOON I DID something I would not have dared think about a few months before. I called the information officer at the Houston Police Department and told him I was a reporter for the *Houston Press* doing a feature on several outstanding members of the department.

"He was with the OSS, right?" I said. "That's something else, isn't it?"

"Yeah, but you ought to talk to him about that," the officer said.

"That's okay. I have most of what I need. I forgot the number of years he was in law enforcement in California. Or was it Nevada?"

"It was Nevada. Five years, I think. Check with him. What's your name again?"

"Franklin W. Dixon," I replied.

"Who?"

I COULD SEE MY mother slipping away by the day, maybe even the hour, convinced that her public humiliation of Mr. Krauser had caused his suicide. The western sky could be strung with evening clouds that looked like flamingo wings; rain might patter on her caladiums and hibiscus and hydrangeas and roses and fill the air with a smell out of *The Arabian Nights*, the book that probably saved her sanity as a child. But no matter how grand a place the world might be, my mother's eyes had the hollow expression of someone staring into a crypt. My father and I took her out for Mexican food at Felix's, and as I looked at the misery in her face, I knew that voices no one else heard were speaking to her and soon our family doctor would have her back in electroshock, a rubber gag in her mouth, her wrists strapped to a table.

At that moment in the middle of the restaurant, I made a decision to lie or do whatever else was necessary to keep her from descending into the madness that the Hollands carried in their genes and the scientific world further empowered in its own hothouse of quackery and ignorance.

"I talked to one of the detectives who investigated Mr. Krauser's death, Mother," I said. "The detective says Mr. Krauser may have been abducted and thrown from the roof of the building."

She ate with small bites, her gaze fixed on nothing. I waited for her to speak. My words seemed to have had no effect. Then she looked at me, her eyes empty, focused on a spot next to my face. "Why would they do that?"

"Maybe Mr. Krauser was mixed up with people who send homeless boys to indoctrination camps," I said.

"He did that?" she said.

"No one is sure," I said.

My mother took another bite, chewing slowly. My father watched her as he would someone walking a wire high above a canyon. The only time my father ever drank in front of my mother was when the three of us were at a restaurant, as though a geographical armistice had been declared between the forces of his addiction and my mother's intolerance. Tonight he had not ordered a beer with his dinner. It was the first time I had ever seen him not do so, and I suspected it had not been easy.

"Listen to Aaron," he said. "I think he knows what he's talking about."

She stopped eating and placed her fork and knife in an X on her plate.

"Are you not hungry?" he said.

"I shouldn't have eaten a sandwich this afternoon," she said. "Do they have a dessert menu here? I can't remember. What's the name of that dessert made with ice cream and cinnamon and mint leaves?"

"It's called ice cream with cinnamon and spearmint leaves," he said.

"I'd love to have that now. Yes, something that's cold and sweet with a taste of mint in it. When I was a little girl, we used to make hand-crank ice cream on the porch, up on the Guadalupe. It was wonderful to eat ice cream on the porch on a summer evening. We should go up there for a weekend sometime."

"I think that's a fine idea," my father said. "What do you think, Aaron?"

Maybe there was some truth to my lie about Mr. Krauser's death. Or maybe a lie can bring mercy and grace upon us when virtue cannot. I didn't want to research the question. My mother seemed happy. It was a rare moment in what had been the declining arc in an afflicted person's life.

Chapter 20

THE NEXT NIGHT my father drove up to the Heights to introduce himself to Mr. Epstein. Mr. Epstein had told me he was not a Communist "now." I wasn't sure what that meant. To me communism seemed like such a ridiculous system that no rational person could respect or fear it. By the same token, I didn't think anyone who had bought in to such a joyless mind-set could have the ability to rid himself of it.

My father did not ask me to go with him. I hated to think about the political collision he might have with Mr. Epstein. My father returned home in under an hour and went into his small study and resumed work on his book about his family, his fountain pen moving across a fresh sheet of paper, a Lucky Strike burning in the ashtray by his forearm. I knew he was among the horde of men in tattered gray and butter-brown uniforms advancing up a slope in sweltering July heat at a place called Cemetery Hill.

I pulled up a chair behind him. He didn't look up from his work. "Everything go okay?" I finally said.

"Hi, Aaron," he replied. "You gave me a start. I thought you might be a Yankee sharpshooter."

"Was Mr. Epstein home?"

"Yes, he was definitely there."

I waited for him to continue. But he didn't. "That doesn't sound too good," I said.

"Mr. Epstein is a cradle-to-the-grave ideologue. A leftist but nonetheless an ideologue."

"What's an ideologue?"

"Someone who brings religious passion to a political abstraction only cretins could think up," he said. "When you meet one, flee his presence at all costs. He'll incinerate half the planet to save the other half and never understand his own motivations."

"What are his motivations?"

"Control, power, penis envy, addiction to breast-feeding, the fact that most of them are born ugly, God only knows. In one night, ten men like Mr. Epstein could have New York City in flames."

I glanced over his shoulder at the ink drying on his manuscript page. "Are you still working on Pickett's charge?"

"In part, but there's another story about the charge that not many people know of. After the slopes were littered with Confederate wounded and dead, the federals tamped their muskets on the ground and chanted, 'Fredericksburg, Fredericksburg, Fredericksburg' as a taunt for the pasting they took going up Marye's Heights."

I wasn't sure what his point was. He anticipated my question. "There's no glory in any of this. Nothing good comes out of war. It only breeds more hatred and suffering and killing. Freeborn Negroes, man, woman, and child, were taken from their homes in Chambersburg and sent to the auction block in Richmond. Louisiana outfits participated in it, too. Robert Lee witnessed the terrorizing of the town and did nothing to stop it. The kidnapping and selling of Negroes was no different than the behavior of Nazis. That's where ideology leads us, Aaron."

I had never heard him speak this way. I went into the kitchen and made coffee for both of us and went back into his study and drank it with him and watched him work.

THE FIRST CALL to the River Oaks police station concerning Clint Harrelson's property came at 10:33 P.M. The neighbor who called refused to give her name but said, "The jungle music coming out of that house is destroying my sleep and rupturing my eardrums and upsetting my husband, who happens to be stone deaf. Would you kindly do something about it?" The second, third, and fourth calls came from neighbors who heard shouting and then gunfire and saw from their balconies or through the bamboo at the back of the house the bizarre denouement of Clint Harrelson, anthropologist, oilman, rice producer, and apparent Aryan supremacist.

A song was blaring from the high-fidelity speakers in the game room. The pounding drums, the thumping bass chords exploding out of the piano, the peal of the clarinet and the wailing of the horns and the driving four-four backbeat were an assault on the sensibilities of the neighborhood. The underwater lights were on in the swimming pool, the surface dimpled with rain rings. The glass door on the game room slid back violently, then Clint Harrelson burst outside, barefoot and in boxer shorts, his skin as sickly as a toadstool. He began running and slipping along the side of the pool, looking back over his shoulder like a man caught inside the pop of a flashbulb. A figure in a hooded windbreaker stepped out of the game room and aimed a semi-automatic with two hands. The first shot tore through an umbrella and smacked against the brick wall at the rear of the estate. The second one punched through the back of Harrelson's knee and kicked his leg from under him. The shell casings bounced on the concrete.

Harrelson had fallen across a canvas recliner. He gripped his knee as though trying to pull it to his chest. His fingers were shiny with blood, his mouth wide with rictus, his pain clearly beyond sound or words. "Why are you doing this?" he managed. "Please. We can turn this around. This will be no good for you or anyone else. Listen to reason. We have alternatives if you'll only listen."

The figure in the hooded windbreaker walked toward him. Harrelson tried to run again, grabbing pieces of pool furniture, dragging one leg as though it were boneless. The next shots exited his chest and stomach and throat. He fell headlong into the pool, his arms floating at his sides. He sank halfway to the bottom, red smoke funneling from his wounds, then rose to the surface and remained still, his hair pasted on his scalp, the blue water rippling across his back.

The shooter walked the length of the patio and onto the grass and through a cluster of camellia bushes into the darkness, closing the gate, shaking it to make sure it was snug. At first none of the eyewitnesses could move. Later all of them said they felt time had stopped, that in the aftermath of the shooting, they felt trapped inside a slow-motion film and traumatized by the fate visited on poor Mr. Harrelson. They gathered on a common porch in their bathrobes and drank straight whiskey poured by the owner of the house and shared their bewilderment. By the next day, their lawyers indicated that their clients could not swear to the accuracy of their earlier statements because of the previous night's inclement weather. They also asked that names not be released to the press and that authorities contact the attorneys if they needed any more information.

In the morning the pool was drained and the tile and concrete scrubbed with lye and the filters cleaned with disinfectant by Mexican workers. Aside from the remains that lay on a slab in the county morgue, all the earthly fluids and chemical signatures of Clint Harrelson were hosed with the pine needles into the sewage system.

THE STORY GOT a banner front-page headline in all three of the city's newspapers. The *Houston Press* ran a photo of Grady arriving at the funeral home in dark glasses and a white suit, a black carnation in the lapel, his jaw set, his hands balled at his sides like a New York gangster barely suppressing his sorrow and anger. The cutline referred to him as a former honor student, football quarterback, and marine. Behind him in the photo was Vick Atlas.

The story stated that Grady was sailboating when he received news of his father's death. After I read the story, I drove to Valerie's house. I was sure we were all going to be dragged into the investigation. I had become as cynical as Saber about the legal system, and not without reason. As soon as I got to Valerie's, she told me Merton Jenks had already questioned her father.

"Why?" I said.

"Jenks thinks he might have done it," she said.

There was a beat when I avoided her eyes. "Your father wouldn't really do something like that, would he?" I said.

It wasn't an honest question. I knew better. Mr. Epstein was not one to sneak through life on side streets. I hoped Valerie had an alibi for him. I didn't want to think of him as a man who could commit murder.

"What is the difference between somebody 'really' doing something, as opposed to simply doing it?" she said.

"What people say and what they do aren't always the same thing," I replied.

"I know he wouldn't shoot an unarmed man," she said.

"That's it? Armed people are okay?"

"In Yugoslavia he saw the SS hang civilians with wire on the village square while their families were forced to watch."

Valerie could create images that were like a rubber band snapping inside your head.

"But he was home with you when Mr. Harrelson was killed, right?" I said.

"No, he wasn't. He was returning from Beaumont. Jenks asked if you were with me when Mr. Harrelson was killed."

"Why me?"

"He wanted to know if you really had spells."

Jenks was a master at messing up people's heads. "So anything you said would indict me? If I didn't have spells, I was a liar. If I did have them, I could be guilty of anything and everything."

"Something like that."

"What did you tell him?"

"That anything you told him was the truth. That he needed to get his fat ass out of my house."

"You said that to *Jenks*?"

She smacked her gum and didn't answer. How much can you love one girl?

* * *

JENKS WAS AT my house that afternoon. I knew he was coming, and by this time I knew his mission was no longer about me or my mother and father or Clint Harrelson's murder or Krauser's suicide or the death of the Mexican prostitute named Wanda Estevan or Saber's vandalizing of Krauser's house or his boosting Grady's convertible or the torching of Loren Nichols's customized heap or the terrorizing of Valerie by the two ex-convicts who ended up naked in a ditch with their hands stubbed off at the wrists. Detective Jenks didn't have an agenda; he was at war on a global scale. He was right out of medieval mythology, the Templar knight who slept in his armor and gave tribute to God while loading the heads of decapitated Saracens into a catapult and flinging them back into their own lines.

I sat with him at the redwood table in the backyard with all my pets in attendance. It was strange how they seemed to know when I needed them. Major lay spread out with all fours in the shade, his belly and dong pressed into the grass. Bugs and Snuggs and Skippy sat on the tabletop, which they had crosshatched with seat smears since they were kittens. Jenks was wearing a short-sleeved shirt and kept lifting his forearms from the redwood and wiping them without realizing the source of the gelatinous material on his skin. "Is that a mulberry tree back there?"

"I think it is."

He wiped at his forearm again, his face a question mark. "When are your folks due home?"

"Hard to say. They're at the grocery. My mother doesn't drive, so my father has to take her."

"Does your father believe in home protection?"

"Yes, sir, that's fair to say."

"What kind of firearm does he keep?"

"He's never been big on firearms."

"That's not what I asked."

"I thought it was."

"You should have been a baseball pitcher," he said. "Did you ever see a pitcher pull on the brim of his cap or fix his belt just before the windup? That's what you make me think of."

"I put Vaseline on baseballs?"

"I can come back with a warrant. Or somebody a lot less sympathetic can."

"You asked Valerie if I was lying about my spells."

"Yes, I did. Do you think you're capable of killing someone like Clint Harrelson while you're in one of them?"

"Maybe."

"I don't," he said.

"Can you say that again?"

"I can smell a killer. Men can kill other men, but that doesn't make them killers. A killer comes out of the womb with a stink on him that never goes away."

"Then why are you here?"

"I went to the gun store where your father bought the army forty-five. That's the same caliber weapon used to kill Mr. Harrelson."

"You think my father would commit a murder? That's insane."

"I'm going to let you in on a secret," Jenks said. "Sometimes the state doesn't care who gets head-shaved and has cotton stuffed up his colon before he's strapped down and bucked through the ceiling. Sometimes they don't care if it's a woman, either. As long as somebody rides the bolt, the average person doesn't give a shit. You think cops are your problem, son. You're wrong."

"I'm not going to talk to you anymore, Detective Jenks."

He had opened his notebook on the table but had not written one word in it. The wind was blowing the pages on the metal rings. "You know who Jack Hemingway is?"

"Ernest Hemingway's oldest son."

"I jumped with him behind German lines on D-day. He was shot and captured by the SS. The SS didn't take wounded prisoners. Jack was going to be executed, but an SS colonel who'd skied with Jack's father had him transferred to a hospital. True story."

"What happened to you?"

"I escaped."

"Why tell me this?"

"Because you kids in Southwest Houston read a couple of books and think you know it all."

"Why don't you stop lying, sir?" I said.

He was wearing his fedora, but the darkness in his face was not from the shadow of the hat. He closed his notebook and lifted his forefinger. "I'm not above hitting you. I'll do it."

"You never told me you were a cop in Nevada."

He got up from the bench, a gray odor like nicotine and antiperspirant and beer sweat wafting off his body. He dropped his business card on the table. "Tell your father to call me. He's not a suspect. We found his name in a journal kept by Clint Harrelson. Evidently he considered your father a subversive and was going to report him to Harrelson's fellow paranoids in Dallas. Tell your father I need to ask him a couple of questions so I can eliminate him from the investigation."

"Was Miss Cisco your girlfriend?"

He didn't seem to hear me. Or he pretended not to. Instead he sniffed his forearm. "Is that what I think it is?"

"I still think she has qualities. Maybe her life would have been different if she'd gotten a break or two."

"Kid, you deserve everything that will probably happen to you. By the way, a vice officer told me your friend Bledsoe is dealing goofballs in the Heights. If you see him, tell him he'd better find me before I find him."

Chapter 21

SABER'S FATHER HAD gotten a job with Jolly Jack ice cream. I suspected it was a terrible humiliation. The Jolly Jack carts were pedal-powered and usually driven by teenagers who had dropped out of school. Each morning Mr. Bledsoe reported to a warehouse next to a horse pasture and, alongside the kids, packed his cart with dry ice wrapped in newspaper and boxes of Popsicles and fudge bars and Dixie Cups, then pedaled off in ninety-five-degree heat, unshaven and unbathed and smelling of bulk wine and sometimes vomit from the previous night. Who could blame Saber for being in a funk?

Of course, the problem was more than a funk. He had given himself over to a couple of bad Mexican huckleberries. I went by his house; his mother told me she had no idea where he was.

"He's still living here, isn't he, Miz Bledsoe?" I said.

"Like you give a damn," she replied, and closed the door in my face.

I knew where to find him, though. At least on a balmy summer evening, I did. Saber had fantasies. One of them involved meeting a beautiful girl at the roller rink on South Main. He would drive his heap out to the big tent filled with organ music and the grinding of roller-skate wheels on the hardwood floor and the steady hum of the giant fans in back, and park by the entrance so he could see the skaters inside. He would comb his hair in the rearview mirror, sweeping it back on the sides, and smoke cigarettes and drink from a quart bottle of Jax and pretend he was waiting for someone. Finally he would wander inside and eat a Baby Ruth and watch the girls roaring past him, all of them holding hands, speeding up and slowing down, sometimes skating backward. They wore pastel angora sweaters and poodle skirts and wide shiny black belts, and the bold ones might have on hoop earrings and uplift bras, and when they went by in a group, he could smell them like a garden full of flowers. Their eyes never met his. He could have been a wooden post.

He would return home and go to bed and probably masturbate and hide his underwear in the bottom of the clothes hamper and, in the morning, resume his role as the carefree trickster who looked down on the romantic rituals that governed every high school in America.

I had to remind myself of all these things about the private world of Saber; otherwise, I would forget the vulnerable and innocent boy who had been my best friend since elementary school. Even though he was hanging with bad guys, I knew Saber would eat a bayonet for me. When you have a friend like that, you never let go of him, no matter what he does.

At sunset I pulled into the parking lot by the tent. There was Saber's heap, the windows down, the dust blowing inside it. Next to it was a 1946 canary-yellow Ford convertible with whitewall spoked tires and blue-dot taillights and chrome bells on the twin exhausts. Saber was nowhere in sight. A man in a crisp paper hat was selling hand-shaved sno-cones out of a cart by the entrance. I bought a spearmint cone and went inside the flap and sat down on the wooden seats that had been taken out of baseball bleachers. I saw Saber at the snack counter, paying for his order with bills he took from a hand-tooled wallet attached to a chain. I had never seen the wallet before. The two Mexicans from the jail were standing next to him, sipping sodas through straws, wearing patent-leather stomps and dark drapes sewn with white thread and long-sleeved rayon shirts buttoned at the wrists, the tails hanging outside their belts.

Saber and the two hoods were talking to four girls of about fifteen or sixteen, the kind with bad skin who lived in the welfare project and wore the tightest shorts they could get into and tattooed their boyfriend's name inside their thighs. They were the roughest girls I ever knew, but at the same time they were easy marks for a slick guy who told them they were beautiful and smart and physically tough and fun to be with, far too good for the project losers they'd been hanging around.

I walked up behind Saber. He was eating a chili dog off a paper plate, dipping into it with a plastic spoon; I didn't think he saw me.

"What's happening, Aaron?" he said without turning around.

"Nothing much. Wondering where the hell you've been," I said.

The Mexicans were offering the girls sips from their straws, grinning when the girls took the straws in their mouths.

"I'm in the used-car business these days," Saber said.

"Whose Ford coupe is that out there?"

"Manny and Cholo's uncle gave it to them. Want to take a spin?"

"No, thanks. I never liked wearing handcuffs. Who are the girls?"

"They hang out here. We're going to Prince's. Want to go?"

"You heard about Grady Harrelson's father?" I said.

"A tragedy of cosmic proportions. I cried my eyes out. Go to Prince's with us."

"No."

He looked over his shoulder to see if we were out of earshot from the Mexicans. "Are we talking about a racial issue here?"

"No. And quit hiding behind it," I said.

He shrugged and continued eating.

"Did you know some guys were going to set Valerie on fire?" I said.

The cavalier expression left his face. For just a second I saw the old Saber looking at me, the false exterior pared away. "No, I didn't hear about that."

"Maybe Vick Atlas set it up. Two guys ended up dead in a ditch. They were naked and their hands were cut off."

His gaze went away from me and lingered in space, finding the justifications he needed to keep doing what he was doing. He started eating his chili dog again. "Manny and Cholo have got connections. Guys who can do some serious payback."

"Vick Atlas's crowd wouldn't let those guys clean their toilets."

"Maybe you wouldn't, either," he said. "Because that's the signal I keep getting, Aaron."

"Sell it to somebody else," I said.

He threw his food into the trash. "Motor on up to Prince's if you feel like it. I got to get back to my people."

"Your people?"

"My old man is selling Popsicles. I'm putting food on the table and paying down the mortgage. That wouldn't be happening if it wasn't for Manny and Cholo. They're good guys. They accept me as I am."

"They'll wipe their ass with you."

"You're just like your old man," he said. "You play the Southern gentleman, but you think you're better than other people."

He walked away from me, his jaw hooked, his shoulders rounded hood-style.

"Don't talk about my father like that," I said at his back.

He paid me no attention. I got into my heap and tooled down South Main toward Herman Park, the lamps coming on along the boulevard and in the live oaks on the Rice campus. I should have kept going, but I couldn't let it rest. I made a U-turn, horns blowing at me, and went to Prince's drive-in and drove up and down the aisles. Saber's heap wasn't there, and neither was the canary-yellow Ford convertible. They didn't want to go there without the girls, I thought. It was all about the girls. I headed back to the roller rink.

Was I being unfair? I wondered. Not a chance.

It was almost dark, the heat draining out of the day. I pulled into the parking lot. Saber's heap and the Ford were still there. I got out and went inside. The tent was more crowded now, the music faster, a tinge of sweat and talcum and hair spray in the air. I went back outside and saw Saber and the Mexicans and the girls gathered between two storage sheds, drinking canned beer, lighting up, giggling. The wind changed and I knew what they were smoking. I started walking toward them.

"Come with me, Sabe," I said.

"Cain't do it," he said. "I'm with my pards."

The girls were passing hand-rolls around, bending over when they laughed, looking at me as though I were a balloon that had broken its tether and floated into their midst.

"I'm Manny," one of the Mexicans said. "This is Cholo. Why you keep showing up wherever we're at, man?"

He was thinner than his friend, wrapped tighter, with darker skin and more ink on his arms and neck. Cholo had eyes that were soft and warm and unthreatening. I believed that either of them was capable of disemboweling me and gargling beer while he did it.

"Hey, you hearing me, *gusano*?" Manny said. "You were in our cell. Then I see you at the drugstore and now at the roller rink. You just keep coming around, man. It's starting to upset me."

"Sorry to hear that," I said.

"That ain't no way to talk, man," Cholo said. "Want to join us? We got a place in the Fifth Ward. The neighborhood ain't just for coloreds. We get along good there. Hey, you like music? We got all kinds of records, man. You like to dance, too?" His eyes shifted at the girls.

"What's a *gusano*?" I asked.

"It means something like *compadre*," Manny said.

"It means 'worm,'" I said.

"You pretty smart."

"He's okay, Manny," Saber said. "We've been pards a long time."

"He don't look like no pard to me. But if you say so, man, that's cool," Manny said. His eyes went up and down my body. "We're friends now? You want a hug?"

I looked back at him and didn't answer.

His eyes were flat and glassy. He puffed on his reefer, pinching it with two fingers, never blinking. "You think because you're tall, you're a macho guy? You was in jail a few hours and now you're an ex-con? First day up in Huntsville, you'd be in the bridal suite. They'd drive a freight train up your ass."

"You damn spic," I said.

I had never used that word before, not once. My mouth went dry.

I tried to swallow, but there was nothing in my mouth, just a bitter taste.

"He didn't mean it," Saber said.

"Oh, yes, this *chico* means it, man. Is all right, Saber," Manny said. He looked back at me. "We like you, man. We don't got no grudges. I was kidding about Huntsville. You'd like it, man. Somebody would take care of you. Bring scarf to your cell. Introduce you to friends. Give you a cigar."

"Step over here," I said.

"Let it slide, Aaron," Saber said.

Manny was grinning, his teeth as white as Chiclets. Saber stepped between us, then shoved me when I didn't back up. "Go home, Aaron."

I looked at him for a long time. The girls stopped giggling. One hung her head. Cholo hooked his thumb on his right-hand pocket. A police cruiser drove fast down South Main, flasher on, siren off. "Have a good life, Sabe."

"Don't be like this," he said at my back. "Come on, Aaron. We're buds."

WHEN I GOT HOME, my father was at the icehouse. My mother was washing dishes.

"You should have left those for me," I said.

"I don't mind. Detective Jenks called," she said. "He wants you to call him back."

"What about?"

"He said he would like to consult with you."

"'Consult'?"

"That's the term he used. He was quite gentlemanly."

"Don't be taken in," I said.

"A cynical attitude doesn't become you, Aaron. He was very nice. He's obviously a man of breeding, even though he may be of humble origins."

I had learned long ago that any authority figure who treated my mother with a few words of respect became an immediate substitute for the father she never had. The consequence was almost always a disaster. But I didn't argue. I used the telephone in my father's study to call Merton Jenks at the number he had left.

"What do you want?" I said.

"Why don't you learn some manners?" he replied.

"We're of no help to you, Detective Jenks. We don't commit crimes. Why don't you leave us alone?"

"You know about music. You know what kids listen to. Now shut the fuck up before I have to come out there again," he said.

"Sir, what do you want?"

"A forty-five was playing on the hi-fi in the game room when Clint Harrelson got blown into the swimming pool. The song was 'Boogie Woogie Stomp' by Albert Ammons. You know it?"

"You bet."

"Here's the thing. There was no other jazz or swing or boogie-woogie or nigra music in the record racks. People who knew Harrelson say he couldn't stand any of that stuff and wouldn't allow it in the house. You got any idea who might have been playing that song on his hi-fi?"

"No, sir," I said.

"Grady Harrelson doesn't listen to that kind of music?"

"Guys like Grady listen to crap by Pat Boone," I replied. "Besides, I read that Grady was on a sailboat when he got the news about his father."

"Nobody in your acquaintance would have motivation to shoot Clint Harrelson?" he said.

I was already remembering my conversation with Saber's Mexican friends, particularly Cholo, who had said they were living in the Fifth Ward, the heart of the black district. They had a lot of records at their place. Albert Ammons's music was the kind you bought in a colored barbershop or a beauty parlor, not in a white neighborhood. Saber believed Clint Harrelson was behind Mr. Bledsoe's firing. He had also stolen Grady's convertible and sold it in Mexico. Was his desire for revenge so great that he would break into the Harrelson estate and torment the father with a rhythm-and-blues recording, then kill him?

It sounded ridiculous, except he had broken into Mr. Krauser's house and torn up his most valued possessions and used a retarded boy, Jimmy McDougal, to help him.

"Are you in a coma?" Jenks said.

"Why are you always insulting me?"

"Because you piss me off."

In the background I heard a sound like someone sinking an opener into the top of a beer can.

"*I* piss *you* off?" I said.

My mother came out of nowhere. "Don't you dare use that language in this house," she said. She ripped the receiver from my hand. "Detective Jenks, I could hear you in the kitchen. You are a great disappointment. I feel like washing your mouth out with soap. You are not to call here again."

She set the receiver in the cradle, releasing her fingers quickly, as though avoiding germs on its surface.

I BATHED AND LAY down on my bed in the current of cool air that the attic fan drew through the screen. Major and the cats were piled beside me, snoring in the wonderful way animals snore. I felt a strange sense of peace about my home. That soon changed.

My father came in late, brushing against the doorway and the pictures on the wall in the hallway. A few minutes later I saw him through the partially open bathroom door. He was sitting on the edge of the tub, smoking a cigarette in his shirtsleeves and undershorts and socks, his garters clipped on his calves. His face was furrowed, his stubble gray, his hand trembling when he lifted his cigarette.

"Daddy?" I said.

He turned his head toward me, as though I were speaking to him from a great distance. "Aaron? What are you doing up? Don't you have to work tomorrow?"

"Can I help with something?"

He stared into empty space. "No, not really. None of us can. That's the great joke. It's all gone. Everything. It was just a dream on Bayou Teche. *Parti avec la vent.*"

I could hear the paper on his cigarette crisp when he inhaled. I suspected that one day cigarettes would kill him. But that was not the fear I had as I looked at my father. No one had to convince me about the reality of hell. It wasn't a fiery pit. It lived and thrived in the human breast and consumed its host from night to morning.

Chapter 22

THE NEXT DAY I took Valerie to a hamburger joint for lunch, then dropped her off and went to Loren Nichols's house without telling her. I had reached a point where I realized I had been a fool. I was raised to believe that good triumphed over evil, that justice ultimately prevailed, and that God was on our side. We had rebuilt the bombed-out countries of our enemies through the Marshall Plan at a time when we could have turned the earth into a slave camp. Wouldn't it follow that we would do justice to our own at home?

I still believe in those precepts, but as we grow old and leave behind the pink clouds of our youth, we learn that truth often exists in degree rather than in absolutes. I had believed that the people who'd caused us so much harm would be brought to account. Valerie had almost been burned alive, and no one was in custody. I doubted that anyone of importance had been questioned. I thought Jenks believed her, but probably few of his colleagues did. Why should anyone worry about the fate of a seventeen-year-old Jewish girl in the Heights?

It had just started to rain when I knocked on Loren's door. He came to the screen wearing a white T-shirt and a pair of white trousers, his face blank. The screen was latched, but he made no move to unlatch it. His hair was wet-combed, curled up on the back of his neck. "I'm about to go to work."

"Where do you work?"

"I'm a busboy at Luby's cafeteria."

"I'll give you a ride."

He looked past me to see if anyone was in my heap, then unhooked the latch. "Come upstairs. My mother is sleeping."

The inside of his home looked like a mausoleum furnished from a secondhand store. I thought the banister on the stairs would cave before we reached the landing. The interior of his bedroom was another matter. The walls were covered with pencil sketches of people and classic automobiles and animals; the ceiling was hung with models of World War II airplanes, each delicate piece of balsa wood cut and shaved with an X-Acto knife and glued together and pinned down on a blueprint and assembled and covered with cutouts from tissue paper, then painted with a tiny brush and pasted with decals of Nazi swastikas and the American white star inside the blue circle and the rising sun of Imperial Japan. His electric guitar was on his bed, plugged into the amplifier on the rug. Through the window, I could see the tin roofs of his neighbors in the rain, purple with rust, the palm trees and live oaks and slash pines bending in the wind. It looked more like the Caribbean than a run-down part of town in North Houston.

"How much do you want for the thirty-two you showed me?" I asked.

"Is this about those guys who tried to hurt Valerie?"

I didn't answer.

"I shouldn't have started this," he said. "You going after somebody in particular?"

"I think Vick Atlas was behind it."

"Don't bet on that, man."

"Then who tried to burn her?"

"Believe me, if I find out, there's going to be some guys hurting real bad."

"How much do you want for the gun, Loren?"

"Nothing. It's not for sale. Does Valerie know about this?"

"No, she doesn't. I don't want you telling her, either."

"You're not giving the orders. Who killed Grady Harrelson's old man?"

"Why ask me?" I said.

"Because you don't have a clue what you're doing. Because you'll probably end up popping the wrong guy."

"I need the gun. Will you give it to me or not?"

He held me with his stare.

"I'm leaving," I said.

"It's a big line you're stepping over, Broussard," he said.

"That's another thing that bothers me about you, Loren. You call people by their last name."

"If you smoke somebody, they visit you."

"*Who* visits you?" I said.

"Dead people do. It's not like in the movies."

"You've killed somebody?"

"Shut up."

"You offered me the gun. Now honor your word or don't."

I could see the heat go out of his face.

"Let me get an umbrella," he said.

"How are your guitar lessons coming along?"

"Don't change the subject. You don't want to go to Gatesville, man. I never talk about it because people won't believe me. It's worse than Huntsville, especially in the shower or the toolshed, you get the picture?"

"I don't get *you,*" I said.

"What?"

"Your drawings and your model planes are works of art. With your talent, you could be anything you want. Ever think about going to Hollywood? I'm not putting you on."

He gazed out the window at a garbage can rolling down the street in the rain. "Your father is an engineer or something. You live in the good part of town. You're a musician and you go steady with the most beautiful girl in Houston. But you're coming to me for a drop so you can wax a lamebrain like Vick Atlas? I grew up in juvie and Gatesville. I'm the guy needs straightening out?"

"What's a 'drop'?"

He shook his head. "I'm going to hate myself for this the rest of my life. Follow me."

WHAT I DID NEXT was not rational. But I didn't care. I got the address of the Atlas family's business office in Galveston and told Valerie I'd see her that night.

"You're going down there by yourself?" she said.

"Why not? The cops haven't helped us."

"Then I'm going, too."

"That's not a good idea."

Bad choice of words.

"Aaron, we're in this together or we're not. Tell me which it is."

One hour later we were in Galveston and motoring down Seawall Boulevard, the Gulf slate green, the waves streaming with rivulets of yellow sand when they crested and crashed on the beach. The air smelled like iodine and brass and salt and seaweed. The Atlas realty and vending machine office was located in a nineteenth-century home, painted battleship gray, close by the water. It had a small pike-fenced lawn with flower beds, and a shell parking lot on the side, lightning rods and a weather vane on the roof, rocking chairs on the porch, a gazebo with an American flag protruding at an angle from one of the wooden pillars. A client could not find a more welcoming and reassuring and wholesome environment in which to conduct business.

A bell tinkled above the door when we entered. No one was at the reception desk. Through the doorway of the dining room, I could see four men eating sandwiches, pushing pieces of meat back into their mouths, wiping off their chins with a smear of the wrist or hand.

I was afraid, and I was even more afraid that others would know I was afraid. Through a side window, I could see the Gulf and the waves swelling over the third sandbar, and I thought about the day I swam through the school of jellyfish.

The three men eating with Jaime Atlas were middle-aged and jowled and had heavy shoulders and paunches and wore their tropical shirts outside their slacks. They were the kind of men who abused their bodies with cigarettes and alcohol and unhealthy food and wore the attrition as a badge of honor. Their eyes had the same deadness I had seen in the eyes of Benny Siegel and Frankie Carbo. I wanted to be back among the jellyfish. Atlas stopped eating, his sandwich crimped in one hand, his eyes close-set, like a ferret's. "What do you want?" he said.

"To see Mr. Atlas. You're Mr. Atlas, aren't you?"

"Who are you? What's your name? You make an appointment?"

My palms were tingling; my tongue seemed stuck to the roof of my mouth. "I'm Aaron Holland Broussard."

"The one threw a brick in my boy's eye?"

"That's not what happened, Mr. Atlas. Vick tried to throw a firecracker at another car, and it blew up in his face."

"Where the fuck you get that?"

"The prosecutor's office or the cops didn't tell you? Vick did the damage to himself."

I saw his face shrink, as though his anger were sucking his glands dry. "Who do you think you are, coming in here talking shit? Answer me. You don't come in here and talk shit to me about my son. Who told you you could come here and do that? Don't just stand there. You got a speech defect? You got mutes in your family?"

Then I realized Vick had not only lied to his father, his father had not kept in contact with the authorities. In the meantime, Vick had allowed his father to direct his rage at Saber and me.

"Maybe Vick sent a couple of guys to terrorize my friend Miss Valerie," I said. "He put his mouth in her hair. Is he around? I'd like to talk to him about it."

"You were never taught manners?" he said. "You bust into somebody's luncheon and start making accusations? Where's your father work? Let's get him out here. Who is he? What's he do?"

The accent was an echo of the Bronx or the blue-collar neighborhoods in New Orleans, the vowels as round as baseballs. His eyebrows looked like half-moons of fur glued on his forehead. He wiped mayonnaise off his lip and then wiped his hand on the tablecloth. In the meantime his three friends were visually undressing Valerie, indifferent to my presence or the awkwardness in her face.

"Why don't y'all show some goddamn manners yourselves?" I said.

Mr. Atlas set his sandwich down. He was breathing hard, his eyes heated, a canine tooth glistening behind his bottom lip. But whatever was on his mind, he didn't get a chance to say it.

"I did a study on you at Rice University," Valerie said. "You are known as a terrible person in every place you have lived. Lucky Luciano said you are not to be trusted. You were kicked out of Greece as a pimp and dope smuggler. You killed a taxi driver in New Orleans. You should join a church or a synagogue and see if you can change your life, because people are embarrassed to be around you."

I stared at her profile. It was like the masthead on a ship plowing through the waves.

"She's telling the truth," I said. "I was at the library with her. There's a ton of material on you."

Mr. Atlas's eyes were as black as obsidian. "Out."

"No, we will not 'out,'" Valerie replied. "Your son has serious mental problems. He may have brain damage. Some people say it was you who scarred his face. You should be ashamed of yourself. What kind of example have you set? Look at the men you're with. They bully women because they're moral and physical cowards. Don't look at me. Look at yourselves. What are you? Nothing. Fat men who smell like salami."

Atlas went to the front and dialed the phone on the receptionist's desk. "This is Jaime Atlas," he said into the receiver, looking back at us. "I got some kids causing trouble in my office. Send an officer over here."

He hung up and came back into the dining room. "Say that again about the firecracker blowing up in Vick's face."

"It's what happened," I said.

"If you're lying . . ." he said.

"People in my family don't lie, Mr. Atlas. You asked who my father is. He went over the top five times in World War One. That's who he is."

* * *

As WE DROVE away, I put my arm around Valerie and pulled her against me.

"What are you laughing about?" she said.

"The faces of those guys when you gave it to them."

"They got off easy. If my father thinks they were hooked up with the guys who poured gasoline in my car, they'll be dead. That's no exaggeration, Aaron."

We were about to turn onto Seawall Boulevard when Cisco Napolitano's red-and-black Rocket 88, the top down, came around the corner.

"Stop!" Valerie said.

"What for?"

"I want to tell her something."

"Tell her what?"

"Did you see the way those men looked at me? I want to take a bath. She's in the middle of all this, but she never has to pay a price. She also has a way of showing up when you're around. Now stop the car."

"Take it easy, Valerie."

"She wants to get her hooks into you. I'm sick of these people."

I slowed in the middle of the street. So did Cisco. Her shades were pushed up on her head, her face windburned. "What are you doing here?" she asked.

Before I could answer, Valerie leaned across me so she could speak out the window. "We just left the collection of trash you hang out with," she said. "When we first got here, they were talking about you. I don't know what they were saying, exactly, but they were laughing. If I were you, I'd find another sandbox."

"Nice try, honey," Cisco said.

"Yeah?" Valerie said. "Try this on for size. They said Merton Jenks got in your bread when he was a cop in Nevada. Maybe they just made that up."

Cisco's face drained. Valerie shot her the finger and then mouthed the word "you." I drove away before anything else could happen.

"I can't believe you did that."

"Stay away from her, Aaron. I don't want you around her." She laid her head back on the seat and shut her eyes. "I love the smell of the Gulf and the sound of the waves crashing on the sand. Do you want to go swimming? Out past the jetty, maybe all the way to the third sandbar?"

"We didn't bring our swimsuits."

"We can go to the end of the island. Nobody is there this time of day."

"Hammerheads and jellyfish are."

"I don't care," she said. "Do you like her?"

"Miss Cisco?"

"Yeah, do you have a thing for her?"

"Not at all," I lied, unwilling to admit my fascination with her and my hope that she was a better person than others thought.

"Yes, you do. You think she's good. She's not. She's evil. She'll try to destroy us."

"I don't think that's true at all."

She took her hand from mine and stared out the window. When I asked her if she still wanted to swim at the far end of the island, she didn't reply. She did not speak again until we were on the highway and headed back to Houston.

THE NEXT DAY Saber showed up at the filling station wearing drapes instead of jeans, shined patent-leather stomps rather than his half-top boots with chains on the sides, his crew cut tonicked and combed back on the sides. He lit a cigarette with a Japanese lighter I had never seen, one with an image of Mount Fuji carved on the leather case.

"Where'd you get the new threads?" I said.

"At a store on Congress Street," he said, looking sideways at the street. "They've got Mr. C shirts, too, the ones with the big upturned collars."

"Why not wear a sign that says Arrest Me?" I asked.

There were circles under his eyes. He kept blinking, like a caffeine addict. He released his cigarette smoke a mouthful at a time. I wondered when he'd had his last full night's sleep.

"I squared a beef for us," he said.

We were standing under the rain shed that covered the fuel pumps. I looked over my shoulder to see if anyone was within earshot. "I don't know if I want to hear this."

"I think you'll enjoy it. We boosted Vick Atlas's Buick. He had a security box around the ignition, so Manny's uncle let us use his tow truck and we lifted it out of the driveway." He grinned with self-satisfaction, waiting for me to react.

I folded my arms on my chest. I couldn't look at him. "When?"

"Last night. A broad in a garage apartment off Montrose hauls his ashes. I wrote 'Blow me, Fudd' in chalk on the driveway."

"Put it back. Or dump it somewhere he can find it," I said.

He nodded. "Makes sense. Steal the car of the guy who tried to send us to Gatesville, then return it. Should I leave an apology?"

"Valerie and I 'fronted his old man in Galveston yesterday. They're going to think we did it."

He looked down the street at the cars passing on either side of the boulevard. He puffed on his cigarette. I wanted to hit him. Instead I took the cigarette from his fingers and mashed it out with my foot and threw it into the oil barrel that served as our trash can.

"There's another reason I'm here," he said. "We stripped the Buick before we passed it on to a guy who's helping the economy in Juárez. That chain with rope loops in it was in the trunk. Manny wondered what it was."

"I don't care about Manny. Why are you telling me this?"

"Manny and Cholo don't know the Buick belongs to Vick Atlas. See, I'm what they call a spotter. I find the kind of car somebody wants. Then we go to work. The situation might get a little touchy if they find out they boosted a set of wheels owned by somebody in the Atlas family."

"I don't know what to say."

He started to take another cigarette out of his pack, then put it back. "Remember when we went fishing in the surf down at Freeport? You were in waves up to your chest and hooked a devil ray that was probably three feet across. You dragged it up on the sand and went right back in. You were never afraid, Aaron. You thought you were. But you weren't."

"Walk away from these guys," I said. "We'll start over."

"I owe them money. I paid off the mortgage on our house."

"How much?"

"You don't want to know," he said. "They're muling Mexican brown from the border to San Antone and Houston."

"Heroin?"

"I stepped in a pile of shit."

His eyes glistened. I tried to put my hand on his shoulder, but he stepped away from me, trying to smile, then got into his heap and fired it up. As he bounced into the street, he gave me a thumbs-up. He went through the Stop sign as though it were not there, then floored the accelerator and disappeared into the shadows of the live oaks that arched over the boulevard.

IN THE DARWINIAN world of American high school culture, I had learned only one lesson: The lights of love and pity often died early, and many friendships were based on necessity and emotional dependency and nothing else. I had the feeling that secretly Vick Atlas and Grady Harrelson despised each other, because each saw in the other his loneliness and the abandonment by his father. In the case of Vick and Grady, however, there was another ingredient: their jealousy over the affections of Valerie Epstein.

The following day neither of my parents was home when I got off work. I bathed and put on fresh clothes and tried to think. I had said that my family didn't lie. That was true most of the time. But in an imperfect world, I figured, there were instances when a lie served virtue better than the truth. I fed Major and Bugs and Snuggs and Skippy, then pulled up a chair to the phone in the hallway and found

Vick Atlas's name in the directory. He answered on the second ring. "Hello!" he barked.

"Hey, Vick. How's it hanging?" I replied.

"Who's this?"

"Aaron Holland Broussard."

There was a pause. "What do you want, wise guy?"

"You stopped those two phony cops from hurting Valerie. I owe you one."

"You and I aren't done by a long shot. If you think you can get on my good side, forget it. You're going to be a long red scrape on the asphalt, Buster Brown."

"Maybe your father told you that Valerie and I were in his office a couple of days ago."

"You're lucky you're not on a meat hook."

"Did somebody boost your wheels two nights ago?"

The line went quiet again.

"Did you hear me?" I said.

"Keep talking."

"I was afraid you'd think it was me and Saber."

"The thought occurred to me."

"I know better."

"How about Spaceman?"

"Saber? The same with him. Would we boost your car and then call you up to tell you we didn't do it?"

"Then who did? The Montrose district is not the kind of neighborhood where you get your car hot-wired. You got a comment on that, wise guy?"

He had just set a verbal trap. The ignition had not been jumped. Vick was smarter than I thought.

"I was at Prince's drive-in last night," I said. "Some of Grady's buds were talking loud in the next car. I heard one guy say, 'Vick Atlas was getting laid when we took the Buick. He's never going to find it.'"

"Rich-boy jocks are hot-wiring cars? That's interesting to know. You're a gold mine."

"I thought I'd pass on the information. Do with it what you want."

"Why would Grady want to steal my car?"

"I don't know, Vick. Somebody stole his convertible, and maybe he thinks you had something to do with it."

"No Kewpie doll, earwax."

"Sorry I bothered you," I said. "By the way, your car wasn't hot-wired. Not according to these guys. It had some kind of box around the back of the ignition switch."

I could hear him breathing against the surface of the receiver. "So how'd they steal it, pinhead?"

"Search me."

"No, not *search* you, *fuck* you. A lot of cars have security boxes, toe cheese."

"They said they wrote a message on the driveway that would really get to you. I think it was 'Blow me' or 'Blow me, Elmer Fudd.' Something like that. They said they wrote it in chalk. They thought it was a howl."

I could almost feel his body heat coming through the receiver. "That cocksucker," he said.

"I was trying to do the right thing. I'm sorry I upset you, Vick. I like all the things you called me. One day I might want to be a writer. You've given me a lot of material."

The line went dead.

Chapter 23

RODEO PEOPLE REFER to the two-week period before July Fourth and the two-week period following it as Christmastime. That's when the circuit opens up, and the country remembers a bit of its origins, and the big prize money awaits any cowboy willing to go the longest eight seconds in the world. In Houston the rodeo and the fair and livestock show were grand events. Bottle rockets exploding above the fairgrounds, the Ferris wheel printed against the sky, the smell of caramel corn and hot dogs and cotton candy, the music of the carousel, the popping of the shooting gallery, the spielers in front of the sideshow, a fire-eater blowing clouds of flaming kerosene from his mouth, bull riders eating steak sandwiches under an awning snapping with wind, all the riders wearing butterfly chaps and big-roweled spurs strapped on their boots. For me these images could have fallen from the painting on the ceiling of the Sistine Chapel, but I doubted they would ever be recognized as such.

I took Valerie on the Ferris wheel, which was like rising into the stars, even better, because when the gondola halted at the top to let on more passengers, the whole world seemed to drop away from us, the gondola swaying, the people on the ground no more than stick figures, all of our problems trapped down below us, as though we were cupped inside a divine hand. I hung my arm over her shoulder.

"You said Miss Napolitano would try to destroy us. It's the other way around. She sees herself in you. She believes Jaime Atlas was forcing Mr. Harrelson and Grady to give us a bad time because Saber and I hurt Vick."

"This woman wants to be me?" Valerie asked. "Where did you get this brilliant insight?"

"You're everything she's not. You're admired and loved by others. She's not. She's used by the scum of the earth. You know what the big mystery is, the one I think no one can figure out?"

"No, what is it, Mr. Smarty-Pants?"

"Why a girl like you goes steady with the likes of me."

She tried to look serious, but I saw her eyes crinkle at the corners.

"When people ask me, I tell people you not only have poor vision but you're a terrible judge of character," I said.

She laughed this time. And what a laugh she had. It was like the way she chewed gum. It was an expression of joy.

We ate hamburgers and went to the livestock show. Twice I thought I saw a hulking man in a fedora following us. I sat down on a bench by the entrance to the Coliseum while Valerie looked for the ladies' room. I was staring at the tips of my cowboy boots when I felt the weight of a big man ease down on the bench. I didn't need to look up to know who he was. I could see the Pall Mall cigarette protruding from his cupped fingers; I could also smell his odor, a portable fog of nicotine and harsh soap and breath mints or antiperspirant that didn't work.

"Good evening to you, Detective Jenks," I said.

"You riding this weekend?" he asked.

"Yes, sir, tomorrow. I drew a bull named Original Sin."

"You riding in the junior division?"

"I lied about my age. I'll be with the regulars."

"Is Miss Valerie with you?"

"You should know. You've been following us for the last hour."

"I must be slipping," he said.

"You're a head taller than everybody else."

"I have some information on those two gunsels who terrorized

Miss Valerie. They were running a couple of floating craps games and not piecing off the action. That's what probably got them killed."

"It didn't have anything to do with Vick Atlas or Grady Harrelson?" I said.

"These sons of bitches don't need much reason to kill each other." He coughed and took a small bottle wrapped in a paper bag from his coat pocket and drank from it. He seemed to take strength or comfort from it. "This here is codeine. We used to call it GI gin. It clears the pipes."

"What do you want from us, sir?"

"I've got people on my back. Clint Harrelson got blown into his swimming pool in the richest section of River Oaks. The neighbors are not happy with the notion that his killer might be living close by."

"What does that have to do with us?" I said.

"Maybe everything, maybe nothing. The truth is, I'm not sure who you are, son. I talked to your family physician."

"Our family physician? He's a quack who sent my mother to electroshock."

"He says you have a memory disorder just like you told me, except more serious. He says it's like an alcoholic blackout without the alcohol, which means the person having the blackout can do a lot more damage than a drunk person can. Does that seem a fair assessment of your spells?"

"You think I shot Mr. Harrelson?"

"It seems your whole family has shot somebody. I got to have a talk with Miss Valerie, too."

He dropped his cigarette and covered it on the ground with his shoe. Through the entranceway, I could see the sawdust on the Coliseum floor and the animals in their pens and the lights burning overhead. I wanted to be among them, in the smell of wood chips and dung and ammonia and animal feed in the bins. "Sir, I can't begin to fathom your reasoning. People like Vick and Jaime Atlas and Grady and his friends are on the street, and you're questioning Valerie?"

"Grady Harrelson says he was sailboating down by Kemah the night his father was killed. Valerie's neighbors say Grady was at her house that evening."

I felt the air go out of my chest. "Maybe they got their dates mixed up."

"No, they're aware who Grady is and who his father was. They have no doubt about the date."

"That doesn't make sense to me."

"Because Valerie didn't tell you Grady was at her house?"

I couldn't look at him. "Maybe she wasn't home. Maybe Grady came by and left."

"No, she was home that night," he said. "All the lights were on. Three neighbors gave the same account."

I saw Valerie coming through the crowd in her cotton skirt and tennis shoes and denim shirt sewn with cactus flowers. I stood up, as I was always taught to do when a woman approached me. She was smiling, obviously unsure what Detective Jenks was doing there. He stood up, too, offering the place where he had been sitting. She sat down between us. He told her the same thing he had told me. She gazed at the animals inside the Coliseum, showing no reaction while he talked.

"I don't remember what happened or who I saw that evening," she said after he finished.

"You don't keep track of who comes by your house? The same night your ex-boyfriend's old man is murdered?"

"I stopped seeing Grady, even though he called regularly."

"Your neighbors gave us false information?"

"Ask them."

"I did. That's why I'm here," Jenks said. "Don't try to vex me, Miss Valerie."

"You're being victimized by a seventeen-year-old high school student?" she said.

"That's why I used the word 'vex.' You're an expert at it, missy."

"Was Grady at Kemah or not?" I asked Jenks. But my heart wasn't in the question. I believed what Jenks had said. Grady had been at Valerie's house and she hadn't told me. I felt a chasm opening under my feet.

Jenks coughed as though he had a wishbone in his throat. He put another cigarette into his mouth. "Sounds like somebody is lying. Who's lying, Miss Valerie?"

"I don't have any comment," she replied, turning up her nose.

Jenks lit his cigarette, blowing smoke straight out in front of him. He rubbed his mouth with the back of his wrist.

"Those things will flat kill you, sir," I said.

"No, you kids will. You're a goddamn morning-to-night pain in the ass."

"It's impolite to swear in a lady's presence," I said.

"One or both y'all is on the edge of committing a felony," he said. "It's called aiding and abetting after the fact."

He stood up. His face looked gray, tired, his long nose tubular like a teardrop, his skin rough as emery paper. He dropped his cigarette to the ground and stepped on it, but not before I saw the blood stippled on the butt.

"Miss Valerie, if you're covering up for Grady Harrelson, you're making the worst mistake of your life," he said. "And you, Aaron Holland Broussard, are acting like you were hiding behind a cloud when God passed out the brains. Don't let that punk con you. You're a hundred times the man he is. What's the name of that bull you drew?"

"Original Sin."

"Hope you have a soft landing."

He walked into the crowd, his fedora low on his brow, his coat covering the badge on his belt and his holstered snub-nose, his massive shoulders and confident walk a poor disguise for the death he carried in his lungs.

VALERIE AND I WALKED up and down the aisles among the livestock stalls and poultry and rabbit cages, neither looking at the other. I felt a sense of betrayal that was like a flame burning through the center of a sheet of paper, the circle spreading outward, curling the paper into carbon. If you grow up in an alcoholic home, you learn a lesson that never leaves you: The need to satisfy the addiction comes first; everything else is secondary. Daily betrayal becomes a way of life.

We stopped in front of a stall where a huge York/Hamp sow was nursing a row of pink-and-gray piglets. I always loved animals. My favorite story in the Old Testament was the account of Noah and the Flood, which I believed then and believe now is deliberately misinterpreted by both Hebrews and Christians. In the antediluvian world, man was told by Yahweh that the stone knife should not break the skin of an animal. The first creatures loaded on the Ark were not people but animals who marched two by two into their new home made of gopher wood. When the earth was washed clean and the archer's bow was hung in the heavens, man was made a steward, not an exploiter, and was not allowed to harm his charges. I wanted to tell these things to Valerie. But I couldn't. I believed she had cut loose her boat from mine and was floating toward a place where Grady Harrelson waited for her.

"Why did you lie for him?" I said.

"I didn't lie for him," she said. "I just didn't offer information that would hurt him."

"It's called a lie of omission."

She folded her arms on top of the stall's gate and fixed her eyes on the mama hog feeding her babies. "Grady is a child inside. I never should have gone out with him. I knew it was never going anywhere."

"Then why did you?"

"Because the boy I loved and wanted to marry got killed in Korea."

A man and woman close by looked at us, then glanced away. Valerie kept closing and opening her hands, her eyes flashing. Children were running up and down the aisle with balloons, their shoes splattered with sawdust and the runoff from the stalls. My head was reeling from the smell of ammonia and the sense that either Valerie was a stranger or I was driven by the same kind of jealousy I found so odious in others. The couple standing close by walked away.

"Why didn't you tell me you covered up for him?" I asked.

"I know what obstruction of justice is. I didn't want to make you party to it. Why do you think Jenks said you're a hundred times the man Grady is?"

"He thinks I feel inferior to a guy like that?"

"Yes, that's exactly what he thinks. So don't act like it."

"Put it on another level," I said. "What if Grady isn't an innocent player in his father's death?"

"That's silly," she replied.

"Who broke the neck of the Mexican girl, Wanda Estevan? She didn't do it to herself."

I saw her cheeks color, her nostrils flare. It wasn't from anger, either. I knew fear when I saw it, particularly in a person who was rarely afraid.

"Grady wouldn't do that," she said.

"Remember what you said to him when you threw his senior ring in his face at the drive-in? You called him cruel. You also warned me about what he and his friends could do to me. You had it right, Val. Grady and all his friends are cruel, and they're cruel for one reason only, just like Mr. Krauser was: They know they're unloved and they're frauds and others are about to catch on to them."

I started to say more. I believed that Valerie thought her father capable of killing Mr. Harrelson and she didn't want to see an innocent person blamed for his death. But this time I kept my observations to myself.

"So you know all this, do you?" she asked, her face in a pout.

"Yes, I do, because I grew up scared, just like Grady, and for the same reasons. But I'm not like that anymore. My life changed because of one person, and that's the one I'm with now, the most beautiful girl in Texas. Now let's go see what all these animals have to say about it."

CONTRARY TO MY demeanor, I wasn't done with fear. That night I dreamed of bulls. There is no more dangerous event at a rodeo than bull riding, and in the days before padded vests and helmets with face guards, it was even more lethal. You can get hooked, ruptured, tangled up and dragged, stomped into marmalade, and flung into the boards. A bull can corkscrew, spin like a top, stand up on his front legs with his back feet seven feet in the air, levitate straight off the turf, buck you on his horns, and as an afterthought, break your neck or snap your spine. He can reconfigure the entire muscular network along the backbone from eight to eleven inches so the back is not going in the same direction as the feet. Imagine driving a truck along the edge of a cliff at high speed while the wheels are coming off the axles, the brakes are failing, the gears are stripping, and the windshield is coming apart in your face.

Original Sin was notorious. He hooked a rider in Amarillo and crushed a clown in San Angelo and crashed over the boards into the stands in Big D. I woke up in a ball at two in the morning, shaking from a bad dream. I sat on the side of the bed and tried to clear my mind. The dream was not about Original Sin. I had dreamed of Detective Merton Jenks. In the dream Merton Jenks had become me, or I had become Merton Jenks, and one or both of us was about to die. The dream told me something else, too. The breath I drew into my lungs and took for granted was for him a second-by-second ordeal as well as a luxury he was about to lose. He had survived commando raids in Yugoslavia and parachuting behind German lines in France only to die a painful and humiliating death from the Pall Mall cigarettes. Jesus didn't pass by the blind man on the road when all the travelers did. I felt Merton Jenks was the blind man. In my foolish mind, I wanted to do something to help him.

The light in the bathroom was on, the door half open. My father was sitting on the edge of the tub, smoking a cigarette.

"Can't sleep?" I said.

"I snore. I thought I'd give your mother some rest," he replied.

It wasn't true, of course. Like all depressives, my father suffered from insomnia; he also needed his nicotine, just as he needed his alcohol. I wanted to tell him of my feelings, but I never did, because I knew I would only add to his pain. Instead I told him of my anxiety about easing down in the chute onto the back of Original Sin, eighteen hundred pounds of black lethality.

"I'll be sitting in the stands," he said.

"Mother's not coming?"

"You know how she is. She doesn't like crowds."

"She doesn't like being among what she calls common people."

"People have their quirks. It's what makes us human. If we ignore other people's faults, we don't have to be defensive about our own."

In all my years of growing up, I never heard him speak unkindly or critically of my mother, no matter how harshly she spoke of him.

"I was scared about riding Original Sin, but I dreamed about Detective Jenks," I said. "Now I feel all right. Why's that?"

"Because when we think about other people's problems, our own don't seem so important."

"I have a feeling he still has a crush on Miss Cisco."

"The woman from Nevada? That's one person you need to forget, Aaron. Just like we need to get the Harrelson and Atlas families out of our lives."

"Who do you reckon killed Mr. Harrelson?"

"Somebody cut from the same cloth he was. Somebody who's hateful and twisted and thinks he's the left hand of God."

He dropped his cigarette hissing into the toilet bowl.

"You think Mr. Epstein could have done it?" I asked.

"Is he capable of killing someone? I'd say yes. Would he shoot an unarmed old man? I doubt it. It's someone else's grief. Don't make it your own, Aaron."

"It's hard not to do sometimes."

"I know," he said.

Chapter 24

I DID NOT TAKE my father's advice about not meddling. Early the next morning I drove to Grady Harrelson's house and knocked on the door. When no one answered, I knocked harder. Grady opened the door in a blue silk Japanese bathrobe covered with green dragons. He was unshaved and bleary-eyed and not happy to be awakened. "What's your fucking problem, Broussard?"

"My fucking problem?" I said. "Let me see. The fact that you lied to the cops about your whereabouts the night your father was murdered? The fact that Valerie covered for you and got herself in trouble? No, that's not really what's on my mind. Can you get me in touch with Cisco Napolitano?"

"Why would Cisco be interested in seeing you?"

"A friend of hers is dying. I want to tell her that."

"What friend?" he asked.

"What do you care? Try not being a shit all the time, Grady. Do a good deed."

He tried to grab me by the shirt. "You listen—"

"Touch me again and I'll rip your hand off and shove it down your throat," I said.

Behind him, I could see a girl standing at the top of the stairs. She was barefoot and in a slip, and I could see only her knees. Her skin was brown, her knees puckered. Even though I could not see the rest of her, I felt that somehow she was innocent and out of place in Grady's home. "Go back to bed," he shouted at her.

"Who's the girl?" I said.

"You're always asking questions. A friend. It's not Cisco, if that's what you're thinking."

"I knew that," I said.

He gave me a look. His breath was sour, the whites of his eyes filled with broken capillaries. "Come in. I want to ask you something."

"About what?"

"Vick Atlas."

"I don't want to talk about Vick Atlas."

"Help me, I'll help you," he said.

I stepped inside. He closed the door behind me, the crystal droplets on the chandelier jingling. I followed him to the kitchen. I had a hard time believing he had asked me in. I had taken his girl and hit him in the face and was convinced he bore me nothing but ill will. "I'm sorry about your father," I said to his back.

"He had the last laugh."

"Pardon?"

"My old man put everything in a trust. I get a subsistence allowance until I'm forty. It's like having someone will you a box of diapers. Sit down." He poured water into a coffeepot and dumped the grinds in the water and set the pot on a burner. "Did Vick sic those hoods on Valerie so he could show up and be a hero?"

"Ask him," I replied.

"He swears he had nothing to do with it. I don't know what to believe. The Atlas family is a bunch of psychopaths. They lie when they don't have to lie. I don't even know what country they're from. They look like they're glued together from other people's body parts. My father said they brag on murders they didn't commit."

"So why'd you get mixed up with them?"

"Money is money. You either have it or you don't. If you don't, you get to cut other people's lawns. You're a smart guy. You believe the shit you read in the newspaper? Those guys write what they're told to write. Same thing with business and politics. It's a stage play put on for the little people."

He took a bottle of milk from the refrigerator and a box of cereal from a cabinet. I began to get the feeling that he hadn't asked me inside to talk about the Atlas family.

"Tell me the truth about something, Broussard. You and Bledsoe stole my convertible, didn't you? If you did, I don't blame you. I gave you guys a bad time."

"I don't steal cars."

"Bledsoe did it?"

"I'm not my brother's keeper."

He poured milk into the cereal and sat down. "You want some?"

"No. Who's the girl upstairs?"

"A Mexican girl. What do you care?"

"Because you're acting rude to her."

"Jesus Christ," he said. He got up and walked to the bottom of the staircase and yelled upstairs. "Sophia, you want something to eat?" There was no answer. He returned to the table. "You really have spells?" he said. "People say you have a few beers, or something doesn't go right, and you wander off and do shit you can't control."

"Must be somebody else," I said.

He studied my face, milk and cereal running off his spoon as he put it into his mouth. "My father was putting three hundred grand into a new casino in Vegas. Then he started having reservations about dealing with greaseballs. When you and I got into it, he told the greaseballs they needed to straighten you out and, more important, straighten out Valerie's old man. He froze the funds, and I got no idea where they are."

Through the French doors of the breakfast room, I could see the empty swimming pool and the harshness of the light on the concrete patio and the spartan deck furniture and the potted plants that hadn't been watered and were starting to turn brown.

"What do you want me to do about it?" I asked.

"Your uncle is mobbed up, a business partner with Frankie Carbo," he replied.

"My uncle is a prizefight promoter."

"Do I have to say it again? He knows Frankie Carbo. Do you know how many people Frankie Carbo has killed? I want that money. Frankie Carbo can get it back for me."

"So your father dumped all this trouble on us so he could work out his situation with the Mafia?"

"That's the kind of great guy he was. Plus, he didn't like you getting the best of me."

"What do I get out of this besides the whereabouts of Miss Cisco?" I asked.

"Your friend Bledsoe is running with some drug dealers. I can have them put out of business."

"I don't want to have anything to do with your lowlife friends, and I'm not going to approach my uncle for you, either."

"Suit yourself."

"How about a phone number for Miss Cisco?"

He wiped at his nose. "If you think you're going to melt her heart, forget it. Behind those king-size jugs is an iceberg."

"I'm doing this for someone else, Grady, not myself."

He took a pencil and a piece of paper from a drawer and wrote on it and handed it to me. I folded the number and put it into my pocket. I could see the bare feet of the girl in the slip halfway up the stairs. I wanted to have one more try at his conscience, and I wasn't thinking just about the girl up the staircase but the girl whose neck had been broken two blocks from Loren's burned car. "Why do you like Mexican girls?"

"Give it a rest, Dr. Freud."

"I think Wanda Estevan's death was probably an accident. Why not own up to it and be done?"

He massaged the back of his neck, widening and closing his eyes as though still waking up. He drank a mouthful of coffee straight from the pot, the grinds congealing on his lips. He leaned toward me. "You ask me why I like Mexican girls? They know when to close their mouths and when to open wide. Got it?"

"You're a special kind of guy, Grady. Keep your seat. I'll let myself out."

I didn't call Cisco Napolitano. I used the crisscross directory at the city library and found her address. She lived in the same apartment building in the Montrose district that Vick Atlas did. But I had spent enough time on other people's problems for the day. That evening I would be busting out of the chute on top of Original Sin.

THE STANDS WERE packed with people in their best cotton dresses and starched jeans and short-sleeved shirts. The building hummed with a steady drone, like a beehive. I was behind the chutes, with all the riders milling about. It was a brotherhood not quite like any other. Most of them were from Texas, Oklahoma, Wyoming, Montana, or Canada. No matter their origins, they all seemed to have the same adenoidal accents. They looked sculpted from oak. They were also duck-footed, as though unaccustomed to walking on level ground. I wore chaps, like everyone else, except mine had no fringe and were one color, a sun-faded yellowish brown, because they had been worn by my grandfather as an old man. I had one hour to wait before I would be climbing over the top of the chute and easing down onto Original Sin's back. In the past hour, I had been to the men's room three times.

Valerie was sitting with some of her 4-H friends on the other side of the arena, but I didn't see my father. He always sat in the same places when he attended public events. He sat behind first base at baseball games; he sat in the last pew at Mass; he sat in the last seat of the row at the movie theater; he sat by the rail at horse shows; and he sat ten rows behind the chutes at any rodeo I participated in. I looked up into the stands and didn't see him anywhere. There were only a few empty spaces in the seats, and most were taken by people who had gone to the concessions. I felt my heart go weak, my resolve begin to drain. Then I saw him escorting my mother down the steps toward two empty seats. She was wearing white gloves and a pillbox hat with the veil turned up. I waved at them, but they couldn't see me inside the shadows.

I also saw Saber and Manny and Cholo. Saber waved at me and I waved back. His two friends were eating barbecue sandwiches, licking the sauce off their fingers. I went to the restroom. In the concourse, a black man had set up a shoeshine stand with elevated chairs, and a bunch of rodeo boys from the little town of Tomball were getting their boots shined, eyeballing the girls, smoking hand-rolled cigarettes, while the shine man popped his rag to the R&B coming out of his portable radio. It should have been an idyllic scene, the kind you saw on the cover of *The Saturday Evening Post.* It wasn't.

A group of North Houston hoods, wearing drapes, pointy-toed stomps with taps, and greased duck-ass haircuts, sauntered by in what was called the con walk—the shoulders slouched, the length of the stride exaggerated, arms dead at their sides. I saw Loren Nichols among them, wearing cowboy boots and jeans, although low on the hips and without a belt, greaser-style. Just as they passed the shoeshine stand, one of the boys from Tomball went "Quack, quack."

It was the kind of moment that would not pass. There was no way the insult and the challenge would be undone. The groups despised each other, worse than whites and people of color or Hispanics did, and if you asked them why, they would not be able to explain except to say, "They're always asking for it, man."

Loren went into the men's room by himself. I followed him inside and stood one urinal down from him. He hadn't noticed me and was looking back at the entrance to the room while he relieved himself.

"Hey," I said.

"Is that you, Broussard? You look good in that hat and chaps," he said.

"I'm riding in a few minutes. Loren, get away from those guys."

"Which guys?"

"The hoods you're with."

"Those are my friends. Don't be calling them names."

"Okay, I won't. I know those kids at the shoeshine stand. They're from Tomball. They don't mean anything. Blow it off."

"They *do* mean it."

"Don't get into it, man," I said. "It's not worth it."

"It's not my call."

I zipped up my pants and washed my hands and went to the lavatory where he was combing his hair in the mirror. I took out my wallet. "I have two passes, reserved seats. They were for Valerie and a friend, but she went in with her 4-H clubbers. You take them."

"No, man."

"Yes, man," I said. I punched him in the sternum with my finger.

"You worry too much, Broussard."

"Don't call me by my last name."

"Okay, Aaron. You're from outer space. But you're not a bad guy." He took the tickets from my hand.

"I'd better see your butt in one of those seats," I said.

"What are you riding?"

"Bulls."

"I knew you were suicidal." He held up the tickets. "Thanks."

I walked out of the men's room ahead of him and didn't look back. His friends were gathered at a concession about twenty yards from the shoeshine stand. None of them had bought anything. They seemed to be waiting on Loren. I walked through the concourse and a security gate and past the rough-stock pen into the loading area behind the chutes. I looked up into the stands and tried to locate my parents but couldn't see them in the glare. But I saw Manny, a smirk on his face. He stood up and shot me the bone, then cupped his phallus. Behind me, I heard one of the bulls tearing the chute apart.

When I lowered myself down onto Original Sin, my teeth were clicking so loudly I was sure the gate man could hear them. I pulled the bull rope tight and felt Original Sin swell like a thunderstorm between my thighs, then crash against both sides of the chute; I touched my holy medal with my left hand, said the first words of a Hail Mary under my breath, then couldn't remember the rest of the prayer and hollered, "Outside!"

The gate swung open. Original Sin and I burst out of the shadows into a world of blazing spotlights, bullfighters in football cleats and outrageous costumes and clown grease, the metal bell clanging on the bull rope, Original Sin slamming down on all four feet, bending my spine like a bicycle chain about to snap, the shock so hard I believed I was ruptured, all the while my spurs raking at Original Sin's neck, my head stretched back to his rump.

The bullfighters seemed to be rotating around me, the spotlights an eye-searing blur, my chaps flapping, my buttocks starting to slip sideways with each bounce as I waited to hear the buzzer and didn't. I thought I heard my father say *Hold on, son. The bull hasn't been born you can't ride.* Original Sin corkscrewed and reversed his spin. For just a second I saw the other riders up on the boards, their faces full of alarm; I felt blood on my face and knew I had been hooked and was about to go over the side; I also knew my left arm was hung up and there was a good chance I would be rope-dragged under Original Sin's hooves or impaled and whipped like a rag doll.

But it didn't happen. I heard the buzzer like the voice of God. Then I was flung through the air, my arm free of the rope, and even though I crashed to the ground on my side, I knew I was in one piece and the bullfighters were diverting Original Sin away from me. My hat was still on my head, the slice below my eye a badge of honor, the audience applauding and shouting and coming to their feet, the other riders dusting me off and patting my back and saying things like "One hell of a ride, kid" and "Casey Tibbs better look out."

But I was disqualified. I had touched the bull during the ride with my free hand on the first bounce out of the chute. It wasn't important, though. Earning the approval of professional rodeo people is reward enough. A medic cleaned the cut on my face and put a bandage on it. "Get yourself some stitches or you'll have a scar," he said.

I heard a sound outside the arena, somewhere down the concourse by the concessions. At first it was a single scream, perhaps a woman's, then the sound began to grow like a wind swirling through a woods, gaining strength, gathering organic debris in its maw. These are the words I could hear people saying:

"Stabbed."

"How many?"

"*Who* was stabbed?"

"A lady out there said it was her son."

"Somebody's dead?"

"It ain't for sure."

"I hope they kill the bunch who done it."

"A boy pulled a stiletto, one of those Italian kind. That's what they're saying."

With a three-inch square of gauze taped on my face, I went out in the concourse and headed toward the crowd that had formed around the shoeshine stand. I stepped up on the railing behind the stadium seating so I could see over their heads. A blond kid in jeans and a cowboy shirt and a crew cut, his hat stuffed under his head, was lying on his back, his shirt open, the cellophane from a cigarette package pasted over the wound below his left nipple. Two ambulance attendants were trying to push a gurney through the crowd. An open switchblade, its wavy surfaces rippling with light and streaks of red like fingernail polish, lay on the concrete. Loren's greaseball friends were lined up and leaning on their arms against the wall while three uniformed cops shook them down, kicking their ankles apart, ripping their pockets inside out, splattering coins and keys and a couple of knives onto the concrete. I didn't see Loren among them.

A soapy wine-colored bubble formed on the boy's lips. A woman who must have been his mother was inconsolable. She beat her fists on a man's chest as he tried to calm her. One of the boy's hands was gripped on the wrist of a man in slacks and a clip-on bow tie and a white shirt kneeling beside him, a Bible held open by his thumb. The boy's face was drained of all color; there was a dark triangle in his jeans where he had soiled himself. The attendants got through the crowd just as the boy looked straight into the ceiling and stopped breathing, as though someone had pulled a plug loose from the back of his head.

Everyone in the crowd became silent, even those who could not see what was happening. They all seemed to sense at the same time that the boy had died. I stepped off the rail into the crowd. A man in front of me whispered to a friend, "Back home, this wouldn't make the jailhouse."

Someone touched me on the back. It was Loren Nichols. "What happened?" he said.

I didn't answer. I grabbed his upper arm and pulled him with me toward the men's room. He tried to free himself, craning his head to see over the crowd. "Answer me, Aaron. What's going on?"

"One of those boys from Tomball is dead. Where were you?"

"In the seats. A girl and I used the passes you gave me. Are the cops busting somebody?"

"That's the least of it." I pushed him along the wall, away from the crowd. "Don't look up."

"What are you doing?"

"They know you. I said don't look up."

"Who knows me?"

"The cops."

"Those are my friends back there."

"Yeah, and one of them just killed a high school kid."

"Over what?"

"Nothing. Absolutely nothing. That's where all this hard-guy crap finally ends up. A kid makes some quacking noises and somebody sticks a knife in him. That was his mother screaming back there. You want to explain to her why her son is dead?"

"Lay off that. I never carry a shank."

"Yeah, but those guys do. What do you think is going to happen if the crowd gets their hands on them?"

"They're still my friends." He started to pull away from me.

"They're not your friends. They're pack animals, just like the rich kids who hang with Grady."

"I'm not like Grady Harrelson, and neither are my friends."

"Shut up."

There was a clutch of phone booths against the wall. I pushed him into one and stood in the doorway so he couldn't get out. His hair was in his eyes, his face flaming. "Let me out."

"I told you to shut up. Where's your girl?"

"In the ladies' room."

"You have wheels?"

"My brother's truck."

I took off my hat and put it on his head. "Walk with me. Look at the ground."

"Why are you doing this?"

"Because you're too dumb to take care of yourself."

"You're sure that kid is dead?"

"The knife wound was to the heart."

"Jesus. I got to get my girl."

"So she can get busted or torn apart with you?" I said.

People were streaming past us on their way toward the shoeshine stand. Through a window I saw the emergency lights on an ambulance, its siren dying as though descending into a well. I could almost smell the heat in the crowd, a collective stench that was close to feral.

"I saw one of them," someone said.

"Where?" someone else said.

"By the can. He was just here. He came in with them."

"Keep walking," I said to Loren. "Don't look back."

I squeezed his upper arm tighter, but he no longer resisted. Someone heading in the opposite direction knocked against me; he didn't apologize or even look at me but kept going, with others behind him. I could hear the mother wailing, which was drawing more and more people out of the stands into the concourse.

"I don't like running away," Loren said. "I didn't do anything wrong."

"There's another one of them!" someone yelled. "That greaser down there!"

A cop was blowing a whistle. The crowd that had been flowing past us seemed to shift into slow motion, their heads rotating slowly, their eyes coming to rest on us. I pulled Loren along with me. Up ahead was the entranceway that led to the loading area behind the chutes. "Hey, you," someone yelled. "Somebody stop that guy! That's their goddamn leader. The one with the duck-ass."

We went through the entranceway, then through a side door that opened onto an empty space with a dirt floor beneath the stadium seating. I shut the door and pulled off my boots and unbuckled my chaps and peeled them off my jeans. "Put these on. I'll get them back later. Don't let anything happen to them. They were my grandfather's."

"I ain't afraid," Loren said.

"I am," I said. "Now get these on. If you say anything back, I'm going to hit you upside the head."

The band began playing "The Eyes of Texas," then there was a great thumping that shook the floor and the girders, like elephants charging up a staircase, so thunderous it sent dust and grit cascading down on our heads. The crowd was either leaving the stands or flowing back, I couldn't tell which. Someone kicked open the door and shone a flashlight inside. Behind the glare, I could see his badge and cap and holstered revolver. "What the hell y'all doing in here?" he said.

"Taking a leak," I said. "We didn't want to go into that mob in the concourse."

"Why you got your boots off?"

"I went over the side and got dirt in them."

"Well, get finished and get out," he said. "We got a murdered boy up there. Maybe the guy who did it got away."

"How old was the boy who got knifed?" Loren asked.

Shut up, Loren.

"Seventeen, eighteen, along in there," the cop said. "He was here with his mother. You know those boys from Tomball?"

"No, sir," Loren said.

"They're good boys," the cop said. "This is a goddamn shame." He shone his light over our faces and bodies again, then clicked off the light and went away, leaving the door open. Loren's legs looked long, like stovepipes, inside Grandfather's chaps.

"Don't stop till you get to your brother's truck," I said. "Don't look around, either. No matter how bad you want to."

"Was that cop trying to say something to me?"

"No, you didn't have anything to do with it, Loren."

"That boy must have done something. Maybe he pulled a shank himself."

"Stop fooling yourself. Those kids from Tomball think a John Deere tractor exhibit in the high school gym is a big event. So is the rodeo. Their only sin is their innocence. They think a fight is with fists."

I didn't mean to make his situation worse than it was. But the disbelief and fear in the boy's face and the helplessness in his eyes were not images I would easily get rid of. Secretly I hoped Loren's friends were pounded to pulp.

"I feel bad about that kid, man," he said. "Who takes shit-kickers seriously? If I'd been there, I could have shut it down."

"Think they're worrying about you? The switchblade was on the concrete. I bet there're no prints on it. I bet it's pin-the-tail-on-the-donkey time."

"No, the guy who did it will stand up."

"Yeah, that's why they were all being cuffed," I said.

"They were?"

"Getting knocked around, too. Nobody stood up. The guy who knifed that kid was a punk."

Loren widened his eyes and looked over his shoulder. "What about my girl?"

"Those are reserved seats. I know where she'll be. I'll take her home."

"I got to say something. I went to Gatesville for almost killing a guy with a pellet pistol. He felt up my sister at her junior high picnic and had it coming, but it bothered me just the same. I ain't that kind, Aaron."

"I know that."

"How?"

"You're like me. You never gave yourself credit for anything."

He walked down the concourse, my straw hat slanted over his eyes, Grandfather's chaps swishing on his legs. No one gave him a second look. Then he was out the door and gone.

I never found his girl, but I did find Valerie, and we went up into the stands and sat with my parents. I did not tell them what I had seen in the concourse, nor did I mention Loren. The rodeo resumed, but we left early, and I had twenty-one stitches put in my face in an emergency room, and we went to a barbecue joint and ate a late dinner.

I said a silent prayer for the boy who had been murdered and tried to forget the look I saw in his eyes. After all these years, it is still with me. The look was one of regret, not because of the incautious words he may have uttered but because he had not been given time to appreciate how ephemeral life was. I thought about my father's account of the Yankee soldiers who tamped their musket stocks on the ground atop Cemetery Ridge and chanted "Fredericksburg, Fredericksburg, Fredericksburg," and I wondered if they were stained forever by their visit to the Abyss, or if they had become willing caretakers of it.

For some reason I couldn't explain, I felt I had gained a greater understanding of my father's loneliness.

Chapter 25

THE NEXT MORNING I went to Cisco Napolitano's high-rise apartment building, located on a flower-planted traffic circle in the Montrose district. When she opened the door, she was still in pajamas and not wearing makeup. She leaned against the jamb. I could see the tops of her breasts, but she didn't seem to care. I wasn't even sure she was going to speak. "What's the haps, kid?" she said.

"No haps."

She didn't invite me in. Her face looked older, dry, on the edge of flaking, her eyes red-rimmed and set more deeply, as though she were staring out of a mask.

"May I come in?" I said.

"May I? That's why I love you. Yes, you may come in, you little honey bunny."

I wondered if she had crashed and burned on some toxic goofballs. She closed the door behind me and pointed at the bandage below my eye. "You get out of line with what's-her-name?"

"Valerie? We don't have that kind of relationship."

"You got hurt at the rodeo?"

"I went to the buzzer, but I got disqualified."

"Let me get dressed. I'm a little sick this morning. I'd like you to drive me somewhere."

The curtains were closed, the ornateness of the room suffused with a warm yellow light that accentuated its colors and clutter of Oriental and Arabian-style furnishings. "I came here to tell you about Detective Jenks," I said.

"Him again?"

"I think he's got emphysema or cancer in his lungs. I think he's going down for the count."

She was looking through a crack in the curtains at the traffic circle or the flowers inside it or the cars on the street. "Why tell me about it?"

"Because I know y'all were an item in Reno or Las Vegas. I think he's a good fellow in spite of his redneck manners."

"You have your nose in too many things. Where'd you come up with this emphysema stuff?"

"He sounds like he has metal filings in his chest, and there's blood on his cigarette butts."

"Let me tell you something about Merton Jenks, kid."

"Can you call me Aaron?"

"Merton was undercover vice in Vegas. Believe me, he fit right in. Catch my meaning?"

She waited. When I didn't answer, she said, "He gave me up in court. I spent eleven months in county jail as a material witness. I'm lucky I wasn't killed."

"Maybe that's why you bother him."

"You're a laugh a minute."

"Where are we going?"

"To La Farmacia, in the Fifth Ward, honey bunny. I've got a mean case of something." She paused, her face empty. "Merton's really going under?"

"What do I know?"

She closed and opened her eyes as though she had lost the thread of the conversation. I could not remember if I had ever seen her arms uncovered. I knew the signs. Drugs were just starting their journey from the slums and the border to middle-class neighborhoods throughout America. The culture had always been in Houston in cosmetic form.

Hoods put lighter fluid on a folded handkerchief and walked around sniffing it, both for show and for a 3.2 high. Sometimes there were reefers at a gig. Shit-kickers had been rolling Zig-Zags since they were knee-high to a tree frog. But smack or H or horse or joy juice or tar or China pearl, as we called it indiscriminately, was the dragon just firing up.

Miss Cisco went into the bedroom to dress. Her drawstring bag was on the table by the window. I had never looked into a woman's purse without permission. The drawstring was loose, the top of the bag drooping over. I put my little finger inside and widened the opening. I was sure I'd find her works—a spoon or a hypodermic needle or a rubber tourniquet, at least a cigarette lighter. Wrong. Among her cosmetics and Kleenexes and wallet and car keys and loose change was an army .45 automatic, the same 1911 model my father had purchased when he thought we were in danger, the same-caliber weapon that killed Grady Harrelson's father.

I stepped back from the bag and folded my arms across my chest, as though I could undo the discovery I had just made.

"What are you doing?" Miss Cisco said.

"Pardon?"

"Are you looking at the flowers in the traffic circle?" she asked. "I water them sometimes."

She walked toward me. Closer. Then closer. She had put on a long-sleeved magenta rayon shirt that seemed to change in the light, and a pair of khakis that had pockets all over them, and unzipped soft-leather, half-topped boots with white socks that a little girl might wear. I stepped backward.

"Hold still," she said, her eyes a few inches from mine. She peeled the bandage halfway off my skin and kissed the stitched star-shaped puncture that Original Sin had left with his horn. She smoothed the gauze and tape back into place. She had brushed her teeth or used mouthwash; her eyes were hazy, iniquitous.

"You use redwings?" I said.

"Is that what you call them here?"

"They'll melt your head," I said.

"You like me?"

"Sure," I said.

"How much?"

"I came to see you, didn't I?"

"Why?"

"Because I don't think you have any other friends. Because I wanted to help Detective Jenks."

She leaned forward and put her mouth on mine. I stepped backward, knocking into the table.

"Don't worry," she said.

"About what?"

"What you're thinking." She picked up her bag, disconcerted. "If you didn't have a girlfriend, maybe it'd be different. The French call it a transition, from the mother to the girlfriend. Why were you looking in my bag?"

"I didn't mean to."

"Don't lie, Aaron. You wonder why I carry a gun?"

"No," I lied.

"Grady's father committed three million to a consortium. It's bottled up in banks somewhere. That money was not only pledged, it's already been spent on two casinos under construction. You think the guys in Kansas City and Chicago are going to let a spoiled shit like Grady keep it?"

"What does that have to do with you?" I asked.

"I'm supposed to get it back."

"With your looks and brains, Miss Cisco, you could be a movie star. Why do you hang around with troglodytes?"

"Because I don't want acid thrown in my face."

I tried to follow her logic and my head began hurting. She brushed the hair out of my eyes, studying my features as though putting makeup on someone. It was obvious that I would never understand her frame of reference or the world she lived in. "I think I should leave, Miss Cisco."

"You can drive my Rocket 88, every teenage boy's wet dream. I think I'll put back the seat and sleep. I'm not myself right now."

"Why are we going to this Farmacia place?"

"It's where I get well. I need you to help me. Don't argue."

"I won't."

"Hold still." She cupped her hand on the back of my neck and bit softly into my neck, then released me.

"Why did you do that?"

"I'm perverse," she said. Then she winked. "Tell me I didn't give you a little rise."

I don't know why I liked Miss Cisco. I guess I figured that what we sometimes call evil is simply a form of need. Plus she had gone out of her way to protect me when she had nothing to gain and everything to lose.

I DROVE HER INTO the same neighborhood where I had bought the switchblade knife. It was Sunday morning, and few people were on the streets. A blind woman of color was playing bottleneck guitar under a canopy in front of a liquor store. The neighborhood reminded me of the spells that had caused me so much trouble. They could hit me with a paralysis that left me nonfunctional and barely able to breathe. I didn't want them back, and I didn't want to think about them. Miss Cisco seemed to read my mind. Just before we reached our destination, a drugstore with a perpendicular sign on its facade that stated simply La Farmacia, she turned her head on the seat and said, "What kind of train are you pulling, kid?"

"What kind of what?"

"Don't pretend. Everybody has a secret shame. My mother told me that. She learned it from her clientele. She was a whore in New Orleans."

"I have blackouts. Later I have holes in my memory I can't fill in. Booze can bring it on. Getting angry can, too. Sometimes I go into a deep sleep and walk around like a zombie and can't wake up till someone gives me a good shaking."

She closed her eyes again. "Count your blessings. I'd like to forget half the things I did in my life."

"What I mean is, I don't know what I'm capable of. So I imagine the worst. Then I'm not sure if I'm imagining things or remembering what happened."

She felt the Olds slow and looked around. "We're here. Time for a little medication."

"The store is closed."

"Not for me," she said.

"Did you hear what I was saying, Miss Cisco?"

"Yeah, I did. Lose the crap. You wouldn't bruise a butterfly if you were coked to the eyes. I'll be back in a few minutes. I'm about to puke. It has nothing to do with you. Mr. Jones got into my sandbox real bad this morning."

Fifteen minutes later she had not returned. On a back street I thought I heard the throaty rumble of Saber's twin mufflers echoing off the storefronts. I didn't know if he was living with his criminal friends or not. I had a hard time thinking about Saber and the way our friendship had disappeared like water down a drain. My mother never had friends or a father or a home growing up. Most of her life was spent in misery. That was how I knew the importance of a friend like Saber. We met in the seventh grade. He saw two bullies shoving me around at a bus stop and shot them both in the face with a huge water gun loaded with urine he had collected from the veterinary clinic where he worked.

I heard the twin mufflers thin at the end of a street. A moment later I heard them again. I looked in the rearview mirror and saw Saber's heap headed toward me, oil smoke streaming out of the hood and tailpipes. I got out of the Olds and tried to stop him. "Hey, Sabe! It's me!"

I could barely see through the smoke. He passed me, the back bumper almost hitting my leg. I didn't know whether he saw me or not. I began running alongside the car, trying to catch him. "Saber, what are you doing? It's Aaron!"

I was still waving my hands at him when he went through the intersection, running the light. I stood in the middle of the street, dumbfounded, trying to convince myself he hadn't recognized me.

The blind woman playing guitar under the liquor store canopy slid her glass bottleneck along the frets and sang, "I was sitting down by my window, looking out at the rain. Something came along, got ahold of me, and it felt just like a ball and chain."

As I looked down the street at the empty sidewalks and closed stores and the abandoned filling station under a live oak on the corner and the ragged clouds of oil smoke left behind by Saber's heap, I believed I was looking into the face of death itself, and not in the metaphorical sense. It was as real as a freshly dug grave on the edge of a swamp, the dirt oozing with white slugs.

I knocked on the front door of the drugstore, then rattled it against the jamb. The windows were dirty, the counter and shelves inside coated with dust. I went around to the back door and looked through the glass into a room furnished only with a table and two chairs, lit by a solitary bulb hanging from a cord overhead. Miss Cisco was sitting with her back to me, her black hair tangled on her shoulders. A man with a face the color and shape of a tea-stained darning sock was bending over her, untying a necktie from her upper arm. A stub of a candle flickered inside the neck of a wine bottle. A bent spoon, blackened on the bottom, rested next to it. She turned her face into the light. It was aglow with peace and visceral pleasure, like that of a person in the aftermath of orgasm. I thought I saw her look straight at me, then realized her eyes had become cups of darkness that probably saw nothing.

She opened the door and stepped outside and clung to my arm. "Oh," she said. "Oh, my. The white horsey got loose on poor little me. Walk me to the car and then drive it home. Can you do that, big boy? You know how to drive it home?"

She was beautiful even when impaired, and I had certain thoughts that I would carry into the night, the kind of thoughts I guessed all men had and that made them feel ashamed and treacherous and unworthy of the real woman in their life. But at least I didn't think about acting on my desires, even if I could have. I guess I was learning that when you get close to death, you'll trade everything you own for one more day on earth.

* * *

THREE DAYS LATER I drove to Loren Nichols's home in the Heights. Just as I pulled to the curb, I saw him get off the bus at the corner and walk back toward his house, wearing a white T-shirt and dirty white trousers, a black lunch box swinging from his hand. I never saw a guy who could walk as cool as Loren.

"You just get off work?" I said.

"I'm working at a supper club now."

"They make you bring your own lunch?"

"You must not have worked in a restaurant."

"No, I haven't."

"If you do, you'll never eat out again. Half the people in the kitchen are winos who sleep at the mission. If the meatballs get spilled, somebody sweeps them up in a dustpan and sprinkles them with shredded cheese. They wipe the tables down at night with the bathroom mop because it takes too long to hand-wipe them. You here for your chaps?"

"Yeah. And I wondered how you're feeling."

"About the kid who got stabbed?"

I didn't reply.

"I saw his picture in the paper," he said. "To be honest, I cain't get his face out of my head."

"Valerie and I are going to play miniature golf tonight. We thought you might want to join us."

"I don't know about that."

"You don't like miniature golf?"

"It's not my first choice."

"I brought you something."

He looked down at my hand. "A book?"

"It's called *The Song of Roland.*"

"What's it about?"

"Courage and the battle of Roncevaux. My cousin Weldon carried it with him during the war. He had three Purple Hearts and the Bronze and Silver Star."

He scratched his cheek, his gaze leaving mine. He took the book from my hand. "Thanks. You're not trying to talk me into going to church or something?"

"I wouldn't dream of it."

"Come in back a minute."

We went into his workshop behind the house. He set his lunch box on the workbench and took Grandfather's chaps off a wood peg and handed them to me. "I had to rethink some stuff after that kid was killed. I shouldn't have given you the thirty-two. You don't need blood on your hands. You wouldn't be able to handle it."

"I really appreciate that," I said.

"Shut up. A couple of friends came by this morning. They said you're in the wind. Bledsoe, too."

"In the wind how?"

"Grady Harrelson and Vick Atlas were at Prince's drive-in with a pair of sluts. They're buds now. The word is you called up Atlas and told him Harrelson's friends boosted Atlas's car. One of my friends knows Atlas pretty good. My friend says Atlas saw you with this broad from Vegas. Atlas says she's Mob property."

"She lives in Atlas's apartment building. I drove her to a pharmacy in the Fifth Ward Sunday morning."

"She has to go to the middle of colored town to fill a prescription?"

"It's a little more complicated than that."

"You're talking about Mexican skag?"

"Yep."

"You busted a vessel in your brain or something?"

"I thought I was doing a good deed. She used to be an item with Merton Jenks. He's dying of cancer or emphysema."

He tapped at the air with his finger. "That bull, what's-his-name, Original Sin, he must have stepped on your head."

"I hope you enjoy the book."

"I'm not done," he said. "Your man Bledsoe is dealing horse for a couple of Mexicans. They're not piecing it off, either. They're going down, man. Both Bledsoe and the Mexicans. You don't deal heroin in Houston or Galveston without permission."

"I can't change that."

"I just tried to join the navy," he said. "They told me to beat it."

"You think somebody is going to take you out, too?"

"It's a possibility," he said.

I hung Grandfather's chaps over my shoulder. "Val and I will pick you up at seven."

"I don't know how to say this, Aaron. I think they're going to kill you. Atlas's old man might put a bomb in your family car."

"My father was at the Somme and Saint-Mihiel."

"I got no idea what that means. Blown apart is blown apart. Dead is dead."

"Seven o'clock," I said.

When I fired up my heap, my stomach felt as though I had poured Drano in it.

I HAD THE NEXT day off. I called the Houston Police Department and asked for Detective Jenks.

"He's out today," a sergeant said.

"Is he all right?"

"Who's calling?"

"Aaron Holland Broussard. I'm a friend of his. Could you give me his home number?"

"Yeah, I've heard him speak of you," the sergeant said. He hung up.

I waited an hour and put a pencil crossways into my mouth and called again. The same cop picked up.

"This is Franklin W. Dixon, features editor at the *Houston Press*. Our photographer is supposed to do a shoot at Detective Jenks's home. Evidently he screwed up the address, and the staff writer is out of the office. Can you confirm Detective Jenks's address for me?"

"Hang on," the sergeant replied. "I got it in the file."

THE HOUSE WAS located in an old rural neighborhood off the Galveston highway. It was a place of tin roofs and slash pines and dirt streets and a volunteer fire department and a general store. At night you could see wisps of chemical smoke that hung like wraiths above the electric brilliance of the oil refineries in Texas City. Jenks lived in a decaying biscuit-colored bungalow with ventilated storm shutters on the windows, a tire swing suspended from a pecan tree in the front yard. The pillars on the porch were wound with Fourth of July bunting, the path to the front steps lined with rosebushes.

The inside door was open, the screen unlatched. I tapped on the jamb. Jenks came to the door in his socks, a newspaper in his hand, glasses on his nose. "How'd you know where I live?"

"I think you told me."

"No, I didn't."

"Can I have a few minutes?"

He pushed the screen open and went back into the living room. There was a flintlock rifle over the mantel, a framed array of medals on another wall, a rack of magazines and paperback books by an upholstered couch. On the coffee table was a bouquet of flowers wrapped with blue and silver foil. I didn't see or hear anyone else in the house; there was no sign of a woman's presence.

"You've been pretty busy," he said, indicating the flowers.

"Sir?"

"Look at the card."

I picked it up from the pot.

"Read it aloud," he said.

"'Merton, you're probably a dick on several levels, but I've known worse. Call me if you need your battery charged. I've always been a sucker for losers.'" I put the card back on the flowers. "Pretty poetic."

"You told Cisco I was sick?" he said.

"Yes, sir, I passed on my impressions."

"I love the way you put things."

"She said you did her dirty."

"You came here to tell me that?"

"No, sir, I don't believe you'd do her dirty."

He sat in a stuffed chair and put his feet on a cloth-covered stool. "Sit down."

I sat on the couch. He took a fresh pack of cigarettes from his shirt pocket and looked through the window at a bird on the porch rail. He seemed to forget I was in the room.

"I got something weighing on my mind," I said. "I can't take it to anybody else, at least not anybody who'd understand."

His eyes refound me in the gloom. "Maybe you should talk to a preacher."

"Most of them aren't built for serious problems."

"I never thought about it like that." He pulled the red strip off the cellophane on his cigarettes.

"You're going to smoke those?" I said.

"When you're on third base, you don't tend to worry about a cigarette or two." His face held no emotion, neither fear nor animus nor pity nor regret. After he lit the cigarette, he gazed at me through the smoke.

"I have dreams," I said. "In one of them I see Mr. Harrelson dying by his swimming pool. In the dream I have a forty-five in my hand. You told me you could smell a killer and I wasn't one."

"You think you killed Mr. Harrelson?"

"Not me. Maybe another me, one that I don't let come out except in my dreams."

"That crap belongs in motion pictures."

"That's the kind of thing ignorant people say. You're not ignorant."

I waited for him to get mad. But he didn't. He drew in on his cigarette, the ash reddening. "What else did you want to know?"

"Loren Nichols says Vick Atlas's father might put a bomb in our family car."

"He told you that, did he?"

"Yes, sir."

"And you want to know if Jaime Atlas is that vicious or crazy?" I nodded. He stared into space. "You want something to eat or a cup of coffee?"

"No, sir, I want you to tell me the truth."

"Jaime Atlas was an enforcer for the Mob in Chicago and New York. He crushed a man's head in a vise. He used a blowtorch on others. He'd start with the armpits and work down to the genitalia."

I could feel my eyes shining, the room going out of shape.

"You okay?" Detective Jenks said.

"Yes, sir, I think so."

"No, you're not. Pure evil has come into your life through no fault of your own. That's how people are destroyed. They blame themselves as though somehow they deserve what's happening to them."

"What can I do?"

"Not a thing. You wanted the truth. That's the truth."

He coughed into his hand as though a piece of glass were caught in his lungs. He put out his cigarette in an ashtray and rubbed his hand on his knee. I felt helpless, floating away. Supposedly the courts, the police and sheriff's departments, the prosecutors, the FBI, the parole system, and the jails and hospitals for the criminally insane were there to protect the innocent. Why was my family being made a sacrificial offering to evil men? Outside, the wind was blowing from the Gulf, the air peppered with salt and rain, the pine trees glistening in the sunlight.

"I'd like to kill them all," I said.

"Kill who?"

"Jaime Atlas. His son. The people who work for him. The people who allow these guys to stay on the street. Every one of these sons of bitches."

"You're starting to worry me."

I got up to go. "Who's going to take care of you?"

"Take care of *me*?"

"It's obvious you don't have anybody. There's blood on your cigarettes. Your lungs sound like a junkyard."

"Cisco told you I did her dirty?"

"What?" I said, unable to follow the way his mind worked.

"That I betrayed her?"

"Not in those words."

"You've got a lot of anger in you, son," he said. "Don't let it turn on you. It'll flat tear you up."

Chapter 26

By the time I got home, the sky was turning black and the house creaked with wind, even though it was made of brick. I brought Major and Skippy and Bugs and Snuggs inside and sat with my guitar in my father's study. His manuscript pages were placed neatly in a stack on his desk pad. I began to read the account told him by his grandfather about the events at Marye's Heights on December 13, 1862. The boys in butternut were entrenched with muskets and artillery behind a stone wall at the top of the rise. All afternoon, Union troops went up the hill, wave after wave, and were slaughtered by the thousands, to the point where they slipped in their own gore and the Confederates no longer wanted to fire upon them.

I wondered how anyone could be so brave. I also wondered why I could not rid myself of the well of fear that seemed to draw me into its maw. The answer was simple: I feared for my family, and I resented myself for placing them in harm's way. I was also experiencing a syndrome that I would one day learn was characteristic of almost everyone who has been a victim of violent crime.

I had no answers. I was just short of eighteen. I loved my mother and father and Valerie and my animals. All I wanted to do was be with them and forget the Atlases and Harrelsons of this world. Unfortunately, the fury and mire and complexity of human veins do not work like that.

* * *

THE RAIN HAD started falling in solitary drops when Saber's heap bounced into the driveway, its pair of fuzzy dice swinging from the rearview mirror. He got out, laughing before he could start his narrative.

"What is it?" I said.

He was shaking his head, unable to stop laughing. He fell back against the car, trying to catch his breath.

"Are you loaded?" I said.

There were tears in his eyes. "You won't believe it."

"Believe what?"

He started to speak again, then went weak all over and had to open the car door and sit on the seat. "I just pissed inside Grady Harrelson's head," he said, losing control again. "Oh, it was beautiful. It'll take him weeks to figure everything out. He's royally screwed six ways from breakfast and in serious danger." He was doubling over, laughing so hard he had to hold his ribs, his face turning red.

"What did you do?" I said.

"Grady's been shacking up in a motel on Wayside Drive with the wife of a guy who drives a wrecker on the night shift, a total animal who's been in Huntsville twice for felony assault. Grady bought a convertible just like the one we boosted and sold in Mexico. I followed them to the motel last night and waited until they went to eat, then gave the maid two dollars to put a plateful of chocolate fudge laced with Ex-Lax in their room." He started laughing again.

"Will you stop it?" I said.

He wiped at his face with a handkerchief. "Hang on. It gets better. I boosted his new convertible, then waited a couple of hours for the Ex-Lax to kick in so they'd be fighting to get on the bowl. I called the husband's emergency number and told him Grady was putting the blocks to his old lady and gave him the motel address." Saber was stamping on the driveway. "I watched it from across the street. The animal arrives and kicks the door off its hinges. Grady is inside in his Jockey underwear, and the broad is going nuts, and Grady is trying to explain himself, then he realizes his new car is gone and accuses the animal of stealing it." Saber tried to stand up, then fell back on the car seat wheezing, his nose running, his entire face slick with tears.

"Saber, when are you going to grow up?"

"Never. Come on, don't be so serious," he replied. "You should have seen Grady. There was a brown stripe through the seat of his Jockeys. People were coming out of their rooms, and cops were shouting at them to get back inside. Grady started cussing at a cop, and the cop shoved him on the concrete. His face was white. I thought he was going to have a nervous breakdown."

"What are you going to do with his car?"

"Dump it in colored town."

"That doesn't sound like your friends," I said.

"Manny and Cholo? They don't want any more heat from guys like Vick Atlas and Grady. You know what Manny said? 'Don't mess with guys who got juice.'"

"I'm really impressed with their great knowledge. When are you going to stop listening to these liars?" I said. "Come inside."

"What for?"

"To wash your face."

"You got to lighten up, Aaron," he said, starting to get control of himself. "Things will work out. We'll always be buds, right?"

"I didn't bust us up," I said.

"Okay, so I was wrong. Look, you're already smiling. We've got senior year coming up. It's going to be a gas."

"Promise me you're going to dump the car, Saber."

"What do I want with it?"

"Where is it now?" I said.

"Manny has it in a garage for safekeeping. It's fine. You're always worrying. Let's get a couple of beers and drink them in the park."

"Jaime Atlas might kill my whole family," I said. "Detective Jenks told me he was an enforcer in Chicago and New York. He burned his victims' armpits and genitalia with a blowtorch. That's why I'm not laughing a lot."

The mirth went out of his face. He wiped his eyes. I never realized how long his eyelashes were or how much they reminded me of a girl's. "Jaime Atlas did what?"

THE RAIN POUNDED down for almost an hour, flooding the streets, then the storm was gone and the sky was once again as bright and hot as tin. I drove to Valerie's. Mr. Epstein was on his hands and knees weeding around the rosebushes in front of the house, bare-chested in cutoffs, in full sun, the gold hair on his back soggy with sweat. He grinned up at me, his arms thorn-pricked and speckled with dirt. "She's inside."

"How you doin', sir?" I said in the same way my father always addressed another man.

He didn't answer. He just continued to grin into my face. I was never comfortable around Mr. Epstein, perhaps because I was intimate with his daughter. Or maybe there was another reason. I knew little of the violence that is a constant in the lives of some men and a last resort for others and for some an option that doesn't exist. I knew Mr. Epstein was not a member of the latter group. But where did he fit? He was a leftist and perhaps an ideologue; as a commando, he must have killed enemy soldiers or even civilians with a knife or his bare hands. How do you wash that kind of guilt off your hands?

I sat down on the steps and tried to hold his gaze. "I talked with Detective Jenks today."

"Is Merton okay?"

"I think he's real sick. In the lungs. Maybe the heart, too."

"Sorry to hear that. Merton knows how to take it to them."

"Sir?"

"He carries a badge, but he writes his own rules. They all do."

"Who's 'they'?"

He grinned again. "They."

"Mr. Epstein, I'm sorry for bringing all this trouble into Valerie's life."

"You didn't have anything to do with it."

"You could fool me, sir." Again he didn't reply. I went on, "Detective Jenks told me some terrible things about Jaime Atlas."

Mr. Epstein sat up on his haunches and wiped the mud off his hands on his cutoffs, his eyebrows beady with moisture. "The man who comes after you is only a man. Most assassins are cowards."

"Jaime Atlas crushed a man's head in a vise."

"Don't believe everything you hear."

"Detective Jenks made it up?"

"No, Jaime Atlas probably did. Put it to his kind, and they'll cut and run. They don't serve in wars. They make money off them."

I wasn't interested in his thoughts on the Atlas family. The question on my mind was one I couldn't force myself to ask.

"It's not going to offend me," he said.

"Pardon?"

"Whatever you're wanting to say, it won't offend me."

"Who do you reckon killed Mr. Harrelson?"

He picked up a trowel and began digging at a clump of weeds, chopping hard. There were dirt rings on his neck.

"Did I say something wrong, sir?"

"Nope. Go talk to Valerie. A woman you know called for you. Tell her not to call here again."

VALERIE WAS WASHING dishes in the kitchen. I picked up a towel and began drying them. I could see the color in her throat.

"Your father said I had a phone call."

"Yes, the woman named Cisco."

"She called here?"

"What did I say? Why are you in contact with this person, Aaron?"

"I tried to help Detective Jenks. He's dying."

"All right, but what does she have to do with it? Why does she have to call my house?"

"I don't know. Did she leave a number?"

"Yes, she did. Maybe you'd better hop right on it."

"Don't be like that, Val."

"Like what?"

"May I use your phone?"

"Help yourself." She dropped a plate into the drying rack.

The telephone was in the hallway. I dialed the number Valerie had written down. Miss Cisco picked up on the first ring. "Where have you been?"

"Where have *I* been?" I said.

"Do you realize what has happened?"

"I don't know what we're talking about."

"Where are you calling from?"

"Valerie's house. What difference does it make?"

"Can they hear you?"

"I suspect. What's going on?"

"Go somewhere else and call me back."

"Not unless you tell me what this is about, Miss Cisco."

"Stop calling me 'Miss.' I don't like that hypocritical Southern formality. Do you have any idea what your stupid friend has done? Any idea at all?"

"You're talking about Saber?"

She hung up. Valerie was still at the sink, her back to me. "Would you take a ride with me?" I said.

She didn't answer.

"Please," I said.

She dried her hands and turned. "Fine," she said.

I put my arms around her and held her tight, my face in her hair. I didn't care if her father saw us or not. "I love you," I said. "I'll love you the rest of my life."

WE DROVE TO a local drugstore. It was cool inside, fans spinning on the ceiling. I ordered chocolate milkshakes for both of us and went to the phone booth and closed the door. I could see Valerie reading a magazine at the counter. I could also see the front door and the traffic on the street and the newspaper delivery boys rolling their papers on the corner. It was a scene no different from any other working-class neighborhood in America in the year 1952. Except for one difference. The light outside was like the glitter of thousands of razor blades. The air blowing through the door smelled of hot tar and sewer water. The sounds of the traffic were metallic, shrill with horns. I dialed Miss Cisco's number.

"That you?" she answered.

"Yes," I replied. I stared out the plastic panel at the street, at the jittering light, at the harshness of the colors.

"Your friend stole Grady's convertible, didn't he? The one he bought to replace the other one your friend stole?"

"Which friend?"

"Don't get cute unless you want your friend roasted on a spit. Where's the car, Aaron?"

"I don't know."

"Where's your friend?"

"Same answer."

"I want to grind you into salt."

"I saw the flowers you sent Detective Jenks. I thought that was real nice."

"Tell your friend to leave the car any place of his choosing. Then he can call you and tell us where it is. It's that simple."

"Who's this 'us'? I'm not part of any us, Miss Cisco."

"I thought you were a smart kid."

"No, I'm dumb. I've proved that by having this conversation," I said.

"You know what Ben Siegel used to say? 'Don't get involved with squares.' I should have listened. Goodbye, Aaron. I tried."

"What's with the car? What's the big deal about the car?"

She broke the connection. I replaced the receiver and opened the door of the booth. Out on the street, a lime-green '49 Hudson with a whip antenna and lowering blocks passed the front door; then a pickup truck painted a shade of yellow that was ugly in the way the color of urine is ugly; then a souped-up drag racer with an exposed Merc engine decked out with duel carbs and chrome air filters and chrome nuts on the cylinder heads; then a shirtless guy in greasy jeans and cowboy boots mounted on a Harley.

I sat down next to Valerie and drank from my milkshake. Through the doorway, I could see heat waves on the sidewalk and hear the roller-skate wheels of a crippled man pushing himself on a board along the concrete. The pickup truck passed again. So did the guy on the Harley and the two guys in the drag racer. The lime-green Hudson had pulled up to a hamburger joint, one that had a canvas canopy over the parking area, where carhops in red uniforms carried the orders out on metal trays. "You know any of those guys out there?"

"Which guys?" Valerie asked.

"The guys who have been circling the block."

"I don't see anyone."

I went to the doorway. Across the street, the guys from the Hudson were smoking cigarettes under a tree. They wore drapes and needle-nose stomps and shirts that hung outside their belts. They had left their car under the canopy and obviously had not ordered anything to eat. I stepped outside and looked directly at them. If they noticed me, they showed no reaction. The drag racer was at the light. The guy in the passenger seat resembled one of Grady's buds, a crew-cut football player with upper arms like smoked hams. In the trainer's room at my high school gym, I'd once seen him shove a skinny kid's face into his crotch and say, "What's happenin', fart?"

I headed for the drag racer. The light changed and he drove away. Neither the driver nor his passenger looked back. I went back inside the drugstore. "My imagination is probably on overdrive."

"What did that woman say?" Valerie asked.

"Miss Cisco?" I tried to keep my face blank.

"That's who you came here to call."

"Grady Harrelson bought another convertible to replace the one somebody stole," I said. "It got stolen, too."

"Nobody has luck that bad."

"Grady does."

"This sounds like Saber Bledsoe's work."

"You know how Sabe is. Trying to control him is like trying to reverse the course of Halley's Comet."

"He starts trouble and pulls you into it," she said. "I'm tired of it, Aaron."

I couldn't blame her. The yellow pickup went by again. "Stay here. Don't talk to anybody who comes in. I'll be right back."

I went to the rear door and looked in the alley. One of the guys in drapes was smoking a cigarette by the sidewalk. At the other end, the bare-chested guy on the Harley was messing with his chain as though he had a mechanical problem. The vertebrae in his back arched against his skin, and he wore a knife in a scabbard attached to his belt. I stepped into the alleyway. It was paved with old bricks and lined with garbage cans. Even though the temperature was above ninety, the wind felt cold on my face.

I touched the bandage on my cheek. I can't tell you why. Perhaps for the same reason university duelists in Germany preserve their facial scars. "I'm here, if you guys want to talk."

Neither guy seemed to hear me. Then the guy working on the Harley stood up and turned in a circle until he was looking straight at me. His jeans hung below his navel, his pubic hair showing, his skin pale and shiny with grease and sweat. He took his comb out of his back pocket and combed his ducks into place with both hands, his head tilted, his armpits festooned with hair.

"You guys working for Grady?" I said.

Neither of them answered.

"I got no beef with you," I said.

The biker put away his comb and slipped a switchblade from his right pocket. He pushed the release button and began cleaning his nails as though I were not there. I could hear the guy at the other end of the alley walking toward me. I looked around for a weapon, then picked up a garbage can lid.

"We thought you could he'p us," the guy in drapes said. "You run with Bledsoe, right?"

"Saber Bledsoe?"

"You know him?" he asked.

"He's my friend."

"That's good. You're an honest man," said the guy in drapes. His hair was mahogany-colored, combed straight back, waved across the top. There were pits in his cheeks; his nose and eyes and mouth seemed too small for his face, like lead birdshot that rolled to the center of a plate. "Bledsoe is tight with a couple of spics?"

"I don't know anything about that."

He lifted his hand for me to be quiet. "My point is, we're only interested in the wets. Bledsoe gets a pass. One of them is named Manny. Know a guy named Manny?"

"I think I heard of him," I said.

"Know where we can contact him?"

"Maybe he's screwing your sister. Give her a call," I said.

"That'll get you in trouble, man," the biker said. I had taken my eyes off him. He was closer now, the knife in his palm, sharp edge up. "I got an extra shank, man. Want to go one-on-one?" He was grinning.

"No."

"I didn't think so," he said. "Starting to wet your pants?"

In for a penny, in for a pound, I told myself. I stepped farther into the alley. "Put the frog-sticker away and let's see what happens."

The guy in drapes flicked his cigarette into a wall. "Cut this crap out. Where'd they put the convertible, buddy? Wise off one more time, we're going to break your sticks."

"I don't know where it is."

The guy in drapes and the biker looked at each other. There wasn't a sound in the alley.

"Cut him," the guy in drapes said.

That casual and indifferent. An arbitrary command to mutilate someone unarmed and outnumbered. I looked at him as I had never looked at anyone before. I wondered if it would be held against me should I kill someone under these circumstances.

I turned around to go back into the drugstore. Grady's crew-cut friend was standing as big as a house in the doorway.

"Where's Valerie?" I said.

"Ladies' room, I think," he said. He smiled as though full of goodwill.

"Get out of my way, please."

"Sorry," he replied.

"You were a linebacker. You were all-state runner-up."

His eyes dulled over as though he were trying to remember somebody he used to know. Then he came out of it. "Cain't let you by. Sorry."

My options were gone. "Valerie Epstein isn't part of this. If you hurt her, her father will kill you. That's not a line."

"Nobody is going to hurt a girl," he said. Then he whispered, "Hey, man, give them what they want."

I turned back to the alley. The guy in drapes was five feet from me. He was scratching the back of his neck with one finger. His other hand was behind him. "Open your palm," he said.

"What for?"

"You dealt it, boy. You know what for. Nothing's free."

"My father will catch up with you."

"I'm shaking." He waited. "Come on, Broussard. Get with it."

"Get with what?"

"Give me your hand. It'll be over."

"What will?"

"It's going to end in only one way. You know that. Why put it off? Take your medicine."

"Fuck you," I said. I shoved him and said it again: "Fuck you."

Then I saw the barber's razor in his left hand. He reached for my wrist. I heard the pickup truck stop at the end of the alley and the passenger door open, squeaking like a tin roof being wedged up. It was Loren Nichols, an oiled chain as supple as a snake swinging from one hand.

"What's happenin', Loren?" said the guy in drapes, his eyes askance.

"You sprouts beat feet. You ever try to touch my buddy Aaron, I'll be looking you up," Loren said. He looked at the crew-cut guy in the doorway. "That includes you, fat boy."

"We got no grief with you, Loren," the guy in drapes said.

"You can say that again," Loren replied.

They had no place to hide their shame except in their silence.

Then they were gone. That fast. Loren draped his chain over my shoulder. He cupped his hand on my neck and bent his forehead into mine. "Get out of town."

"I won't run."

"I knew you'd say that," he replied, tapping his head into mine. "Some guys just got to be a hero."

Chapter 27

I DROVE VALERIE HOME, and later, when my parents were gone, I put the .32 Loren had given me under my car seat, and put the stiletto I had bought from the pawnshop in my jeans. I had no idea what I would do with either of them. I sat in the backyard in the gloaming of the day, with Major at my feet and the cats on top of the redwood table, and tried to play my Gibson and forget about what happened at the drugstore.

I couldn't concentrate. I saw images of a human face dissolving into porridge, of blood slung across a garbage can, of a guy in drapes begging for his life. I put my Gibson into its case and threw Major's rubber ball across the yard. When he returned, waiting for me to pull it from his mouth and throw it again, I was lost in my thoughts. The phone rang inside the house.

At first I didn't want to pick it up. I was sure the person on the other end was an enemy. "Hello?"

"Hey, Aaron. It's Saber. I'm in a pile of it, man."

"I heard."

"Heard what?"

"Grady knows it was you who boosted his convertible. Three guys trapped me in an alley. A guy was going to cut me with a barber's razor."

"For real?"

"You think I made this up?"

"How'd you get out of it?" he asked.

"I didn't. Loren Nichols showed up."

"Who were the guys?"

"I never saw two of them. The third one was Bud Winslow, the football player. Remember him?" Saber had been chewing gum. I heard him stop and the line go quiet. "Saber?"

"Yeah, I remember him. In ninth grade, he held me down on a wrestling mat and parked his package in my face."

"Well, he's a hump for Grady now."

Saber started chewing again. "Grady's convertible was leaking money."

"It was what?" I said.

"A hundred-dollar bill was sticking out of the panel on the driver's door. We pulled off the panel. The door was loaded. So was every other panel. The same under the floor. Not just cash. Small gold bars were pushed inside the padding in the backseat. Grady was driving Fort Knox on wheels."

"How much money are you talking about?"

"Nine hundred thousand and change. I don't know what the gold is worth."

"Park the car on the street and make an anonymous call to the cops."

"I don't have it."

"What happened to it?"

"We took it to a chop shop that Manny's uncle runs. Except Manny's uncle doesn't know about the money. Manny put everything back and drove off with the convertible before the uncle got wise."

"You don't know where it is?"

"No. Neither does Cholo. Why is Grady driving around with all that money in his car?"

"His father probably had it stashed. He owed it to the Mob. There's probably more stashed somewhere else."

"I don't know what to do," Saber said.

"We have to brass it out."

"I'm sorry I pulled you into this, Aaron. You were my best friend. I've been a real shit."

"Blame it on the jellyfish," I said.

"What do jellyfish have to do with it?"

"Everything. Where are you now?"

"At a pay phone."

"Are you living at home?"

"The old man threw me out."

"Stay away from Manny and Cholo," I said.

"They used me, didn't they."

"It's the way things are," I said. "The good guys put their faith in people they shouldn't."

I heard him crying on the other end.

I BROUGHT MAJOR AND Skippy and Bugs and Snuggs inside the house and went into my father's office. My father had spread twenty pages of manuscript across a table. He had been working on an account of Lee's failed attack on Malvern Hill. Without artillery, Lee had thrown fifty thousand men at the Union line. The result was a disaster. It would be repeated later at Cemetery Ridge. In his account, my father included a story he had always told me about the rebel yell. He said it was not a yell but a fox call. When he was a little boy on Bayou Teche, there were many Confederate veterans who entertained the children by re-creating the strange warbling sound that rose from the throats of thousands of boys and men dressed in sun-faded butternut and moss-gray rags when they charged through the smoke and dust at the Union line. My father's point was not the sound itself but what it represented. The sound was like a series of "woo's," similar to an owl hooting, the vowel both rounded and restrained, pushed out by the lungs rather than shouted. I tried to imagine advancing with an empty musket through geysers of dirt, trying to control my voice and my fear, while cannon loaded with canister and grape and chain and explosive shells blew my friends and fellow soldiers into a bloody mist. How do you find that kind of courage? Wouldn't your legs fail? Would not normal men throw their weapons to the ground and run away? Where did you go to learn courage?

I knew the answer. You were brave or you weren't. You didn't get the Medal of Honor for swimming through a school of jellyfish. I knew my trek up Golgotha was waiting.

I BOUGHT A QUART of ice cream and drove to Valerie's house. Her father was on a job at the refinery in Port Arthur. We had the house to ourselves. Valerie owned a Stromberg-Carlson high-fidelity record player. We plugged in an extension cord and took it on the back porch, and she loaded six 78s onto the spindle. We spread a quilt on the grass and ate the ice cream out of the carton, and I laid my head in her lap. The sun was gone, the sky turning from purple to dark blue. I could smell the cleanness of her dress and feel her fingers stroking my hair and tickling the back of my head. I closed my eyes and felt myself drifting away. The record changed, and "Marie" began to play. When the record changed again, the slow momentum of "Tommy Dorsey's Boogie-Woogie" rose and fell and filled the yard and echoed off the walls of the house and garage as though we were seated in the midst of the orchestra.

"I didn't know you had any Tommy Dorsey records," I said, my eyes still closed.

"Those are the only two I have."

"Your dad likes Tommy Dorsey?"

"Grady gave them to me."

"Oh?"

"Oh what?"

"Nothing. I never thought he was a guy who'd like 1940s jazz or swing."

"He liked it because his father didn't. His father didn't like anything connected with Negroes or Jews."

I picked up her hand and stuck her fingers into my mouth.

"Why'd you do that?" she said.

"Because you taste good."

"I'm afraid for you, Aaron."

"Don't be."

"My father left me a gun. He said if any of those guys come to the house, I should call the police."

"That's good advice."

"No, he said I should call the police, then kill the guys who were at the house."

I opened my eyes. She was looking down at me. "Don't listen to him. There's always another way," I said.

"Do you believe that?"

I wanted to say yes. But I couldn't. I was carrying a stiletto; under my car seat was a .32 revolver rigged to circumvent forensic examination. I also had revenge fantasies. The truth was, I wanted to forget the New Testament and escape into the orgiastic violence of Moses and Joshua and my namesake Aaron. I wanted to paint houses and the countryside with the blood of my enemies.

"What is the other way?" she said.

I pressed her back down on the quilt and buried my face in her hair. I held her there for a long time, saying nothing, then placed my head against her breast and listened to the quiet beating of her heart.

BEFORE I WENT BACK home, I did something I had never done. I drove into the black district and asked a black man to buy me a six-pack of Lone Star and a half pint of whiskey. Then I drove to Herman Park and sat under a tree in the dark and drank all the whiskey and four of the beers. I think the only reason I didn't drink the remaining two was because I passed out. When I awoke—or rather, when the world came into view again—I was driving my heap down Westheimer at 11:48 P.M. I did not know how I'd gotten from Herman Park to Westheimer. I passed the Tower Theater and the wood-frame ice cream store and the firehouse where we used to take our used tires and bundled newspapers and clothes hangers for the war effort after the bombing of Pearl Harbor.

When I came in, my mother smelled alcohol on me and was upset.

I hated that I had hurt her, but I hated worse the probability that she would punish my father for my drunkenness.

The next day creaked by in slow motion. I could not remember where I had been or what I had done between driving into the park and awakening miles away on Westheimer. At work I listened to the local news on the tiny radio in the office, wondering if I had sought revenge on the three guys who had trapped me in the alley. I bought the early-afternoon edition of the *Houston Press* and searched the crime reports. Nothing. I convinced myself I worried too much.

Just before five o'clock, Cisco Napolitano's Rocket 88 pulled to the pumps, the top down. She was wearing black sunglasses and a white peasant blouse that exposed her breasts almost to the nipple. What was new about that? Nothing. But I couldn't say that about the guy sitting next to her. It was Bud Winslow, the guy who liked to shove the faces of smaller kids into his genitalia.

I went out to the car with a rag and a bottle of window cleaner. "Fill her up?"

"Get in," Cisco said.

"I'm working," I replied.

"Better do what she says," Bud said.

"Didn't Loren tell you to get lost?" I said.

"What were you doing at Bud's house last night, Aaron?" Cisco said.

"I don't know what you're talking about," I said.

"I saw your heap," Bud said. "I saw it twice. You got out with something in your hand. Then you acted like you changed your mind about something and drove away."

"You live in Bellaire, don't you?" I said.

"You *know* where I live."

"That's why I don't go into Bellaire. I heard the neighborhood has turned to shit."

I saw my boss looking at me through the glass in the office. I unscrewed the gas cap and started fueling, my gaze fixed on the numbers clicking on the face of the pump. She got out of the car and stood behind me. "What were you doing at his house?"

"I wasn't doing anything. I was home. What do you care, anyway?"

She either lowered her voice or spoke through clenched teeth. "Because his father is a business partner of Jaime Atlas. We want Grady's car back. Got it?"

"No."

"You dumb little twerp."

The gas tank ran over. She stepped back before it could splash on her tiny shoes.

"That's a dollar seventy-eight," I said. "Need your oil checked?"

Her nostrils looked like she was breathing the air in a meat locker. "Give my number to your stupid friend and tell him to call me."

"I think the Sabe left town. He said something about going out to Hollywood."

She took off her glasses. The skin around her eyes was white and wrinkled, her pupils like drops of ink. "My ass is on the line."

She didn't call me "kid"; she didn't call me by my name. I think her fear was such that she couldn't muster more words than it took to admit how scared she was.

"What about my family?" I asked.

"They're grown-ups. Let them take care of themselves. What'd they do for you? It's obvious that someone did a mind-fuck on you."

I looked into her eyes. I wondered who lived inside her. No, that's not true. I thought I knew exactly who lived inside her, the figure from the shade we've all been warned about, and the thought of it frightened me.

"I'm sorry for any injury I've caused you, Miss Cisco. You seemed like a nice lady. I always thought you were a lot better than the people you ran around with."

I saw her lips part and her face quiver. She reached into her purse for her billfold to pay for the gas. The top of her right hand was sprinkled with sun freckles or perhaps liver spots. It was trembling.

* * *

WHEN I CAME HOME, I found a note from my mother on the icebox door: "Your father and I went to Walgreens. I have a terrible headache. Your dinner is inside. Please do not drink today. I didn't have time to feed Major and the cats."

I brought Major and Bugs and Snuggs and Skippy inside and filled their food bowls and put fresh water in the big bowl they shared. My grandfather, the former Texas Ranger, had an axiom all the Hollands followed: Feed your animals before you feed yourself. Then I put on clean jeans and a starched short-sleeved shirt, and took the plate of cold cuts and deviled eggs and potato salad from the icebox, and sat down to eat. I did not want the telephone to ring. I knew of no one except Valerie who had a worthwhile reason to call. I bit into the deviled eggs and eyed the phone in the hallway as though I could force it to remain silent. I had not finished the first deviled egg before it rang.

"Hello," I said.

"This is the only call of this kind I'm making," the voice said. "Make the smart move or it hits the fan in the next twelve hours. You think I'm manic? You don't know manic. You think you can handle shit, I'll show you shit. You think you're some kind of rodeo cowboy can steal our money and tell us to fuck off? You'll learn what getting fucked is all about."

"Vick?"

"*What?* You deaf? You got wax? Want me to come over there and unplug your ears?"

"Is this about Grady's car?"

"Is this about the car, he says. I asked my father to let me have a run at this. That's the only reason nobody is holding a hot cigar to your eyelid right now. Think I'm kidding? You got a dog and three cats. I saw them in your front yard. How about we put on a warm-up? I don't like cats. I don't like funny little bird dogs, either. Are you listening to this? Don't pretend you're not listening. Hey, answer me!"

"You'd better not come near my house or my animals or my family, Vick."

"He says 'don't come near my house.' That takes some nerve. The guy who can't keep his nose out of other people's business, he doesn't like me around his house. The guy who's taking food out of my family's mouth."

"I'm eating dinner now."

"His lordship is eating dinner now. That's going to get Little Lord Fauntleroy off the hook. You deliver that car. You deliver it by this time tomorrow. I'll light you up, man. I'll pull your insides out with a pair of pliers."

"Stay away from us, you sick bastard."

I hung up, then stared at the phone as though it were alive. I took the receiver off the hook and put a pillow over it so I wouldn't have to listen to the buzzing sound filling the house.

I KNEW WHERE MY father would go when he returned from Walgreens with my mother. I asked if I could go with him.

"I never thought you were keen on the icehouse," he said. "Thirsty for a Grapette?"

"Yes, sir. I'd like to talk with you about a concern of mine also."

"What would that be?"

"Sleepwalking and such."

"Your mother said you had a snootful last night."

"Better wait till we're at the icehouse, Daddy."

We walked the three blocks to his hangout and sat at an outdoor plank table under a striped canopy riffling in the breeze. It was dusk. The sky was speckled with birds slowly descending into the trees that shaded most of the neighborhood.

"Three guys threatened me in an alley up in the Heights," I said. "One wanted to cut me with a razor. Loren Nichols bailed me out."

His face never changed expression, but his eyes did. "*Who* was going to cut you with a razor?"

"I don't know his name. Bud Winslow was with them. He was a linebacker who used to run interference for Grady Harrelson."

The waiter brought my father a Jax and a glass and a salt shaker on a tray and set them down one by one in front of him. Then he served me a Grapette and went away. My father's eyes never left my face. "Go on," he said.

"I think I might have gone to Winslow's house in Bellaire last night."

"Why do you think that?"

"Winslow came to the station today with Cisco Napolitano and said he saw me get out of my heap in front of his house."

"You have no memory of that?"

"No, sir." I paused. "I had a shank."

"A what?"

"A stiletto."

He was still, not a hair moving on his head, even though the canopy was flapping. "I think a predictable phenomenon is occurring in your life, Aaron. It's the nature of evil."

"The knife?"

"No. Evil is like a flame that has no substance of its own on which to feed. It needs to take up residence within us. You imagine yourself committing acts that are in reality the deeds of others."

"But what if I harmed someone?"

"You didn't. You never have. And you won't, at least not deliberately."

"Vick Atlas called."

"I don't want to hear about it. These people don't exist. If they come around, we'll have to make a choice."

"Sir?" I said.

"Maybe it won't come to that. You know what we need? A slice of that Hempstead watermelon at the stand on Westheimer."

He put seventy-five cents on the table to cover the beer and the soft drink and the tip for the waiter. I had never seen my father walk away from a glass or bottle that contained alcohol.

Chapter 28

THE NEXT MORNING Saber moved back into his house. I was surprised. I had thought Mr. Bledsoe was an unforgiving and angry man. He was probably like most people, better than we think they are. It probably took a lot of courage for him to humble himself and go to work as a Jolly Jack ice cream cart driver, on a route in his own neighborhood, where people concluded he had been fired from his job at the rendering plant for drinking, which wasn't true. Anyway, the Sabe motored into my driveway and parked under the porte cochere and announced he was through with Manny and Cholo and boosting cars and dropping goofballs and smoking Mexican laughing grass. I wasn't quite sure Manny and Cholo were through with him, and I knew Grady Harrelson and Vick Atlas weren't.

Saber's return home presented another problem, too. Our enemies knew where he was.

"Where'd you get the mouse?" I asked.

The bruise was dark blue and purple, in the corner of his eye. "I had to straighten out Cholo." He grinned, knowing how absurd he sounded.

"What'd they do with Grady's car?"

"You got me. They're out of their league and dumping in their pants. They wanted me to drive it to Mexico. How's that for smarts?

'Hello, *señor,* got anything to declare? Oh, almost one million dollars? Come on in.' "

"Vick Atlas said he might do something awful to Major and the cats."

"He's been watching your house?"

"He or somebody else," I said.

"That's one guy who should be cut off at the knees. You told your folks?"

"My dad."

"What'd he say?"

"That we might have to make some hard choices."

"Come on, blow it off," Saber said.

"I think I had a blackout and went to Bud Winslow's house with a shiv."

Saber squeezed his eyes shut as though trying not to hear me. "Let's play miniature golf tonight. We got to get back to our old ways."

"It doesn't work like that."

"Yeah, it does," he said. "You got to be upbeat. I'll pick you up at eight, Gate. Tell Valerie we'll be motorating over to her place. We're back in action, Jackson."

I watched Major and the cats walking down the driveway toward us, trusting, innocent, full of curiosity.

"I got a new one for you," Saber said. "What did the bathtub say to the commode?"

"I don't know. Tell me."

" 'I get the same amount of ass you do, but I don't have to take all that shit.' "

Saber was Saber. Destiny was destiny. I felt myself falling through a black hole. As he backed out, he gave me a thumbs-up to show that he had everything under control.

BEFORE I LEFT THE house, I called Merton Jenks at home. "How you feeling?" I asked.

"Worry about yourself," he replied.

"Did Miss Cisco come see you?"

"You got a big problem, Aaron. You want to believe in people."

"That's bad?"

"For you it is. You have the judgment of a hoot owl sitting in the middle of the highway on a bright day."

"Vick Atlas and his father or their people are going to hurt my family or my animals."

"You know this for sure?"

"I have no doubt about it."

He waited so long to speak that I thought we had been disconnected.

"Are you there?" I said.

"What the hell are you up to, boy?"

"See you around."

I hung up and headed for Vick's apartment building.

I RODE UP TO the penthouse in a birdcage elevator. Vick answered the door in a pair of red Everlast boxing shorts, flat-soled gym shoes, and a strap undershirt. His shoulders and chest were covered with black hair. He had on a pair of blue bag gloves, the kind with a wood dowel inside. "How'd you get up here?"

"On the elevator."

"What happened to your face?"

"This?" I said, touching the bandage on my cheek.

"Yeah, *that*."

"A bull got me."

"A cow or a cop?"

"Guess."

Behind him I could see a heavy bag hanging from a steel frame. The air was fetid, his eyes like two ball bearings out of alignment. He looked up and down my person. "Are you calling me out?"

"Why would I call you anything?"

"God, you're stupid. Are you making a play? You want to mix it up? You want to shoot off your mouth? Tell me what it is."

"I want you to kill me. Then you'll be on your way to Old Sparky, and my animals and my family will be safe."

"You're a nutcase, man."

"I guess we'll never be buds. So in that spirit, see how you like this."

I hooked my fist just below his eye and felt the skin split against the bone. I'm not proud of the rage and violence of which I now knew myself capable. I know he had no expectation of what was happening to him. I know he got up once and tried to run for the bathroom. I know he knocked the phone off a hall table. I remember his taking the shower curtain with him when he went down in the tub. I also remember the horsetails of blood on the wall. He was mewing on his knees and holding both hands to his nose when I left.

I took the stairs down to the first floor and went out the back exit. A black woman was picking stuff out of a garbage can. A rag was tied on her head to keep her hair out of her eyes. "You hurt, suh?"

"I'm fine," I said. "Are you all right?"

"Yes, suh. There ain't nothing wrong wit' me."

"Don't you have food at home?"

"My welfare got cut off."

I gave her two dollars from my wallet. Her palm and the underside of her fingers were the gold-brown color of saddle leather. She closed her little hand on the bills and put them into the pocket of her dress. "There's a police car out yonder. Don't be going near them with what you got on you."

"No, ma'am, I won't. Thank you."

I got into my heap and drove away. I thought I heard a fire engine screaming, but I could see no emergency vehicles in the vicinity. At the red light, the sound was so loud that I was sure my heap was about to be cut in half. Then the light changed and the world went silent and I drove home like a man who had been struck deaf.

* * *

After I bathed, I rinsed my clothes clean under the faucet and wrung them dry before I hid them at the bottom of the clothes hamper. Then I scrubbed the tub with Ajax. When my father came home, I told him everything.

"I wish you hadn't done that," he said.

"I didn't see any other way out of it, Daddy."

"That's an interesting perspective. Can the rest of us do the same thing? 'I don't like this, I don't like that. So I'll just punch someone in the face.' Sound reasonable to you?"

"Not when you put it in that context."

We were in the kitchen. The backyard was in shadow. The cats were sitting on top of the redwood table, and Major was jumping in the air at a mockingbird that kept dive-bombing him from the telephone wire.

"How bad was the Atlas boy hurt?" my father said.

"I didn't ask. He's not a boy, either."

"It doesn't matter what he is. You shouldn't have attacked him."

I gestured out the window. "How about Major and Skippy and Snuggs and Bugs? Who speaks for them?"

He cut his head. "You make a point." He opened the icebox and looked inside as though a bottle of beer or wine waited on a shelf. As I said, my mother didn't allow alcohol in the house. If that was what he was looking for, he was out of luck.

"Want to walk over to the icehouse?" I said.

"No, not really." He sat down at the breakfast table.

"What are we going to do, Daddy?"

His collar was unbuttoned, and there was a V of bright red sunburn on his chest. His fingernails were clipped and pared and clean, every hair on his head in place. "It's time to make some people do their job."

"Which people is that?"

He made an appointment with Detective Dale Hopkins, the plainclothes investigator who had busted Saber and me for vandalizing

Mr. Krauser's home. We met with him in a tiny windowless room that contained no furniture except a wooden table and three chairs and a D-ring inset in the concrete floor. The door was made of solid metal. Through the crack, I could see officers in uniform walking back and forth in the corridor. Hopkins wore a suit the color of tin. He did not bother to shake hands with me or my father. The skin of his face was as taut as a drumhead. He carried a clipboard with him. Perhaps intentionally, he clattered it on the table when he sat down. He had the worst nicotine odor I had ever smelled. "This is in reference to Vick Atlas?" he said.

"Vick Atlas and my son," my father said.

"So what about Vick Atlas and your son?" He smiled as though trying to be polite and pleasant.

"We want to know if Vick Atlas is all right," my father said. "We want to apologize. You're the same gentleman I spoke with on the phone, aren't you?"

"We're not in the apology business, Mr. Broussard. Vick Atlas isn't pressing charges. So all sins are forgiven."

"I don't think I've made myself clear," my father said. "My son is sorry for what he did. If he's not, he should be. That is only part of the reason for our coming here. We believe the Atlas family plans to do us harm. What my son did was wrong. But he was acting in defense of his animals. Can you tell me why people like Jaime Atlas and his son and their ilk are allowed to do anything they wish, including the murder of others?"

Hopkins's eyes were like glass, the pupils like seeds. "I got no opinion on that."

"That's remarkable," my father said.

"I didn't catch that."

"Isn't it obvious something besides a teenage squabble is going on? The Harrelson and Atlas families are involved, a schoolteacher has committed suicide, my son lives in fear for his life, and you seem to see or hear nothing."

"I don't appreciate your tone."

"Do you plan on talking to Vick Atlas or his father?"

"No."

"Do you care to explain that?"

"No charges have been filed. There won't be any, either."

"Why not?"

"Vick Atlas and his father told me it was an argument and a fair fight. For them, it's over."

"Do you believe them?" my father asked.

"What I believe is irrelevant. If you want my opinion, the issue is your son."

"Aaron is the catalyst?" my father said.

"The what?"

"Corruption has a smell. It's an infection a man carries in his glands."

The room seemed pressurized. I could see a pencil drawing of a cock and balls on the back of the metal door. Down the corridor, someone was yelling for a roll of toilet paper through the bars of a holding cell.

"I went out to the apartment building myself," Hopkins said. "I talked to the desk clerk who called in the incident. He saw your boy go out the back door. He also saw him talking to a nigger woman by the garbage cans. Your son was giving her money. Know why he would be doing that just after he beat the hell out of someone?"

"No, I don't."

"Maybe they had a previous relationship. Is that a possibility?"

"Would you clarify that, please?" my father said.

"She used to work in a crib."

"I have a hard time following your implication," my father said.

"The situation speaks for itself, doesn't it?" Hopkins said.

"I gave her two dollars because she had no food," I said to my father.

He wasn't looking at me anymore. He was looking at Hopkins in a way I had never seen him look at anyone.

"I say something against the grain?" Hopkins asked. There was a smirk at the corner of his mouth.

My father touched me on the arm. "Let's go, son."

Don't let him get away with it, Daddy, I thought.

But he picked up his fedora from the table, and we walked silently side by side down the corridor. I looked over my shoulder. Hopkins was talking to several cops in uniform, his back to us. They were laughing as though listening to a joke. My eyes were shimmering, my heart a lump of ice.

Then my father said, "Stay here, Aaron."

He walked back down the corridor. I followed him, disregarding his instruction. The attention of the cops in uniform shifted from Hopkins's story-in-progress to my father. "Forget something?" Hopkins said. One uniformed cop laughed.

"I've known every kind of man," my father said. "Desperate men in transient shelters, convicts in Angola Penitentiary, psychopaths who enjoyed mowing down German farm boys. But there was an explanation for all of these men. You're of a different stripe, Detective Hopkins. You flaunt your power and gloat at your misuse of it. You see humor in the suffering of others. You have the tongue and the instincts of both the coward and the bully. One day these men will realize that you dishonor everything they stand for. When that day comes, they'll turn on you. Don't you dare come near us, and don't you dare slander my son."

We walked away, his arm across my shoulder. There was not a sound in the corridor except the man yelling for toilet paper. Then even he was quiet.

Chapter 29

I HAD THE NEXT day off at the filling station. The police department put a guard on our house. Valerie and I drove down to Freeport and waded into the waves and fished with cane poles and bobbers and shrimp for drum and catfish and speckled trout. The wind was up, the waves yellow and cascading with sand, gulls cawing and wheeling overhead. We caught one gaff-top and one stingray and turned them loose and ate po'boy sandwiches in an open-air beer joint on the beach that had slot machines and a jukebox and a shuffleboard inside. It was wonderful to be away from all the problems that awaited us in Houston.

I didn't want to think about Vick Atlas and what I had done to him. Nor did I wish to think about possible retaliation. I had started to wonder about all the events that had happened as a result of my argument with Grady Harrelson at the Galveston drive-in. I had thought the issue was jealousy. To an extent, it was. But the larger pattern seemed linked to money or power and not the angst of teenage romance.

How about the shooting death of Clint Harrelson? The more I thought about it, the more I felt there were elements in the story that I hadn't given adequate scrutiny. For example, the theft of Grady's convertible, the one loaded with currency and gold. In a city the size of Houston, how had Saber found out where Grady and the wife of the wrecker driver were making out? What about Grady's ties with Mexican girls and Mexican gang members? Was Grady a lot smarter than I thought? Were Saber and I getting played?

After we got back to Valerie's, she went upstairs to shower. Her father was gone. I used the phone in her hallway and dialed Grady's number. "I need a minute of your time," I said.

"If you're looking for a life preserver, you called the wrong guy," he said.

"Why should I want a life preserver?"

"Because you pounded the shit out of a sadist and five-star nutcase? What's in your head? You thought he was going to leave you alone after you kicked his ass?"

"Harsh words for a guy who was at your side right after your father was killed."

"I'm looking at my watch. I'll give you fifteen more seconds," he said.

"Why aren't you making a stink about the investigation into your father's murder?"

"Because I know why he was killed."

I wasn't ready for that one. "You know who did it?"

"Not specifically. My father liked boys. Just like that closet stoolpacker Krauser. Those kids in his indoctrination camps were given multipurpose roles, get it? He was a geek and deserved to die the way he did. Any other questions?"

"You killed Wanda Estevan."

"Yeah? Who's in the cookpot, pal? Get a life. Oh, I forgot. You don't have one. Vick is about to strip your skin off. That's not a figure of speech."

"I think her death was an accident. I think you can get loose from all of this, Grady, if you're willing to get honest."

He hung up.

Valerie came down the stairs in her bathrobe, a towel wrapped around her hair. "Who were you talking to?"

"Grady."

"He's not worth the effort, Aaron."

"Did he ever tell you his father was a pederast?" I said.

She looked at me blankly. "No."

"Did he have young guys hanging around his house?"

"I wouldn't know. I was never there. Mr. Harrelson didn't like Jews. He didn't like my father in particular."

"Grady said his father deserved the way he died. Was Grady molested?"

"If he was, he never mentioned it. He joined the marines to prove he was a man. Then his father got him discharged behind his back. I don't think Grady ever forgave him."

"Maybe his father didn't want him killed in Korea."

"The discharge wasn't about Grady. It was about his father. He believed Grady was a coward and would disgrace the family name."

"Grady knew this?"

"Mr. Harrelson told him he needed him 'behind the lines,' helping train these pitiful boys who went to his indoctrination camps."

"I have a bad feeling, Val. I think we've been set up."

"Who's 'we'?"

"You and Saber and me."

She touched my cheek. "You worry about all the wrong things. You give people dimensions they don't have."

She put "Tommy Dorsey's Boogie-Woogie" on the record player and draped her hands on my shoulders and started to dance, her eyes closed. I began dancing with her slowly, in two-four time, Dorsey's orchestra swelling around us. I held her against me and put my face in the dampness of her hair.

"Can we go upstairs?" I said, my voice hoarse.

"Stay here. This is so good. I wish we could be like this forever."

"I'll turn up the volume."

"No, hold me. Just like you're doing."

Then I realized she was crying. "What is it?"

"Everything. It's as you say. I try to pretend otherwise. I think something horrible is going to happen. My father—" She couldn't finish.

"What about your father?"

"He left a note and a hundred-dollar bill. He said if he wasn't back by supper, I should go to my aunt's house in Austin. I looked in his closet. His grease gun is gone."

"His grease gun? I don't understand."

"It's a machine gun with a folding stock. Paratroopers used them in the war."

"Where was he going?"

I stared at her. The record ended. In the silence I felt as though I were slipping down the sides of the earth. "Tell me Grady killed his father."

"Why do you want to believe that?"

"I don't want to think the killer is somebody who wants us dead, too."

"I don't know what Grady did. He was here a few hours before his father died. His friends say he was on a sailboat that evening, when Mr. Harrelson was killed. Grady is probably telling the truth."

"Let's go to Mexico."

"And do what?"

"Get married."

"You need to go to college."

"What for?"

"To be a writer."

"I'll be a writer and your husband. Let's go upstairs."

She wouldn't meet my eyes. "Can we do it another time?"

"Yeah, sure," I replied.

"You don't mind?"

I shook my head. "It's not because of me, is it?"

"No, never."

But I wasn't convinced.

VALERIE CALLED ME at seven P.M. Her father had just gotten home and was in the shower.

"Is everything all right?" I asked.

"He said all this is going to pass."

"What is he? Some kind of Tibetan holy man?"

"That's not very respectful."

I paused, trying to suppress my anger. "Want to go out for some ice cream? The sun doesn't set until after nine."

"Maybe tomorrow."

"Then I guess I'll say good night."

"It's still evening."

"No, it isn't," I said.

IN THE MORNING I looked through the newspaper for stories about violence, bodies discovered in a ditch, a shooting by an unknown assailant at a business property owned by the Atlas family. There was nothing I might link to Mr. Epstein.

My mother's greatest fear was that someone would look at her and see an impoverished little girl standing barefoot by herself in front of a house that was hardly more than a shack.

I was in the backyard when I heard her come home early from work. Through the kitchen window, I saw her trying to boil water to make tea, the pot shaking in her hand. I went inside, closing the door carefully. "You all right, Mother?"

"I had a dizzy spell at work," she said. "I think I ate some tainted food." Her vocabulary for depression and her justifications for the pharmaceuticals were endless. Her contradictions were also. She was physically brave and did not fear disease, mortality, or notions about perdition. She believed most men were meretricious by nature, yet these were the same avuncular men who usually ended up victimizing her.

"Sit down. I'll fix that for you."

"Thank you, Aaron. You're such a good boy. I left that salad too long in the icebox. I'm sure that was it. This man came in. He was from San Angelo. He wanted to open an account. I told him that wasn't one of my duties. He seemed to pay no attention to what I told him. He insisted he knew me." She was sitting at the table now, looking into space as though speaking to herself. "He used my childhood nickname with a smirk on his face," she said. "He told me who my brothers were, as though I didn't know their names. I told him to please go to Mr. Benbow's desk and open his account. I told him I didn't appreciate his presumption. Then I went into the lunchroom and ate that salad even though it had a funny taste. I'm so distressed and angry at myself. I'm sorry to bother you with this, Aaron. I just get so confused."

"He's just one of those worthless fellows we have to forget about," I said.

"That is exactly what he is. There is nothing lower than that kind of white man. They abuse Negroes and use social situations to let their eyes linger on a woman's person. They're common and coarse and invasive and enjoy humiliating the defenseless. Sometimes I want to do violent things to them. I really do." She was knotting her hands, the nails leaving tiny half-moons on the heel. "Would you take me to Mrs. Ludiki's house? I need to order my thoughts. I don't know why I allowed myself to be upset by this common, rude man."

She had never learned to drive. In my opinion, Mrs. Ludiki was a curse; she was a fortune-teller raised in the caves outside Granada who spoke a dialect she called gitano. She lived in a small paintless frame house surrounded by persimmon and pomegranate trees that left rotting fruit all over the lawn. I didn't believe she was a confidence woman, nor did I believe she practiced black arts. It was the other way around. I believed she had a natural insight into people and their propensities, and her "readings" were foregone conclusions about a person's behavior. The problem was the credulity and desperation of my mother. Mrs. Ludiki listened and gave warnings that grew not out of the zodiac but out of my mother's emotional and mental illness.

I didn't argue, though. There were worse people than Mrs. Ludiki. She had hair like a porcupine that she tried to mash down under a bandana, and she wore so many gold chains and glass necklaces and so much hooped jewelry that she rattled when she walked. Her "reading room" was a gas chamber of incense and perfumed candles. The centerpiece was her deck of tarot cards; the iconography had its origins in Egypt and Byzantium and the legends of Crusader knights seeking the Grail. The deck was a pictorial history of the Western world's cultural debt to the Middle East.

My mother's conversations with Mrs. Ludiki were always circuitous. She could not bring herself to say she was afraid; she could not admit her addiction to pharmaceuticals; she could not admit that she was forced to quit high school in the tenth grade and go to work, nor that she had married a man much older than she when she was seventeen, as though poverty and loneliness and desperation were unacceptable in the sight of the Creator.

"I've felt terribly out of sorts," she said to Mrs. Ludiki. "Nothing on a grand scale, of course. Like this morning at the bank. A man was discourteous and kept insisting he knew me when he didn't. Actually, it doesn't bother me. I'm quite all right now, except for a mild case of food poisoning. How have you been, Mrs. Ludiki?"

"I think we can get to the root of these problems quickly, Mrs. Broussard," Mrs. Ludiki said, laying out the tarot cards in a wheel. "Look. There's the man carrying staves on his back, his burden about to break him. He takes out his unhappiness on others. He resents spirituality and goodness in others and is to be pitied and not feared."

"You think that's the man I met this morning?"

"Yes, I do. So I'll put him back in the deck and leave him to his fate."

I thought we were finished. But Mrs. Ludiki, like all people who toy with the delicate membrane that holds the soul together, had unlocked doors that my mother never should have walked through.

"Who is the figure tied upside down on the tree?" my mother asked.

"That's the Hanged Man." Mrs. Ludiki tried to pick up the card and replace it in the deck before the conversation went further.

"That's the death card, isn't it?" my mother asked. She pressed her finger on the edge of the card.

"The Hanged Man is Saint Sebastian, the first martyr of Rome. He was a soldier executed by his fellow soldiers."

My mother studied the card carefully. The figure was pale-bodied and effeminate, covered only by a loincloth. "He bears a resemblance to Aaron. Look. It's uncanny."

"No, we mustn't transfer the wrong meaning from this card, Mrs. Broussard."

"Are those arrows?"

"They're darts. The Legionnaires fired darts from their crossbows."

"What's the next card in the deck?"

"I don't know. Let's move on and look at these other things in our wheel," Mrs. Ludiki said, her eyes veiled. "There is certainly prosperity here. Good health as well. Yes, there are very positive indicators working in your life."

"No, the Hanged Man is at the apex of the wheel. When there is an ambiguity in the card, you always supplement it with another. Please show me the next card, Mrs. Ludiki."

Mrs. Ludiki turned over the top card on the deck and placed it below the Hanged Man. It showed a skeleton wearing black armor and riding a white horse.

"That's the Fourth Horseman of the Book of Revelation," my mother said.

"Yes, it is," Mrs. Ludiki said.

"Death?"

"Yes."

"I see," my mother said. She stood up, groping in her purse. She squeezed her eyes shut. "I forgot how much our session is. I'm sorry. It's a dollar seventy—"

"There's no charge today," Mrs. Ludiki said. "I'm happy to see you. Please don't take away the wrong ideas from the tarot."

"Yes, I'm sure you're correct," my mother said. "It's been an unusual day. I must be running. Aaron, say goodbye to Mrs. Ludiki."

"Goodbye, Mrs. Ludiki."

Her eyes couldn't meet ours. She rose from her chair, a basically good woman wreathed in scarfs and tinkling jewelry and fumes from her candles and incense bowls, unable to dispel the misery she had helped fuel.

Outside, I took my mother's arm, then opened the car door for her. "Would you like to go for a drive? Maybe to a show?"

"No, I don't feel well. Thank you anyway, Aaron. He looked like you. You saw the resemblance, didn't you?"

"The Hanged Man? Not a chance, Mother. That guy looks like the ninety-pound weakling getting sand kicked in his face in the Charles Atlas ad."

Her face blanched. Could I have chosen a worse metaphor? Nope. I had found the absolute worst.

I drove my mother to a soda shop and bought her a lime Coke. I thought I heard a clock ticking inside my head. I don't think the sound was imaginary.

Chapter 30

My anxiety had become almost as bad as my mother's. I called Valerie. "I have to talk to your father," I said.

"He's at his club."

"What club?"

"The one he hangs out at by the driving range. What is wrong with you, Aaron?"

"What's wrong with *me*?"

"Is it about yesterday?" she said. "About not wanting to do it?"

"No, I understood perfectly," I said. "Don't worry about a thing. Not for one minute."

"So why do you want to talk to my father?"

"Because I don't like all this secrecy crap."

"Come by the house and I'll go with you."

"No, I need to talk to him on a personal level."

"You feel you're doing something wrong?"

"I feel like we're slipping around."

"My father treats me like a grown woman. I don't keep secrets from him."

"But he does," I said.

"What?"

"I always have to guess at what he's talking about. He's always indicating that he knows something he's not sharing."

She gave me the address of his club, then asked if I would be by later.

"If you'd like me to," I said.

"What do you think?" she replied.

THE DRIVING RANGE was in a semi-rural part of Houston where urbanization had not had its way. The late nineteenth century was still visible, including pastureland and clumps of live oaks wilting in a savannah and a general store and saloon with a wide gallery that had barrels of pecans on it in the season. Mr. Epstein's "club" was a former American Legion bar now owned collectively, mostly by men who had served in World War II. It was dark and cool inside and smelled of tap beer and cheese and heavily seasoned smoked meats. The ceiling was made of stamped tin and hung with wood-bladed fans. The bartender told me Mr. Epstein was in the men's room and that I could wait at the bar and have a soft drink if I wanted.

It was a strange setting, a hybrid one that seemed disconnected from the Texas where I had grown up. There were newspapers printed in Hebrew attached to poles along one wall, and tables for dominoes and cards and chess games, and a long glass case filled with athletic trophies, an inflatable flight vest, a Flying Tiger jacket, a photo of the Times Square celebration on V-J Day, an Israeli flag, a shot of French paratroopers coming down in a rice paddy.

One photo reached out to me like a fist in the face. Six men dressed in military fatigues without insignias, all of them bearded and wearing flop hats, stood with their arms over one another's shoulders in front of a burned tank, a sand dune in the background. The man in the center was Mr. Epstein. The man next to him was either a look-alike or in reality someone I had hoped I would never see again, even in a photo. At the bottom, someone had written "Palestine, 1947."

I felt rather than saw Mr. Epstein standing behind me.

"Valerie called and said you were on your way," he said. "Want to sit down in a quiet corner?"

"Is that you in the photograph?" I tried to smile.

He squinted at the glass case. "That's me."

"You were in the Israeli-Palestinian war?"

"I popped in and out a couple of times. Nothing to write home about."

"The man next to you looks like my metal-shop teacher."

"Yeah, that's old Krauser. He was quite a character." Mr. Epstein sat in a booth and waited for me to sit down across from him, his attention occupied with everything in the room except me. "What's on your mind?"

I tried to suppress the vague sense of resentment I always felt around Mr. Epstein; he seemed to suggest that others were supposed to adjust to his perception of the world, his experience, his knowledge.

"Mr. Krauser was one of the worst people I ever knew," I said.

"He wasn't everyone's cup of tea."

"He was OSS?"

"For a while."

"In my opinion, he should have been on the other side."

"With the Krauts?"

"No, with the Nazis," I said.

"What do you know about Nazis?"

"They're bullies. Like Krauser. They feed on the weak."

"Nazi scientists built our intercontinental missiles," he said.

He went into a digression about Operation Paperclip and the missile program in Redstone, Alabama, his gaze roving around the room. Then he stopped and picked at his hands as though he had given me more time than he'd intended.

"Mr. Epstein, Valerie said you went off somewhere with a grease gun and then came home and said, 'All this is going to pass.' What is 'all this,' sir?"

"I talked with a couple of people." He paused to see if his meaning had settled in. "I mean I 'talked' with them. Do you understand what I'm saying?"

"People who work for the Atlas family?"

"I didn't say who they worked for."

"You 'talked' to them in a way they won't forget?"

"They're not interested in you. They're after the Harrelson money. Stay out of their business and they'll stay out of yours. You also need to stay away from Grady Harrelson. Do that and all this will pass. It's not a complicated idea."

"I'm not in their business. I never wanted to be around Grady. He was abusing Valerie at a Galveston drive-in. That's how I got involved with him."

"I'm trying to tell you about the world you've stumbled into, son."

"How do you know these people, sir?"

"I know them. What difference does it make?"

"Valerie told me why the government let Lucky Luciano out of jail."

"Yes?" he replied, folding his hands.

"So Luciano could keep the shipyard workers broke. That's how you know these guys? You or your friends worked with the Mafia?"

He told the waiter to bring us two Nesbitt's oranges.

"Why don't you answer the question, Mr. Epstein?" I said.

"Luciano was let out of jail to stop espionage on the docks."

"I read there was no espionage. Luciano ordered a ship burned so his people could get him released and transformed into a patriot. He introduced heroin to the Negro slums. He murdered people for two decades."

Mr. Epstein leaned forward, his brow knurled. His skin was dark, his hair like a curly gold wig, his pale blue eyes as mirthless as ice at the bottom of a cocktail glass. "Deal with the world in kind or be its victim, son. But you won't take my daughter down with you."

"Krauser called me that."

"Called you what?"

"Son."

"I'm not getting your point."

"It was an insult," I said.

"Excuse me?"

"I think all this stuff you've told me sucks pipe, Mr. Epstein."

"Sucks pipe? I don't think I've heard that one."

The waiter put down our drinks. Mr. Epstein watched him walk away, then his gaze moved back to my face. "Merton Jenks showed you photos of the two men who poured gasoline on Valerie?"

"Yes. They were naked. Their hands were gone."

"But they had it coming, didn't they?"

"I can't make that kind of judgment."

"You're still not hearing me. I'm saying they made a mistake."

I could feel my mouth drying out. Under the table, I kept clenching my thighs with my hands, unsure whether I was more scared than angry. "I don't know if I want to hear more. Who would cut off a man's hands?"

"That's the world you walked into. That's what I'm telling you."

"Maybe I don't want to hear any more about it."

"You may not have that choice," he said.

"I asked Valerie to run away. I suspect we'll get married one day. Nobody is going to run me off, Mr. Epstein."

"I'm not trying to run you off. Valerie's choice is Valerie's choice. I'm telling you to be careful. You're not a listener."

"No, sir, you're threatening me."

He opened a penknife and began cleaning his nails. "Drink your orange."

"Drink it yourself," I said.

I got up from the booth and walked outside into the wind. Across the street, men and women and teenagers whacked golf balls high into a sky marbled with crimson-tinted thunderheads, the balls dropping and bouncing like hailstones on a green carpet that once was a feeder lot. I heard the screen door of Mr. Epstein's club swing back into place behind me.

As a young person on the edge of discovering the world and shaking away the scales of your youth, did you ever have a day when you knew that for the rest of your life, you would be grateful that your father was your father and your mother was your mother, no matter how flawed they might be?

* * *

THAT EVENING SABER picked me up in his heap and we headed out to Bill Williams's drive-in across from Rice University. Saber also wanted to go to the roller rink.

"Valerie's old man was buds with Krauser?" he said.

"Maybe they were just fellow commandos or intelligence guys, something like that," I said.

"Lose the doodah, Aaron. You're talking about the guy who might become your father-in-law."

"Okay, it's a depressing prospect. What's that tinkling sound?"

"I didn't hear anything."

I looked at the backseat, then down at the floor. "What's in those bottles?"

"Security," he said. They were dark green, tapered at the neck, plugged with corks, rags tightly wrapped and taped around the bottom.

"Are they Molotov cocktails?"

"For backup, that's all."

"Your heap is a potential firebomb."

"That's the breaks. There's worse things than going out in a blaze of glory."

The summer-evening regulars were dragging South Main—low-riders, hoods, convertibles full of girls, bikers hunting on the game reserve, football jocks, scrubbed kids who went to church on Wednesday night, somebody lobbing a water bomb, music trailing from radios, Hollywood mufflers throbbing on the asphalt.

Saber pulled up to the drive-in and ordered fried chicken for both of us. Jo Stafford was singing "You Belong to Me" through the loudspeakers.

"This song haunts me," I said.

"What for?" Saber asked.

"Because it's the way things should be. Except they're not."

"You'd better stay out of your own head."

"I think we got sucked in, Sabe."

"Are you kidding? You're a rodeo hero, and I'm back in action and at the top of my game. We're unstoppable."

I watched a car full of hoods go down the aisle, the radio blaring. "How'd you know Grady was shacked up in that motel?"

"Manny saw him and followed him there. Then he ran it by me."

"In a city the size of Houston, Manny just happens to see a guy from River Oaks on the wrong side of town, a guy we happen to hate and whose car you boosted?"

"That's what I said."

"You didn't think there was anything unusual about that?"

"No."

"Did Manny tell you to boost the car?"

"I forget who had the idea first. What difference does it make?"

The hoods parked at the end of the aisle. One of them got out and walked to the men's room. He was wearing drapes, a long comb sticking out of his back pocket, his shirt outside his belt, unbuttoned in front. He looked straight at me as he passed the car. He had a narrow face, a small mouth with crooked teeth, bronze-colored hair glistening with oil, and the thickest ducktails I had ever seen.

"Grady once told me he had connections with some Mexican hoods," I said.

"So you're saying Manny and Grady were working a scam to get me to steal Grady's wheels with his money and gold bars inside?"

"No, I don't guess that makes much sense. But it's something similar."

"You've got a worry machine in your head instead of a brain. On top of it, you don't worry about the things you should."

"Like what?"

"Vick Atlas, a guy who's not only a psycho but whose father blowtorches people."

"I cleaned his clock, and so far he hasn't done anything about it," I said foolishly.

"Because the cops put a cruiser in front of your house."

"My father got rid of it. He said it was dishonorable."

"After y'all went to the cops?"

"He said he didn't ask for protection. He wanted the cops to do their job and put the Atlas family in jail."

"I bet they got right on it," Saber said.

The waitress brought us our chicken dinners and french fries and milkshakes on a tray. The hood came out of the men's room combing and shaping his hair. Then he abruptly changed directions and walked to my window, sticking his comb in his back pocket. He leaned down, his breath sweet with chewing gum. "What's happenin', man?"

"No haps," I said. "I know you?"

"I used to go to Reagan. I saw you at a couple of football games and a dance or two," he said. "Loren find you?"

"Loren who?"

"Nichols, man. Loren Nichols. You're Aaron Broussard, aren't you?"

"Loren is looking for me?" I said.

"Yeah, he was here earlier. I thought I'd tell you." He propped his elbow on the roof of the car, the wind riffling his shirt. "He was going to Herman Park with a couple of girls from Bellaire."

"Loren is going out with girls from Bellaire?"

"I'm just passing the word, man. You guys want to smoke some tea?"

"No, thanks."

He leaned down farther so he could look into Saber's face. "Is your name Bledsoe?"

"What about it?" Saber said.

"I heard about you. You hung your johnson through a hole in the ceiling over a teacher's head. That's something else, man."

Saber looked at him. "I just washed my heap."

"So?"

"Try to keep your pits off it."

"I'll tell Loren I saw y'all," the hood said. He tapped the window jamb and walked away.

"You know that guy?" I said.

"No."

"You think he's hooked up with Vick Atlas?"

"You know it," Saber said. He put the wishbone he was eating back on the tray. "Man, oh, man." He got out of the car.

"What are you doing?" I said.

"I cain't take this anymore."

"Take what?"

"Getting jobbed by these guys all the time. Dangle loose."

"Come back here, Saber," I said, getting out of the car.

Saber walked to the driver's window of the hoodmobile and leaned down. "I don't know what that guy in the backseat told you, but he's on the stroll. He just propositioned us and tried to get us over to Herman Park. I'm going inside now and call the cops. This is a class joint. If I were y'all, I'd dump this guy somewhere. Talk about no class."

I thought we were dead. But nothing happened. Saber was glowing. In his innocence, he believed he had confronted evil and defeated it with guile. I don't think that was the case. I believed the fear of the kids in the hoodmobile was so great that they would eat any insult rather than report back to Vick Atlas with information he didn't want to hear. They were born poor and hid their insecurities by wearing the clothes of 1940s zoot-suiters, and they didn't even have the vocabulary to describe the impulses that controlled their lives.

"We stuck it to them, didn't we?" Saber said as we headed down South Main toward the roller rink.

I looked out the window without answering.

"Did I tell you I had a conversation with the organ player at the rink?" he said. "I think she digs me."

"You're the best, Saber," I said.

The clouds were as yellow as sulfur and roiling in thick curds all the way to the horizon, as though we were trapped beneath an ocean that was sliding over the edges of the earth.

Chapter 31

I COULDN'T FALL ASLEEP that night. I didn't get up until nine. My parents had already gone to work and my mother had fed our pets, which was usually my job. I made coffee and opened the morning paper. On the first page of the local section was a photograph of a pickup truck that had been hit broadside by a locomotive and mashed into scrap. The story stated that the driver of the pickup had tried to beat the rail guard and that he and his passenger probably died upon impact. Their names were Manuel Delgado and Cholo Ramirez, age twenty-one and twenty-two, respectively.

I felt perspiration break on my forehead. My stomach flared as though someone had dragged a match head across the lining. I called Cisco Napolitano. She picked up and cleared her throat before she said hello.

"I need to talk with you, Miss Cisco," I said.

"You again?"

"Can I come to your apartment?"

"No. Stay out of here."

"Why?"

"*Why?* You actually asked that? That wasn't you who painted Vick Atlas's shower wall with his head?"

"I need help," I said. "I have to ask you some questions I can't ask anyone else."

I heard her make a brief sound, like air leaving a balloon. "Where are you?"

"At home."

"Is anyone else there?"

"No, ma'am." I gave her my address.

"I'm doing this for only one reason," she said. "I called you a twerp. I regret that."

"Are you in danger, Miss Cisco?"

"I'm going to bring needle and thread and sew your mouth shut."

I SCRAMBLED EGGS AND chopped cheese and green onions and made more coffee and cut three roses off the trellis and put them into a bottle of water on the breakfast table. She pulled her Oldsmobile deep into the driveway, past the porte cochere, out of sight from the street. I almost didn't recognize her. She was wearing a pair of bib overalls and a white T-shirt and checkered boat shoes without socks, her hair tied in a ponytail. I pushed open the back screen. Major and Skippy and Bugs and Snuggs ran inside with her.

"What's all this?" she said, looking at the food on the breakfast table.

"A late breakfast or an early lunch or an omelet my dog would like."

"I must have done something unpardonable in a previous incarnation," she said. She sat down and looked up at me. She was not wearing makeup. The skin around her eyes was gray. "What did you want to know?"

"Last night I think some guys tried to set up Saber and me. I think they were humps for Vick Atlas."

"They tried to lure you somewhere?"

"Herman Park."

"What did you tell them?"

"Not much. Saber stuck it in their faces. There were five of them. They didn't do anything about it."

"They're probably punks doing favors for Vick. What else do you want to know?"

"How did you know Saber boosted Grady's convertible from in front of the motel?"

"One of the ignorant peons with him tried to fence a gold bar at a pawn store."

I pushed the local section of the newspaper toward her. She glanced down at the photograph of the pickup truck twisted on the tracks.

"The two Mexican guys working with Saber were named Manny and Cholo," I said.

She looked at the photograph and the lead paragraphs of the story a long time, then at me. "You believe they were murdered?"

"I don't know," I said.

"They weren't. At least not by Atlas's people."

"Atlas's hirelings have their standards?"

"They don't disguise their work. They advertise it."

"You want some coffee? Or eggs? Here." I scraped them out of the skillet onto her plate. "I've got some toast coming up."

She rested her forehead on her fingers. "All right, here it is. Two guys just arrived from Palermo. Real greaseballs. They never know the hit. The hit doesn't know them. Their fingerprints aren't on file. They've got figures like dildos and inkwells for eyes. After they do the hit, they go back to Sicily and bounce their children on their knee."

"Who are they here to kill?" I said. My words sounded apart from me, hollow, deceitful. I didn't want to hear the answer to my question. No, that was not it. I wanted her to say someone else was the target, not me or my family.

"Whoever Jaime Atlas tells them to kill," she replied. "You split open his son's face. It got infected. Maybe the old man will let it slide, maybe not. He wants the Harrelson money from Grady's convertible. Don't ask me how this is going to play out. I just want to get a lot of distance between me and people who smell like a garlic farm." She picked up her fork and ate two bites.

"You look different," I said.

"Yeah, I just joined the Mormon Choir."

"You look like a lady who's been working in her garden. I mean, your hair and your clothes. You look nice."

I could see the irritation growing in her face. "You're too young to be talking to me like that."

"I'm sorry."

"I've got six days off the spike," she said. "I'm going to meetings where people follow some steps and get rid of the kinds of problems I have. I don't know if it's going to work or not. It probably won't."

She took a brown envelope from her overalls and set it on the table. It was tied with a piece of red cord. "There's six hundred dollars in here. Take your parents and yourself on a vacation. Take Bledsoe with you. I'll try to talk with Vick. The old man is out of the question. Ten years ago he bit the nose off his business partner."

"I'm supposed to tell my parents we need to hide?" I said.

"If that's what it takes."

"That's not the way my family does things."

"Know how the South lost the Civil War?" she asked. "They never learned that after you're dead, you can't fight anymore. Sit down and eat, will you? You make me nervous. Look, maybe all this will go away. Give it time."

"That's what Mr. Epstein said. I think he's just as much a killer as the Atlases are."

"I'm not going to tell you what Jaime Atlas has done."

"Detective Jenks has already told me."

"Merton doesn't know the half of it. There was a girl in a brothel in Reno."

"Go on," I said.

"You get your mother out of town."

"Why my mother?"

"Jaime Atlas likes killing women. Who do you think you're dealing with? Jaime Atlas is the devil."

The toaster popped behind me. I jerked all over.

"Shit," she said. Then she stared at the roses. "Did you cut those for me?"

"I was trying to brighten up things."

"I've got no magic, Aaron." She got up from the table. "Close your eyes."

"What for?"

"Just do what I tell you."

"Miss Cisco, I'm not sure this is appropriate."

"Do it," she said.

I shut my eyes. Then I felt her place her arms lightly around my shoulders and touch her lips against my cheek. When I opened my eyes, she stuck one of the roses into my shirt pocket. "You've got a nice home and family. Hang on to them."

"Why did you put the rose in my pocket?"

"Probably because you deserve it and I don't. Or something like that."

She picked up the envelope with the money inside it and went out the screen door without saying another word. Major went to the screen and watched her walk away.

THAT EVENING I TOOK Valerie to see *Viva Zapata!* at the Loews Theater downtown. At first I wanted to see *High Noon*, but Valerie said it was an allegory about the House Un-American Activities Committee and Joseph McCarthy and the prosecution of the Hollywood Ten.

"How do you know that?" I asked.

"My father said so," she replied.

Her information was probably correct, but if it came from Mr. Epstein, I didn't want to hear it.

"I hear Brando is great as Zapata," I said. "Anthony Quinn plays his brother. Joseph Wiseman plays Judas. I love Joseph Wiseman."

"Okay, by all means, let's see *Zapata*," she said.

For two hours we got lost in revolutionary Mexico. When we came out of the theater, the sky was turquoise, the wind flapping an American flag on a building across the street, the image of Marlon Brando in a sitting position and shot to pieces in a cattle lot imprinted upon our memory. I put my arm across Valerie's shoulders. She looked so beautiful in the glow from the marquee that I ached inside. For just a moment I thought about the two of us throwing our suitcases into my heap and heading west on Highway 66, following the sun to Hollywood and the beaches of Santa Monica and Malibu.

Then I saw a man across the street, in a boxlike 1940s four-door black sedan, wearing a suit and fedora despite the heat, his features barely visible in the shadows.

"Why are you stopping?" Valerie said.

"That guy in the black car."

"What about him?"

"He has a camera. There, see? It has a telephoto lens."

He pointed the camera at us. I shielded Valerie from his view, my back to the street. A dozen people surged by us on the sidewalk. When I looked again, the car had pulled into the traffic. This time I saw the driver clearly. His face had the texture of bad wallpaper; his eyes were wide-set, his fingers like sausages on the wheel.

A pedestrian collided into me. "Sorry," I said.

"If I had a gal like that, I'd be distracted, too," the pedestrian said.

The car turned the corner and was gone. I didn't have time to get the license number.

"Who was he?" Valerie said.

"Cisco Napolitano says Jaime Atlas has brought in a couple of guys from Sicily."

"Killers? Why didn't you tell me?"

"I thought maybe she exaggerated."

"Did you tell your parents?"

"That's just piling more grief on them."

"I'll tell my father."

"Maybe the guy was a tourist. Let it go."

"You don't want my father to know?"

"Everybody has to carry his own canteen," I said.

"What?"

"That's a pipeline expression." I put my arm around her again. The muscles in her back were as hard as brick. "We'll be okay," I said. "Straight shooters always win."

She took my arm from her shoulders and entwined her arm in mine. "It's not going to pass, is it."

"You up for a chocolate shake?"

THE NEXT MORNING Loren Nichols came into the filling station. He was driving the skinned-up dirty-vanilla pickup truck owned by his brother. He had washed his hair, and it hung on his head like a black mop. "How's it dangling?"

"Pretty good. How's yours dangling?" I replied.

"Got to ask you a favor. I got a job driving a church bus on Sundays, three dollars for the afternoon. They talked me into playing with a quartet at their picnic and assembly tonight. I'm going to be singing lead on two of the songs."

"That's great, Loren."

"Except my guitar shorted out and caught fire." He gazed at the live oak growing out of the concrete next to the station.

"You want to borrow my Gibson?"

"Valerie told me how much you treasure it."

"Can Valerie and I come with you?" I said.

"I'd like that." He pushed his hair back. "You know a plainclothes peckerwood pile of shit named Hopkins?"

"Yeah, I do. He busted Saber and me."

"He pulled me in. He tried to squeeze me about you and Bledsoe and Vick Atlas and Grady Harrelson's convertible."

"Why should you know anything about Harrelson's convertible?"

"That's what I told him. He asked me about those two guys Bledsoe was hanging with, the ones who got killed on the train tracks. You heard about that, right?"

"I saw it in the paper."

"Hopkins said somebody was chasing them when they tried to beat the guard."

"What did you tell him?"

"That I didn't know anything. He said, yeah, I did. He said gutter rats like me always had their noses to the sewer grate."

"What did you say?"

"To shove it up his old lady's ass because it was obvious she hadn't been coming across lately."

"You said that to a plainclothes cop?"

"Another roach hit me in the back of the head with a shoe. That was about it. What's the deal about Harrelson's convertible?"

"It's stuffed with money. The two Mexican guys killed on the train tracks took off with it."

"How much money?"

"Close to one million. Maybe more."

"You're pulling my crank?"

"No, that's the truth, Loren. The Atlas family brought in a couple of Sicilian hit men to find it."

He straightened his collar and glanced sideways down the street, his hair blowing in the wind, his shirt flapping. "Hopkins is dirty, isn't he?"

"Corrupt? I don't know."

"He was a vice cop in Galveston. That means he was either on a pad for the Atlas family or he quit or got fired because he was on the square. Does Hopkins strike you as a guy on the square?"

"You think he knows these hit men?"

"A guy like that has his finger in anything that pays a buck. Did Bledsoe boost Harrelson's convertible?"

"Ask him."

"That's what I thought. Okay, why hasn't somebody picked him up and torn him apart? Why haven't they torn you apart?"

"Maybe they're fixing to."

"Maybe. But why haven't they done it so far? Wise up."

"Somebody already knows where the convertible is?"

"See what a smart guy you are?"

"What do you think I should do?"

"Know what I learned at Gatesville? Stack your own time. Don't let people know what you're thinking. Silence scares the shit out of them. That's why the hacks put guys in solitary. It's the thing they fear most themselves. They're always playing their radios or yelling at each other in a locker room. When they don't hear sound, they've got to deal with their own problems."

"What time is your performance?" I said.

"At seven. It's at the Baptist campground. First I got to pick up all these kids on the bus. I read that book you gave me. *The Song of Roland*? It's pretty good. Did all that stuff really happen?"

"It never stopped happening," I said.

"You're a weird guy, man. I mean deep-fried *weird*."

I STOPPED IN A church on the way home and sat in a pew at the back, deep in the shadows. There was no one else there except a janitor knocking a push broom among the pews. I had come to believe that my spells were not simply blackouts but a way of hiding my true personality from myself. Amid the smell of incense and holy water in the stone founts and the candles flickering in their blue and red vessels, I admitted I wanted to kill Vick Atlas and his father and, for good measure, Grady Harrelson, and I wanted a divine hand to give me permission.

My thoughts seemed obscene, an offense to my surroundings and the powers I believe live on the other side of the veil. If I expected help with my request, it wasn't there. I walked outside, blind in the glare of the sun.

Chapter 32

I ATE AN EARLY supper with my parents, then picked up Valerie and drove to the campground where Loren's Baptist friends held their assemblies. A milky brown stream ran through it, and there were cedar and pine trees along the edges of the gulley, and swings and seesaws on a playground, and a big green ramshackle building with Ping-Pong tables and a basketball court inside. I had never been to a Protestant gathering. Back then, at least in the South, Catholics were often looked upon with suspicion. We in turn were taught to avoid regular company with the descendants of Martin Luther and John Calvin.

"I feel like I'm in hostile territory," I said.

"Why should they be upset with you when they've got a Christ killer like me available?" Valerie said.

How do you argue with that?

An empty yellow bus was parked by the building among rows of pickup trucks and old cars. Loren was smoking a cigarette outside the bus door, wearing navy blue slacks high on his hips and a white long-sleeved cowboy shirt with a silver tie and clasp, his hair wet-combed over the collar. I parked by the bus and took my guitar case from the backseat and handed it to him. "There're a couple flat picks and a thumb pick inside."

"Thanks," he said. He dropped his cigarette to the ground and mashed it under his shoe. Then he picked it up and field-stripped it and let the tobacco blow apart in the wind. He took a deep breath and worked his neck against his shirt collar.

"Nervous?" I said.

"Sweating through my clothes," he replied.

"You're going to do fine," Valerie said. "I learned this in speech class: Don't look at any person in particular. Look at the back wall. Everyone will think you're looking at him or her."

That was how Valerie talked. She never made a grammatical error; every word she used gave a sentence a more specific meaning than it needed. As I looked at her profile in the twilight, and at the glow on her skin and the happiness in her eyes, I knew I would never be able to separate myself from her, no matter what else occurred in our lives, even death. I felt as though we were already one flesh, one spirit, lovers who were almost incestuous, like brother and sister, companions unto and beyond the grave. It was a funny feeling to have.

"What are y'all singing?" I asked.

"'Keep on the Sunny Side' and 'Blue Moon of Kentucky' and a couple of others, if we don't get thrown out."

"That's swell, Loren," I said.

"You reckon I can do it?" he said.

"We'll be in the front row," Valerie said. She didn't need to say anything else.

He went through the back door of the building with my guitar case, and Valerie and I went through the front and sat down in the bleachers that surrounded the basketball court. In a few minutes the building was packed. Children ran around on the court with balloons on sticks while the musicians set up on the stage. The people sitting by us were sun-browned and had the rough hands and narrow features of people for whom privation and hard physical work were as natural as the sunrise. Their clothes were wash-faded and starched and ironed, their eyes full of expectation and pleasure at attending a function that for them was a communal validation of their lives.

Loren's band came out on the stage. If he was nervous, he hid it well. Because of his height, he had to lean down to the microphone when he sang "Blue Moon of Kentucky." The spotlight bathed him, his moist hair black and shining, his cheeks sunken, the range of his voice like Porter Wagoner's. The audience began to applaud slowly, and then they went crazy. I don't think anyone was more surprised than Loren. He looked around him as though they were yelling and stomping their feet for someone else. He went immediately into the Carter Family's theme song, "Keep on the Sunny Side." Then he did Hank's "Lovesick Blues." Then he did "I Saw the Light" and came back for five encores.

Valerie looked around. "I've never seen anything like this."

"I'm going to call Biff Collie tomorrow. Biff's a good guy."

"Who?"

"He's a disk jockey and the master of ceremonies at Cook's Hoedown."

"You did this, Aaron."

"Nope."

"Loren pretends he has everything under control, but he has no confidence at all. He told me you showed him his first chords. You don't know how much that meant to him."

At the intermission, we bought hot dogs and Cokes at a long table covered with food. Loren came through the crowd with my guitar case, shaking hands with people, nodding, embarrassed by their praise and affection. He slipped the handle of the case into my hand. "I've got to go outside."

"What for?" I said.

"My head feels like it's full of helium. I'm about to faint."

"Have a hot dog," Valerie said.

"I did okay, huh?" he said.

Valerie and I both grinned.

"You liked it?" he said.

"What do you think?" I said.

Then the girls were all around him. Valerie and I went outside. The western sky was as red as a forge. A purple MG turned off the state two-lane and drove across the grass and parked not far from the church bus. Grady Harrelson got out and looked over his shoulder, then stared at us without moving. I didn't know if he was self-conscious about his British sports car or afraid of the class of people he found himself among.

"What's he doing here?" I said.

"I don't know, but Loren had better not see him," Valerie said.

"Loren said something?"

"He thinks Grady is responsible for his cousin's death."

"So do I."

"Let me talk to him," she said.

"How about we both talk to him? How about we both tell him to leave us alone?"

"Look at him. He's pitiful," she said.

I didn't argue. She was probably right. But I was learning that people who are pitiful and have nothing to lose are the ones who can leave you in shreds.

As it turned out, Grady didn't want to see "both" of us. "Hi, Valerie," he said. "What's happening, Aaron? Take a walk with me."

"How'd you know where we were?" she said.

"One of your neighbors told me. Can I have a word with Aaron?"

"Talk to both of us or neither of us," I said.

He was wearing jeans and sandals and a golf shirt with an alligator on the pocket. A thick strand of hair hung across one eye. Somehow Grady always struck a pose that seemed to capture our times—petulant, self-indulgent, glamorous in a casual way, and dangerous, with no self-knowledge. "I've got a duck camp south of Beaumont. Why don't y'all get out of town for a while? Let all this stuff blow over."

"What stuff?" I said.

He turned around and gazed at the sky. "It looks like the clouds are burning, doesn't it?"

"What's bothering you, Grady?" I said.

"Things got out of control. It happens. That's what I'm saying. I don't want y'all hurt."

"Then stop acting like an idiot," Valerie said. "Are you here about those Sicilian murderers?"

The blood drained from his cheeks. "You've seen them? They're here?"

"Did Vick send them or did his old man?" I said.

He stepped backward and didn't answer.

"Did Vick send them?" I repeated.

"Vick doesn't confide in me. Talking to y'all is a waste of time. I wish I'd never seen you, Broussard."

"I never wronged you, Grady," I said. "I always felt sorry for you."

"You feel sorry for *me*?" he said. "Where do you get off with that?"

"Thanks for coming by," I said.

His face was like a wounded child's. His gaze shifted to the front of the green building. "I didn't know you were with *him.*"

I turned around. Loren was walking toward us.

"Go home, Grady," Valerie said. "Now."

"Tell Broussard to go home," he said. "You were my girl till he messed us up."

Loren's stride was eating up the distance between him and us. Grady stepped backward again. Loren pointed his finger at him and said, "*You!*"

"Go on," Valerie said to Grady, almost whispering. "I'll talk to him."

"No, you won't," Grady said. He stepped away from us, his hands hanging at his sides. He swallowed.

"What are you doing here?" Loren asked.

"Talking to my friends," Grady replied.

"This is our place," Loren said.

"What do you mean, your place?"

"What I said. You don't have friends here."

"It's a free country," Grady said.

Those were the exact words I had used to Grady when I'd interfered in the argument he was having with Valerie at the drive-in.

"No, it's not a free country, Harrelson," Loren said. "You got my cousin Wanda killed, and you got away with it because nobody cares about a Mexican hooker getting her neck broke. You're a River Oaks punk who couldn't cut the Corps, so you came back home to Daddy and pretended you were a hard guy by getting it on with a poor girl who went to the ninth grade."

"I came out here to do a good deed," Grady said. "I think that was a mistake."

"You got that right. Go back to your part of town," Loren said.

"You people are too much," Grady said.

"'You people'? You want me to put you in your car and show you up for the yellow-bellied douchebag you are?"

"Bugger off. I'm leaving," Grady said.

"Do what?"

"Ask Valerie to take you to the library. They've got a book there called a dictionary. You'll dig it."

I could see the confusion in Loren's face, his powerlessness over a word he hadn't heard before.

"My father dumped us when I was a kid," he said. "But if he was around today, I wouldn't be afraid to play my music in front of him."

Grady's hands closed and then opened at his sides. His face was turned slightly to one side, as though he were trying to avoid a hot wind. "What are you talking about?"

"One of your friends was laughing about your old man not letting you play Gatemouth Brown in your house," Loren said. "Wanda was too good for you. I think that's why you hurt her. Every time you look in a mirror, it doesn't matter where you are, you see a punk looking back at you."

If I ever saw someone's soul flinch, it was then. Grady's mouth seemed to collapse and his eyes to lose focus, as though the earth had shifted under his feet. "Yeah?"

"Just blow," Loren said. "It's our part of town. Those are the rules, man. You should know. Y'all made them."

Then Grady did the strangest thing I had ever seen a young guy do in public. He worked his golf shirt off his shoulders and turned around, arching his tanned back at us. VALERIE was tattooed across his shoulder blades, each letter formed by a chain of red hearts. "She'll always be with me, and there's nothing you can do about it, Broussard. As for you, Nichols, you were a loser when you came out of the womb. I hope you're with Broussard when he gets his."

I felt myself moving toward him.

"I'm going," he said. "Y'all have a great life. See you, Val. Believe it or not, I thought you were the one."

He walked away from us bare-chested, his shirt clenched in his hand. I suspected Grady's father had taught him many lessons, and one of them involved probing for bone and nerve to leave the most ragged of wounds. I caught up with him before he got to his MG. He was smiling to himself.

"I don't know what it is, but there's something I missed," I said. "It was a detail, something you said or Valerie said or a cop named Jenks said. It has to do with your alibi."

The sky was a dull red now, the campground falling into shadow. His eyes searched my face. "You'd make a lousy poker player."

"It's not me who has sweat on his upper lip," I replied.

THE EVENING WASN'T over. After Grady drove away, I spotted a black boxlike sedan parked among the cedar and pine trees bordering the gulley that wound through the campground. A heavyset man in a fedora was behind the wheel. He raised a pair of binoculars to his face.

"Don't turn around," I said.

"What is it?" Valerie said.

"The car we saw outside the theater is parked by the trees. A guy is looking at us through binoculars."

"The one with the camera?" she said.

"I can't be sure."

"You're talking about those hit men?" Loren said, his eyes riveted on mine.

"Just one. The guy in the car," I said. "That's the car we saw outside a theater with a guy in it who took our picture."

"You're sure it's the car?" Loren said.

"There's no doubt about it."

Then the man behind the wheel made a mistake. He put down the binoculars and lit a cigarette, the flame flaring on his face. Just before he flicked away the match, he turned and looked straight at me and I saw his wide-set eyes and the coarseness in his skin, the fingers that resembled sausages.

In spite of my admonition, Loren turned around. Then he looked back at me. "That's the guy?"

"I'd bet on it."

"Start your heap," he said.

"Whatever you're thinking, don't do it," I said.

"Thinking makes my head hurt."

"The cops will send you to Huntsville, Loren," Valerie said. "If they don't kill you first."

"They're not interested in fender benders," he said.

"Fender benders?" Valerie said.

Loren walked away, spinning a key ring on his finger.

I COULD HAVE STOPPED him. I didn't want to see him hurt or beat up by the cops or sent to a mainline prison, although I didn't know that any of those things would happen. I guess I respected him too much to stand in his way.

But I tried. "Loren! Come on back! A lot of people inside want to talk to you! I'm going to call Biff Collie! I'm not kidding you, I know him!"

I suspect I sounded like a fool, shouting about a local disk jockey. Valerie put her hand on my arm and squeezed it. "Let him go. It's just Loren's way. That's why he's not like the others."

My father said that those who are crucified usually seek their fate, because it is only after we murder them that we make them our light bearers. I hoped Loren wasn't trying to find his own set of hammer and nails. He got behind the wheel of his bus and began revving the engine. With the door open, he backed in a semicircle, straightened out, aimed in the outside mirror, and floored the accelerator.

It was beautiful to watch. The bus whined in reverse across the grass, swaying and bouncing over the bumps, bearing down on the man in the boxlike sedan. At first the man seemed unable to grasp what was happening. Then his mouth opened in dismay and he recoiled backward as though a wrecking ball were swinging into his face. The impact flattened the doors and running board and front fender and tilted the car halfway over. Then the car fell back on all four tires, the front windshield bursting like crushed ice on the hood.

Loren shifted into first, straightened out, then backed the bus into the sedan again and began pushing it in bulldozer fashion over the rim of the gulley. The sedan tipped sideways and slid down the embankment in a cloud of dust and landed in the water. People began running from the building and the parking area. The driver of the sedan crawled up the opposite embankment, his shoes digging for purchase in the dirt, his fedora gone, exposing his tight gray haircut. He grabbed a tree root and pulled himself onto flat ground, then got to his feet, his suit and dress shirt streaked with mud. He was a huge man, his cheeks swollen like a chipmunk's, his neck ringed with fat. He stood still, as though making a decision, then disappeared into the cedar and persimmon trees, sticks and dead limbs breaking in his path.

Loren jumped down from the bus and ran to my heap. He piled into the backseat. "What are you waiting for?"

I couldn't move. Neither could Valerie.

"Fire it up," he said. "Time to boogie."

Valerie shook my arm. "He's right. Let's go, Aaron. Snap out of it."

I wasn't thinking about the damage he had just done to the church bus, or the chaos in the parking area, or that Loren might soon be on his way to jail. He had said the word I couldn't remember, the key to the lockbox, the detail I had missed, one that had lain in plain sight and would expose the blood-bespattered world of regicide and guilt and ambition in which Grady Harrelson lived.

Chapter 33

WE WENT TO a northside drive-in and parked in the shadows, away from the glow of the neon and the lighted dining area inside. Loren kept looking out the back window. "Y'all stay here. I'm going to use the pay phone and get my brother to pick me up. This stuff will die down in a couple of days."

"Die down?" I said.

"This is how it will go. The car I smacked is probably hot. The guy driving it wasn't hurt and doesn't want to talk to cops. The cops couldn't care less about the guy or the car. I'll square the bus damage with the preacher who gave me the job. I probably won't be driving the bus anymore. End of story."

"It's that simple?" I said.

"I'll get lost for a few days," he said.

"You said 'boogie' back there."

"What about it?" he asked.

I looked at Valerie. "You told me Grady gave you his Tommy Dorsey records because his father didn't want jazz or Negro music in his house."

"That's right."

"He gave you 'Tommy Dorsey's Boogie-Woogie' and 'Marie'?"

She nodded.

"When did he give them to you?" I asked.

"On the afternoon his father was killed."

"Those were the only records he had with him?"

"No, he had a stack of them. He said he got them from some Mexicans."

"Did he have another boogie-woogie record?"

She looked out the car window at the shadows and the strips of neon wrapped around the restaurant. "He had an Albert Ammons record."

"What was the title?"

"'Boogie Woogie Stomp,'" she replied. "He loved that recording."

I shuddered. "That was the song playing in the Harrelson house when somebody blew Mr. Harrelson apart."

She stared at me. "He went from my house and killed his father, then went out on the sailboat?"

"That's what it sounds like," I said.

"Y'all are surprised by this?" Loren said. He got out of the car and leaned on the roof. "Let me make a suggestion. Don't let Harrelson know you're on to him. Don't tell the cops, either."

"Why not?" Valerie said.

"You think they're on our side? Even your old man knows better than that."

"Merton Jenks is on the square," I said.

Loren looked at the dining room window and at the people eating inside. "That's why I like you, Aaron. When the whole world is a cinder, you'll still be a believer. You kill me."

I watched him walk away. "You know what that guy could do if he went to school?"

Valerie squeezed the back of my neck and laid her head on my shoulder.

"Did you hear me?" I asked.

"Yes," she replied. She pulled herself closer to me and held my hand and rubbed the top of her head against my cheek.

"Why the silence?" I asked.

"You believe. Others don't. Loren knows that. You don't. That's why I love you."

She said nothing else until Loren returned from making his call.

* * *

When I went home, the house was dark except for the desk lamp in my father's office. I unlocked the front door and walked through the living room and past my parents' bedroom and into my father's office. He was sleeping with his head on his arms. A cigarette had burned to ash and collapsed in the tray. His uncapped fountain pen and an empty coffee cup sat by the edge of his manuscript. I picked up the cup and smelled it. He kept the whiskey bottle hidden in either the garage or the trunk of his car. He never took it into the house. To my knowledge, this was the first time he'd drunk whiskey in the house.

I sat down in the spare chair by the wall. The attic fan was drawing a nice breeze through the screen. Bugs and Snuggs and Skippy were sitting on the sill. I wanted to wake my father and tell him about the hit men the Atlases may have brought to town; I also wanted to tell him about Loren plowing the car into the gulley. But I knew nothing good would come of it. Had he been at Cemetery Hill, he would have gone straight up the slope with the others, Yankee canister and grape ripping holes the width of barn doors in their lines. And every confession to him of my own fear only added to the burden that sent him back to the icehouse or into the garage after my mother had gone to bed.

I heard Major's nails clicking on the floor, then his tail knocking against the bookshelves as he walked into the office. My father raised his head from the desk. "Oh, hi, Aaron, I didn't hear you come in."

"I didn't mean to wake you," I said.

"Is everything all right?" he asked.

"Yes, sir, I'm fine."

"I was having a dream," he said. "We were back in Louisiana. You were five years old and I was taking you to the circus. Do you remember that?"

"Yes, sir, I do."

"You were amazed by the giraffe you saw in the animal pens. You couldn't believe there was an animal that tall."

"I remember."

"Are you sure everything is all right?" he repeated. "Did you and Valerie go with your friend to the church campground?"

"Yes, sir. We had a grand time."

"Your friend sang?"

"He sure did. People liked him."

"That was a fine thing you did, Aaron. I'm sure he will always remember your kindness. Is your mother awake?"

"She's asleep."

I could see his disappointment. "I guess I'd better take a little walk. If I take a nap before I go to bed, I wake up in the middle of the night and can't go back to sleep. Lock the door. I have my key."

"Why don't I heat us some milk and fix some pie. There's a whole apple pie in the icebox."

"That's too much trouble. I'll be back shortly."

He removed his hat from the rack by the door and went out on the porch and eased the door shut behind him so as not to wake my mother. Through the window I saw him walking in the moonlight, his shadow moving along the sidewalk like a disembodied spirit that would never find its way home.

THE NEXT MORNING I looked in the mirror. I'd had the stitches in my face removed after six days, but I had kept a medicated bandage over the wound to prevent infection. I peeled off the bandage and dropped it into the wastebasket. The scar resembled a broken red exclamation mark that had drained from my eye. I wanted to think of myself as a Prussian duelist or a soldier of fortune or a deputy marshal backing Doc Holliday and Wyatt Earp's play at the O.K. Corral. Or maybe I just wanted to be brave in the way Loren had been brave, forgetting about himself and risking time in Huntsville for a friend. But all I saw in my reflection was a seventeen-year-old pale-eyed kid who realized that to help his parents, he would have to accept that he might not reach age eighteen. I barely got my hand to my mouth before the bilious surge in my stomach had its way.

I went to the filling station without figuring out I had reported to work an hour early. At eleven A.M. Merton Jenks drove up in a dented black-and-white cruiser and parked it on the grass by the men's room. The vehicle's disrepair was the kind you saw only in the cruisers driven by Negro patrolmen in the black wards. Jenks didn't get out. I walked to the passenger window. "Yes, sir?" I said.

He put a quarter in my palm. "Get me a Coca-Cola."

"Anything else?"

"Don't be smart," he said.

I brought him his Coke and change.

"Get in," he said.

I sat down next to him, the door open to catch the breeze. He chugged half the Coke and burped. "Where's Loren Nichols?"

"At home or at work, I guess."

"Lose the act."

"I don't know where he is, Detective Jenks."

"After you fled the church campground last night, where'd you take him?"

"To a drive-in. He made a phone call and went off on his own."

"He went off where?"

"I don't know."

"Who did he leave the drive-in with?"

"I can't tell you that, Detective Jenks."

"How'd you like to be sitting in a jail cell?"

I shook my head.

"That means no, you don't want to be in a jail cell or no, you're not going to tell me anything?"

"It means Loren is a good guy and was trying to help us."

"Right," he said. "Photo time."

He opened a manila folder on a black-and-white photograph of a large man in a baggy suit hooked to a wrist chain with several other men stringing out of a police van. "Does this guy look familiar?"

"He was at the church campground."

"Driving the car Nichols pushed into the ditch?"

"That's the guy."

"His name is Devon Horowitz. He was doing hundred-dollar hits when he was fifteen. His partner in bargain-basement murder was Jaime Atlas."

I could feel my heart thud. "You have him in custody?"

"Would I be here?" he replied.

"They're planning to kill me, aren't they."

He propped his elbow on the window jamb and kneaded his brow. "The word is that two or three button men are in town. They're here about Clint Harrelson's money. Nobody stiffs the Mob. Maybe they're not after you. Maybe they just want the money. I can't say for sure. I'm trying to be square with you, Aaron. You know why I'm driving this beer can?"

"No, sir."

"I'm on half-time because of a medical condition. I'm also fixing to pull the pin. So I was given a pile of junk to motor around in. Are we starting to communicate here?"

"What's a button man?" I asked.

"A hit man. He pushes the 'off' button on people. I asked if you understood why I was driving this pile of junk."

"Your superiors have no use for you now, so you're going out of your way to help me."

He fiddled with a pack of Lucky Strikes in his shirt pocket, then tossed it onto the dashboard. "I'm going down to Mexico. A place called Lake Chapala. I'll be training some Cubans who're planning to invade their homeland. What do you think of that?"

"Mexico doesn't have very good health care," I replied.

"You missed your calling. You should have been a funeral director."

"Miss Cisco told you about the Mob getting stiffed and the button men coming here, didn't she."

"She didn't have to. I was working vice in Vegas when Siegel built the Flamingo. I knew the guy who popped him. I once hung him out a train window by his heels."

"She told you," I said.

He took a cigarette from the pack on the dashboard and stuck it into his mouth. "You've got a talent for pissing me off."

"I'm going to let them do it," I said.

"Do what?"

"It."

He removed the cigarette from his mouth. "Want me to slap you?"

"Shoot me. I don't care what you do. Look in my face and tell me I'm lying."

"Maybe things will get set right. Give it time."

"Your colleagues are going to help me? You are? The courts are going to put the Atlas family in prison?"

He held his eyes on mine and didn't reply.

I LEFT WORK EARLY and went home and bathed and put on a clean pair of khakis and my cowboy boots and a short-sleeved white shirt with a spray of small pink roses on the shoulders. I called Valerie, but no one answered. I wrote my father and mother a note that said "I'll be over at Saber's. See you later." Then I put on my cowboy hat, the one I wore the night I rode Original Sin, and went into the backyard. The sun was red and veiled with dust. I picked up Major and Bugs and Snuggs and Skippy one at a time and hugged each of them.

When I arrived at Saber's, he was on the swale changing the oil under a flatbed loaded with drill pipe. I wondered how his neighbors liked having an industrial service truck parked in their neighborhood. He crawled out barefoot and bare-chested, flakes of dried road grime in his hair and on his face. "What's shakin', rodeo man?"

"Need you to back me up."

"Doing what?" he said.

"I have to end all this stuff with all the people who are out to get me."

He got to his feet. His narrow chest was white and shiny with sweat, his eyes blinking with moisture. "We fight like the Indians. From behind a tree, right?"

"I need somebody to be my witness."

"Witness to what?"

"To whatever is fixing to happen."

"I'll get us a couple of RC Colas."

"I don't have much time, Saber. Are you in or out?"

"I just need something cold to drink. How you like the old man's truck? He got a job delivering pipe in the oil field. I'll be right back."

Saber walked into the house, his ribs and spine printed like sticks against his skin. Through the front window, I saw him talking with his father, gesturing. He came back out with two sweating bottles of RC Cola. He sat down against the truck tire, one leg stretched out. "So run that by me again."

"You always said you were backing my action."

"I meant it, too," he said, looking straight ahead. "I just don't know what the action is."

"I'm going to make them hurt me or leave me and my parents alone."

"Back off and take a second look at what you just said."

I sat down next to him. I didn't drink from the bottle. "I need your help, Saber."

"The old man hasn't touched the sauce in four days. I've been racking pipe for him and riding shotgun and such. We might have to go to Beaumont tonight."

He waited for me to speak, to tell him that I didn't need him, that I was wrongheaded, that it was okay for him to cut me loose and let me down.

"Don't worry about it," I said. "Could I have those two Molotov cocktails that were rolling around in your backseat?"

"Come on, what do you want those for?"

"I'll find a reason."

"Come on," he repeated.

"Will you give them to me or not?"

He looked away. "They're not real."

"What?"

"They're full of water. They were just for show."

I could hear the chimes of the Popsicle truck at the end of the street. Children were running from their houses with the nickel or dime their parents had given them.

"Forget it," I said, resting my cola on the grass. "I figured out something the last day or so, Saber. I never could understand why Grady hung with a guy like Vick Atlas. Then I thought about why you and I always hung together. Both of our fathers have problems with alcohol, but we've always stuck with them. That's when I realized where the bond between Grady and Vick came from. Both of them grew up hating their fathers. It's funny, isn't it? We don't think we're anything like those guys, but in some ways we are." I got up and took off my hat and wiped my brow. My legs felt weak.

"Where you going?" he asked.

"I haven't thought it through, Sabe." I said. "Check with you down the track."

I walked to my heap, accidentally knocking over my drink, the cola seeping into the swale.

Chapter 34

I DROVE TO THE north side of the city and stopped in a dusty park. Mexican children were having a birthday party and hitting a piñata hanging from the crossbar of a swing set. I parked behind the concrete restrooms and took Loren's .32 revolver from under the seat and walked into a cluster of pines behind the backstop of a softball diamond and dumped the shells from the cylinder into my palm and sprinkled them into a trash can. I slipped the revolver back into my pocket and clicked open my stiletto and inserted it under the base of a water fountain and snapped off the blade. Then I closed the stub and put it in my pocket with the revolver. I sat down in the bleachers and watched the children split the piñata into shreds, showering paper-wrapped taffy in the dust.

I do not know how long I sat there. I was sweating inside my hat. I set it crown-down on the bleacher seat and propped my hands on my knees and lowered my head and shut my eyes. There was a red glow inside my eyelids, a warm finger of sunlight on the back of my neck. I could smell a drowsy odor on the wind, like flowers left too long in a vase. My mother's father, Hackberry Holland, used to say death was like a field of poppies. He said every third night he rode deep into them, the husks smearing the legs of his horse, the red petals gluing to its skin. He said that death was a long field that had no fences but led to a precipice the other side of which was a blue sky. Grandfather had left us the previous year and, I believe, joined the drovers and lawmen and saloon girls and Indians whose companionship had defined his life. I wondered if he waited there to show me the way across.

"Are you okay, mister?" a tiny voice said.

I opened my eyes and looked down at a little Mexican girl. Her shiny black hair resembled a cap. She was wearing a pinafore and had a pink ribbon in her hair. "You looked like you was asleep and about to fall over," she said.

"I'd better not do that, then," I said.

"You want some cake?"

"Whose birthday is it?"

"Mine. We have ice cream. You want some?"

"That's nice of you. But I already ate."

"Did somebody hurt you?"

I had to think about her meaning. "You mean this bandage? A bull did that."

"Are you a cowboy?"

"Not really. Maybe a weekend cowboy. What's your name?"

"Esmeralda."

"Happy birthday, Esmeralda."

"Are you sad about something?"

"No, it's a fine day. A grand one for your birthday."

"You talk funny."

"It's the way my father talks."

"Your father must be funny."

"You can say that again. I don't have a present for you. But here's a quarter. How's that?" I stood up, the tops of the trees tilting; I wondered if I had been asleep.

"Thank you," she said. She started to run away, then stopped and said, "Don't get hurt no more. Bye-bye."

I watched her run back among the other children. I wanted to join them, to give up a decade of life and return to my childhood during the darkest days of the war, when gold stars hung in people's windows and we were united against those who would extinguish the light of civilization and transform the world into a slave camp. I walked to my heap like a drunk man and drove to a bar and poolroom in the middle of the Heights.

TO SAY IT was a rough place doesn't get close to it. Back then, Houston was the murder capital of the world. It was only forty miles from a town called Cut and Shoot, supposedly named because of a fight among the townspeople over the design of their church building. Violence was an inextricable part of the culture; it hung in the air, perhaps passed down from the massacres at Goliad and the Alamo and the Battle of San Jacinto or the feuds during Reconstruction or the systematic extermination of the Indians. One of Houston's most famous beer joints was called the Bloody Bucket.

The patrons at the place in the Heights were nine-ball hustlers, drifters, grifters, gamblers, and midnight ramblers. Driven less by passion than necessity, they had an encyclopedic knowledge of bail bondsmen, local flatfeet (whom they called roaches), shylocks, floating craps games, call girls (there were no brothels in Houston), hot-property fences, money washers, Murphy artists, jack-rollers, street dips, safecrackers, prizefight fixers, arsonists, and dope dealers. In its way, the bar and poolroom represented another country, one that didn't quarrel with human nature and the perfidious tendencies that hide in the unconscious.

I went inside the phone booth in back and closed the folding door and dialed Vick Atlas's number. There was no answer. I had a cup of coffee at the bar and waited fifteen minutes and called again. This time he picked up.

"Hey, Vick," I said. "I'll try to make this brief."

The line was silent.

"Are you there?"

"I assume this is my favorite hemorrhoid calling."

"I just came from the police station and wanted to update you,

Vick. They were talking about your hit man, the one who used to murder people with your father for a hundred dollars a hit. His name slips my mind."

"Like always, I got no idea who or what you're talking about. You trying to be cute again? That's what we're doing here? You got a tap on this?"

"Your man had an accident at the church campground, Vick. He got knocked in a gully by the church bus while driving a stolen car. I remember now. His first name is Devon."

"Where are you?"

"It's Devon Horowitz," I said. "The cops said he's an imbecile, just like you and your father. They said y'all have the reverse King Midas touch. Everything you touch turns to shit."

"Say that to my face."

"That's why I called. I'd like for us to get together."

"You think I'm stupid?" he asked.

"Not at all. I think you're scared. I think you hate your father and your father hates you. Anyway, I'm in the Heights." I gave him the name of the bar and its address.

"What are you up to, asshole?"

"Don't just send your guys, Vick. Bring yourself, too. Prove you're not the chickenshit, gutless dimwit everybody says you are."

I hung up and sat at the bar and watched two men shooting nine ball, my ears popping so loudly I couldn't hear the balls drop into the leather pockets.

I WENT INTO THE men's room and washed my face and looked in the mirror. My heart was tripping, my breath coming hard in my throat, beads of water trickling down my face like moisture on a pumpkin. The room looked a hundred years old. There was a flush tank with a chain high up on the wall; the floor was wood, dark with stains and soft as cork from toilet overflow or urine that had missed the bowl. A dirty towel hung in a loop from a machine above the toilet. There was not one inch of graffiti written or carved on the walls. These may seem strange details to notice, but they each represented in some aspect the situation I found myself in. I had broken the hands off my own clock and sealed myself inside an era and a culture that had more to do with the past than the future. Maybe my spells were an incremental journey to this spot, a retrograde place that was grimed and smelled of piss, where you dared not scratch your name on the shithouse wall unless you wanted your fingers broken.

I went back to the telephone and called Valerie. Through the plastic panels in the door, I saw the bartender watching me. Valerie picked up on the second ring. "Is that you?" she said.

"It's me."

"Where are you?"

I told her.

"What are you doing in there? It's full of criminals."

"So is the whole town."

"What *is* going on with you, Aaron?"

"Nothing. I just wanted to talk."

"Saber called and said you were at his house and talking crazy."

"He's exaggerating. Look, I have to take care of some things, Val. Will you do me a big favor?"

"What?"

"I'd like for you to talk to my mother. I'd like for you to be closer to her. She's strange in her ways, but her heart is in the right place."

She made a sound like she was blowing her hair out of her face. "Either come to my house right now or I'm going to that pool hall."

"I'll try to get there directly."

"Directly? I hate that word. It's what ignorant people say when they want to sound folksy. When did you start talking folksy?"

"I love you, Valerie."

The line went silent.

"Did you hear me?"

"What's wrong, Aaron? Is it that man from the campground? Did you see him again?"

"No, I didn't. Don't worry anymore. Tell Saber I've got it under control."

"I'm babysitting the child from next door. I can't leave. Don't do this to me."

"I've got to go now. Remember what I said about my mother, okay?" I eased the receiver back onto the hook.

I ASKED THE BARTENDER for another cup of coffee. His shoulders and chest had the solidity of concrete; the backs of his fingers were tattooed with illegible letters. He poured into my cup but set the coffeepot down on a towel rather than back on the stove. "What are you doing in here?"

"Waiting on somebody," I replied.

"This isn't a social center."

"I didn't mean to bother anybody."

"Who you waiting on, kid?"

"They didn't give me their names."

He put the coffee back on the burner and picked up the towel and wiped the wet spot the pot had left on the bar. "Where you from?"

"Houston."

"Where in Houston?"

"The southwest side."

He gazed through the front door at the street. "The warm-up is on the house. Drink up."

"You're telling me to leave?"

He huffed air out of his nostrils and filled his chest with air. "Don't complicate my day. That's the operating rule here. Think you can abide by that?"

"Yes, sir. Have you seen any strange guys around?"

"What do you mean by strange?"

"Greaseballs."

"This isn't a cuddly place. That's not a good word."

"Guys who carry guns and shoot other people," I said.

He threw his towel into the air and caught it, then walked away.

I watched the clock. Five minutes passed, then ten. The two nine-ball shooters stacked their cues and ordered draft beers and started peeling hard-boiled eggs at the end of the bar. The bartender was reading a newspaper he had flattened on the bar. I saw him look up and study something or someone out the front window. When I turned on the barstool, I saw a maroon Packard station wagon, one with real wood paneling and whitewall tires and chrome-spoked wheels; it drove to the end of the block and disappeared. The bartender folded his newspaper and walked toward me, trailing one hand on the bar top.

"A couple of guys out there have been around the block twice," he said.

"The ones in the station wagon?"

He nodded.

"I don't know anybody with a station wagon," I said.

"They were in the alley a little bit ago." I didn't reply. He leaned on his arms. "They're hitters. One of them was trying to see through the back door. Want to tell me what's going on?"

"You know Merton Jenks?" I asked.

"Everybody knows Merton Jenks."

"Call him if things go bad in here."

"Are you out of your fucking head?"

"I don't think so."

"Scram. Now."

"I'd appreciate it if I could stay a little longer."

"You'll appreciate being alive if I have to repeat myself."

"Was one of them a big guy? His name is Devon Horowitz."

The bartender stabbed his finger an inch from my nose.

I went out the door. An old gas-guzzler packed with children passed by. I thought I saw the little Mexican girl from the park waving at me. I raised my hand in reply, but the car turned a corner and was gone.

On the next block, I saw the station wagon parked at the curb in front of a pawnshop, the sunlight's reflection as bright as an acetylene torch on the windshield. Inside the glare, I thought I saw a man step out on the curb, but even with my hat brim shadowing my eyes, I couldn't make out his features.

The driver shifted into reverse, turned around in the middle of the intersection, and drove away. I got into my heap and headed for Vick Atlas's apartment building in the Montrose district.

THE CONCIERGE STOPPED me at the desk. "Sir, you can't go upstairs."

"Why not?"

"Aren't you the person who attacked Mr. Atlas?"

"I have no memory of that. Is Vick in?"

"Mr. Atlas went somewhere. Please leave."

"You mean he's not here?"

"If you go upstairs, I'll call the police."

"I'll go up there and check. You're doing a good job. I'll tell Vick."

I rode up to the penthouse and knocked on the door. There was no answer. I walked to the end of the corridor and looked down into the alley. Two men in dark trousers and immaculate long-sleeved white shirts billowing with wind, the cuffs rolled, were talking by the maroon station wagon. They were young and lithe and had long black hair combed straight back, a small pigtail like a matador's on the nape of the neck. I opened the window and stepped out on the fire escape, the steel grid screeching under my weight. They both looked up. I leaned over the handrail and lifted a hand in greeting. Neither reacted. They started talking again, glancing at the street and at the other end of the alley where my heap was parked. They didn't recognize me. Cisco Napolitano had said Jaime Atlas's hired killers were imports who never knew their target. The only one who might recognize me was Devon Horowitz. He had taken a photo of me at a bad angle in poor light in front of the theater.

Vick Atlas had not shown up at the bar and poolroom in the Heights. Now he had eluded me again. I stepped back inside and took the elevator down to the lobby. "You're right," I said to the concierge.

"Vick isn't here. Two of his friends are in the alley, though. They're killers from Sicily. I'll tell them you want them off the property."

I walked outside. The sun was a reddish-purple melt in the west, the clouds aflame, the breeze out of the south, fresh and cool and smelling of rain and flowers. I saw no sign of the maroon station wagon or the two men who looked like matadors. I got into my heap and drove to River Oaks, my mufflers purring on the asphalt in the cooling of the day.

Chapter 35

But first I stopped at a drugstore and called home. My mother answered. "Decide to have supper with us?"

"Sorry, Mother, I got tied up."

Then she surprised me. "That's all right. I put your plate in the icebox. Where are you?"

"Out on Westheimer. I'll be there soon. Is Daddy there?"

"I'll put him on. Are you all right, Aaron?"

"Sure."

"Just a minute."

She set down the phone. A moment later my father picked it up. "Have trouble with your car?" he said.

"No, sir. I need to take care of some things. I want to ask you something."

"Hold on. Take care of what things?"

"When you were in the trenches, how did you get the courage to go over the top the first time?"

"I didn't get the courage," he replied.

"Sir?"

"I never had courage. None of us did. We ran at Fritz because we were too frightened to run in the other direction. Where are you, son? What are you into?"

"I've got to get these guys off our backs."

"Tell me where you are. Let me help you."

"You already have. I'll be fine. If I'm a little late getting home, don't wait up."

He started to argue. I took the receiver from my ear so I couldn't hear his words. When he stopped speaking, I placed it to my ear again. "I'll be swell. The circus is coming to town in August. We'll be in the front seats."

I set the receiver back on the hook and got into my heap and drove into that giant island of oak trees and wealth and faux antebellum splendor that was Grady's homeland. There was a squall in the Gulf, and horse tails of purple rain were spreading across the blueness of the sky. I glanced in the rearview mirror. The Packard station wagon was two blocks behind me. A piece of wet newspaper slapped against my windshield and disappeared into the vortex of wind and trees behind me; the gearshift knob was throbbing like an impacted wisdom tooth inside my palm.

BY THE TIME I got to Grady's block, the sky had gone dark. The rain was blowing in sheets, leaves floating in the gutters. All the lights were on in Grady's house. I parked at the curb and cut the engine and waited. Two or three cars with their headlights on were coming up the street. Each of them passed me without slowing down. The station wagon was not among them. I could see two cars parked by Grady's carriage house, but I couldn't make out what kind. I thought about my father's words regarding the nature of courage. I believed he was telling the truth about himself and his friends. They had been terrified, but they had stepped across a line and surrendered to their fate, whatever it might be.

The Midwestern boys who died at Marye's Heights or the Southerners whose bodies littered the slope at Cemetery Hill would have understood my father's statement. You had to find courage in yourself; no one could pay your dues for you.

As I sat in my heap, the rain pounding on the roof and windows, I began to feel a sense of anger. I had been the random target of Grady

Harrelson and his friends and the Atlas family, though I had done nothing to harm any of them. Like the rape victim or the molested child, I'd felt that I deserved what had been done to me, that I was alone, that no one cared, that I was odious in the sight of others. I now regretted that I had dumped the shells from the cylinder of the pistol and snapped off the blade of the stiletto. I took the pistol and the knife from my pocket and placed them on my thigh. Far down the street, I saw a pair of yellow headlights wobbling through the rain.

I twisted in the seat and waited as the vehicle slowed. The rain turned to hail, clicking on the trees and lawn and street and the top of my car. There was no mistaking the vehicle heading my way. It was a Packard station wagon, its windows streaked with ice. Suddenly I felt all the rage and pain I had experienced since I had tried to help Valerie at the drive-in in Galveston. I pulled my hat tight on my head and got out of my heap and ran toward the station wagon. I couldn't see the two occupants well, but I doubted they were expecting someone to charge at them during an electric storm. I threw the pistol at the windshield and clicked open the broken blade of the stiletto and tried to break the passenger window with it. The driver swerved toward the curb, trying to knock me sideways. I threw the knife at the back of the car as it drove away. Then I walked through the pools of water in Grady's front yard and hammered on the door.

Grady jerked it open. Vick Atlas was standing behind him in the foyer, the crystal chandelier shining on both of them. Vick was wearing a bandage over the split I had put in his cheek.

"What are you doing here?" Grady said.

"The hired help screwed up," I said. "How's it going, Vick? Your face looks a little swollen. I heard you got an infection. I think it adds to your mystique."

"Why'd you bring this asshole here, Vick?" Grady said.

"I didn't have anything to do with him coming here. Don't be saying I did, either."

"Vick didn't have the guts to come up to the Heights, so he sent his greaseballs and hid out at your house," I said. "You guys have been working together all this time, haven't you."

I stepped inside. Grady closed the door behind me and looked at Vick as though he didn't know what to do next. Vick was wearing half-topped boots, and tailored brown slacks that looked like Marine Corps tropicals, and a pink kerchief tied around his neck. "Where's Bledsoe?"

"I don't know," I replied.

"He's always with you," Vick said.

"Not tonight. You guys have the convertible and the money and the gold stashed, don't you?"

"You're pretty dumb, coming here like this," Vick said.

"What are you going to do that you haven't already done?" I said. "I'm not afraid of you or your people anymore, Vick. Same goes for you, Grady. You guys are bums, and the guys who work for you are stupid and inept."

"You think you can talk shit to me?" Vick said. "Nobody talks shit to me. That's what you think, you can walk in here and talk shit? Answer me. I'm talking to you."

"That's exactly what your father said to me. Why do you imitate the person who disfigured your mouth? Isn't that humiliating?"

"Ease up," Grady said.

"The Vickster can take it. Right, Vick?"

"You need to towel off, Broussard," Grady said. "We'll work this out."

"No, we won't," I said.

"Walk with me," he said, cupping his hand on my bicep. "There's a bathroom at the end of the hall. I'll get you some dry clothes."

I lifted Grady's hand from my arm. That was when Vick picked up a gold-encased anniversary clock and smashed it against the side of my head. The floor slammed into my face.

I WOKE IN AN embryonic ball inside an elevator that had a collapsible gate for a door. My stomach was sick, the side of my head sticky with blood. I pushed myself against the wall of the elevator and looked at my watch. No more than ten minutes had passed since Vick had hit me. The elevator was stopped under the house in a broom-clean parking garage lit by low-wattage bulbs inside wire guards on the ceiling. The gate on the elevator was locked. There were several collectible automobiles parked in the garage; among them was Grady's pink convertible, the one Saber had boosted from the motel. I could hear Vick and Grady talking through the ceiling. I got to my feet and almost fell down.

I tried the buttons on the elevator. Either the power had been cut or the elevator had been locked in place. I tried to jerk the gate loose from the jamb, then got down on the floor and tried to push it with my feet until it caved onto the concrete. I held on to a handrail and kicked until the elevator was shaking. A light went on in a stairwell on the far side of the convertible. Vick walked out of the stairwell, a hypodermic needle in one hand, a pair of handcuffs in the other. "Sorry to keep you waiting down here. I had to get some items from my car. I'd like to tell you there's a hard way or an easy way, but that wouldn't be true."

"My heap's out front," I said. "My family knows where I am."

"So you came here and you left," he replied.

"Why the needle?"

"Maybe I got a kind heart. Been to any junkyards recently? The compacting process puts me in awe."

"I'm not going to help you hurt me."

"I'm going to drag you," he said. "Not here. Out there." He fed a stick of gum into his mouth and waited for my response. He began to smack his gum, smiling. "I did it once. At spring break in Fort Lauderdale. A guy thought he was going to get laid. He got laid, all right."

"Are the money and gold still in the convertible?"

"What do you know about money and gold?" he asked.

"That money is owed to your father."

"Turn around and poke your hands through the gate."

"Why should I do that?"

He removed a .25-caliber semi-auto from his pants pocket. "So I don't shoot you in both kneecaps and anywhere else that hurts."

My vision was starting to go out of focus. I pressed my hand against the side of my head and then looked at my palm. It was matted with blood and hair. "What about the hit men?"

He closed his eyes as though processing the question. "Which hit men?"

"The ones you sent up to the Heights because you wouldn't go yourself. What if they see the convertible? What if they tell your old man you're about to steal a million dollars from him?"

"They don't know me, asshole. You're really dumb. That's why people like me win and people like you lose."

"Grady will screw you, Vick. After I'm out of the way, he'll want Valerie back. That means he'll have to get you out of the picture because he knows you for the lowlife you are. You have another problem, too. Grady thinks that money and gold are his. Why would he share them with you?"

For just an instant I saw the focus change in his eyes, like he was watching a bird fly into a distant tree. "I didn't quite get that."

"In your mind, you're stealing from your father or the Mob. In Grady's mind, you're stealing from him. Would you give away fifty percent of your money to take back what's already yours?"

There was a smirk on his lips, the kind stupid people wear when they convince themselves they long ago solved the great mysteries of the world and now float high above them. He dropped the handcuffs through the gate. "I'm going to enjoy this."

The door chimes rang upstairs. I heard Grady pull open the front door. "I must be hallucinating," he said.

"My heap broke down two blocks up the street," Saber's voice replied.

Chapter 36

Can we come in?" Valerie said. "We're drowning."

"No. Get out of here," Grady said.

"Why are you acting like this?" she said. "Where's Aaron?"

"He left his heap here and went off with some guys," Grady said. "I thought he was with you all."

"That's his hat on the floor," she said. "Where is he, Grady?"

"We had an argument," he said. "It's nothing to worry about. Will y'all get out of here?"

"No, we will not," Valerie said. "Have you done something to Aaron? What are you hiding?"

"A million dollars is what he's hiding," Saber said.

Way to go, Sabe. You just flushed all of us. But how could I be mad at him? The Sabe had gone looking for his old friend.

"Come in," Grady said.

I heard Saber and Valerie step inside the foyer and the door closing behind them.

"Your heap is up the street?" Grady said.

"Yeah, the weld on my manifold cracked," Saber said.

"I'll call a wrecker. It's on me," Grady said.

"We don't want a wrecker. Where's Aaron?" Valerie said.

"Downstairs," Grady said. "We need to work things out. I'm going to bring the elevator up. Vick's here."

"Vick Atlas is here?" Valerie said. "That's why that clock is smashed on the floor?"

"Take it easy, Val," Grady said.

"Don't you dare talk down to me," she said.

"Lower your voice."

"Have you hurt Aaron?" she said.

"I'm bringing the elevator up," Grady said. "None of this is my doing. All of you had your chance, but you wouldn't listen. Now we're either going to work this out, or the shit is going through the fan."

I heard the engine that drove the elevator come alive, then the elevator jolted and began rising. I watched Vick bolt for the stairwell, the hypodermic needle in one hand, the semi-automatic in the other.

Our lives were now in the hands of infantile men. They were irrational, frightened, narcissistic, ruthless, and cruel. One had murdered his father because he wasn't allowed to play a song recorded by a man of color; the other had been disfigured and perhaps neurologically impaired by a father he both imitated and despised. I thought again about my father and his fellow soldiers who went over the top in the Great War. I wondered if my legs would fail me when I had to face my own ordeal.

THE ELEVATOR STOPPED on the first floor and the outer door slid open. At the same time, Vick emerged from the stairwell at the back of the house.

"Aaron, are you all right?" Valerie said. She was dripping water on the floor; her hair was glued to her cheeks.

"Sure, Val," I said.

Then she saw Vick coming toward her. "Is that a gun?"

"It's not my dick," he said.

"You're disgusting," she said.

"I told them we'd work it out," Grady said. "You hearing me, Vick? We've got ties."

"What we've got is the mess you made," Vick said.

"Mess I made? You hit Broussard in the head with a fucking clock," Grady said.

"Shut up. I'm trying to think," Vick said.

"It's still no harm, no foul, Vick," Grady said.

"Repeat what you said about the million dollars, Bledsoe."

"I don't remember saying anything about that," Saber said.

"He doesn't remember," Vick said. "I love these guys. They make up their own reality every five minutes. 'I don't remember.' 'I didn't do it.' 'You're a good guy, Vick.' 'Don't hurt me, Vick.' 'Lend me some money, Vick.' "

"You fall down the stairs on your head?" Grady asked.

"Get some tape," Vick said.

"For what?" Grady said.

"I got to draw you a diagram?" Vick said.

"Don't do this, Grady," Valerie said. "You know what my father will do if you hurt us."

"You'll have a hard time telling him anything if I put you under thirty yards of concrete," Vick said. "Keep running your mouth and that might just happen. Stick out your hand, Bledsoe."

"Screw you," Saber said.

"Bad boy," Vick said. With no expression, without blinking, he pointed the pistol and shot Saber through the foot. The spent shell bounced off a lamp table.

Saber fell against the wall and slid to the floor, blood welling out of his shoe, his mouth wide with pain.

"You're the lowest of the low, Vick," I said. "If we get out of this, I'm going to get you. If I don't, my father will."

"See how you feel an hour from now," Vick said.

Valerie knelt beside Saber and held his head to her breast. She looked up at Grady. "Stop this."

"You shouldn't have come here, Val," Grady replied. "You shouldn't have let Broussard bust us up. You shouldn't have left me at the drive-in that night in Galveston."

"You're breaking my heart here," Vick said. He unlocked the gate on the elevator. "Outside, Broussard. The festivities are just beginning."

A bolt of lightning exploded in a tree in the side yard, dropping a huge limb into the swimming pool, taking down the power line with it. The house went dark. There was my chance, I told myself. Vick flicked the wheel on his cigarette lighter and pressed the barrel of his pistol against Valerie's head. "Keep having those kinds of thoughts and her brains will be in Bledsoe's lap. You lose again, asshole."

GRADY CAME BACK from the kitchen with two flashlights and a roll of tape. Saber was sitting against the wall, one knee pulled up to his chest, his wounded foot sticking straight out in front of him, blood pooling around the shoe. Vick handcuffed Valerie's wrist to Saber's. He reached into his pocket and took out a second small automatic and gave it to Grady. "The safety is above the trigger guard."

"I don't want it," Grady said.

"Yeah, you do," Vick said. "You were born for the life. You were always one of us."

"What about *him*?" Grady asked, glancing at me.

"This baby is mine," Vick said. "We're going out to a junkyard run by a friend of mine."

"I don't get it. What's the plan?" Grady said.

"I got to keep my word on something. About Broussard. He knows what I mean."

"You're going to drag him? That's sick, man," Grady said.

"Look at what he did to my face," Vick said. "Think he doesn't have it coming? I got pus running out of this bandage every day."

"What about Val?" Grady asked.

Vick shone a light on her face. Her eyes watered in the glare. He grinned at Grady.

"Knock that off," Grady said.

"You develop qualms?"

"Maybe I have."

"You got an easy choice, Grady," Vick said. "You can stay a rich man or go to work sacking groceries."

"I'll talk to her. She's practical."

"By now she's figured out you killed your father. How practical is she going to be about that?"

"You better put a cork in it, Vick," Grady said.

Yes, yes, yes, provoke him some more, Vick. But I underestimated him. Vick was a survivor who had spent a lifetime dealing with a disfigured face and the insults it drew.

"I'm just kidding," he said. "Your old man brought it on himself. You're a stand-up guy, Grady. You proved that when you joined the Corps. I think secretly your old man was afraid you'd show him up."

"Grady, please stop and try to think about what you're doing," Valerie said. "You've made mistakes. But this isn't you."

"Tell her," Vick said.

"Tell me what?" she asked.

"About the Mexican girl," Vick replied.

"Lay off that," Grady said.

"Tell her."

"He's talking about Wanda Estevan," Grady said. "It was an accident. We set fire to Loren Nichols's car. She tried to jump out of my car. I was trying to pull her back in. I grabbed her neck the wrong way. I feel terrible. I went to Broussard's church about it."

"Then don't let this creep ruin your life," she said.

"Time to go," Vick said. "I'm going to move Broussard's heap. I'll take Val and the freak with me. Put Broussard in my trunk and follow me. In three hours, we're going to be eating pancakes and sausages and eggs. This won't exist anymore."

"What's the hypo for?" Grady asked.

Vick looked at Valerie again. "You never can tell."

Chapter 37

How do you surrender to death? Or to the idea that your fate lies in the hands of evil men? When these events occurred that dark night in River Oaks, I had no preparation. Death had always been an abstraction, a vague presence that held no sway in my life. The stories that came back from Korea were always heroic in nature; the newsreels showed American F-80s coming in low over white hills at the Chosin Reservoir, sliding balls of flaming napalm into the thousands of Chinese troops that had crossed the Yalu and surrounded the First Marine Division. We cheered inside the warmth of the theater and took heart at the sight of marines with frozen beards who gave the thumbs-up to the cameraman. Death and suffering had been visited on our enemies, not us.

I think there is a clock in all of us that most choose not to see or heed. The clock has a date and an hour and minute and a second on it that are not subject to change. I knew my hour had come, but I couldn't accept it. The thought made my mouth go dry, my colon constrict, my throat back up with bile, my vision go out of focus. I felt like my blood had been fouled. The person I thought of as Aaron Holland Broussard seemed to have taken flight from my breast, and I wondered if the real me was indeed a coward, a pathetic creature whose only accomplishments in life were to ride a dumb animal for eight seconds and to swim terrified through a school of jellyfish.

Vick pulled open the door. All the other houses on the street were without power. Rain was sweeping across the Harrelson lawn and the live oaks and the swimming pool and blowing into the foyer. Grady struggled to get Saber to his feet. Saber tripped and fell and pulled Valerie down with him.

"Get him up," Grady said.

"Let them go. It's me Vick wants," I said.

"It's over. Accept it, Broussard," Grady said.

I lifted Saber to his feet. He kept his weight on one leg, holding on to me, his face buried in my shoulder. "Two guys in a woody," he whispered. "One block south. Greaseballs."

I didn't know how the information could help. But I knew that somehow the two assassins were related to our mutual fate, that their presence was part of the design, that somehow there was a doorway out of the black box we were in.

"Grady?" Valerie said.

"Yes?"

"Look at me."

"There's no point talking about it, Val."

"Look at me, Grady."

"What is it?"

"When you're done with us, you'll always be Vick Atlas's tool. He'll take everything you have. You're weak. You need him, but he doesn't need you. Why do you let him do this to you?"

"Shut your mouth," Grady said.

"That's it," Vick said. He pushed Valerie and Saber out the door. Then he looked at the rain swirling in the trees. He picked up my hat from the floor and put it on. "Okay, you two, let's take a ride. See you in a minute, Grady."

I watched the three of them walk through the puddles in the driveway toward my heap. Saber was holding on to Valerie, his left leg almost collapsing with each step. Grady shoved me between the shoulder blades onto the porch. "We'll cut through the side yard to the carriage house."

A long ragged bolt of lightning split the clouds, and I saw the reflection glimmer on a station wagon parked one block south, just as Saber had said. We were about to enter the gate that gave on to the side yard and the swimming pool and the carriage house and Vick's parked car. I was supposed to climb into the trunk and let Grady lock me inside. Down the street I heard the station wagon start up, backfiring once, like a wet firecracker. Then I knew what was going to happen. I was not prescient; I didn't have an epiphany; it was the opposite.

I was at the side of my father the first time he went over the top. I was in a wheat field golden with heat and misty with blood, and among the martyrs like Felicity and Perpetua who died in a Carthaginian arena, and at the limestone wall among the farm boys from Ohio who charged into Confederate artillery with empty muskets. I knew that death wasn't that bad after all, that it freed me from the earth and united me with brothers and sisters who were among the finest in the family of man.

I began running toward Valerie and Saber, waiting for Grady to take aim and fire at my back. But it didn't happen. Instead, the driver of the station wagon pulled to the center of the asphalt and accelerated toward us, the car's wake rippling over both curbs onto the lawns along the street. There was only one passenger. He was in the backseat, rolling down the window.

As he positioned himself and fitted the automatic rifle to his shoulder, I could see his white shirt, the bloodless pallor of his face, the delicacy of his hands, the flawless sweep of his hair over his tiny ears, the ease with which he sighted on his target and prepared to pull the trigger.

The weapon he held was known formally as the Browning automatic rifle and informally as the BAR. Its effect was devastating. As the station wagon closed on us, the line of fire was perfect. Probably two bursts would kill the four of us.

The driver clicked on his headlights, then hit the high beams, silhouetting Vick, my cowboy hat slanted on his head, his bandaged cheek as white as snow. I piled into Saber and Valerie and knocked them both to the ground and covered them with my body. The shooter opened up. There must have been at least one tracer round in the magazine. It streaked away into the darkness, maybe hitting the bathhouse in the side yard. The other rounds chewed Vick Atlas into pieces. His flesh, his hair, his clothing seemed to dissolve in the headlights, as though he were caught on wires. I could hear the ejected shells pinging against the station wagon's window frame, the bullets thudding into a tree behind us. Then the station wagon drove away slowly, the profile of the shooter as sculpted and serene and immobile as a statue's.

Vick had fallen into the water. I got up and pulled his body onto the swale and found the handcuff key in his pocket. I unlocked the cuffs from Valerie's and Saber's wrists and put Saber into the passenger seat of my heap. My hands would not stop shaking. I thought Valerie was crying. Or maybe laughing. Saber was grinning. I was sure about that.

Behind me I saw Grady running down the sidewalk, staring back at us like a frightened child.

Epilogue

THE POWER WENT back on, and one house after another filled with light, as though the Angel of Death held no dominion in this green-gray, moss-hung urban forest on the rim of the industrial world. I went back into the house and called the police. Then I made a second call, one I have never told anyone about until now.

"Hello?" she said.

"Hi, Miss Cisco."

"Aaron? What kind of mess are you in now?"

"Long story. You have a key to Grady Harrelson's house?"

She paused before she spoke. "What do you think?"

"Detective Jenks said he plans to go to Mexico. I bet he'd like to go there in a Caddy convertible. It's pink. You'll find it in Grady's basement."

The line went silent again.

"Did you hear me, Miss Cisco?"

"Where's Grady?"

"He just barreled butt down the street. On foot. I don't think he'll be back for a while."

"What's happened, Aaron?"

"Vick Atlas got blown apart by the Atlas hit men. Vick shot my friend Saber in the foot. He and Grady were going to put us in a junk-yard compactor after Vick chain-dragged me behind his automobile."

"You're making this up."

"Suit yourself. It's going to be raining cops and newspeople in a few minutes. If you're interested in the Caddy, I'd visit a little later. I doubt they'll pay it any mind."

"Why are you doing this?"

"You've got to do something for kicks," I replied.

I NEVER SAW GRADY again. He avoided prosecution by tying up the process in the courts and eventually going bankrupt. Some said he was terrified of Jaime Atlas and hired bodyguards who beat him up and raped him and left him naked in a ditch. Five years later, I heard he married a former actress who produced pornographic films and lived in the Hollywood Hills. In 1967 he was found dead in a hotel on East Fifth Street in Los Angeles, a hypodermic needle in his arm.

Eighteen months after the shooting, I received a letter from Mexico City. It read:

> *How are you doing, kiddo? I hope you got your life straightened out. I can't necessarily say I have, but at least I'm not putting the joy juice in my arm. You were a sweet kid and you got me a little bit excited on a couple of occasions, so I apologize to you for that, but hey normalcy was never my strong suit, which doesn't seem to bother M. a lot. He says to tell you hello and to ride it to the buzzer. He's on radiation and I'm on wrinkle remover, but we have oceans of money courtesy of you-know-who. Am I regretful for having been in the life? I'd have to think on that. As Benny used to say, "It beats the fuck out of pushing a bagel cart."*

The letter was unsigned.

Saber dropped out of school during the fall semester and joined the army. In the spring of 1953, he was MIA at Pork Chop Hill. His name showed up once on a list of POWs at Panmunjom, but he was not repatriated, and nothing was ever learned about his fate. There were rumors about American soldiers having been moved across the

Yalu into China and perhaps even the Soviet Union, where they were used in medical experiments. Saber's father died and his mother went to work at a record store in West University and for years wrote letters to the government and spoke to anyone who would listen about her son's fate, until she went mad. I have always wanted to believe that Saber survived, that the trickster from classical folklore who had lived in our midst and hung his flopper through the hole in the ceiling above Mr. Krauser's head was still out there, screwing up things, ridiculing the pompous and arrogant, getting even for the rest of us. And that's the way I will always think of him.

The following year the vice president of my father's company invited him to go on a duck-hunting trip down at Anahuac. He asked because of my father's genteel manners and his ability to speak with corporate people on any level about any subject. My father looked upon the trip as an obligation, not a pleasure. On the way back to Houston, he was sleeping in the passenger seat of the vice president's Cadillac. The hour was late, the highway white with fog. The vice president rounded a curve and plowed into the back of a disabled truck. For reasons never explained, the truck driver had not placed reflectors or flares on the asphalt to warn oncoming traffic. My father was flown to Houston. He died the next day from a blood clot, while I was en route from college to be at his bedside.

My mother lived to be one hundred and two years and asked nothing from anyone and took care of herself until the end. I became a writer; I didn't become a musician. But Loren Nichols did, and he dedicated a song to me and Valerie from the stage of the Grand Ole Opry.

What about Val and me? There is a certain kind of love that's forever. It's not marked by a marital vow, or social custom, or gender identity, or the age of the parties involved. It's a love that doesn't even need to be declared. Its presence in your life is as factual as the sun rising in the morning. You do not argue in its defense or try to explain or justify it to others. The other party moves into your heart and remains with you the rest of your days. The bond is never broken, any more than you can separate yourself from your body or soul.

At age seventeen Valerie and I became one person, unable to enjoy pleasure without the presence of the other. The changes in our lives, the geographical separations, the pull of the earth on our bodies, none of these things ever affected the contract and bond that took place in our youth; over the years neither one of us ever suffered a tragedy or bore a burden or celebrated a success without the involvement of the other. I could not draw breath without feeling that Valerie Epstein was at my side.

I guess I've learned by now that the past can be a prison. But there are memories you never give up. They remain painted on the air. They come to you in a song, a sunset on the ocean, a palm tree stiffening in the wind. When I hear of wars and rumors of wars and I tire of my fellow man's destructive ways, I think about Valerie Epstein beside me in my heap on the last day of summer in 1952, the two of us roaring full-out down the boulevard on Galveston Island, the sun a molten ball sinking into the Gulf, the waves slate green, curling with foam just before they burst in an iridescent spray on the beach. The stars were already out, the drive-in where we met wrapped with yellow and red neon, the cars parked under the canopy glowing in the light like hard candy. When she pulled herself against me and held her head tight against my shoulder, her hands squeezing into my arm, I knew that neither of us would ever die, that life was a song, eternal in nature, and the smell and secrets of creation lay in the tumble of every wave that crested and receded into the Gulf. I also knew that the gifts of both heaven and earth would always remain where they had always been, at our fingertips and in the shimmer we see in the eyes of those we love.

ACKNOWLEDGMENTS

I would like to thank my editor, Ben Loehnen; my copy editor, E. Beth Thomas; and my daughter, Pamala Burke, for their invaluable help in making this novel one of the best I have written.

ABOUT THE AUTHOR

James Lee Burke, a rare winner of two Edgar Awards and named Grandmaster by the Mystery Writers of America, is the author of more than thirty previous novels and two collections of short stories, including such *New York Times* bestsellers as *Creole Belle*, *Light of the World*, *The Glass Rainbow*, *Feast Day of Fools*, and *The Tin Roof Blowdown*. He lives in Missoula, Montana.